I hope [illegible]

the wild ride.

God bless you!

Fred [illegible]

The Draegonian Invasion

Fred Jackson

CrossBooks™
A Division of LifeWay
1663 Liberty Drive
Bloomington, IN 47403
www.crossbooks.com
Phone: 1-866-879-0502

First published by CrossBooks 5/17/2012

ISBN: 978-1-4627-1443-8 (sc)
ISBN: 978-1-4627-1445-2 (hc)
ISBN: 978-1-4627-1444-5 (e)

Library of Congress Control Number: 2012903710

Printed in the United States of America

This book is printed on acid-free paper.

This book is dedicated to my wife, Nancy, and my kids, Victor and Laurel, for all of their suggestions, support and longsuffering.

It is also dedicated to all the young people involved with Christian Youth Theater whose lives have been such an inspiration to me.

Also a special "thank you" to Amy Davis and Marjorie Bell for their expertise in editing.

Contents

Chapter 1

The First Night

The sky seemed to take on a pinkish glow, Brad noticed as he started for home. Walking along the street in front of his friend's house, he was reliving the hours of fun he and Luke had playing computer games that afternoon. They had both reached new levels as they attempted to rid the universe of the evil forces of Lord Draegon, who was invading from planet Draegos. He studied the twilight for a second. The stars were just beginning to come into view. As he looked up, he could count three, four—no, six tiny stars twinkling between the reddish horizon and dark blue evening sky.

That's curious, Brad thought, gazing into the heavens. *What's that strange light?* Far in the distance, amid the stars, was a small, undulating light. It seemed to alternate green to gold to red. Starting small, not much bigger than the stars that were beginning to appear, it was definitely getting larger. Brad began to realize he had seen this before. Most boys of fifteen, almost sixteen, who had entered the world of Draegon, would know what this was. Straining, he looked past the strange phenomenon. His suspicions were confirmed as several more, similar luminaries came into view. *What should I do? Who can I tell? Someone needs to be told.* Brad could feel his heart racing.

He looked behind him and saw a guy in his mid-twenties walking a shaggy dog, coming toward him. The thought darted through his mind of how much people's pets can resemble them. This fellow with his scraggily beard and sort of wild hair could have been walking his four-legged child. It was freaky! The young man approached, oblivious to what was going on above him. Seeing the look of worry on Brad's face, as he gazed up into the heavens, he looked up as well. Finally he asked, "What you looking at, dude?"

"Don't you see 'em?" Brad said, pointing up into the seemingly tranquil sky.

"You mean that airliner up there? Yeah, makes you wish you were up there on it and going somewhere fun like Florida, doesn't it?" The fellow replied, grinning as he stared, clueless, into the sky.

"No, I mean those five strange looking lights just over that radio tower," Brad said intensely.

"Well, I can't see very well. I was sort of in a hurry and came out without my glasses, but I don't see anything to be so excited about. You've probably been watching too many sci-fi flicks." The guy chuckled a little and darted forward as his mutt took off, clearly ready to sniff out some unsuspecting kitty. As he bobbled away holding furiously on to the leash, Brad thought to himself, *He's just like most people today. They don't have a clue when evil is sitting right over them, ready to destroy their lives.*

Turning his attention back to the sky, Brad stood there watching. The strange lights were definitely moving closer at incredible speed. Within five minutes they had grown brighter than anything else in the sky—glowing, pulsating balls of light getting larger and larger. It was one thing to experience this in the world of computer games, but, standing there on the street, fear began to grip his heart. These things weren't supposed to be real, yet there they were. *"I'm standing here right out in the open like a dummy?* "Why am I walking anyway? Where's my bike?" Brad asked, confused. Knowing his own house on Morning Star Way was more than five blocks away, he turned to look at Luke's house. Brad could see golden rays of light reaching out into the dusk from his friend's window on the second floor. Brad couldn't stop wondering, what was different about the house? He had spent half his life there since Luke and his family moved in six years ago. Luke's house had become his second home, yet now there was something strange about it. Something about the color was wrong, and now it appeared to be so much bigger than he remembered.

As he stood there wondering what he should do next, Brad saw Luke looking out of the window. Luke waved his hand at his friend down on the street and raised his shoulders as if to say, "What's the problem?" Luke couldn't see the eerie display going on above his home because of the huge oak tree which loomed surreally over their house. Brad waved frantically to his friend and pointed skyward. As he did, he realized that the strange colors around him were getting brighter. The trees and house began to glow with hues of green and red. The first of the strange lights was now close enough for Brad to get a better look at it.

"It can't be!" Brad said to himself. He could now make out a jagged, wedge-shaped forward area like the head of a great flying beast coming into view from behind a patch of low breaking clouds. The mid-section of the craft spread out and gave the impression of huge wings fanning out from a narrower body. Brad's heart fluttered as he recognized the unmistakable form of what could only be a gigantic, Draegonian Battle Cruiser, moving ominously into position right over his friend's home.

Where is everybody? Brad wondered. *Did no one else see this huge shape hovering above the neighborhood? Was everyone on Holloway Lane away for the evening?* Brad looked down the abandoned street and saw no sign of the dog walking his master. He looked up again into the very belly of the beast seeing that the thing he feared was now practically right over him. Having already reached level 52 fighting the dreaded Draegonians on Cronos Four, Brad was quite familiar with what was unfolding in the heavens above him. It was an all-out invasion. He stood there in stunned amazement, virtually paralyzed with fear as the glowing menaces moved closer and closer. He wanted to run but his body simply wouldn't move. Suddenly, hundreds of smaller dragonfly-shaped fighter droids began streaming out of the open bay doors of the larger ship. Organizing into formations, several groups flew off into the horizon, obviously bound for some strategic destination. About twenty of them headed back toward his town, a quiet bedroom community near the city. All at once, they broke formation and began to zigzag across the sky, swooping down to fire laser bursts at various targets. Explosions erupted throughout the town, and the sky was illumined with the reflection of flames shooting into the air.

Brad dove to the ground as a fighter droid screamed close over his head. Lying on his belly under the bushes, Brad peered up at Luke who was now staring bug-eyed out the window at the chaos. At that moment, a laser burst hit the enormous tree beside his house splitting it in half near the base. With a loud crack, it burst into flames. The largest portion fell, crashing into Luke's home, right over his bedroom. Brad watched as flames began to climb the tree toward an opening that was torn into the side of the house near the roof. Looking up, Brad saw that Luke was no longer at the window.

Brad cried out, "God, how can all this be happening?" Although he spent a great deal of time playing computer games, fighting androids and neutralizing evil galactic villains, he did not believe they were real. He believed in God and knew that interplanetary aliens did not fit into God's plan for the earth.

Realizing the desperation of the situation, Brad began to pray for his friend who he knew didn't attend church or understand much at all about God. Luke was a smart kid, who was about six months younger than Brad. He was a bit small for his age and struggled with that, sometimes doing kind of crazy things to be accepted.

Watching the catastrophic events unfolding before his very eyes, Brad decided he had to do something to help his friend, and right now. Amid the peculiar whirring sounds of vehicles streaking over head and the blaze of explosions in the background, he summoned all of his courage and dashed toward Luke's house.

Luke's parents and little brother, Jake, had gone out for the evening and hadn't returned. His older sister, Sandra, was on a trip to the beach with some friends. As soon as Brad reached the front door, he grasped the doorknob, opened it, and barged into the foyer of the house. The lower level was apparently empty. Brad glanced at the dark staircase leading to the upstairs hallway. The house appeared out of proportion, and things didn't seem to be in the right places, although Brad couldn't figure out exactly what was wrong. He stopped, listening. The house was quiet. He could smell smoke and feared that the fire from the tree outside may be approaching the house. Brad called out for Luke and paused. All he could hear now was the muffled commotion of crazy noises outside. Rumblings of explosions, sirens, and the occasional high-pitched scream of a fighter droid penetrated the quietness of the house. Brad also noticed something that sounded like computerized battle music, which seemed to drill into his head. *Totally weird*, he thought as he cried out for his friend again. For a few seconds, there was an unusual hush. It was followed by a faint voice from upstairs.

"Brad, please help me."

"Luke! Where are you?" Brad called out as he raced up the stairs. Smoke was now getting thicker in the house. Brad knew that he did not have much time. He reached the top of the stairs, and ran down the hall to Luke's bedroom. He was astounded at the mess. Luke's normal mess of clothes was hanging from every chair and hook. Along with multiple stacks of books, magazines, and boxes of assorted model cars, there were several pairs of shoes strewn about the place. This was all now complicated by the tree, which had fallen into the back of the house. Luke's room looked like a giant tree house that needed some major tree housekeeping. The bed was demolished; a huge branch had come through the window and crashed right across the middle of it. Brad could see outside, right up into the sky, through a place that used to be solid wall. Luke's computer was still on. The computer game they had just spent hours playing was still going. The reptilian face of the villain, Draegon, was illuminated in colors of green, red, and gold. Mockingly, it contorted on the screen. Brad was distracted for a few seconds by its hypnotic movement and wondered momentarily at the strangeness of it all.

Smoke and flames were now leaping into the room from the burning tree outside. It was obvious that Luke was not in there. Brad turned and started back down the hall. "Luke! Where are you?" He yelled.

"Here!" came the reply.

"Where?" Brad called back, now totally confused.

"I'm in the bathroom, dufus!"

"The bathroom? I guess all those tornado drills paid off," Brad joked, as he opened the door of the bathroom. "Whoa," He exclaimed, amazed at the sight.

A good portion of the tree had come through the ceiling and was laying right over the sink and toilet. Just beyond that was the bath tub. Brad climbed through the mass of broken limbs and branches. Two big brown eyes peered up at him. Covered in leaves and branches, Luke sat, curled up like a ball. He looked like some sort of flora alien from the planet of the tree people.

"What are you doing, man? We've got to get outta here!" Brad urged as he reached in and grabbed Luke's wiry arm, pulling him out amid a flurry of falling leaves.

"Man, that was some storm," Luke stated, oblivious to what was really going on.

"Yeah," Brad replied, "and it's still going on, but it wasn't a storm."

"What was it, an earthquake?" asked Luke, still clueless.

"You won't believe me if I tell you."

They were making their way down the hall when the lights flickered, and suddenly went out. "What the heck is going on, Brad?"

The nervous pair made their way to the stairs. Holding on to the railing, they slowly descended through the smoke in almost total darkness. Random flashes of light lit up the sidelights around the front door in hall at the base of the stairs.

"You know those computer games we play all the time?"

"Yeah, what about 'em?" Luke pressed.

"As they say, truth is stranger than fiction, at least tonight anyway."

"You're not making any sense. Will you please tell me what's happening?"

At that moment there was a loud mechanical scream followed closely by an explosion which shook the house.

"Aliens, dude! It's an all-out invasion!" As Brad tried to explain what was happening, he found himself having to speak louder and louder as he was being drowned out by a deep, pit-of-the-stomach type of rumbling sound. At the same time, a brilliant light poured through the sidelights, followed by an earth-shaking thud. Too afraid to go near the door, the boys began to back away, up the steps, holding on to each other in fear for their lives. Wide-eyed, with their gaze fixed on the door, they could hear the whining sounds of hydraulics—then, a deathly silence. Brad looked at Luke, who trembled violently as absolute fear gripped him. Before the guys could think what to do next, the door burst open; torn right off the hinges. It slammed into the wall, buckling under the force of the blow. A giant, pewter looking, metallic figure that stood almost eight feet tall crouched to get through the doorway.

The boys were paralyzed as they gawked at the awesome entity, whose glowing, red, laser-like eyes were fixed on them. It was impossible to tell if it was living or purely machine. It didn't really matter. All that mattered was that this thing could quite easily crush them in its four-fingered grip, not to mention incinerate them with the sleek gleaming weapon which was neatly attached to its forearm. It was as if it had stepped out of some computer game or space wars flick, right into Luke's living room and was heading directly for them.

Before Brad could react, the thing reached out its massive mechanical arm, grabbed Luke and yanked him right out of the door. The image of Luke's terror-filled, brown eyes, and his arms reaching out in desperation took Brad's breath away. Alone now, Brad was left with a feeling of utter helplessness. Through an ominous, misty, green light in the doorway, he could see four or five smaller shapes. These slender figures with large heads and long reptilian tails were dragging Luke away.

Brad rushed forward, only to run right into a metal fist that stunned him and sent him reeling backward onto the stairs. His mouth burned with pain. Putting his hand to his mouth he could feel the warmth of his own blood flowing from his gashed lip. The metallic being reached down and grasped him under the chin, forcing Brad up off the floor. Choking now, he was being held completely off the ground by one arm of the demonic hulk. With both hands Brad grabbed its arm and pulled himself up so that he could breath.

I cannot believe this is happening to me, Brad thought. Then, another thought entered his mind. *Where is God? This can't be real. Jesus is real, not aliens.* As he hung there, the being's grip tight around his throat, Brad tried to cry out.

"Jesus, h-help me!" he squeaked out.

There was a sudden, absolute silence for a couple of seconds. The beast abruptly released its grip and Brad fell to the floor, in a heap at the base of the stairs. The metal monster recoiled with what seemed to be a quick, stark look of terror on its shining, helmet-like face. Next, a shaft of light shot from behind Brad and struck the demon's chest which started to glow, like red-hot metal. Beginning from the midsection where the light hit it, a great hole formed. Then, the entire monstrosity collapsed into a huge pool of mercury-like soup.

Emotionally drained, the tears poured forth as Brad turned and looked up to see where the light had come from. Behind him on the stairs, in the haze, stood a man wearing what looked like a long, white coat. The man had an affirming smile on his face as he looked down into the eyes of the startled youth. Brad could only stare at Him, wondering.

Finally, the man spoke. "Fear not, for I am always with you, even unto the end of the world."

At this point Brad totally lost it, and with tears of relief streaming down his face he cried out,

"Thank you, Lord!" Then Brad remembered Luke. "What happened to Luke? Sir, we must save Luke!"

With tears in His kind eyes, the Man looked down at Brad and replied, "Yes, Brad, we must. Right now he is lost and is headed into very dangerous ground."

As Brad continued to focus on the gentle face, it began to fade, but he could still hear the voice.

"Brad, will you help Me help him?"

CHAPTER 2

REALITY SETS IN

BRAD WOKE UP WITH A start and sat straight up in bed. Tears were still on his cheeks. He quickly wiped them away before anyone might see them. Lying there, staring at the ceiling fan whirring overhead, he nearly jumped out of his skin as he heard a loud mechanical sound outside his window. His heart raced at the sound of whining hydraulics. Brad let out a deep breath as he heard loud banging and realized it was just a garbage truck outside. Still somewhat dark, the dawn light was just beginning to brighten his window. He was drawn to it and looked upward, gazing at the sky. Thick bands of clouds were separated by large clear areas as a pale orange glow blended into the deep blue of the early morning sky. Brad noticed a few twinkling stars. He started to study them more closely, then, he heard the distant high pitched whine of a siren. With a shudder, he closed the blinds and dove back into the bed.

"Oh no! I'm not going through all that again," he said to himself, as he lay with the sheets pulled over his head. Then it hit him. *It was a dream.*

"It was all a big stupid dream!" he said out loud. Then, thinking better of the words that he had just spoken, he added, "It was a dream but it wasn't stupid at all." He sat there thinking. *All of the alien stuff was, well, chalk that up to all the computer games Luke and I have spent countless days playing. Mom always said they'd have an effect on me.* Brad realized the part at the end made it all worthwhile. The man in white had to have been Jesus and He had spoken to him in this dream. Luke was indeed lost. He certainly didn't know Jesus, but Brad wondered what the Man meant when He said that Luke was on dangerous ground? Over the last year Luke had been trying really hard to mix it up with some guys that were not the best influences. But was he actually in danger? Brad had never grasped the urgency of sharing Jesus with his friend so clearly.

A droning beep, beep, beep, beep from the garbage truck backing up down the street startled Brad out of the deep thoughts swirling in his mind. He turned over, grabbed his pillow and held it tightly over the back of his head. He soon came to the realization that he wasn't going back to sleep, and after the nights excursion he wasn't sure he even wanted to sleep anymore. Much more sleep like that and he would be too tired to get up. Tossing the pillow on the floor, he turned over, sat up and began to rub the sleep from his eyes. Brad staggered out of bed toward the bathroom. *What time is it, anyway?* he wondered, as he glanced back to look at the clock on the somewhat cluttered nightstand beside his bed. He could barely make out the numbers glowing in green from underneath his drawing tablet. "6:29— Man, I'll be late for school," he muttered. As he hurried into the bathroom it dawned on him that nobody else was up. The house was strangely quiet. Perhaps it hadn't been a dream after all? Had his entire family been abducted by aliens?

He quickly, but quietly moved out of the bathroom back into the hall. Slowly, he crept down the hallway and heard a muffled thump coming from the laundry room. Moving past his sister's bedroom, he noticed light illuminating the cracks around the laundry room door. As he reached for the doorknob, it suddenly flew open, and a huge pile of laundry came barreling out of the door, knocking him to the ground. Brad's mother let out a slight shriek, totally surprised by someone standing in the darkness.

"Bradford Johnson, what are you doing?" Brad stood up slowly, removing the boxer shorts that had fallen over the top of his head.

He stuttered, "I-I thought you were an alien."

"Well!" she declared with feigned indignation and a frown that was obviously not serious. "I know I look pretty rough first thing in the morning, but is that what you really think of your poor old mom?" The frown changed into a half smile.

Brad smiled at his mom with embarrassment. The truth was that Brad thought his mom was one of the prettiest ladies in the world. Her smile was so warm, and although she did look a little different in the morning before the makeup went on, she still had a beautiful face, framing her bright golden-brown eyes.

"No, Mom. I'm sorry," he replied with a sheepish look. "I had a rough night."

"Well, I can believe that. You look a little scary yourself. I like that crazy 'do' you've got going on up there. Maybe you should shoot it with some hair spray and create a new fad. You could call it the lophead or something." She reached over and scratched his head lightly.

He let out a "ha, ha, ha", as he bent down and began picking up the laundry which had fallen out of the basket in their close encounter.

"What are you doing up so early on a Saturday? Did the storm wake you?" she asked.

"Storm?" Brad wondered. "No, uh-h, I had a weird dream."

"That's what all that pizza will get you right before bedtime."

"Yeah," he acknowledged with a smile. "But I want to tell you about this one, maybe at breakfast."

"O-K," she agreed with a slight hesitation of curiosity in her voice. "I'll be down in a little while, after I finish re-folding this laundry." She shot him a glance with that funny scowling frown of hers.

"Sorry," he replied, knowing he had been the cause of the laundry malfunction. As he walked back down the hall toward his room he thought, *it's Saturday. How could I have forgotten that? No wonder no one is up.* He headed into the bathroom, flipped on the light and squinted at the brightness of the row of bulbs illuminating his pale face, which stared back from the mirror. *Why do I always look so pale first thing in the morning, and what happened to my hair?* It looked like he had been through some sort of alien shock treatment during the night. He now understood why his mom had called it the lophead. A good portion of his dark, blondish hair was sticking almost straight up on top of his head, but with a definite tilt to the left, while the right side was smashed tight to his scalp, in sort of a wave toward his cheekbone. Brad turned on the water and started to wet his hair.

His sister Amanda walked by the open door of the bathroom and stuck her head inside, snickering at the unruly sight on top of his head. "What happened to you?" she taunted with a cock-eyed smirk on her bright, brown-eyed face. Did you stick your head in the toilet and flush?"

"Very funny," Brad responded, water trickling down his face. "You're no fairy princess this morning yourself," he retorted, glancing over at her. Her normally carefully maintained curly, blond hair was in its morning "frizz" state, the by-product of the phenomenon of static electricity. Brad chuckled and looked at her through the mirror. "If you put on a big red nose you could join a circus. Maybe we could get you a bunch of little yappy dogs and a hoop. You'd have a great act."

Tightening the sash around her brightly colored, terrycloth bathrobe, she reached up and smacked him on the back of his head. "You're so mean," she huffed as she stood there pretending to be offended.

"Will you please control yourself, girl? You started it, you know, taking advantage of your poor brother in his sensitive state of bad hair. I'm going to tell mom that you're picking on me."

She laughed and shook her head, knowing that she could never really pick on him. His sturdy frame was approaching six feet when he stood up straight. Years of playing soccer had made him lean, but working out had built his strength, making him an impressive looking young man.

She turned to leave and said, "You better be nice to me. I'm going down to help Mom with breakfast. How'd you like your eggs and toast nice and black?"

Brad looked at her, his head down slightly, and with his crisp, sparkling, blue eyes peering up at her, he summoned all of the pitifulness he could muster. "You wouldn't do that to you dear, sweet brother would you?"

She looked back and smiled, "Nice try but you can't con me. Remember you can't fool your own sister." Shaking her head, she disappeared down the hallway.

"Yeah, and I might not have any choice about that burnt breakfast," he muttered to himself. "I sure hope mom is down there with her." He had choked down more than one of her "slightly, well done" meals. *She means well, always trying to help mom out, and is really a fine cook when she's not distracted by a phone call or drawn away by an exciting read.*

Mandy was a very motivated young lady who loved to read and was academically gifted. Brad was very proud of his sister and secretly she was a great inspiration to him. She had on many occasions spoken the truth into his life and challenged him in his faith. Brad had struggled, at times, in understanding the Bible and actually living it every day. Often, he would get so involved in succeeding in sports or seemingly important things like computer games or dreaming about the cool ride he was saving up for, that he didn't spend much time at all with God. As a result, his Christian walk had gotten lost in the constant pursuit of things that seemed more fun and exciting.

His sister Mandy, although a year younger than he, had a very real, close daily walk with Jesus. This seemed to produce a maturity beyond her fourteen and a half years. She wasn't flighty like a lot of girls her age that will do anything to impress some boy or to gain popularity. With a seriousness tempered by a quick sense of humor she had obviously inherited from her mom, Mandy always seemed to understand the root of a problem. She had also developed the discipline to do the right thing, no matter the cost to her popularity. As a result, ironically, she was one of the most popular girls in her class. Other girls were always coming to her to talk about problems that they were facing. Her classmates knew that they could trust her, and that she was faithful to pray for them. Even if they weren't Christians, they seemed to appreciate the knowledge that someone cared enough to pray for them.

At the age of ten, after many years of family devotions and numerous discussions with Mom and Dad dealing with life issues, Amanda had made a serious commitment to follow Jesus. Since that time, she had been faithful to get up early in the morning to spend time with Jesus. No matter how much school work she had, or what else was going on, she was always up early with her door closed, getting closer to her Best Friend for life. Brad knew that he needed more of that in his life, and after the wild ride of last night, the sooner the better.

Brad's attention shifted back to the issue at hand: that of, the now wet appendage sticking out of the top of his head. Brad turned his head slightly to one side, then the other, as he studied his mug in the mirror. *Man, I need a haircut,* he thought as he grabbed a comb and went into action trying to straighten out the mess. Hair, finally under control, Brad returned to his room to get dressed for the day. Surveying his bedroom, he decided it "needed some attention," as his mom would say. *It's not in too bad of a condition,* he thought as he removed a couple of NASCAR ball caps that he had flung atop his soccer trophies. Then, he went around the room picking up various t-shirts, jeans, sneakers, and several pairs of socks which were way overdue for the laundry. It was amazing what he found as he removed the clutter from the room. He'd been looking for that pocket knife for weeks. "Oops, well dad will be glad to have this socket wrench back," he said to himself, as continued the whirlwind sweep of his room.

It was a pretty cool room when you could actually get around in it. One of the centerpieces of the room was a 24-inch-long, scale model of the Starship Enterprise from the original Star Trek series, hanging from his ceiling, in the corner of the room. His dad had put it together when he was a teenage boy, and Brad had inherited it on his eighth birthday. It had been hanging there ever since. On the wall closest to the ship was a colorful poster of the various Biblical names of Jesus, also inherited from his father's college days when he was involved with Campus Crusade for Christ. Brad's dad, Richard, had gotten saved in college and never looked back.

Grabbing an arm-full of assorted books stacked on his desk, Brad noticed the bulletin board hanging over his desk. It was a collage of photographs depicting family and friends through the years. As his eyes roamed from photos of Boy Scout camping trips, to various soccer games, swim meets, birthdays and church events, Brad noticed one face that appeared numerous times. It was a face with very dark, almost black hair. The long bangs which hung down right over his dark brown eyes made you wonder how he could even see. His glowing white teeth and square jaw sort of made his friend Luke look like hair with a smile. Back then Luke smiled a lot. He was the type of fellow that liked to make others laugh. Brad remembered some of the times when Luke would do something stupid like act liked Curly from an old Three Stooges DVD. He had perfected that finger snapping routine right down to the nyok, nyok, nyok. Complete silliness would overtake them, and they would be on the floor laughing so hard that their jaws would ache. Those were happier times for Luke. The two of them had been like two peas in a pod. Along with being in Boy Scouts and sporting activities together, they had attended the same schools for the last almost six years.

Stopping at the picture of the two of them at a church youth retreat in the mountains, Brad remembered the time, just over two years ago, when Luke came to that retreat. He had been so interested in learning more about Jesus that weekend. He asked so many questions, participated in the Bible study time, and even enjoyed the Praise band.

Luke loved rock music, and he loved the drums. He had a set in his room and would play for hours with his headphones on listening to old rock CD's. Brad just knew Luke was going to give his heart to Jesus. Then it happened. About three weeks later Luke's parents separated. It was a bad, bad time for Luke. His dad left, and in less than a year had re-married. Luke never seemed the same after that. Slowly, he began to act as if he just didn't care about life anymore, like he blamed God for letting it happen.

"God, why did you let that happen?" Brad asked out loud. "He was so close to coming into your kingdom. We could have grown together in The Truth and helped each other." Brad questioned, prayerfully.

Luke became bitter, and when Brad tried to talk about God, Luke just didn't want to hear it. He got more into his music, listening to vintage groups like AC/DC, Aerosmith and KISS and then moved into the heavy metal stuff. Now, it was something called black metal. Brad had a hard time with going over and listening to some of that stuff. It seemed to drain him spiritually. He could only wonder what it was doing to his friend. *Why does life have to be so hard? Why couldn't Luke's parents have stayed together and worked things out?* They had gone to church, although, with their busy lifestyle and his dad's work taking him out of town so much, it was sporadic at best.

"Why don't people give more thought to how these things devastate their kids?" Brad wondered, openly talking to God.

After the divorce Luke hardly ever saw his dad, even though he lived in a neighboring town only an hour away. Luke had said that it wasn't much different when his parents were married. His dad was either away on business or too tired to do anything but sleep in front of ESPN on the tube. Brad felt a deep sadness come over him for his friend Luke. Through God's Spirit, he could feel the burden Luke carried.

A still, small voice arrested Brad from his thoughts. "It doesn't have to remain this way," Brad heard in his spirit, "Luke can be found." Brad felt the Spirit of God was calling him to read His word. He looked down and saw his Bible sitting on his now less-cluttered desk. He picked it up and opened it, as he strolled over and plopped down on his bed. Turning the pages through the New Testament, he stopped in Romans chapter two and noticed some scribble he had written in the margin, next to verse four. "It is God's kindness that leads us to repentance," he read out loud. He studied the verse that talked about how good and patient God is. "It's totally true, Lord," Brad said, as he thought back on the many times he had blown it because of his own selfishness and rebellion. "I've failed you so much, and I've pretty much given up on Luke. How could I be so foolish, blaming you for Luke's rebellion? He could have run to you at that difficult time, but instead he listened to the wrong voices. Those voices hate you and try to separate us from you. And I just backed off and let it happen," Brad lamented, as a deep sadness welled up inside him.

"Is he even savable, now?" Brad asked. As he gazed at the words on the page, Brad came back to the part about God's kindness and patience.

He felt God say to him, "I haven't given up on Luke. Why should you?"

"Wow, then there is hope," Brad declared. *I've got to see if I can find Luke today and see what's going on with him. Maybe it's not too late for him. After all, he's not even sixteen yet,* Brad thought as a glimmer of hope overcame his discouragement.

A piercing, feminine voice suddenly called from down the hallway, "Brad, are you going to come down to breakfast? Your burnt eggs and toast are getting cold," Mandy spoke with some exasperation.

Oh great, Brad thought, *there's only one thing worse than burnt eggs and toast, and that's cold burnt eggs and toast.* He jumped up and started quickly toward the door. As he did, he tripped over the pile of clothes he had been collecting around his room. Careening out of the door into the hall and then sort of bouncing off the wall, he found himself on the floor staring up, right into the upside down face of his smirking sis.

With arms folded and head wagging, she retorted, "Now, that was a smooth move. I bet you impress a lot of girls that way."

"Some loving sister you are. You could offer a guy a little sympathy. I might have broken my shoulder or something," he whined as he grabbed his shoulder and grimaced.

Feeling a little guilty, she asked with more compassion, "Are you really hurt?"

With an expression of pain on his reddening face, he opened one eye, smiled, and said, matter of factly, "Na-ah." He then jumped to his feet with a triumphant grin on his face.

"I can't believe I ever feel sorry for you!" she exclaimed, faking frustration, as she punched him in the side.

He laughed out loud at the slight pain in his ribs which made him flinch. "Come on, Sis. Cut it out. You're getting awfully violent in your old age."

At that moment, Mom, who had obviously been monitoring the ruckus, called up the stairs, "OK, Jethro and Ellie May, you better knock it off, and get down here unless you want a real whuppin'. Your vittles are gett'n cold." Mom grew up watching reruns of the old Beverly Hillbillies series and loved to quote Granny and Uncle Jed.

When the yung'ens finally made it to the breakfast table, Mom and Dad were already in the middle of a Saturday morning breakfast feast. There were no burnt eggs and toast. Instead, there were blueberry pancakes, hash browns and bacon. Saturdays were great because it was usually the only morning the family could sit down and enjoy a nice breakfast without rushing off to school or work.

"Good morning, sleepy head. Glad you could join us. That was some storm we had last night. Did it keep you awake?" Dad asked, as he greeted Brad in his usual jovial way.

Brad's dad was a slightly above average-sized man, about six feet tall, with a friendly smile and a kind heart underneath his sometimes firm nature. He was a conservative fellow, with a clean cut look about him and anyone could tell that he and Brad were father and son. Richard Johnson, like his son, had dark blond hair that tended to curl a bit around the edges when it was longer. Richard's, however, was never long enough for that, and was graced with a little graying around the edges of the almost military style haircut. Although his father had never actually been in the armed services, he always looked and acted like he could have been.

Everyone expected Brad to be about the same height as his father, since they had a similar build as well as identical shoe sizes. When Brad was about twelve, his feet began to grow first, and his friends nicknamed him "Battleship Feet." His dad had consoled him by confiding that the same thing happened to him when he was twelve, and that it took his body less than two years to catch up and come into proportion with his feet. This brought great relief to Brad, who feared that he would become some sort of freak wearing gigantic shoes like Ronald McDonald.

"What time was that storm going on?" Brad asked.

"Oh, it woke me about three thirty and must of gone on for an hour and a half after that," Dad explained, while reaching over to load some buttery spread onto his knife.

"The TV news said that the local fire departments were busy putting out a half dozen fires caused by all that lightning. It was incredible, and the thunder was deafening. I'm surprised that you slept right through it, Brad," Brad's mother commented as she got up to skim another stack of steaming pancakes off the electric griddle.

"I'm not, his snoring could drown out a freight train," Mandy teased. She forked a couple of pancakes onto her plate.

As Mom sat down she asked, "Are you feeling better, Bucky?"

"Yes ma'am, I feel fine now. Boy, am I starving," Brad responded. Brad wasn't exactly sure where the nickname "Bucky" had come from, but the best he could ascertain from his investigation of the matter was that it started when he was a baby. According to Dad, he would get on his hands and knees and begin to rock back and forth. Mom thought he looked like a little bucking horse and started calling him Bucky. She also called him "Bradford," his full name, when she was upset at him. His mom was funny about names. Brad's mom, Constance, grew up in Pennsylvania not far from Philadelphia, but her mother's family was from near Plymouth, Massachusetts. She was a direct descendent of William Bradford, leader of the Pilgrims, of Mayflower fame. Thus, her firstborn son could have no other first name than Bradford. Connie Johnson had developed a great interest in genealogy through the years and had spent many hours on the computer and in libraries researching all of her family tree. Brad liked his name and was proud of his family heritage. He was just thankful she wasn't a direct descendent of some guy named Etheldred or worse.

"Mom says you had a rough night last night, some sort of bad dream?" Dad asked, blowing gently on a fresh mug of steaming coffee in his hand.

"Dad, do you think dreams mean things?"

A little furrow formed over his dad's left eyebrow as he pondered the question for a few seconds.

"Well," his dad started slowly, "that all depends."

Brad looked in puzzlement at his father and asked, "It depends on what?"

"Exactly how much of that leftover pizza did you eat last night before bed?" Mom and Mandy were now snickering and glancing at each other as Dad's attempt at humor jabbed Brad.

"Da-a-ad," Brad protested in mock exasperation. "Where do you and Mom get that, anyway? I don't believe there is any scientific evidence that pizza causes you to dream crazy dreams."

"Oh, no. What about the time when you were six and went to that pizza party?" Dad retorted, ready to defend his hypothesis. "You know, a-ah-m, who was it dear? Oh yeah, little Bernie MacAlister's party. You woke up that night, petrified of this giant rat that was chasing you through the house."

"Well, Dad," Brad responded defensively, "that might have also had something to do with the fact that I had never been to Chuck- E Cheese's before. I couldn't help it if people in large rodent suits freaked me out, no matter how well they were dressed. Something about his eyes made me really nervous, and he was so big I felt like I couldn't breathe when he tried to hug me." Brad remembered running away from the large character in terror, and hiding in the giant maze of tubes.

Mandy laughed, and then had to add the fact that it was a recurring dream, for her brave, big brother.

"Look, Dad, I'm serious. I had a crazy dream last night about alien forces attacking the neighborhood as I was coming from Luke's house."

"Hmm, "Dad wondered, "this sounds serious, what did these aliens look like?"

"The main battleships looked kind of wedge-shaped. There were fighter droid ships that looked like dragonflies, and a huge metallic looking dude with red laser-like eyes."

"Wow," Dad replied, "that sounds like a fun dream. Too bad I can't ever have one like that." Dad was plagued by recurring nightmares about college exams for which he couldn't find the text book, and hadn't been to the class in six weeks; never any fun things like fighting aliens.

"Dad, you don't understand. This one seemed so real, and Luke was in it."

Brad had been so involved with telling his dad about the dream, that he didn't notice his mom slip out of the room. When she came back to the table, she laid a computer game case down in front of Brad and took her seat beside him. "Brad dear, did any of the characters in your dream resemble anything on this game cover?"

Brad stared down at the black case emblazoned with exciting pictures of wedge-shaped battle cruisers, dragonfly-shaped droid ships, and right in the middle of it all was a gleaming metallic villain. "Yes, Mom there are some things in the dream that were from the Draegonian Invasion game. I guess the flashes of lightning and loud crashes of thunder intensified the effects," he admitted as he picked up the case and studied it. "But, there were things about the dream that definitely weren't in the computer game."

Finally Dad asked, "Son, what makes you think there was anything significant about this dream? Do you think we're actually in danger of being invaded by alien beings? As much as I enjoy good science fiction, I know that it's just someone's vivid imagination."

"Yes, Dad, I know that. The alien part isn't real. But, do you think that God can speak through a wild dream involving all these characters that I'm so familiar with?"

"Well," Dad thought, pulling on his chin, "I can't remember where it is, but I believe there is a scripture that says that in the last days our young men shall dream dreams."

"Oh, I was just reading that last week. Wait just a minute," Amanda stated, as she ran off to find her Bible.

Mom spoke up and added, "I don't know if this is quite the same, but Jesus did use stories of the day, to make the truths that He was teaching clearer."

"He also said that these parables would be understood through the explanation of God's Spirit and that those who didn't know God wouldn't understand them," Dad added.

"Cool," Brad agreed. "It's almost like it was written in, like a heavenly code or riddle that God only explains to those who are in His Kingdom."

About that time Mandy came bouncing back to the table, her Bible in hand. She announced with a chuckle, "I found the scripture you were thinking of, Dad, but there's a slight problem. It's in Joel chapter 2 verse 28." Through the prophet Joel, God says:

> 'I will pour out my spirit on all mankind; and your sons and daughters will prophecy, Your old men will dream dreams; your young men will see visions.'

So, I guess you've aged quite rapidly big brother," she joked as she closed her Bible.

"Brad you still haven't told us why you think that this dream is from God," Dad queried as he swirled his last fork-full of pancake through the thick maple syrup left on his plate. "What did God say to you through this?"

"Well, Dad, it was more about Luke. When this alien devil finally came, he grabbed Luke and took him away. It picked me up, right off the ground, by the throat. As I was hanging there in his grip, choking, I cried out to Jesus. All of a sudden, the thing let me go, as a light from behind me shot through its chest, and he sort of melted. When I turned to see where the light came from, I saw a man dressed in white."

Mandy interrupted. "Dad, do you really think that was Jesus or maybe an angel?"

"Just wait a second and let him finish," Mom interjected. "Go ahead, Brad, what happened next?" Mom asked excitedly.

Brad started again, blinking back tears, "The Man spoke and said, 'Fear not, for I am always with you, even until the end of the world.'"

"Those are indeed words that Jesus spoke," Dad confirmed, seeing the impact that they had on his son.

"Then, I remembered Luke, and I asked the Man about saving him. With tears in His eyes, He said that Luke did need saving because he was indeed lost. He also added that Luke was in great danger. What I can't figure out is, if that is a different type of danger than the danger of being lost and going to hell? I know that is the greatest danger of all because it's final, but what if it means an imminent danger, now?"

"That's a good question Brad," Dad pondered. "One thing I believe for sure is that God is definitely trying to tell you something."

"What was the main point you think you got from what Jesus said, dear?" Mom asked as she reached out and laid her hand on his arm.

"The main thing is that Luke needs to be saved and the situation is urgent."

"Son, why don't we start by praying for Luke right now?" Dad suggested as he reached first for Brad's hand, then Connie's. "Would you like to pray for Luke?"

"That would be great, Dad." Brad prayed, "Dear Lord Jesus, thank you for speaking to me about Luke in that wild dream last night. I know that You did it because of Your love and concern for him. Help me know what to say to him. Help me to never give up on him. I pray that You would lead him to repentance because of Your great kindness. Open his eyes and heart so that he might realize his need for you. Thank you for never leaving us, or forsaking us. I love You, Lord, Amen." As Brad finished, the entire family echoed "Amen."

Mom got up from the table and began clearing plates and silverware. Clearly moved by her son's prayer, she affirmed, "Brad that was a wonderful prayer. We're all going to be praying for Luke and his family too. I know that the divorce was traumatic for all of them. I just hope Marcia's new husband is a faithful man. I don't know much about him. Richard, maybe we could invite them over for a cookout or something soon," she suggested to Dad with a hopeful smile.

Dad nodded his head in agreement. "Sweetie, I think that would be a great thing to do. It would give me a chance to get to know Marcia's new husband. Ah-h-m, his name is . . ."

Mandy intervened, "I believe his name is David Finney."

"That's right," Mom acknowledged enthusiastically, "I wonder if he is a distant relative of that famous preacher from the turn of the century."

"You mean Charles Finney?" Dad asked with a thoughtful look.

"Yes, he's the one. He was an amazing preacher and part of a great spiritual awakening in this nation," Mom explained, now carrying dishes to the sink.

Brad got up and grabbed the butter dish and syrup and moved toward the fridge, "Mom, what do you think the odds of that are?

She turned to him, smiled, and replied eagerly, "I don't know, but it sure would be fun to find out."

Brad shook his head and jokingly asked, "Have you looked into getting treatment for this genealogical obsession of yours?"

Dad laughed out loud, "Yes, son. It's called research therapy. She spends hours on the computer and in libraries getting her fix.

Mom, who was laughing as well, replied, "I can hardly wait to invite them over." Then she stopped and thought, "I hope Mr. Finney is open to it. You know some people are sort of private. Brad, you've met him haven't you? What do you think?"

"Hm-m," Brad thought a second. "I've only seen him a few times and that was a while ago. But, he seemed like a nice guy. He smiled a lot, and even tried to joke around, but he acted a little nervous. I know that Luke was having trouble accepting him. I think he's still angry at his own dad, although he doesn't talk about it much. I haven't even seen Luke though, in three or four weeks."

Mandy spoke up, "You two used to be inseparable."

"Yeah, like Batman and Robin," Dad interjected.

"Well, I was thinking more like Abott and Costello," she chuckled as she glanced at Dad. "Anyway, now it seems this past year you've rarely seen him."

"Well, people change, unfortunately," Brad replied somberly. "Luke doesn't seem like the same guy at times, and he's busy with new friends."

"You mean those guys in that band he got hooked up with? What do they call themselves?" she asked, putting her plates in the dishwasher.

"The Slammers," Brad responded.

"I have seen some of those guys around school, and they are sort of scary," Mandy continued.

Dad spoke up. "Well, let's not pass judgment too quickly. Remember, Jesus died to save everyone, even those who may look a little different or even scary. Some people might even think I'm a little scary at times." Dad opened one eye really wide and sort of screwed up his face giving his Quasimodo impression.

Brad laughed at him, and announced, "As soon as I finish my Saturday chores, I'm going to see if I can find Luke. I made a commitment to God that I wouldn't give up on him. I believe God wants to do something major in his life." Brad looked up at the bird clock on the kitchen wall and noticed the little hand was almost on the cardinal, "Man, it's almost nine o'clock. I better get moving!" he announced, realizing he was still in the knee-length athletic shorts and t-shirt that served as his pajamas.

As he darted out of the kitchen, his mom called to him, "Bradford, don't forget the trash and to sweep out the garage." Then she added in a lower voice almost to herself, "and be careful."

Richard came over and put his arm around his wife and whispered, "Lord, guide him—watch over him, and give him wisdom."

CHAPTER 3

CLOSE ENCOUNTERS AT LUKE'S

IT TOOK UNTIL ALMOST ONE o'clock for Brad to straighten his room and finish his Saturday chores. He then jumped on his bike and took off down the street toward Luke's house. *Man, I can hardly wait. Only four more months, and then I'll have my license and no-o-o more pedal power,* Brad thought, smiling. His mind drifted to the possibilities of cool cars he could buy with the fourteen hundred dollars he had saved up over his entire life. Perhaps there was the slightest possibility that he could persuade his dad to let him spend it on a car sometime before his eighteenth birthday.

The sun was bright overhead although it had been in and out of clouds all day. Brad wondered if it might storm again before the day ended. The street he was traveling down was an older street with houses built before he was born, Dad had said, in the late seventies. Most had well manicured lawns with nice shade trees. Several people were out cleaning up after last night's storm.

As he rounded a corner, he noticed a black Beamer coming toward him. *Nice ride,* Brad thought. It passed him, and he could see that the driver was motioning for him to stop. Recognizing the fellow who had graduated from his high school two years ago, named Sammy Dornburg, Brad stopped to find out what he wanted. Sammy was the manager of "The Slammers" band. He had been in trouble with the law and had even done a six month stint in jail for possession of illegal drugs. That's where he got the name for the band. It was commonly known that Sammy was involved in drug trafficking. Brad figured that the band was either a front for Sammy's drug dealing, or he used the band to attract new customers to get hooked on his wares.

Sammy called over to Brad in his elitist tone. "Hey, Johnson—where you headed, man?"

Brad wondered why he would care, but responded, "I'm headed over to Luke's."

Sammy sort of frowned, "No need—he ain't there. He hasn't been there since yesterday. He played with the band last night at the Rat Race Club. Besides, they had a slight problem at their house last night. Look, if you see Luke somewhere, tell him I'm looking for him, OK."

Brad thought a second and replied, "Well, if I see him today, sure." Brad could not understand how Luke's parents would let him play in this band and at the Rat Race Club. That was about the seediest place around.

As Sammy sped off in his slick ride, Brad wondered about how in the world a guy like that could pay for such an expensive car. *It must be something illegal. He couldn't possibly make that kind of money managing a third rate band.* Brad started off on his bike. He was wondering what might have happened at Luke's house during the night, when out of the corner of his eye, he saw something—or someone, dart from behind a trash can sitting on the edge of the street and slip behind a parked car. Brad stopped his bike and slowly pedaled toward the car. Suddenly, a figure in dark clothes raced into the nearby woods before Brad could get a good look at him. Brad stared into the woods for a minute, and then decided it was probably just some goofy neighborhood kid trying to be funny. He shrugged, and continued down the street toward Luke's, wondering who it could have been and why they ran off that way.

Still unnerved by the shadowy figure, Brad's jaw almost dropped right off of his face when he rounded the corner and Luke's house came into view. The house was a long brick, split-level with the two story part on the end where the yard sloped downward. Luke's room was on the second floor on that side of the house. Brad could not believe what he saw before him. The large oak, which was not quite as big it was in his dream, was split at the base and half of the tree had fallen over onto the Finney's house. "Whoa, this is just too incredible!" Brad exclaimed. He dismounted his bike and walked over to the house through a web of yellow caution tape, obviously put there by the fire department. Surveying the damage, Brad saw that the tree trunk was black and scorched as if it had caught fire, just like in his dream. Brad again wondered if it really was a dream. *What else could have done this?* Then Brad remembered the storm. *I guess this was one of the lightning strikes that kept the fire department so busy last night.* Studying the tree further, however, he realized that it had not burned much at all. *I guess the rain kept it from burning more.* Looking past the jagged trunk, Brad noticed that most of the lower limbs had been removed from the house and sawn up into smaller pieces. This was done so that a large blue tarp could be draped over the back corner where the limbs had compromised the roof. Branches had also gone through the double windows on the end of the house right into Luke's bedroom. Those had not yet been removed. The overall damage to the house didn't seem quite as severe as Brad remembered from the dream.

Brad wondered if the Finney's were still out of town. He decided to go around the front of the house to see if anyone was home. As he came to the front door, he was astonished to see that the front door was all boarded up and crisscrossed with yellow caution tape. "Wait a minute," he wondered aloud. His mind flashed back to the vision of the door flying off the hinges and the huge metallic being standing in the doorway. *Why would the door have been all messed up?* He pondered, as he stood there in stunned disbelief on the bottom step of the porch. He was about to pinch himself to see if he was awake, when a somewhat muffled, squeaky voice from behind him announced,

"May, I help you sir?"

He turned with a start to face his challenger and gasped. He was now gazing down at a four foot tall alien being with large droopy eyes, a grayish-green complexion and long pointed ears that protruded horizontally from the sides of his head. He was also armed with a plastic light saber.

It spoke again and asked, "Do you seek Yoda?" followed by muffled giggling.

Brad laughed and replied, "Who's that in there?" He grabbed the top of the creatures head and gave it a yank. The rubber mask popped off to reveal the smiling face of a boy, about eight or nine years old, with matted up golden hair and sparkling brown eyes.

"He-ey, be careful. Don't tear my head off," he declared, fixing his mussed up hair.

Brad bent down to look at the boy and asked, "Who are you?"

"Jake Finney," came a cheerful reply.

"O-oh, ye-eah, you're Luke's new little brother. He told me about you."

"He did? Co-ol. I know who you are too. I've seen pictures on Luke's wall over his desk. You're Luke's friend, Brad, who plays soccer."

"Yeah, I guess I am." Brad responded. Luke had told Brad that his new dad had a kid from a previous marriage. His wife had died in an auto accident when Jake was about four. Jake had been staying with his grandparents down in Florida while his father got settled in a new job here in North Carolina. With Mr. Finney remarried now, Jake would come and live with his new family.

Jake looked up at Brad, squinting one eye in the sunlight, and asked, "Do you want to play Star Wars with me? I have another light saber you can use, and I think I saw Darth Vader run into the woods just before you came."

Brad replied, "Nah, not today. I'm . . ." Brad paused, thinking about what the boy had just said. Remembering the figure in black darting into the woods earlier, he asked, "Jake, who did you really see running into the woods?"

Jake wrinkled up his brow, thinking hard. "It looked like him, you know, Darth Vader, but he wasn't wearing his helmet. Well, he was dressed in black, but I couldn't see his face."

"Was it a man or a kid?"

"I think it was a teenager, kind of like Luke."

"Luke?" Brad wondered. "By the way, where is Luke? Is he at home?"

Jake shook his head, "No, he was out playing in the band last night and didn't come home all night. Mom and Dad have been looking for him."

"Really," Brad said, considering the possibilities.

A lady's voice called from around the house, "Ja-ake."

The boy yelled out, "I'm over here, by the front porch."

A second later an attractive woman in her early forties with blond highlighted hair falling around her shoulders came into view. Walking up to the boys, she greeted them with a big smile, "Hi Brad, it's so good to see you. We've missed you around here lately."

Brad returned the smile and joked, "Yes Ma'am, it must have been quite a while. The place has kind of fallen apart since I was here last."

She laughed, "Yeah, how about that storm last night? What a mess it made," she agreed, turning to look at the yard.

"Was anyone hurt when the tree fell on the house?" Brad asked, as he watched Jake run off to chase a squirrel which had ventured into the yard.

"No, no one was at home. We had all left for the beach yesterday. Well, everyone except Luke, who wanted to play a gig with his band last night. He evidently never made it home, which I'm sort of concerned about. He hasn't called or anything. You haven't seen him have you?"

Brad thought, with concern, *my Mom would have the entire town looking for me if I didn't come home without calling.* "No Ma'am, I came over looking for him myself." He paused, "Mrs. Finney, I'm a little worried about Luke and these guys he's hanging out with."

She nodded in agreement. "Yes, Brad, I thought maybe this band thing was just a phase, an outlet to deal with his father's leaving, but he has changed so. It's so hard to figure out how to handle a boy his age, who has been through so much hurt. I thought that having Dave in his life, as a father-figure, would help, but Luke won't even give him a chance. Dave's a good man. He tries to talk to Luke, but Luke is so cold to him."

"I'm sorry to hear that, Mrs. Finney. I guess replacing a Dad isn't that easy." Brad said with a heavy heart.

She looked away sadly, then back at Brad and lamented, "I am so sorry that life had to change so for Luke, but sometimes we have no control over what others choose to do."

He noticed her wipe a tear from her eye, "Mrs. Finney, I'm going to try to spend more time with Luke and maybe see if he'd like to come to youth group at church."

"I think that would be a fine thing, Brad. He needs a good influence right now. I hope he comes home soon. Since there's no electricity in the house, we're headed back to the beach until Monday, when the repair work starts," she explained with a look of concern.

"Well, if I see Luke I'll tell him to call you, and if you've left town I'll invite him to stay over at our house," Brad replied, hoping to comfort her.

"Brad that would give me such peace, knowing Luke was at your house," she affirmed, reaching out to give him a hug.

As she turned to leave, Brad stared at the front door, thinking. He called to her, "Mrs. Finney, what happened to the front door?"

"Isn't that something?" she replied, shaking her head as she walked back toward him. "The firemen broke it down when no one came to the door. They were afraid someone might have been hurt inside. I am glad Luke wasn't at home. He could have been severely injured by the tree limbs that came right into his room. I guess God is looking after him." The thought seemed to give her hope.

"Mrs. Finney, you can be sure of that," Brad responded confidently.

She smiled, closed her eyes as she nodded in agreement and said quietly, "Thank you." She turned and walked back toward the garage.

Brad prayed quietly, "Lord, help her. Draw her to your truth. Lead her back to you." Brad had known Mrs. Finney for many years. He felt she knew about God in her mind, and at one time had responded to God, but had never fully given her whole heart to Jesus. She was a very nice person, but she was just sort of a spectator and not a player in God's kingdom. As a result, some of the choices she had made in life; ignoring God's word, had brought her great pain. Abruptly, Brad was awakened from his thoughts by a shrill voice, shouting.

"Storm troopers, run! The storm troopers are advancing, draw your weapons!" Jake announced, as he stopped, waving his light saber sporadically in front of Brad. Brad noticed a silvery-metal, cylinder-shaped flashlight sitting on the steps, perhaps left by the fire department. He quickly grabbed it up, clicked it on and began artfully wielding it against the imaginary forces of evil arrayed before him.

Jake grinned and yelled, "Watch out behind you!" as he rushed over and slew the foe that was about to strike down his new partner in the galactic fight against the evil empire.

After a few minutes of valiant battle, they heard a feminine voice calling. Could it be the brave heroine, Princess Leia, coming to join the battle?

"Ja-ake, it's time to go," came the voice of Luke's older sister. "Where are you?" she called as she rounded the corner.

Jake cried out, "Oh no, it's the evil emperor!" Jake turned and held his light saber with both hands in front of him, ready to strike.

Luke's sister was a cheerful but no nonsense nineteen year old. She had been in all the right clubs at school, a cheerleader, and class vice president. Sandie, a striking young woman whose dark brown eyes matched her shimmering brown hair, seemed to have a good head on her shoulders. She knew what she wanted out of life and was determined to get it. Brad figured she would be a lawyer or something.

Sandie insisted firmly, "Jake, you come back here this instant or we're going to leave you." Seeing Brad standing there, she exclaimed in her bubbly way, "Oh, hi Brad. How's it going? I haven't seen you in forever. I was wondering who mom was talking to out here."

Brad smiled back and stammered awkwardly. "Hi, ah-h, I came over to find Luke, but he seems to. . ." He was cut off by a voice that came in front of the garage.

"Where did everyone go? San-die! Ja-ake! We're ready to go," Mr. Finney called, walking toward them. "Hi Brad," he called, "Hope you're doing well."

"Hello sir—doing just fine," Brad responded respectfully, as he set the flashlight back down on the step.

"Sorry we have to rush off, but we are heading back to the beach. The condo is paid for through Monday, and we've missed almost a whole day thanks to that storm last night. If you see Luke, tell him he's missing all the fun. I sure wish he would have come with us," Mr. Finney explained.

"Yeah, I don't know what he sees in that grungy band of his. He seems to care more about them than his own family," Sandie interjected.

"I'm sure it's just a phase," Mr. Finney responded, trying to keep the peace.

Brad nodded, "Yes sir, I hope so."

Mr. Finney rounded up Jake, and everyone piled into the Explorer. They headed down the street waving at Brad who was walking toward his bike.

He picked up the bike and started toward the street. He was about to mount it when the black Beamer came roaring up to him. As the tinted window came down Brad felt a nervous knot in the pit of his stomach.

"Yo Brad, you haven't seen my drummer, Luke, have you?" Sammy asked again, this time in a more annoyed tone.

"No, you were right. Luke's family said that it appeared he hasn't been home all night," Brad affirmed, trying to put on a friendly demeanor.

"Is that right? Well, if you see him, you'll let me know, won't you? I'll make it worth your while, if you know what I mean." Sammy proposed, as he glanced down the street as if scanning the area for some sort of prey.

Brad was now more concerned than ever for Luke, and asked, "So, why are you looking for Luke anyway? Maybe if I see him I could give him a message."

Sammy got an annoyed, distant look and with a slight clinching of his teeth, sneered, "I think maybe, you just need to mind your own business. This is between me and Luke. You had best, just stay out of it. You just tell him to see me. Got it?"

Brad felt a mixture of anger and fear welling up inside. He just looked at Sammy, not saying a word. Sammy hit the gas and sped away. Watching the sleek black machine take off down the street, Brad noticed the personalized license plate on the back of the car. It read DRAGON2. For a few seconds Brad thought that it had read DRAEGON2. He marveled briefly at how similar the two names were. As he stood there watching Sammy's car stop at the corner, he shuddered as the tail lights lit up and brought back an eerie feeling. *What was it?* He wondered, *The dream.* The red taillights and the blackness of the car looked very similar to the eyes of the metallic-looking dude in the dream. For a few seconds Brad was staring back into the face of a huge force holding him up by one powerful arm, once again gripped by the fear of the moment. Brad shook his head and declared out loud "No!" He would not let fear dominate his life. What his sister had inferred at the breakfast table was in large part true. All his life, he had been afraid: afraid of the dark, afraid of creatures lurking under his bed, and afraid of strangers. But most of all, Brad was afraid of death while he slept. Brad had been plagued with nightmares about someone trying to kill him as he slept. He was almost sixteen years old and wanted to be brave. How could God use him if he was so afraid? Would fear stop him from talking to people about the gospel? *The Bible says that God has not given me a spirit of fear, but of love, joy and a sound mind,* Brad thought as he let the words from the Bible encourage him.

Coming back to reality, Brad picked up his bike and started down the street. He had gone about two blocks when a curious thought struck him. The flashlight that was sitting on the porch, which had turned into his imaginary light saber; he had seen it before. It had been at many Boy Scout camping trips. It was just like one that belonged to Luke. *I guess there could be more than one person with a flashlight like that.* Brad thought, as he slowed his pedaling. Luke's flashlight however, could be easily indentified. It had a metal casing, and Luke had taken a nail and etched his initials in the bottom cap, which screwed off of the battery compartment. Brad quickly did a 180 and headed back to Luke's. He had a funny feeling about that flashlight. *Maybe Luke did come home last night!* Brad raced into the driveway, and across the front yard. Hitting the brakes hard, he skidded to a stop right in front of the porch. To Brad's surprise, the porch was empty. The flashlight was nowhere to be found. His mind ran back through the events of the afternoon. He had held on to that flashlight through much of the conversation with Mrs. Finney. *I put it back on the step when I was talking to Mr. Finney. Jake could not have picked it up because he had run off to the side of the house, near the fallen tree. No one else picked it up because I was standing near the porch until everyone walked around the house to get in the car to leave. It had to have been on the porch after everyone had left. So what could have happened to it? Who could have taken it?*

As Brad stood there, like one of the Hardy boys thinking through the day's events, he heard the muffled sound of a door closing inside the house. Brad's heart skipped a beat, and he wondered who could be in there. He crept up to the boarded front door, got down on his hands and knees and peered into the bottom pane of the sidelights around the door. Brad saw the back of a figure, dressed in dark clothes, the hood of his sweatshirt pulled over his head. The intruder was doing something in the hall closet. Brad backed away from the door, off of the porch and, crouched behind the bushes in front of the house. He sat there a moment, thinking. *What should I do? Suppose they have a gun or knife.* Brad grew angry at the fear trying to keep him from doing anything. He decided he had to at least find out who it was.

Chapter 4

Facing The Intruder

Brad moved quickly and quietly around the house to the back door which was on the lower end of the house. He looked through the glass into a basement storage room. Brad was familiar with this room, as he and Luke had built various Boy Scout projects and other fun stuff down there. Brad tried the door knob. It turned. He hesitated for a moment, considering if what he was doing was right. Then he wondered what the intruder might do when they met. He hadn't seen a weapon, and Brad believed he was bigger than this person. *Maybe it's just a wayward kid, taking advantage of the Finney's misfortune— trying to lift something for a quick sale, needing drug money.* He had to find out what the person was doing.

Slowly, Brad opened the door. He had it about one-third of the way open when the door started this loud cre-e-ak. Brad stopped immediately and listened. He waited for a minute or two, which seemed like an eternity. He then slipped between the space in the doorway without moving it further. Stealthily, Brad crept past the furnace and some old shelves stacked with dusty boxes and jars. Just past a utility sink was another door and a short stairway that lead up into a small laundry room, near the garage. The door from the laundry room to the kitchen was open. Brad stopped and listened again. As he entered the kitchen, he crouched and moved behind the island. About that time he heard a door shut and footsteps going up the stairs. Brad walked along with the steps, to cover the sound of his footfalls. He came to the entry hall and stopped, seeing that the staircase was empty. He waited there a minute, watching. Ever so quietly, he started up the stairs, his heart beating so loudly that he wondered if the intruder could hear it.

Brad decided to get down on all fours and climb the remaining steps down low so that if the mysterious person rounded the corner, Brad could tackle him at the knees and knock him down. He reached the top step. Peeking round the corner near the floor, Brad saw movement through the partially open door at the end of the hall.

What would they be doing in Luke's room? Brad wondered. *I bet it's a looter, a kid trying to steal Luke's computer.* Brad was incensed at the thought of someone trying to take advantage of the Finney's troubles. Emboldened now, he sneaked to the door and watched.

The room was somewhat dark because of the tarp over the window and the lack of electricity, but Brad could see someone crouching in front of Luke's drum set. Luke's room was still a mess of broken glass, leaves, branches and debris, because of the shattered windows and the fallen tree. However, the damage was not nearly as severe as in his dream.

The person in the room had his back to Brad and was taking the cover off of the front of the bass drum. *Was this person dumb enough to try to walk out with an entire drum set?* As Brad watched, the prowler moved some pillows used to muffle the sound of the bass drum and pulled out a small black pouch, like a money pouch, which he put into a gray satchel. That's when Brad noticed the flashlight from outside, lying on the bed.

At that moment, a phone started ringing. The startled burglar turned and jumped to his feet. Brad drew a quick breath, set his stance and in the deepest voice he could muster announced, "What do you think you are doing in here?"

Abruptly, the burglar in black rushed at Brad and tackled him, knocking Brad backward against the wall. Brad immediately grabbed his assailant and being the bigger of the two, wrestled him through a doorway into what was now Jake's bedroom. They stumbled together onto the floor. As they rolled around, the hood of the foe slipped off his head. It revealed, to Brad's complete astonishment, the battered and bruised face of his friend, Luke. About that same time Luke recognized Brad.

"Luke!" Brad exclaimed dumbfounded. "What's going on?"

Luke began to laugh in nervous relief. "I could ask you the same thing. You scared me to death. I thought you were. . ." Luke stopped in mid sentence. His tone became more serious. "What are you doing here?"

"Well, let me up, and I'll tell you," Brad replied, a little miffed that his smaller friend had wound up on top of this scuffle. But, Luke had always been lightning fast. Brad chalked it to the nervous energy of a drummer type. "I was looking for you. Man, where have you been? Don't you know that your family is worried sick about you?" Brad sat up and leaned against the wall.

"They don't worry about me. They know I can take care of myself. Besides, if that guy my mom married thinks he can step in and be my dad and tell me what to do, he's got another thing coming." Luke stated defiantly.

"Luke, he's your Dad now. Why don't you give him a chance?"

"I don't need a Dad. I have done perfectly well without one for almost sixteen years. I also don't need some goodie-two-shoes telling me how I should live my life. I'm doing just fine on my own, so you can just butt out and leave me alone." Luke glared at Brad.

Brad returned an intense look into Luke's face and noticed how beat up he was. He wanted to be angry at Luke for calling him a goodie-two-shoes, but Luke looked so pitiful. He could feel nothing but compassion for him. His lip was swollen, and he had a cut on his left cheek as well as a black eye. Brad wanted to quip that it really looked like he could take care of himself—not. Instead he got control of his sarcasm, realizing he was just a convenient target for his friend's bitterness. Finally Brad admitted, "Luke, I know we've sort of drifted apart in the last year. But, I'm here because I care about you, and I'm afraid that you're in some sort of danger."

Luke's expression softened momentarily, and he asked with a hint of nervousness, "Danger? Why would you that think I am in danger?"

Seeing that Luke was indeed a little fearful, Brad responded slowly, "Well, you've been hanging out with some real rough company. Your family didn't even know where you were for days, and that Sammy Dornberg has been asking me if I've seen you, like he's after you for something."

At that Luke was clearly shaken, although he did his best to cover it up. "Sammy? What did he want?"

"He said he needs to see you. Said he'd pay me if I told him where you were. Sounds like trouble to me, man. Also," Brad paused, considering what he was about to say, "I know this might sound weird to you but I just have to tell you. I had a wild dream, and someone in the dream told me that you were in danger."

Luke raised one eyebrow and asked, "Yeah, who?"

Brad thought for a second, wondering if Luke would freak or something, but finally said, "Jesus."

"Jesus!" Luke repeated, shaking his head in dismay. "So Jesus is talking to you now. I wonder about you sometimes, man."

"Luke, Jesus can speak to our hearts through His Spirit. I believe He's trying to speak to you."

"Look," Luke stated with obvious annoyance, "I don't believe in all that stuff. It doesn't work for me. My life is in my music and the group—I mean the band. They are my family now. They take care of me, and one day we'll be rich and famous and I won't need anybody. I don't want to hear anything about that loser, Jesus. He's never done anything for me."

"Except die on a cross for you," Brad responded calmly.

"I didn't ask Him to die for me, and I don't need a bunch of religious mumbo jumbo in my life right now," Luke retorted belligerently.

"You're right, you didn't ask him to die for you. None of us did, because we don't know what's good for us. But Jesus knows and cares. He's constantly trying to get our attention." Brad explained, while silently asking God to help him say the right thing.

"Man, I don't need your help or your so called "God's" help. I just want to be left alone!" Luke scoffed, pointing an angry finger in Brad's face.

A great sadness swept over Brad as he studied Luke's angry eyes. "Luke, I came over for another reason, really."

Brad hardly finished the sentence when Luke cut him off, "I don't want to be preached to, OK? So, what is it you want?"

Brad looked at him, trying to suck up the emotion and sighed, "Luke, I want to say that I'm sorry and to ask for your forgiveness."

Luke was taken aback and asked, "Forgiveness? For what?"

"For not being a better friend when you were going through a rough time. I was in my own little world of comfort, and you were feeling all alone, like no one cared about you, not even your own father. I was stupid, and at that time I was not really following God, and I'm sorry for that."

Luke's expression turned to one of deep thought, considering Brad's words. He didn't respond but walked out of Jake's room back into his and picked up his satchel and flashlight. Finally Luke stated coolly, "I gotta go."

Brad asked, "Go where?"

"Look Brad, I appreciate your concern and all. But, I don't want you to get involved. This is my life, and you don't really understand it," Luke huffed, stuffing a t-shirt into the satchel.

"Tell me something Luke, how'd your face get all beat up? Who did that to you?"

"I just did something dumb, OK?" Luke replied.

"Was it one of your new friends? If so, I wouldn't want friends like that."

Luke looked up at him with a frown of disgust. "They're alright. At least they stick with you."

Brad thought, *yeah, but at what price?* Then he suggested, "Luke, you really ought to call your Mom and let her know you're alive. She's really worried. They all are."

Luke sighing, responded, "OK, OK, I'll call her as soon as I get to The Snake Pit, or rather, the Dragon's Den. They're renaming it, you know."

"The Snake Pit," Brad responded in amazement. "They let someone your age in there? That's one of the worst bars in town. What do you mean they are renaming it?"

"This big shot from up north bought it out and has made a lot of changes. It's a really cool place. He's trying to make it more of a hangout for teenagers."

Brad hesitated then dove in head first. "Aren't these guys involved in illegal drug trafficking? Luke, how'd you get involved with these guys anyway?"

Luke smiled and responded in a cocky manner, "You just have to have connections, my friend. Besides, the band needs the money and the exposure. I'm a talented drummer, and they give me whatever I need. Well, dude, it was good to see you, but I got to run." Luke picked up his bag and headed out the door.

Brad wondered if he should ask Luke what was in the pouch he had pulled out of the bass, but instead asked, "Luke, are you in any kind of trouble?"

Luke shook his head and declared, "Brad, you worry too much."

The two walked down the stairs into the kitchen and Brad offered, "If you need a place to stay while your room is being fixed, just come on over. If you need anything at all, call me. OK?"

Luke turned to him and just said, "Thanks, man, but I'll be fine." They left through the garage door, and Luke started walking down the street in the opposite direction of Brad's house.

As Luke walked quickly down the street, Brad called to him, "Luke! Be careful!"

Luke stopped and turned back, "Dude, I'm not a little kid!"

Brad thought to himself, *no, you're right. You are a whole fifteen years old.* Brad looked down at his watch. *Oh man, I'm going to be late for dinner.* He jumped on his bike and peddled hard all the way to his house. In his haste, Brad missed the black BMW that rounded the corner behind him. It pulled up slowly behind Luke. Two guys got out and confronted Luke, who then got into the back seat. Slowly, the car continued down the road, and disappeared around the corner.

Brad arrived home just after the family had sat down for dinner. He apologized for his tardiness and began to explain what had happened at the Finney's house.

"I can't believe that he's going to play at that Snake Pit place," Mandy balked. "Haven't people been killed there?"

Mom agreed, "If his mom knew he was playing there, I believe she would do something."

"Mom, she knows. She knew he was playing at the Rat Race Club last night. I don't think she feels that she can control his life. She believes she needs to give him his space." Brad explained. "By the way, Luke said they are changing the name to the Dragon's Den."

"What's the deal with the names of these bars anyway? They can't come up with anything a little more inspiring than some vermin's home?" Dad joked. "Where are they playing tomorrow, The Tarantula's Web?"

Brad smiled, "Well, I was thinking about going over there to hear Luke play."

His mom almost choked on the tea she was about to swallow, but managed to get out among the sputters, "B-Bradford Johnson, have you lost your mind?"

Brad just said it for the reaction, and he thought he would see how long she would fall for it. "But Mom, I'm curious to see what kind of place it is and I'd like to support my friend's talent."

His mom sat there speechless with her mouth open. Then she caught the grin he was trying to keep from spreading across his face. She reached over and smacked him across the back of his head and asked, "What are you trying to do, add more gray to my head?"

They were all laughing now, and Brad chided, "Mom, don't you know me better than that? Besides, I think you have to be eighteen to get into that place."

Brad's dad questioned, "I wonder what the authorities would say to a boy Luke's age being in that environment? I bet they could get into a lot of trouble for that."

"I guess as long as he's not drinking or anything, it's OK," Brad reasoned. "Luke also mentioned that they were trying to make the place more of a teenage hangout. But, I'm concerned that Luke might be getting into real trouble with his new friends. I'm just not sure what kind."

"It sounds like we all need to continue to pray for Luke and his family," Mandy added, as the family agreed, and finished up their dinner.

"Well," Dad asked, glancing at his watch, "is anyone up for going bowling?"

Mandy replied, "I would love to, but Sherri and several of us are going over to Wren's house to watch *Anne of Green Gables*."

Brad smirked, "*Anne of Green Gables*? How many times have you seen that snoozer anyway?"

"I've only seen it once this year," she replied defensively. "I know it's not nearly as intellectually stimulating as the Star Wars movies that your friends watch endlessly, but it is fun."

Brad just rolled his eyes and ran upstairs to find his sneakers.

"Dad, could you drop Sherri and me off at Wren's house?"

"Sure, I think that can be arranged." He replied, slipping his shoes on.

"Is Sherri going to walk over or would you like for us stop and pick her up?" Mom asked while searching her purse for some bowling coupons she had clipped out of the newspaper.

"Would you mind if we picked her up?"

"No problem," Dad smiled. "We go right by there anyway. Is everyone ready to go? I'm ready to do serious damage to some bowling pins." He said, throwing an imaginary bowling ball down the hallway, practicing his form.

"Dad, I'd be happy to beat you guys at bowling again," Brad announced confidently as he barreled down the stairs.

Richard laughed at his son's cockiness, but Mom smiled and exclaimed, "Ha, when is the last time you've beaten me, kid?"

Brad shook his head as if to say, "We'll see." He knew, however, that she had a mean spin that was hard to beat. Brad replied. "Would you like to make a small wager on that?"

His mom in mock exasperation, responded," Bradford, you know I don't gamble." Then, smiling slyly she added, "But, since this is a sure thing, it's not gambling. I tell you what, how about the looser treats us to ice cream afterward."

This made Brad a little nervous, but the gauntlet had been thrown down. "OK, you've got a deal." Just to egg her on, he added, "It will be very close to taking candy from a baby. "

"In your dreams, fella," his mom asserted.

"Plea-se, Mom, don't use that expression," Brad replied jokingly, "I'd really like a decent night's sleep tonight."

Chapter 5

The Second Encounter

It was almost ten o'clock when Brad and his parents returned from the bowling alley. As they entered the house Brad's mom taunted, "Thanks for the hot fudge sundae, dear. It was yum-my." She leaned over and kissed his cheek with a smack.

"Well," Brad replied, "at least you're sweet in the way you rub it in." Brad didn't at all mind buying his mom the ice cream, especially since his Dad had picked up the tab for everyone else including his.

"Boy, am I tired," Dad admitted, while bringing his hand to his mouth to cover a big yawn. You guys wore me out."

"Me, too," Brad agreed as he opened the closet door to hang up his red NC State jacket. "I can hardly wait to hit that pillow tonight." Everyone said goodnight, and Brad tromped slowly, feet heavy, up the stairs and got ready for bed. He had barely laid down when he noticed flashes of light from his bedroom window. *Oh, no,* he thought, *not another thunder storm.* He rolled over and looked at his alarm clock, which gleamed 10:26 and made sure that it was set correctly. "Lord, I could really use a better night's sleep tonight. After all, tomorrow is Sunday and we get up pretty early for Youth Fellowship and church." Instantly, there was a low, growling roll of thunder in the distance. Brad quickly added, "Nevertheless, Lord, Your will be done." Brad believed that God had a sense of humor, mainly because he gave people the ability to laugh. As he watched the room flicker with the bluish brightness, he thought about God's great and awesome power, and His amazing creativity. "There is no one else like You, God," he whispered lifting his hands up toward heaven. The thunder rumbled again, and Brad felt as if Jesus were giving him a big bear hug. *Wow, that's cool,* Brad thought. Lying there, he began to pray for his family and friends.

As the lightning flashed in his eyes, and the thunder got louder, Brad thought, *I will never get to sleep.* He got up and walked over to the window to pull down the blinds. Just as he grabbed the cord for the blinds, a flash of lightning lit up the entire front yard below. Brad did a double take. Standing in his yard near the street was a figure dressed in dark clothing. Brad moved to the side of the window and peered around the edge waiting for the next flash. Sure enough, as soon as it flashed he could make out a person standing in the corner of the yard nearest the street. The mysterious person appeared to be wearing a dark hooded sweatshirt. *Could it be?* Brad wondered. *Is that Luke?* Brad stood in front of the window so that the next time the lightning flashed, whoever it was would see him. Immediately the sky lit up, and Brad waved his hands. Brad could barely make out the outline of the figure from the pale light of the street light, who waved back in response. Brad raised his window and stuck his head out into the cool, muggy night air. "Luke, is that you?" he asked in a loud whisper.

"Yeah, man, it's me," he responded. "Can you come down? I need to talk to you. I-I need your help."

Brad looked at the clock which read 10:54 in brilliant green. He turned back, "Just give me a minute to get my shoes on, and I'll be right down." Brad stumbled around his room until he kicked a shoe. He managed to get them on and find his way to the door of his room. On his way out he grabbed his old Mudcats baseball jacket which was hanging on a hook on the back of the door. All the lights were out and Brad assumed that everyone was asleep. *Thank God for night lights,* Brad thought as he worked his way downstairs to the front door. His dad had them scattered around the house because he hated tripping over things in the middle of the night. Brad opened the front door to the chirp of a little frog singing somewhere in the bushes. He closed it quietly and ran over to where Luke was still standing near the street. As he did, the sky lit up again, followed a few seconds later by a crash of thunder. The cool, clammy night air sent a shiver through his body. "Luke, what's going on? Don't you want to come inside? I know it's fun to watch the lightning and all, but this is a little crazy," Brad said, putting on his jacket.

"Brad, I really need your help. They're after me," Luke confided, his voice shaking with fear.

At that moment, a car rounded the corner, moving slowly down the street. Luke grabbed Brad's coat and pulled him into the shrubbery at the edge of the yard. As the lights from the vehicle approached, Brad got a strange feeling in the pit of his stomach. *Is that some kind of jacked-up Hum-V?* It seemed to be way too high off the ground, and the headlights were too far apart. That's when Brad realized that it wasn't a car at all, but a very strange-looking vehicle that didn't have any tires. It appeared to have nothing actually touching the pavement at all. The thing was hovering about six feet off the ground. "What is that?" Brad asked, as he studied the machine through the branches of the azalea bushes. The craft was about as long as a school bus, Brad figured, but wasn't boxy. It was more rounded, like a cylinder with a glass encased compartment on top, toward the rear of the craft. There were two wing-like appendages which flared out on each side toward the rear. Each supported what looked like a giant computer mouse. Their undersides pulsated with an orange glow. There was also one similar device on the lower front end of the vehicle. Brad speculated they were enabling it to hover. He was amazed at how quiet it was. A slight humming was all he heard, along with an occasional soft but deep rumbling. There was a flat square apparatus protruding from the top that made a slight high-pitched whine whenever it moved. Brad believed it to be involved in surveillance.

Brad studied what was obviously a cockpit area in the front. Inside, the glass the interior was aglow with assorted screens and lighted panels. He gasped as he could make out two large round shapes moving about. *Are those their heads, or are they wearing helmets?* He strained to see, but couldn't tell for sure.

Mounted on the ship were three gun-like weapons, two in the front and one just forward of the glass covered observation area near the back. Small lights of various colors illuminated various parts of its hull revealing vents and ports, some of which emitted gray clouds of steam. Near the rear of the craft, toward the top, was a cryptic form of lettering. In red, edged in black, all capital letters, on the side of the dull, silvery, metallic hull, was printed *A B Y S S*. Beneath it, in smaller print, was a line of some sort of hieroglyphics.

Luke whispered, "Pray that they don't see us."

Brad replied, "Believe me, I am. Luke, what is that thing?"

"Sh-h-h, they can hear us. We've got to get out of here." Just then a bright beam of light emanating from near the cockpit broke the darkness. When the light began to move away from them, the two boys crept away as thunder rolled in the sky. They moved a little further into the wooded area next to the Johnson's yard and came to a drainage ditch that ran under the street through a large cement pipe. Luke and Brad had explored it many times as kids. Luke motioned to Brad. The two crawled over, and then into the pipe which was big enough to sit up in.

Brad was thankful that it hadn't started to rain, and the water in the pipe was only a few inches deep. They sat there in silence until Brad finally asked, "Now tell me—what is that? Are you in trouble with some sort of government agency?"

"No dude, that's not from the government. They're not from this world at all. They're from some place called Abyss, and they are here to destroy our way of life. They come out on stormy nights, which I believe they have a way of initiating. These guys roam the streets and grab people to brain wash them into following them. They play off weak people's fears and off strong people's desires, to get them to basically destroy themselves. Mindlessly, they're drawn into stuff like drugs, easy money and partying."

Brad thought, *sounds like some people in government to me.* "You mean the people are knowingly serving these alien beings?"

"No. At least, most of them aren't. Most of them go through a procedure that erases the memory of being captured. Their mind is dulled by the procedure, and they just follow their own selfishness."

"Luke, how do you know all of this?"

"Like, how do you think? I was captured by them once."

"So why wasn't your memory erased?" Brad asked with a bit of suspicion.

"I'm friends with one of the guys who's a Control Leader. That's what they call those who have sold their soul to the devil, so to speak. They've been promised power and money when the Draegonians have taken over."

Brad could not believe his ears. "You mean like the computer game? This can't be. It's just a silly game. This sounds like some kind of crazy futuristic movie." Brad thought, *God wouldn't let something like this happen.* "Luke, are you high on some kind of mind altering drug?"

"Brad, do you think I'm making all of this up? I guess I made up that scout ship out there. If I'm on drugs, then you are, too. Look, the computer game was designed to get people hooked into their system. At a certain level of the game, they can begin to control the minds of the players. If people respond a certain way, they know they have a subject who will fit into their plan. That's where they get the Control Leaders," Luke declared irritably.

Brad had a sudden thought, which sent shivers up his spine. *If this is real, then what about my family?* Pictures of strange metal-like creatures coming into his home raced through his muddled brain. Thoughts of big four-fingered androids picking up his parents and sister flooded his mind. Brad grabbed Luke's arm stating fervently, "I've got to get back to the house. My family! They must be warned."

"No, Brad, wait!"

But before Luke could stop him, Brad crawled down the pipe, leaned out, and looked up into the sky. He couldn't hear anything but a distant rumbling, which sounded like thunder. The wind was picking up, and it was beginning to rain. Brad could see that the ship had moved further up the street. It seemed to be hovering further from the ground now, about parallel with the height of the houses. He turned to Luke who had caught him by the leg and was pulling him back. Brad turned, "Let go, man, it's beginning to rain. We better get out of this drain pipe."

"Is it still out there?" Luke asked, letting go of Brad.

"Yeah, but it's moved up the street a-ways."

The trees were now swaying to and fro as the wind whipped the branches fiercely. Lightning flashed more brilliantly than ever. Before climbing out of the creek bed, the boys crouched and watched the ship hovering down the street. Suddenly, it was as if the beast had discovered its prey. A couple of laser bursts from one of the weapons mounted on the top of the craft lit up the area in rapid succession. The first struck the top portion of a tall pine, which crashed to the ground next to a house. The second one hit the roof of the house near the chimney, sending bricks flying and sparking a small fire. Shortly after that, a man and a woman in bathrobes came running out of the house. The couple stopped for a minute, holding each other, blinded by a beam of light emanating from the ship. As they stood there in utter confusion, the scout ship lowered to about eight feet from the pavement. Several metallic-looking troopers marched out, via a hatch which lowered from the underside of the craft to form a ramp.

After a few moments, the boys saw another man come running out of a neighboring house toward his car, bent on fleeing the horrific scene. Before he was halfway across his yard, the small pointed weapon on one side of the ship whipped around. It fired a laser burst, which hit the brand new Dodge Challenger near the rear side panel. An explosion sent the car flipping up into the air, like a toy. The bright yellow vehicle landed upside down on the edge of the yard, crushing the mailbox like a twig.

"Whoa!" both boys exclaimed, almost in unison. They watched the man, who had stopped dead in his tracks, fall face down on the grass, frozen with fear. The silver demons rounded up the terrified victims and herded them toward the ramp. Several smaller, wiry figures with oversized heads and reptile-like tails appeared from inside the craft. They seemed to take charge of the captives, escorting them into the vehicle. Once they were all inside, the hatch closed. The eerie craft lifted from the ground as the wind howled.

The weather had completely deteriorated, to the point that they needed to seek cover. "Follow me!" Luke shouted, barely audible above the roaring wind. They moved quickly through the woods until the beam of Luke's flashlight exposed a small wooden shed. They were about to enter it when Brad looked up, into the threatening sky. Fear gripped him as he glimpsed an ominous dark wedged-shape silhouetted above the clouds, amid the flashes of lightning. *It just can't be,* he thought to himself.

With a cre-eak, Luke door opened the rustic door. Luke's flashlight revealed several shelves on the wall. On one of them was a battery operated lamp, used for camping. Brad took it off of the shelf and placed it on the floor. To his amazement, it worked. It lit up, giving the spider web filled room a creepy dim glow that exaggerated the shadows cast by various pieces of lawn and garden equipment.

The wind was now so loud that Brad shouted, "Freight train!" Every kid who watches the weather channel knows what that means. They instantly crouched down on the floor beside the lawn mower and rotary-tiller, curled into a ball. The wind and rain raged so powerfully that the little wooden structure actually began to shake, and things began to fall off shelves and crash around them.

Brad was crying out to God, "Lord, please save us." After what seemed to have been an hour, even though it was only about twenty minutes by Brad's watch, the torrent began to die down. As it quieted Brad stared at the shed door. With all that had happened to them that night, Brad couldn't help wondering if they'd open that door to reveal a bunch of little Munchkins and a yellow brick road. He looked over toward Luke and asked, "Do you think we're still in Kansas?"

Luke, who didn't get it, asked, "Kansas? What are you talking about?" Brad shook his head. Finally, Luke laughed nervously, then muttered, "Oh yeah, that Kansas. Dorothy and Toto, I get it."

"Finally, a smile," Brad replied. "So, Luke, tell me again why your memory wasn't erased.

"Well," Luke began, "A bunch of the guys in the band were serious Players of the Draegonian Invasion game. They told me how awesome it was at level 66. They said it opened a door into a whole new world, especially if you were high on this particular drug. I got to level 66, but not on any drug. I wanted to see what it really was. It was basically a plan for controlling our society. Draegon said that this method was proven and that those who followed him would have guaranteed fame and riches."

Brad, who found all of this beyond belief, finally contested, "But it's just a game. Who would really believe all of this? It's just some sort of marketing gimmick isn't it?"

"That's what they want you to believe. Most people never make it to level 66, because to do so you have to have the cryptic keys, which are really difficult, nearly impossible, to find without the help of the Controllers. If a person responds correctly and follows the directives of the controllers, the keys appear. They say that the drugs help you see, but in reality they just get you hooked, so they can control you."

"But you still haven't told me how you got away from it," Brad wondered impatiently.

"I'm getting there," Luke replied. "I think the main reason I didn't get sucked in is: I stayed away from the drugs. I did it the first time, but saw how it messed with your mind and decided that was stupid. I needed to keep my mind clear."

"That was smart," Brad agreed.

"I wasn't too smart," Luke continued. "I thought I could play the game, pretending to go along, using my own rules. At first I got into all the stuff they were promising. The fame, girls, and money sounded great. Sammy, who is one of the controllers, said he was my friend, and that I could really go far in their new world. Then one day I actually saw Draegon. He's like their ruler, or Lord, they call him. He can appear in different forms."

"Really? Like one those shape-shifters on Star Trek?" Brad interrupted.

"Sort of, I guess. I know that at times he's a man, but sometimes he's a giant lizard with wings, like a dragon. Anyway, Draegon talked about ruling the world and turning kids against their parents. He tells them they need to be freed from the oppression of slavery from their parents, to be able to fulfill their hearts' desires."

"You're kidding," Brad marveled. "I can see how a lot of kids could be sucked into that. But, why would they be crazy enough to follow such a weird creature?"

"You'd be surprised at what people will do for enough money," Luke admitted. A look of shame and remorse filled his eyes. "I soon came to understand that Draegon only wanted to free them from their parents so that "he" could enslave them."

Brad was amazed at the spiritual truth in all this. Luke seemed to understand the gravity of the world's fallen state and how that there was really only two kingdoms. Brad wanted to explain the spiritual aspects of all of this, when Luke continued.

"The worst of it is, he says that Jesus was a fake, and Christianity is the greatest evil in the world. He says it was all made up by the disciples. Draegon teaches that all the Christians want to do is keep others from enjoying all the freedoms of life. He says that we should be able to do whatever we please without worrying about anyone else. When he started talking like that, I got this sick feeling in my stomach. My dad sort of believed that way. He did whatever he wanted and left us high and dry. I remember going to church with you, hearing the Bible read, and how Jesus went around helping people."

Wow, Brad thought, *he got more out of it than I realized.*

Luke continued. "I decided this Draegon dude was really lame, so I took off."

"So, that's why they're after you?" Brad asked.

"Well, that's part of the reason. The other reason is this." Luke pulled out a little black pouch and showed it to Brad. "This will blow the lid off of their whole plan."

Brad felt the bag which seemed almost empty. "What is it?"

Luke started to speak and then stopped and put a finger to his lips, listening to noises outside of the shed. They heard distant high-pitched mechanical screams followed by either explosions or thunder.

Brad whispered, "It sounds like the dragonfly droids are back." Luke stuffed the pouch inside a box of old newspapers. He whispered to Brad, "If anything happens to me, come back and get this. Take it to Sergeant Shackleton. He'll know what to do."

They sat quietly and didn't hear anything for about five minutes. Finally Brad spoke, "Luke, how have you managed to stay away from them this long?"

Luke looked at Brad intensely for a few seconds in deep thought. Brad could see that he wanted to say something but was hesitating. "What is it?" Brad pressed.

"This man, dressed all in white, I don't know exactly who he is. But, I was almost recaptured once, and he showed up."

"What happened? Brad asked excitedly.

"These Drae-goons I call them, had cornered me in an old warehouse where I was hiding. Evidently, one of my friends had sold me out. They opened-fire inside the warehouse with their laser cannons, and the building was soon engulfed in flames and smoke. I tried to get out, but I was trapped and they caught me. They were carrying me out to their scout ship when they saw this dude dressed in white standing by the door. When they saw him, they seemed confused and they came to a complete halt. He just spoke to them. All he said was: 'Loose him!' Immediately the goons let go of me and I fell to the floor. It was as if those huge, powerful troopers were paralyzed, trembling with fear, at the sight of this one person. I ran over to the man and thanked him."

Brad couldn't believe his ears and sat there speechless.

"I asked Him who he was, and he answered, 'Emmanuel.' Emmanuel who? I asked. He looked right into my eyes, like he was looking right through me, and said, 'Luke, you must choose whom you will serve, darkness or light. Make the right choice.' When I asked Him what He meant he said,

'Find your friend Brad. He is a true friend who will explain the truth to you.'"

Brad interrupted, "Did He tell you anything else?"

"No, he disappeared, and the Draegoons came back to life and started after me. It was funny though. They were after me and almost caught me again, when suddenly, it was like a giant imaginary bowling ball hit them and they all fell down like so many pins."

Brad replied, "Yeah, Jesus made a strike!" Brad laughed with excitement.

"Do you really think that's who it was, Brad?" Luke asked.

But, before Brad could answer, a loud mechanical screaming from above, broke off his words. The explosion shook the ground. It was followed by a loud cracking and then a crashing sound that rattled the shed.

"We've got to get out of here." Luke exclaimed, jumping up. He ran to the door with Brad following right behind. They struggled, trying to open the door.

Finally, both pushing together, they managed to open it enough for Luke to squeeze through.

"What is holding the door?" Brad asked. The darkness made it impossible to see what had happened.

"Tree branches," Luke called back shining his flashlight through the broken limbs. He began pulling the branches away from the door until finally, Brad was out. A tree had fallen right in front of the shed, barely missing it. They had to climb through the tangled mess of limbs and over the trunk.

The rain and wind had stopped. However, in the distance, the boys could still hear the menacing sounds of dragonfly fighter droids, along with periodic explosions. The two headed back into the wooded area that was next to Brad's house. Fighting through the brush, for about five minutes, they neared the edge of the woods.

Brad began to wonder again about the safety of his family. "Luke, I've got to get back to my house to make sure they haven't taken my family."

"No, Brad, you don't. Your family is safe for now."

"Safe? Those dudes are right next to my house! They're not safe!" Brad protested, a bit frantic.

"You don't understand. That's not their plan. For some reason, it seems that the only people they cannot control are serious Christians—you know, people like your family who read and study the Bible and go to church all the time. They call them religious fanatics."

"But," Brad wondered, "I saw them take Mr. Alexander Smith, the guy whose car got blown up. He goes to church."

"Well, obviously not everyone who goes to church is serious about it. Even though he goes to church, everybody knows that a fifty-plus-year-old man who hangs out at bars and drives a car like that is messing around. You know—like stepping out on his wife, not to mention the fact that he's involved in some shady businesses in town."

"How do they know all that stuff?" Brad asked.

"Are you kidding? This is the computer age. Let's just say they keep tabs. That's why I've got this pouch. . ." He stopped in mid sentence and exclaimed, "The pouch! I left it in that shed! I've got to go back and get it!"

As he turned to run back through the woods Brad noticed some bright, bluish lights over the brush from the direction of the shed. "Luke! Wait! Stop!" he called. It was too late. Luke was out of hearing range. Brad thought, and then prayed, "Lord, what should I do?" In his spirit, Brad clearly heard, "Go!"

Brad took off in the direction of Luke. The bluish colored lights were now moving away from him toward the street. Brad got to the shed which was completely dark. Stumbling around in the darkness, he tripped over something and fell head first into a mass of snarled branches and leaves. He grimaced as he felt a broken branch jab his abdomen and rip his skin. He grabbed hold of his stomach and winced, "Ou-ol, ma-an. I bet that leaves a scar." As he struggled to free himself, it was as if the tree were actually holding on to him. "Let me go!" he demanded, as he jerked his way free.

He stood upright and listened for a few seconds. Then called out, in what amounted to a loud whisper, "Luke! Are you here?" He listened . . . nothing. *Where is he,* Brad wondered? Then, he noticed the same bluish light. It shone through the woods now, near the street. Brad began feeling his way through the brush in the darkness. As fast as he could, he made his way back to the creek. Following the creek to the street, he peered up to see what was going on.

The scout ship was back, and there were about six of the Draegoons, as Luke called them. They were conferring around something lying in the street. Brad's heart fluttered as he realized that it was the body of a person. *It couldn't be. Oh, Lord Jesus, no.* Brad thought. About that time, one of the monstrous gleaming beasts scooped up the seemingly lifeless body of his friend. Brad could see Luke's shiny black hair falling away from his upside down face, as his assailant carried him up into the ship. The rest of them marched up the ramp. The ramp disappeared, into the ship which rose slowly into the night sky. With an incredible burst of speed, in a matter of seconds, it was totally gone.

All Brad could hear now was the sound of a lone cricket as he sat there in the darkness, horrified at the fate of his friend. "How could this happen?" he whispered. "God, how could you let this happen? You helped him before; why not now?" Brad was shaking over the trauma of what he had been through. With tears filling his eyes he cried out, "Why, Lord. Why is this all happening?"

Suddenly, Brad realized that he was no longer alone. He turned to face the Man in white once again. Light radiated away from Him in a way that made Him appear as though He were under water. "Why didn't you save Luke this time, Lord? He's trying to get away from those evil beings."

"Luke has not yet decided which path he will take: the narrow or the wide. He is placing his security in something other than my truth and my kingdom. I would like you to help him understand," the Man explained with an understanding smile.

Then he's not dead, Brad thought. "But, how can Luke be free now that they have captured him?" Brad asked rubbing the grime from his face.

"Don't lose hope, Brad. Persevere. Stand firm and be bold. For the Lord, your God is with you." Brad fell to his knees and lifted his hands in praise. For a minute or so he was warmed by the radiance of a growing light. Then, it was gone.

Brad, although totally exhausted, felt encouraged by his encounter with the man known as Emmanuel. He made his way across the yard and up to the front door of his house. He was amazed that everyone had slept through all of this.

He was too tired to think. Heading up to his room, he removed his jacket, then flipped off his shoes and fell into his bed.

Chapter 6

What Happened To Luke?

Brad awoke to a siren blaring outside. *What in the world is going on now?* He wondered, sitting straight up in bed. Brad opened his eyes to a room pulsating with diffused, red light coming from his window. His mind was swirling with thoughts of alien ships and Drae-goons, as he stumbled to the window. Two fire trucks were parked down the street among a sea of blue and red flashing lights. A couple of dozen people were moving around the scene, and Brad could see the glimmer and smoke of a small fire through the trees. He remembered, although his brain was still in a fog, that the scout ship had destroyed Mr. Smith's car. *I bet that's what is going on.* Suddenly he gasped, as a bright light shone down from the sky, illuminating the commotion below. *Oh no! Those people will be incinerated,* Brad thought, turning his eyes to the sky to see what awful alien craft would annihilate the helpless crowd below. About that time the clouds parted to reveal the blue and white colors of the Sky Five helicopter. Brad heard the muffled fop-fop-fop of the blades. *Man, that was close,* he thought, *I don't know how much more of these mind games I can take.*

Brad turned back to look at the clock. *3:16,* Brad thought, *I must have barely fallen asleep. It seemed like I was out half the night. Boy, my clothes sure dried fast. They were soaked.*

Light was coming from the hallway. Brad realized he was not the only one awake. He opened his door and made his way down the hall. A lamp was on in his parent's room, but it was vacant. Brad reached the stairs and slowly descended them. As he reached the base of the stairs, he could hear the muffled chatter of the TV coming from the family room. Suddenly, the front door opened unexpectedly, causing Brad to nearly jump out of his skin. His Dad was standing there, dripping, in a yellow poncho. Before entering the house he removed the poncho, leaving it on the porch.

"Dad, what's going on?" Brad asked.

His Dad laughed and remarked, "Son, I think you could sleep through a freight train hitting the house, or at least a tornado."

That's what you think, Brad thought to himself.

"It seems that a tornado touched down just three houses away and you slept right through it, "his Dad continued.

"No Dad, I didn't sleep at all," Brad contested, as he followed his father into the family room.

The news broadcaster was reporting scattered damage of what appeared to be tornado activity in the area. "And now we will go live to our eyes-in-the-sky reporter for a full report on the damage in the area," the reporter announced excitedly, and with perfect diction.

Mandy, who was watching intently said, "Look, there we are! There's our neighborhood." The TV revealed downed trees, and some partially torn off roofs. Next, the camera zoomed in on an upside down automobile lying partially on the lawn of a house just down the street. "Can you imagine a tornado so close to our house? Isn't that scary?" Mandy declared as she hugged a pillow from the sofa.

"I'm so thankful that God is watching over us and protected us from that awful storm," Mom acknowledged, as Dad nodded his head in agreement.

"It wasn't a tornado," Brad muttered sort of under his breath.

"What did you say, dear?" Mom inquired.

Brad thought a minute, wondering about revealing the night's exploits. "Mom, it wasn't a tornado. It was a scout ship."

"A what?" Mom asked, with a slightly raised pitch to her voice.

Brad slowly realized how dumb that sounded, but he had said it, and now had to continue. "Last night a Draegonian scout ship came into the neighborhood and took some people away."

His entire family sat there with their gaze fixed on him in total silence for a second. Then, emanating from his father's mouth came, "Duh-de-du-duh, duh-de-du-duh." The familiar opening from the old Twilight Zone series wafted through the air, along with the laughter of everyone.

Brad, somewhat irked, retorted, "Look, Dad, I'm serious. I was there last night. I saw that car flip up into the air, not by a tornado but a laser blast from the ship."

"Brad," Dad replied, trying to calm his son, "You weren't outside last night. I've been up since the storm started about an hour ago and I checked on you. Son, you were fast asleep."

Brad sat there in deep thought.

"Brad," Mom spoke up kindly, "Don't you think you could have had another dream."

Brad was stunned at the very idea. "It couldn't have been a dream. It was too real."

"Dreams can seem very real," Dad continued. "Was Luke in it?"

"Yes!" Brad admitted with surprise, "How'd you know?"

"I was just reading online yesterday how our dreams are often about things that are concerning us deeply. Son, you've been very concerned about Luke. It's very likely that this would show up in your dreams."

Brad shook his head, thinking. Then he realized his stomach was hurting and he remembered his fall into the downed tree. *This will prove it was real.* "Look here," he insisted. "What about this?" He reached down and pulled up his t-shirt. Nothing—not even a scratch. It was then that he realized something. He had to go to the bathroom—badly. The pain was from a natural bodily function.

"That's good, son, I see that you've been working your abs. But what has that got to do with flying saucers?" His dad remarked, with a look of concern.

Brad muttered, "They aren't flying saucers."

"Well, I think we're all tired, and we have church in about five hours. We should try to get some sleep," Mom suggested, rubbing her eyes.

Brad thought, *no, not that.* Sleep and the dreams that followed were about to do him in.

As they were about to turn off the TV, an attractive young reporter standing near an area of storm damage was commenting, "This has been a strange night indeed. There have even been reports of sightings of aliens." The entire Johnson family stopped dead in their tracks, glued to the TV. The camera then panned to an older couple in their pajamas and bathrobes. The scruffy-looking man also sported a ball cap and was holding a shotgun. The reporter continued, "The Simpsons live two doors down from this damaged home. This couple is telling us that just before the storm, three strange looking creatures with large heads tried to enter their home. Is this correct, Mr. Simpson?"

"Yes, I was awakened by the storm and came downstairs. I heard a noise at the back door. So I grabbed the shot gun. The door flew open and these three small creatures just like I've seen in the National Inquisitor, were standing there. I raised my shot gun and warned them that I would shoot. All of a sudden, it was as if all the cabinets in the kitchen came open. Pots and pans came flying right at me. Then the beings just disappeared," the wide-eyed fellow reported.

"You should see my kitchen, it's a big mess," the woman complained in frustration. The camera then panned a kitchen that looked as if a tornado had occurred inside, although there was no other damage except pots, pans and broken dishes.

"See!" Brad exclaimed and pointed to the TV screen, "It wasn't a dream."

The young lady appeared again on the screen, "We spoke to the police, following this interview, who explained to us that this was not the first time they had been called to this home. It appears that Mr. Simpson also claimed that a large hairy creature, known as a Yeti, destroyed his trash cans two months ago." The perky reporter continued, "We have also learned that Mr. Simpson frequents a local bar where he was tonight until about 12:30 pm. Mr. Simpson has also been known to have taken pot shots at neighbors on occasion, during the night, thinking they were strange creatures attacking his property."

Brad's dad looked up, trying to contain his laughter. Soon, the others in the family were cracking up. Brad frowned in disgust.

Dad, still smiling, declared, "I guess we've had enough excitement for one night. Let's go to bed."

Brad's mom, seeing her son's distress, followed him upstairs to his room, and sat on his bed. She prayed for peaceful sleep, as Brad drifted off.

It seemed like only about fifteen minutes later, when Brad's alarm clock was beeping at its loudest pitch. Brad fumbled around until he hit the off button. Within minutes he heard the loving voice of his mom calling from down the hall. "Brad, it's past seven. You better get a move on, and get yourself out of that bed or you'll be late for Ultimate Praise."

Ultimate Praise was the name of the high school life group at Creekside Community Church. Brad's family had attended this church as long as he could remember. Rubbing his eyes, trying to wake up, Brad thought, *I have some major prayer requests today.* After his family's response however, he decided to keep mum about last night's events. Brad still couldn't decide if it had really happened or not. He pulled his shirt up and looked at his stomach. It did look a little red. Maybe he hadn't hurt himself like he thought. He jumped up, got ready for church, and headed down to the kitchen. Pouring himself a bowl of cereal, he listened while his family chatted around the table.

"Boy, am I beat," his father sighed. "It was some night. I bet I didn't get four hours sleep."

"Sounds like that was a lot more than Brad got, flying around on those spaceships all night," Mandy teased, thinking she was funny.

"Mandy," Mom scolded, "that's enough."

"It's OK Mom. I guess I just got—carried away," Brad joked, trying to steal the humor.

Mandy and Dad burst out laughing.

Mom, trying to control herself, let out a chuckle and quipped, "Well, son, I'm glad they brought you back."

Brad laughed but something about that statement gnawed at his insides. *Did Luke get brought back? I just don't want to think about all of this right now,* he thought, as he wolfed down the bowl of cereal. He was almost finished when the phone rang.

Mom answered it in her cheery manner. "Oh, hello, Matt, how are you this morning? Yes, here he is." She smiled and handed the phone to Brad.

Matthew Shackleton was Brad's closest friend and had helped him through many struggles as a young Christian. If anyone could understand what was going on, he was sure Matt would. "Hi, Matt." The rest of the family could hear that Matt was concerned about the news report of a tornado in their neighborhood. "Yeah, I'll tell you all about it after church." He paused. "Yeah, we're all doing fine. . . Sure, I'll meet you there and catch a ride home with you after. . . OK, great. I'll see you there." He hung up the phone and joined the family in cleaning up the kitchen. Soon they were in the car heading to Creekside Community Church.

The Johnsons arrived at church and entered the sanctuary, greeting the many friends they had made there through the years. The church had two services, along with Life Groups during each service. As they took a seat in the auditorium, waiting for the musical praise and worship time to start, Brad could not help looking at various people in the auditorium. He wondered if anyone of the four or five hundred people there had been taken on board a ship and was, as Luke had put it, not a serious Christian. Surely, all these people were true believers.

Brad's friend Eddie Lawless leaned forward and spoke into his ear, "Brad, you missed it last night. We were out 'til midnight riding in Bryson's new car. We had a blast."

Brad smiled at him, "Oh. Well, I was kind of busy last night."

As the music began to play, Brad thought, *I guess, maybe not everyone is so serious about following Jesus.* Brad knew Bryson. He seemed to always have a story of girls and partying that certainly wasn't holy.

"Lord help me know what to do, and do it," Brad prayed as he joined in singing, "Our God is an Awesome God."

The song ended and Brad sat down, pulling out his spiral notebook, thinking he might take some notes on the message. During the announcement time, Brad started doodling on the page in his notebook. He looked down at his creation. Over the years he had gotten pretty good at sketching things. It was a very good likeness of a Draegonian battle cruiser. He stuffed it in the back of his notebook to add to his collection and tried to focus on the pastor's words. Thoughts were hitting him from all directions, but Brad was soon engulfed in the message. Pastor Jason taught on the dreams of Joseph, and how God had revealed the truth of His Word through his dreams. "God," Pastor Jason expounded, "showed Joseph things that the boy, Joseph, did not fully comprehend. However, through his trials, he came to gradually see the unfolding of God's amazing plan."

Brad's heart was racing with excitement, as he felt like God was speaking directly to him. The first service ended, and Brad saw some of his friends in the hallway as he made his way to Refuge, the large room that used to be the fellowship hall, before the new one was built. It now served as the youth hangout.

"Brad, Brad!" He heard a rather high-pitched voice call to him from near the door of the Refuge. Brad turned his head to see a thin, blond, curly-haired fifteen-year-old boy named Shad Reiner running over to him. He had trouble stopping, and Brad stepped back a bit to avoid a collision.

"Shad, what's all the excitement about?" Brad asked, knowing that his friend was easily excitable.

"Man, I saw all the destruction in your neighborhood on the news, and I hope your family is OK. Your house wasn't damaged, was it?"

"No, our house wasn't touched," Brad said calmly and then added, "That was some storm last night, wasn't it. How'd your neighborhood make out?"

"Oh, not much excitement at all; a few downed tree limbs, that's all," Shad responded, his braces flashing.

"Did you see the tree at Luke Hunter's house? That was a pretty wild lightning strike wasn't it?" Another voice asserted, entering the conversation from behind Brad.

Brad turned to greet a tall, dark-haired, sturdy fellow who was slightly older than he.

"I hear that Luke Hunter is missing. His parents haven't seen him since the day before the storm."

"Hi, Matt, how's it going?" Brad asked, as he slapped his friend on the shoulder. Matt Shackleton was a serious fellow, whose father was on the local police force. He always had the scoop on what was happening around town.

Brad started to say that he didn't think he was really missing. Remembering what happened the night before, he stopped himself. Instead, he asked, "Have any of you guys seen him?"

"I haven't, but Amy Mackenzy said she saw him in the parking lot of the grocery store carrying a couple six packs of beer," Shad alleged, his excitement building. "He was getting in this slick car with that Sammy dude. She said she hardly recognized him. His face looked like he had been in an accident or something."

"I'm concerned about Luke, "Brad confided. "He needs some serious prayer."

With his usual pensive look, Matt stated, "I hope he's not already in some sort of trouble. Sammy stopped me and asked if I'd seen him."

"What day was that?" Brad asked.

"It was Saturday morning, while I was taking some trash to the street."Matt replied. "I sure hate that Luke's mixed up with that crowd. My dad says that the band they're in has created a cult-like following that seems to be growing, and that whenever they play there's some kind of trouble." Matt's dad was a special investigator with the local police force, who worked on a lot of gang-related problems.

"What kind of trouble?" Brad responded.

"Well, you name it: anything from hateful pranks like tire-slashing and mailbox destruction to stabbings, shootings, and drug busts. A lot of it has involved intimidation and kids younger than us. Dad's investigations have shown that the type of music they're into is a spinoff of heavy metal, something they call Black Metal. Now their show includes this guy they call The Dragon who is some kind of magician. Sort of goes together I guess, black metal and magic."

"Yeah, I hear it's quite a show and draws huge crowds." Brad added.

Shad, who couldn't contain himself, jumped in, "These guys are really weird, and people that seriously follow them have these special parties at that Snake Pit bar. Sean Burton's friend, this guy named Dagger, told him that they steal dogs and cats and kill them in some kind of strange animal sacrifice deal. Haven't you noticed how they're always wearing black and have all those tattoos, and they pierce everything."

Brad laughed at Shad. "Does that mean you're not going to get another earring, Shad?" he ribbed, reaching up and grabbing Shad's ear. "Why don't you wear it on Sundays, anyway?" It was obvious why Shad didn't wear it. None of his friends had one; so they sort of joked about it occasionally. "Shad, you can wear it if you want. We're just kidding with you."

Shad declared, "Really, I don't wear it anymore. I don't need it to be cool. I've got Jesus now, and I don't have to impress anyone but Him."

Matt smiled and affirmed, "Shad, you de ma-an!" Their knuckles met. The guys then took their seats as the "Ultimate Praise" band started playing.

As they stood up to join in the singing, Brad leaned over to Matt and said, "Maybe you could help me find Luke?"

Matt nodded in agreement, "I was just going to suggest that myself."

Brad had several reasons for asking Matt for help. Matt, Brad and Luke had been in Scouts together and were all good friends at one time. Matt knew Luke almost as well as Brad did. He had also helped Brad through some rough times of his own. Brad had great respect for Matt as a Christian. Matt (who was a big tough, guy physically) was on the first string of the high school football team and was very popular at school. Brad, however, most admired his humility and love of God. It was Matt's example which had brought Brad from being a religious fence-sitter to really following Jesus. Matt had challenged him about the dangerous ground he was on with a particular girl Brad thought he was in lo-ove with. Brad knew that he was doing some things with this girl that amounted to lust and worse. Matt cornered him one day and asked him if he would act that way with her if Jesus were standing next to them. At the time Brad was furious with Matt. But when Brad found himself thinking about her in a lustful way right in church, the Spirit of God convicted him. He realized that he was, indeed, in sin. Brad repented to God. Then talked to Matt and they both realized how dangerous it was to get so involved with a girl at their age, if they were serious about following Jesus and living holy lives. They made a commitment to each other: They would help one another pursue holiness in this area and pray for each other. Matt had helped Brad through a rough break-up with this girl, who couldn't understand his "fanatical religious views," as she called them. She promptly dropped him for someone else who would fulfill her romantic desires. Sadly, he had come to see that she was not at all interested in following God.

As Brad sang along with the group, he realized how grateful he should be to God for a friend like Matt. He thought back on the time when Matt, Brad and a few other boys in the youth group had formed sort of a brotherhood of warriors against sin in their lives. They viewed sin as "the enemy" which kept them from serving Jesus. These guys met for prayer every week and discussed the things that made it difficult to follow Christ. They then strategized how to overcome those things. Matt had suggested, that since they all spent so much time playing the Draegonian Invasion computer game, that they rename the villains to teach them how real our battle is in the spirit. One sleazy looking slender alien with a large head and oversized, round eyes called Groatin, they renamed Lusty. Another which looked like some sort of lizard man, they called Liz the Liar, another, Seth Selfish and so on. This helped all of them see the truth of the fact that life with Jesus is a continual battle against spiritual forces. The goal of these forces is to neutralize Christians and keep them from being useful in God's kingdom.

The guys had come up with a special name for the group. They called it The G-Men which stood for God's Men. The G-Men also spent time praying for friends that needed to know Jesus, like Luke. This group was spear-headed by Matt and had been instrumental in helping Brad understand what it really meant to practically follow Jesus every minute of the day.

Matt would be helpful in finding Luke for two other important reasons. One was his Dad's position which enabled him to hear important news about Luke. Secondly, the best thing about Matt in this adventure, was that he was mobile. He had his own car. It would take Brad forever to pedal all over town looking for Luke.

Chapter 7

The Mysterious Black Pouch

As the Youth Pastor, Chuck, started his teaching time, Brad's thoughts drifted back to the events of the night before. Brad was wrestling with the idea that all he had experienced last night was another dream. It was too weird that a car had been flipped over right where it had in the dream. What are the odds of a tornado touchdown causing this, the exact same night of his dream? Brad knew if it was a dream, then God must be trying to tell him something like He did with Joseph in the Old Testament. But, how could he know if it was a dream or not? Then Brad remembered the shed and the black pouch. What could be hidden in that pouch? Brad knew it really existed because he had seen Luke taking it out of the bass drum the afternoon before. But, was it actually in that shed? *I've got to find out.*

The meeting ended as usual with prayer requests. Brad raised his hand and asked for prayer for Luke, and guidance in figuring out God's will. He opted not to mention his dreams, fearing that it might freak some people out.

As soon as the last song was over, Brad asked Matt if he had any plans for the afternoon.

"No, nothing planned—except finding a place to fill this empty spot that's growling like a bear." Matt responded, holding his stomach. He was by no means fat, but his appetite was legendary.

"Do you think your mom would mind if you ate lunch with us today?" Brad proposed.

"No, as a matter of fact, Mom's gone to Winston today for a baby shower, and my Dad's at the station. So, I'm all alone." Matt replied with a big smile."

"Let me check with my mom and make sure it's alright. I'll meet you in five minutes at your car." Brad picked up his Bible and notebook and took off down the hall, then up a flight of stairs to another hallway. Finally, he reached the four through five year-olds class, where his mother taught.

Mom was glad to have Matt over for lunch. Matt was a favorite of hers. She admired his strong character and the way he appreciated her cooking. "Lunch will be around one-thirty," she instructed.

He thanked her and took off down the corridor again. Quickly maneuvering through the busy halls, Brad glanced down at his watch. *That gives us about forty-five minutes. It should be plenty of time to stop by that shed and see if the pouch is in there.* Brad got to thinking; he wasn't even sure whose shed it was. It was sort of back in the woods and could have belonged to either the Guthrey's or the Pearson's.

Once out in the parking lot, Brad walked over to the area where Matt usually parked his car. He scanned the lot for the red 2006 Mustang that Matt had worked so hard to save up for. He had only bought it three months ago and had spent almost all his savings. Matt's grandfather had a large farm outside of town, and Matt had worked for him since he was eleven years old. He had saved practically every penny of his money with one goal in mind, that gleaming red pony. He had hung a huge poster of one in his room, to keep him focused and help him resist frivolous spending. Brad wondered if a cool car was a fringe benefit of not spending all that money on dates. Matt was known for not blowing his money on whims, but was diligent to give to the work of the Lord, and tithed faithfully. Brad figured that was the reason his grandfather had helped to buy the car for his seventeenth birthday.

What luck, Brad thought, wishing he had a rich grandfather. "Thou shall not covet," he recited as he smacked himself on the cheek. He was looking around the parking lot, when, he heard the familiar guttural sound of that sweet machine start up. Brad turned toward the sound in time to see Matt stand up and motion to him.

"Is it a go?" Matt called, as he squinted a little in the bright sunlight.

Brad gave a thumbs up, as he walked over and opened the passenger door. Settling into the black leather seats, the heat from the sun-baked car immediately hit him, "Ouch, I hope your AC works."

Matt closed the door. "Just roll down your window. It'll cool off."

Brad laughed and replied, "You big cheap-skate, you'd rather sit here and sweat than be cool."

"I don't have to have the AC on to be cool in Sweet Ruby here," Matt boasted, putting on his streamlined sunglasses. "But if you'd like to help pay for the gas she drinks, I'll be more than happy to accommodate you, sir."

Brad shook his head, "Point taken." Brad knew that with the price of gas and Matt's tight nature, not to mention the appetite of Sweet Ruby, it wasn't cheap to keep her running. Sometimes Brad thought that Matt believed Ruby was a real pony and had a personality, and that's why he had given her a name. Matt picked the name Ruby because of her deep red color. The guys all joked that the reason Matt didn't have a girlfriend was that he was going to marry his car. It was certainly his baby and he kept it meticulously, but Brad knew it was just a joke. Although Matt was very popular with the girls, he always treated them with honor and respect. He wasn't interested in going with anyone in particular, because he knew from experience it was too difficult to be pure in heart with such temptation to sin. Matt knew that he certainly wasn't ready for marriage, and he had seen too many people hurt by relationships which resulted in sin and even worse, abortion. They all had a great time in groups, anyway, without pairing off and inviting a lot of potential pain.

As they pulled out of the parking lot Brad asked, "Oh, by the way, do you mind stopping somewhere on the way? It's not far from my house."

"No problem," Matt replied, "just as long as we don't miss lunch. Do you know what your mom's making for lunch?"

"Oh, I think she said something about hog jowls and opossum stew," Brad joked as he returned a wave from his sister Mandy and her friend Sherri, who were standing in the parking lot of the church.

"Man, you think you're funny, but you need to chill out with all that Jethro Bodine stuff. What's she really having?" Matt quipped.

"I don't know, man. I've got too many things on my mind to keep up with Mom's menu."

"Really? Like what?" He could see that Brad was serious.

Brad let out a long breath. "It's Luke. I'm really worried about him. I think that he's in some serious danger."

Matt looked at Brad and agreed, "Well, I wouldn't doubt it, knowing the group he's chosen to hang out with."

"I feel like I'm partially to blame for it," Brad admitted sadly. "I sort of stopped hanging out with him when he started all that heavy metal stuff. I was struggling myself with following God. I guess I just didn't think he cared about God anymore, and I didn't care about him."

"Well, that was then. Sometimes when we're struggling with God's will, it's hard to know what to do," Matt responded.

"I know now that God wants me to do something, although I'm still not sure what," Brad declared with a determined look.

"Really, how do you know?" Matt asked, as he slowed for a traffic light.

Brad bit his lip, thinking carefully about how to reply. "I'm going to tell you something but I don't want to be asked about whether or not I've been eating a lot of pizza or anything," Brad started.

Matt laughed and asked, "What a-r-re you talking about?"

"Look, I've had these wild dreams about aliens attacking the town, and Luke gets taken away by them and. . ."

"Whoa, man, I don't know what the pizza thing is all about, but it sounds like you spend too much time with that Draegon game." Matt laughed. Brad was quiet and stared out the window. Matt realized he had offended his friend, "I'm sorry man, but I'm not sure I'm following you."

Brad started again. "I know it sounds crazy, but I have been having dreams; and then stuff happens that's very similar to the dream."

"Really, like what?" Matt asked, trying to take his friend more seriously.

"Like that, right there," Brad pointed out the window. Matt slowed the car, and turned onto the street where Brad lived. A police car was parked with lights flashing. The officer came up to Matt's window. Recognizing Matt, because of his father's position, the officer greeted them:

"Hi, Matt, how's it going? What brings you over this way on this beautiful Sunday afternoon?"

Matt smiled and acknowledged, "Hi, Officer Murphy. I've been invited to lunch over at my friend, Brad Johnson's house, just down the street."

The officer bent down and looked in at Brad and said, "Hi, Mr. Johnson. Your house wasn't damaged by the storm last night was it?"

"No sir," Brad responded.

"You boys be careful driving down the street. There's still some debris on the road. Have a good day." Matt waved goodbye and continued slowly down the street, maneuvering past some large tree limbs still protruding into the street. They came to a stop to watch a tow truck in the process of trying to right Mr. Smith's car which was still upside down.

"You see that, Matt? I saw that happen last night, only it wasn't done by a tornado touching down." Brad pointed excitedly.

"OK, Brad. Tell me. What, exactly, did you see?"

"I saw some kind of alien scout ship, at least that's what Luke called it. It shot—like a—laser burst, which exploded and sent that car flying up into the air."

"Did you say that Luke was with you? Was he in your dream?"

"That's just it, I'm still not sure it was a dream. How could all this stuff have happened for real if it was just a dream?" Brad questioned, with a confused look.

"I don't know about that, Brad. But, if some kind of space scout ship had done this, don't you think someone besides you would have seen it?"

Suddenly, CR-R-ASH! The mangled, somewhat smashed car fell over onto its partially flattened tires.

Brad continued, as they sat watching the man move the cable from the side of the car to the back, "People did see them, but according to Luke they were taken up into a ship or somewhere, and brainwashed into following Lord Draegon. Then their memory was erased so they wouldn't remember what happened."

"That's some wild ride," Matt affirmed as he put the car into drive and continued down the street.

"And that's not the half of it. This was the second dream I had, the first one was the night before last and Luke was in trouble in that one too." Brad pointed and instructed, "Pull over right there by the woods."

"Why here?"

"There's something we have to check out," Brad announced, getting out of the car. "Follow me," he called, as he headed into the woods.

"Where are we going?" Matt responded, catching up with his friend who was focused on his mission.

"After the ship demolished Mr. Smith's car and took the people away, the storm got worse, so Luke and I found our way to a shed back here in the woods. Luke hid something in there and I need to see if it is still there."

"If it was a dream, why would anything be in there?" Matt asked, as he pushed branches out of his way.

"That's what I need to find out: if it really was a dream. Anyway, once the storm settled down, we heard noises and explosions outside. A loud crashing sound shook the ground. We tried to get out of the shed in a hurry, but had to fight through a tree that had fallen in front of the door. We were heading back through these woods when Luke remembered that he had left his black pouch in the shed, and ran back to get it before I could stop him. That's when he was captured by the Draegoons, as he called them. I made my way to the edge of the woods and saw them carrying his body into the ship," Brad recounted, his voice quivering with emotion.

"His body!" Matt exclaimed, "Do you think Luke is dead?"

"I don't know," Brad responded. "I pray to God that he's not, but he sure looked like it." Brad pushed through a thicket of brushy plants and pointed as he exclaimed, "There it is!—I think." There was indeed a tree down in front of a small wooden structure. The tree was smaller than Brad remembered from the night before and the branches didn't totally block the door. *Well, it was dark,* Brad thought, still trying to sort through the events in his mind.

"So, what we're looking for here is a black pouch?" Matt deduced. Brad nodded affirmative.

Matt studied the area and said, "I hope you brought the key."

"What key?" Brad asked about the same time he noticed the big shiny padlock on the latch of the wooden door. "Where did that come from?" Brad wondered, dumbfounded. "That wasn't on there last night."

"It looks to me like, unless you have the key or an ax or something, we won't be getting into this shack today," Matt stated, pulling on the lock. "Why is this pouch so important anyway? What's in it?"

"I don't know, but Luke said it was very important. He called it "his insurance" and said that if anything happened to him we should give it to your dad. Is he working on some special investigation of Sammy Dornburg and his gang? " Brad asked as he looked into a small window that was a little higher than his chin.

"Well, I think that they are constantly monitoring the activities of those guys."

"Hey," Brad exclaimed suddenly, "maybe whoever owns this place has hidden the key. If we look around, maybe we can find it."

"No way," Matt replied incredulously. "If we unlock this door and go in without permission it's called breaking and entering."

"Oh, give me a break. Dude, it's just an old shed. Who's going to know?" Brad retorted.

"If we get caught, my dad will, and that won't be pretty. I can see it in the papers now; 'Local Police Investigator's Son Arrested For Breaking and Entering.' No way. Besides, you don't even know whose place this is. It's just wrong to go in without permission."

Before Brad could offer a rebuttal, an older man's voice called from behind them, "What are you boys doing back there? This is private property, not a public park."

"Uh-oh," Brad muttered. "I guess we know whose place this is now. Hi, Mr. Guthrey," Brad spoke up, putting on a hopeful smile. He had helped old Mr. Guthrey with yard work a few times and was now hoping he had been pleased with his work and would know who he was. The small, silver-haired man slowly moved closer to them and squinted through gold wire-rimmed glasses.

"Who is that?" Mr. Guthrey asked studying the two boys with some suspicion.

"It's Brad Johnson from next door, through the woods." Brad pointed in the direction of his house.

"Oh yes, Brad. How are you doing?" he acknowledged with a smile.

"And this is my friend Matt Shackleton."

Matt reached out to shake the man's hand and said, "Hello, sir," in his deep quiet voice.

Then Mr. Guthrey asked the question Matt was hoping he wouldn't. "Can I ask why you fellows are back here?"

"Well," Brad started, still thinking of what he could say and not tell a lie. "Last night I followed someone into the woods from my house and I was wondering where he might have gone."

"Really?" Mr. Guthrey remarked with interest. "It was probably the same kids that have been messing in my shed. I finally had to padlock it. I just put it on a few hours ago because someone was in it last night. I'd appreciate if you would let me know if see any one roaming in these woods."

"I sure will, sir. I'll keep a sharp eye out." Then, a brainstorm hit Brad and he suggested, "By the way, Mr. Guthrey, if you need some help cleaning up this fallen tree, I'm available in the afternoons this week."

"Why, that would be a big help young man. How about Tuesday?"

"Great, I'll come over about three-thirty, after school."

The man smiled, his blue eyes sparkled through bushy gray eyebrows. Mr. Guthrey thanked him again and headed back down the path.

"Brad, that was a great thing to do. What a good witness," Matt affirmed.

"Well," Brad admitted, "I kind of had an ulterior motive, to be honest."

Matt thought a second, "I get it, you expect that he'll have the shed open to get the tools out, and then you can legally check out what's inside. Shrewd, Dude! As a matter of fact, I would be happy to help you. It would still be a blessing to the nice old gent. Besides, he really got my curiosity up when he said someone was in there last night." Matt paused. "Brad, do you really think God is trying to tell you something through these dreams?" he asked, while kicking around loose branches looking for any evidence.

"I'm convinced that Luke is in trouble, and Jesus wants me to help him," Brad replied seriously.

"What makes you think that Jesus is saying this?"

Brad looked at his friend and stated boldly, "He told me."

"What do you mean? You mean you feel it in your spirit?" Matt wondered with a confused smile.

"No," Brad stated nervously, not knowing how Matt would respond to what he was about to spring on him. "At the end of each dream a man dressed in white appeared and spoke to me about Luke. He used some of the same words of Jesus and said that Luke needed to be saved. I just know it was Him. He came when I called out to Jesus in the dream. Don't you think it could be Jesus, Matt?" Brad asked searching for confirmation.

"I don't know. This is all beyond me, man. I guess it could be God speaking to you. I've read accounts of Jesus appearing to people. I do know that Luke needs to be saved, and if that happens out of all this, I am all for it. We're G-Men, aren't we?" Matt said, slapping his friend on the back.

Brad smiled and nodded, grateful for a friend who shared his desire to help Luke.

Matt looked at his watch and announced, "I thought my stomach alarm was going off. What time did your Mom say we were to be there for lunch?"

Brad glanced at his watch and exclaimed, "Five minutes ago, let's roll!" They both took off through the woods. The guys arrived in the doorway just as Mrs. Johnson was serving.

Following a grand meal, the two boys thanked Brad's mom, then strategized about how to go about finding Luke. Brad called over to Luke's on the phone, but got the rapid busy signal indicating that the phone was still out of order due to the storm. They also called a few of their friends to see if anyone had seen Luke in the last day, but had no luck.

"We could always ride over to that Snake Pit place and see if he's there," Brad suggested.

"I don't know. My dad has warned me that I should stay away from that place."

"It's not like we are going there to patronize the place. We're just going to look for Luke." Brad struck a sly smile and added, "You're not afraid of that place are you?"

"Afraid! Why would I be afraid?" Matt responded indignantly.

"You know, all those stories about the weird stuff that goes on there." Brad remarked eerily. "Beatings, stabbings, and it's the last place some people have been seen. The guy that owns the place is a scary old biker dude who has all these pet snakes. Some people even think he's some kind of Satan worshipper."

"Cut it out, man. You trying to creep me out or what? You're talking about old Rattlesnake Pete. I'm not afraid of that old dude, even if he does worship the devil. Jesus is more powerful than the devil, and He's our protector and deliverer. Besides I don't think Pete even runs the place anymore. Let's go."

Brad laughed, knowing that's all it would take to get Matt fired up. He loved to feel the fear and jump into a challenge. "Seriously, though," Brad continued, "you said that they were changing the name of the place. Has it been sold or something?"

"Yeah some guy from up north has taken it over. I'll have to ask my dad. He keeps his eye on that place. They've been called out there a lot for various disturbances. He says the guy is kind of strange."

Walking across the yard, Matt's crimson, Hotrod Magazine picture-perfect machine came into view. As they got nearer to it, Brad said, "Matt, you know that you are my very best friend, don't you?"

Matt was sort of caught off guard by the comment. Not knowing what to say, he replied, "Uh, I guess so. Yeah, we're best friends."

"Well," Brad continued, "you know that I got my learner's permit two months ago and if you're tired of driving everywhere, I would be happy to drive your car today, dear friend."

Matt was now looking at the cheesiest, hopeful grin on his friend's face, he ever saw. Matt lowered his head and shook it in disbelief at the brazen attempt of his friend to get behind the wheel of his beloved Ruby. "You know I can't do that. You can only drive with someone over eighteen."

Brad's smile lowered a bit, "You can't blame a guy for trying. Maybe in the parking lot then, I just want to see how it feels."

"Maybe, one day," Matt conceded apprehensively.

"Really?" Brad asked.

"Sure, especially since all of a sudden we're best friends and everything," Matt said, as he opened the car door, glanced back at his friend and rolled his eyes. As they seated themselves, Matt started the motor, and joked, "I know Ruby here has a best friend, anyway."

As he adjusted the seat belt, Brad remarked, "You know I was just kidding, don't you?"

"Yeah, I know." Matt affirmed, "So was I."

Brad responded with a laugh, "No way. You said you'd let me drive Ruby, and I'm holding you to it." They continued bantering all the way down the street.

As the boys drove through town, Matt remarked, "Now that we've been fed, I guess Ruby needs some attention." Brad leaned over to look at the fuel gauge and saw that it was just under a quarter of the tank. He knew that Matt never liked to get below that mark. His father had told him to never take a chance of running out of gas, because if he had to leave this type of car in some out of the way place to go get gas, it would surely become a target for car-jacking.

Matt pulled into a gas station and both boys got out. As Matt fueled the car, Brad called, "Do you want anything?"

"Nah, I'm stuffed," Matt called back.

Brad continued toward the brightly colored convenience center, entering to buy a candy bar. As he was perusing the assortment of sugary delights, a familiar voice called out from behind him.

"Brad, wha-sup?"

"Oh, how's it going, Jeremy?" Brad replied, as he continued to search the aisle for just the right tooth decay promoter.

"What are you doing way over on this side of town?" Jeremy asked with his usual annoying curiosity.

Everyone at school, who knew Jeremy Medlyn, figured he would grow up to be some sort of gossip columnist or something. He seemed to have a voracious curiosity about everything that happened at school. He was a skinny fellow who was a year younger than Brad, and at least six inches shorter. His wavy blondish hair and dark eye brows gave him a sort of a young Albert Einstein look. Brad knew that he had to watch what he said to him because it would be all over school within a day. Finally, Brad responded, "I'm just looking for a friend of mine." Then he wondered if Jeremy might know something about Luke and his predicament.

"Who in the world could that be in this neck of the woods?" Jeremy asked right on cue.

"Maybe you know him, Luke Hunter?" Brad suggested unassumingly.

"Yeah, the Slammers' band drummer. He's good. I've seen them play. They are pretty wild, and really jam. You're not by chance going over to the old Snake Pit are you? That's where they've been playing lately. That's a rough place. My cousin used to work there, but when a friend of hers disappeared, she quit. That girl is still missing, you know."

"We thought we might ride by there and see if anyone has seen Luke," Brad replied and immediately wished he could have taken the words back.

"You mean Luke is missing, too? Oh, man that's scary."

"No, I don't mean he's missing. I saw him last evening. I just wanted to see if he had a place to stay since his house was damaged in the storm. Do you know much about that Snake Pit place?"

"I've only been there once and before dark. I understand the place gets kind of strange the later it gets. Those guys who own the place are a real creepy pair," Jeremy admitted with almost a shiver.

"Two guys own it?" Brad asked, "I thought the place was owned by that old biker dude they call Rattlesnake Pete. You know, the guy that has all those pet snakes."

"No, he doesn't own it at all anymore. He lost it somehow. My cousin says she thinks he owed them a bunch of money for drugs and was forced to sell the place to 'em cheap."

Brad, thinking, asked, "So who are the two guys?"

"You know, one of them is your friend Luke's buddy, Sammy. The other guy is really strange and has just been coming into town every few weeks to sort of manage things. I don't know his real name, but he goes by this freaky nickname. I think he's is like the controlling partner in the place and has dumped a lot of money into renovations. He's some sort of magician or something and has this wild magical performance while the band is jamming. I hear it's a real blast, but he seems to call all the shots, and whatever he says goes."

Brad started going through his memory, thinking of all the people he had seen Luke with lately and asked, "Have you ever seen this guy?"

"No, but my cousin says he's an older man who likes to hit on the younger girls. He's got black hair, but is graying on the sides and he has dark goatee. He also has tons of money and usually drives this big black hummer."

About that time Matt came in, looking around. He spied Brad and called over to him, "I'm ready whenever you are."

Jeremy did not turn around. Recognizing Matt's deep voice, he just stood there nervously. Jeremy had spread the rumor that Matt was deathly afraid of the water five years ago. It had occurred when Matt first joined the Boy Scout troop, but had never learned to swim. He was indeed afraid of the water because of a childhood mishap in a farm pond where he almost drowned. A fellow scout had told Jeremy about big, strong, athletic Matt's unwillingness to go into the water. Jeremy thought it was amusing and told everyone he knew. Matt was so upset with Jeremy that he confronted him after school and punched him a few times before getting control of himself. Matt realized that with his size he could have really hurt Jeremy badly. Matt had confided to Brad, it was that episode that caused him to really turn his life over to Jesus. He didn't want his anger to ever rule him like that again. It had also caused him to face his fear of the water. That very summer, he got the swimming merit badge.

"Is he gone?" Jeremy asked, his eyes wide.

"Yes," Brad said trying to keep himself from bursting into laughter. "You know, Matt would never hurt you, man. That swimming bit happened a long time ago. He's over it."

"But, he never says a word to me, not even "hi" or something. I think he hates me," Jeremy sulked, trying to get Brad's sympathy.

"He doesn't hate you. But, can you blame him for not wanting to talk to you? You're not the most trustworthy person with people's feelings, you know."

"I was just trying to be funny. I can't help it if he has no sense of humor."

Incensed Brad blurted out without thinking, "Well then, I guess sometimes you will get what you ask for." Regretting his quick words and feeling the conviction of God's Spirit, he softened his tone. "Look, you can't go around saying whatever you please about people and expect to have any respect from them. The kindest man who ever lived said that we should treat others the way we want to be treated. You wouldn't want people to go around broadcasting all of your personal problems, would you? You should ask yourself why you do it. Isn't it just to make others look bad, so that you can look good?"

With this Jeremy dropped his head a little and agreed.

Brad noticed Matt looking in the window impatiently. "Jeremy, I've got to run right now, but I'll see you at school, OK?"

Jeremy, mulling over the words Brad had spoken, looked up and replied, "Sure Brad. Hope you find Luke."

Brad started walking to the counter, then turned back, wondering, "Jeremy, what was the strange guy's nickname?

His thoughts elsewhere, Jeremy paused a second and remembered, "Oh, yeah, Dragon, they just call him The Dragon."

Dragon, Brad thought. *Too weird, that Dragon guy actually owns the Snake Pit.*

Brad paid for his Butterfinger and was out the door.

"Man, I thought you would never get out of there. What were you doing talking to that guy anyway?" Matt contested, obviously miffed.

"Look, G-Man, you need to talk to him, sometime." Brad remarked.

"Why? So that he can spread some of his bull all over town? No way!" Matt snapped, opening his car door a little faster than normal. Matt realized that Brad's evoking the name G-Man was significant. Part of the commitment of their Christian brotherhood gave him the right to challenge something in his fellow G-Man's life. "Matt, the boy is petrified of you," Brad replied.

"He is?" Matt asked with a look of profound delight. "Naw!" He said in disbelief. Then, in a split second his feeling changed to one of deep regret, as he felt the conviction of God's Spirit. Matt's head lowered and then nodded. "You're right. I do need to talk to him."

They belted themselves in the car, and Matt started her up. Matt turned and confided, "I did tell him I was sorry that I punched him. But, I guess I never really forgave him, because I haven't forgotten what he did, and it was like three or four years ago."

Brad nodded in agreement and stated, "It was five years ago." Trying to lighten the mood, Brad added. "Well, it did work."

"What worked?" Matt asked.

"To my knowledge, Jeremy has never said one word about you since. I guess it proves that he can have some self control. Fear of punishment is a powerful motivator."

"Yeah," Matt sighed, "but I'm not God."

Brad let out an, "Ahah! Did you just figure that one out?"

Matt reached over and popped him on the back of the head as Brad tried to dodge the blow.

Chapter 8

Entering The Den Of The Dragon

A couple of miles down the road an unusual sign appeared on the left side of the road. The sign was about twenty feet high and stood on two poles. Ascending one of the poles, in a spiral fashion, was a giant snake with its head perched over the top of a white sign. In big black and red lettering it read: THE SNAKE PIT. Underneath, in smaller lettering it included "Bar and Grill" and "Live Entertainment". The sign had obviously been there quite a while and needed some attention. Large sections of paint were peeling off of the snake, and Brad joked that it appeared to be shedding its skin.

Matt pulled into the parking lot, which only had a few cars in it, since it was Sunday afternoon. Brad pointed to one interesting vehicle: a glossy black hummer with tinted windows and gleaming chrome rims. The personalized license plate read "Dragon 1." Matt parked his car on the edge of the lot near the woods and in the shade, of course. The two got out and walked cautiously toward the building.

"It looks like the new owners have spruced the place up quite a bit," Matt remarked as he noticed a new covered entry way and fresh grayish brown paint as well as new heavy gothic-style light fixtures. The building itself was an old barbeque restaurant which had changed hands many times and had several additions over the years. Rumor was the original owner drank himself to death on hard liquor. A tough old cuss named Pete acquired it after that. Pete was a kind of strange guy, who collected snakes as pets. He decided to create sort of a biker bar about twelve years ago, using the snakes to create just the right atmosphere. Needless to say it wasn't billed as a family-friendly place and had sort of gone downhill over the years. They were surprised to see what had been done with the place.

"Man," Matt marveled as they walked toward the morphed structure, "That Dragon guy has really dropped some money into this place." Quite a bit of new construction on the back of the building looked as if it had just been completed. It was a two-story addition, which looked like a small auditorium with a metal roof that sloped down toward the back of the building.

"Do you think we can get in?" Brad wondered aloud. They walked beneath the arched entry held up by four, large heavy, cement columns. The oversized wooden doors were stained with a green wash, giving them an ancient look, like something one would find in an old castle. Brad reached out and pulled one of the heavy metal door handles. To his surprise it opened, and the curious pair went inside. The light was dim, accentuating the interesting décor. The boys didn't see a soul. There was no one at the little podium where it seemed that a hostess might stand. "Looks like they aren't open yet," Brad suggested almost whispering.

"Maybe someone who works here could tell us if Luke's around." Matt replied. As they walked further into what appeared to be the dining area, they saw pictures of various musical groups, all in the hard rock and heavy metal style. There were framed posters of vintage bands like KISS, AC/DC, Metallica, Styx, along with Slayer. There were also groups that they had never heard of, like something called Slipknot and More-Bid. Also, interspersed were pictures of grotesque figures and dark gothic knights. Brad stopped to study one painting depicting a huge, muscular knight who appeared to have a skull face under its horned helmet. The Dark Knight was engaged in battle, and obviously killing a large golden lion. "Matt, look at this," Brad called.

"Sh-sh!" Matt urged, as he came over to find out what incredible thing Brad had found in this wild place. "I'm not sure we should even be in here."

"Why not? The doors were unlocked. What do you make of this?" Brad asked still studying the picture. "Is that a crown falling off the lion's head?"

Matt studied the picture becoming incensed at the connotation. "Yeah, and see there. Those gargoyle-looking creatures in the background are slaying angels. This is just the devil's wishful thinking."

"What does it mean?" Brad asked. "Is this supposed to symbolize Satan being victorious over Jesus or something?"

"Ridiculous, isn't it? That slimy dude is in for a rude awakening one day."

The walls in the place were painted different colors: khaki, deep green, and dark red. With tables and booths around the walls, it looked like a restaurant done in a Dungeons and Dragons theme. There were also unusual art objects, some in the form of shiny silver orbs, some with snakes wrapped around them or dragons atop them. In two of the corners there were seven foot high marble obelisks. Beside them were two large cement balls about three feet tall, each with a gargoyle perched on top. "I wonder what happened to all the snakes that old Pete used to have." Brad whispered.

"Maybe they keep them downstairs in the dungeon where they throw all the uninvited guests," Matt replied with a smirk.

Brad shook his head and rolled his eyes. "Dufus—don't say stuff like that. It might be true in a place like this. Maybe, they just let them loose to roam the place to scare off intruders." Brad knew how much Matt hated snakes. "Look –there's one, watch out!" Brad quickly slid a chair out from a table as Matt jumped behind him. Brad laughed, seeing Matt jump at his imaginary snake.

Matt punched him in the shoulder, "Man, will you cut it out? Someone might hear us." Walking through the dimly lit dining area, they could see the bar room through a tall, wide doorway to the right. Matt pointed and Brad could see some large, lit, aquarium-like glass boxes that did, indeed, seem to contain live reptiles. Straight ahead of them was an archway trimmed heavily in dark, stained wood. Above and around the arch was a mural painted with brilliant colors of a dragon, a goat's head, flames, and various figures of men in metallic armor suits with demonic-looking head gear along with some scantily-clad women. It could have been on the cover of any Behemoth CD or a Warcraft computer game. On each side of the archway were heavy six foot tall columns crowned by winged creatures, with frog-like bodies, and heads that resembled a mad bulldog. The wings were like those of a bat which spanned almost four feet in width. Looking through the arch they could see a statue of a Viking-looking fellow with a helmet covering over half of his face, ivory colored horns protruding from each side. His body armor covered all the essential organs, but revealed his Mr. Universe physique underneath. In one hand he raised a huge sword, appearing ready to strike down anyone who entered. In his other hand he held a sphere, while one foot rested heavily on the back of some helpless soul hugging a large stone, upon which the entire work of art was built.

Matt looked closely at the sphere and saw that it was actually a globe. He shook his head in disgust. "He thinks that he has the whole world in his hands. It's a direct challenge to God." Going through the archway, he turned the corner to the left. Suddenly—his heart jumped, and he gasped. "Man! That stupid thing almost made me jump out of my skin," he exclaimed, motioning for Brad to come over.

"What is it?" Brad responded excitedly. "Whoa," he exclaimed as he turned the corner and followed a long green scaly neck almost to the ceiling. Gazing down at them, from a huge, twisting snake-like body was the head of a teeth-baring, nostrils-flaring, evil-eyed dragon. It was a brilliantly painted and detailed winged statue, which was lit strategically by small spot lights meant to bring the beast to life. The silvery head of the creature arched over, and its eyes looked down glaring at them. They walked through a short, towering hallway with two double-door entries into a very large room with a soaring ceiling and walls painted in black.

"What do you suppose that means?" Brad asked, staring down at the marble base on which the beast was perched.

"The Guardian Of The Abyss," Matt read aloud the engraving in the stone. He shrugged his shoulders, "Sounds sort of occult-ish, doesn't it?

Over the entry way, in shiny gold gothic script, were the letters ABYSS, which the boys didn't even notice, being so taken with the scaly receptionist that greeted them.

They cautiously entered a large room, which was dimly lit by funnel-shaped up-lights mounted on the walls, obviously meant to simulate flames. The room was actually a small auditorium with rows of seating and a raised multi-level stage area at the lower end. Stage lighting of various colors surrounded the stage. It appeared to be set up for a rock concert. Behind the stage was a sheer black curtain covering a black wall with a shimmering dragon design. Printed on the wall, in a shiny silver, gothic style script, was the word, ABYSS. The SS was in the shape of lightning bolts.

"I guess this is what Godzilla out there is supposed to be guarding." Brad said, pointing to the stage back drop.

"What is that all about?" Matt asked as he studied the letters.

"I've seen that word before," Brad stated, trying to remember where.

"I'm pretty sure that I've seen it in the Bible. I think it's in the book of Revelation," Matt submitted. Matt and Brad started toward the front to get a better look.

"Excuse me," A female voice interrupted their self-guided tour, "but we're not really open right now."

The boys turned to see a young woman who was barely eighteen years old. She had long straight black hair with a bright-red streak going down one side. "Sorry, we didn't . . ." Matt stopped in mid- sentence, and the girl got a funny sort of smile on her heavily made up face. "Brittany?" Matt said, wondering.

"What are you guys doing in here? Straying off the path?" she asked, arms folded.

Suddenly, Brad recognized her as well. It was Matt's old girlfriend of two years ago, the same girl who caused Matt to give up solo dating. He found that he could not keep his vow of purity under such temptation. She didn't share his views and was terribly offended at his stance. Although Matt tried his best to explain and tell her about his desire to please God, she took it personally. Since then, she had moved to the other side of town. Neither Matt nor Brad had seen her for over a year. “Hi, ah, Brittany,” Brad stumbled as he stood there amazed at how much she had changed. She had on dark reddish eye shadow and displayed numerous piercings including several in her ears and a small silver ring on one side of her nose. She was dressed all in black and sported a small tattoo just below her collar bone. It appeared to be an insect, like a dragonfly.

“Do you work here or something, Brittany?” Brad asked.

“I’ve been working here as a hostess for several months. It’s a really happening place. Sammy and Mr. Dragon have some amazing plans for it.”

“Mr. Dragon? Is that really the guy’s name?” Brad asked, with a laugh.

“Yeah, it’s kind of fun, isn’t it? It works out well with the theme of the place. As a matter of fact, they are changing the name of the place as soon as the new sign arrives. Soon it will be called, “The Dragon’s Den.” That will complete the theme,” she explained with a hostess smile.

“I wonder. Do they have a dungeon around here somewhere?” Brad asked, joking with a bit of sarcasm.

“Don’t you find all this dark stuff a little depressing?” Matt asked, as he finally got the courage to speak up.

“No,” she said defensively. “I don’t have all those hang ups about sin and being perfect, like you do, Matt. I just like to have a little fun. It’s not like people here worship the devil or anything. It’s all just fun and part of the theme.”

“O – OK,” Matt stammered. “Sorry, I didn’t mean to offend you. I was just asking.”

“Maybe you guys would like to come back later when the place is open. I’m sure that you would have the time of your life. Then you could see that the place is harmless.”

Brad replied, “Thanks for the invitation, but don’t you have to be eighteen to get in?”

“Well, the rules are changing. The main thing is you can’t buy any alcohol, but you can still eat and listen to the band. They really rock.” She added once again in her “hostess with the mostest” tone.

“Speaking of the band, that’s why we are here. We’re looking for Luke,” Matt persisted.

“Luke? Luke who?” She asked.

”You know, the guy who plays the drums for the Slammers, Luke Hunter,” Brad explained impatiently.

“O-oh, you mean Bam Bam. That’s what I call him. He’s so cute.”

“Bam Bam?” The boys repeated almost in unison as they exchanged glances, trying to control their amusement. Matt finally inquired, “Well, where is Bam Bam? Have you seen him today?”

“No, I haven’t seen him since last night about one in the morning. That’s when I left. I think he was still here. You know, I was a little worried about him.

I could tell that Sammy was not at all happy with him, and Bam Bam looked kind of rough."

Brad asked, "Do you think it was Sammy who beat Luke up?"

She paused, glancing nervously behind her toward the bar and said in a quiet voice, "I don't know but Sammy does have a very violent temper."

"Do you have any idea where he's staying?" Matt asked.

"Some of the guys in the band have a place a few miles away. It's an old house in the country. A place they can play music without some nosy neighbor calling the law. I'm sure he must be staying with them."

About that time they heard noises, laughing and talking, coming from the back of the auditorium. Brittany listened a second and said, "Maybe you're in luck, I think that's the band coming in to practice. Since you're friends of Bam Bam, I don't think they would mind if you guys stayed and listened to them jam a while. You wait here and I'll check with them."

She walked down the aisle toward the stage and waited a second until one of the guys noticed her and called, "Hey Brit. Wha-s going on, Babe?" A tall fellow who was in his mid-twenties greeted her. A black tank top undershirt hugged his slender torso. Long, bottled-blonde hair falling down past his shoulders in a mass of frizzy curls, completed the rock star image.

"Hi Tommy," she replied, obviously infatuated. Beaming at the sight of him, she asked, "Is Bam Bam with you guys?"

"Who? Oh, you mean Luke. Yeah, he's right here."

Luke looked up from adjusting some cymbals and said "Yo!"

Brit waved and greeted him, "Oh, hi, sweetie. There are some friends of yours looking for you."

"Really? Send them over," he replied as he continued to work. Brad and Matt walked down the aisle toward the front of the stage, into the lights. Brit followed Tommy as he went through some doors into the hallway to bring in some equipment. Luke looked up, but didn't acknowledge them.

Finally Brad spoke up, "Hey, Bam Bam. What's going on in Bedrock, today?" Brad and Matt were both smiling, hoping Luke would lighten up.

Luke was trying to contain a smile, but couldn't. "Man, I hate it when she calls me that."

Matt spoke, "She just thinks you're the cutest thing."

"I am." Luke stated with a chuckle.

"You just need to start calling her, Pebbles," Matt remarked. "I bet that would stop it."

"That's a great idea," Luke smiled and nodded in agreement. "What brings you guys all the way out here?" He asked as he wiped sweat from his forehead and continued to tweak his instrument.

Brad and Matt looked at each other awkwardly, not knowing exactly what to say, especially when they noticed Luke's face. He was in a sad state. Surrounded by his battered face, his bloodshot eyes were sunken into dark circles.

"We just wanted to see what this place looked like and how you were doing." Luke raised one side of his mouth in sort of a half smile as if to say, "yeah, right." Then he asked, "So, what do you think of it?"

"Very interesting," Matt responded. "It's kind of like walking into a Warcraft game."

"Yeah, isn't that cool?" Luke replied.

Brad was looking up at the black curtain hanging behind the stage, and before he realized how the question he asked sounded, he blurted out, "What's the deal with all the dragon stuff and that word Abyss?"

Luke looked up at Brad with a bit of a dazed look, a little nervous about the question. After a second of silence Brad noticed that all of the band members were staring at him. Finally, Tommy who had come back onto the stage and was plugging in his silver and black electric guitar, came over to Brad. His wild hair seemed to glow in the stage lighting. He stared at Brad through piercing green eyes which caused Brad to almost shudder. He reminded Brad of someone's portrayal of Jesus in a movie he had once seen.

He spoke with an intentional smile, "Dude, I don't believe I know you. I'm Tommy Warwick, the lead guitarist and singer with our band. I know the atmosphere in this place is a little unusual. But, the guy who owns the place, his last name is Dragon, so he thought it would be cool to play up that theme. It's really no big deal. It's just meant to be kind of a fantasy place where your imagination can run wild."

Brad nodded his head, wondering why Luke hadn't answered the question and why they seemed a little sensitive if it were "no big deal." "I can see that the imagination certainly can run wild here. What does ABYSS stand for?" Brad pointed up to the large gold lettering.

"Oh that?" Tommy glanced up at the emblazoned black background. "It's just a unique mythological word that Mr. Dragon came up with to name this auditorium. It gives it sort of a gothic, D & D feel. I think it goes great with the style of music we play. It's easy to get into the mood of the blac . . . I mean heavy metal stuff we play. You guys are welcome to stay and listen. I'm sure you could feel the power of the music and get totally hooked on it." Tommy walked back and strapped on his guitar motioning to the sound guy.

Matt spoke up, "Well, we'd like to, but we've got a Bible study group to get to in a little while."

Abruptly, there was the ear-piercing whine of an electric guitar followed by various vibrating screaming sounds. The boys brought their hands down from covering their ears, to the laughter of some of the band members.

"Isn't that awesome?" Tommy boasted, as he turned to the other guitarist who was testing the sleek silver and white instrument he was holding and gave a thumbs up.

"I think we're about ready to rock. Let's get a sound check," announced a frizzy red-haired guy, working on a sound board near the back of the room.

Tommy raised a thumb to the guy and turned to Brad, "Sorry, we've got to get started."

Brad nodded and turned to say something to Luke who was now sitting on his stool ready to test his drums. Brad saw that Luke was as white as a ghost and sweat was beading up on his face. About the time Brad was saying, "Luke are you feeling all right?" Luke toppled over, taking one of the cymbal stands with him, with a loud crash. Brad and Matt raced over to see Luke's eyes rolling back in his head as his body shook violently. Some of the band members actually snickered at the calamity.

Brad overheard, "I knew he couldn't handle the stuff," from one of the band members. As Brad reached down to try to help his friend, Luke mumbled something that Brad could hardly understand. He leaned down to listen. Luke, his speech slurred, murmured, "I don't know . . . don't have it."

Luke's head was now moving slowly from side to side. His hand grabbed Brad's shirt and held on. Suddenly Luke's head stopped and he looked right into Brad's face, as if he had just recognized him. With a fearful look, Luke cried out, "Brad?" Then he paused and tried to focus on Brad. Eyes darting to and fro, he asked intensely, "Do you have it?"

Brad, totally confused by the question and the look of terror on his friend's face, shook his head. "Have what?" he asked, remembering that same look of fear from his first dream when the alien creature was pulling Luke out of the doorway.

Luke's wide eyes seemed to roam around trying to focus. Then suddenly, he blurted out, "The pouch!" The next second, his eyes rolled back into his head and closed. Luke lay there motionless.

Oh God help, Brad thought. *He died.* Matt who was right beside Brad kneeling over Luke, immediately went into Boy Scout first aid mode. He put two fingers next to Luke's throat to see if he had a pulse. Leaning over, Matt turned an ear to listen for breathing.

"Is he dead?" Brad asked.

"No, he's just unconscious," Matt confirmed. "But, someone needs to call the paramedics. He really needs to be checked out."

Several of the band members were now standing around gawking and Tommy bellowed, "Guys there's no need to over react, he just can't hold his booze."

Matt responded, clearly upset, "He's not even sixteen years old. I'm sure the authorities would have a major problem with a fifteen-year-old drinking, much less doing whatever drug that's obviously still in his system."

"You better just watch your mouth man," Tommy remarked harshly. You're making a lot of accusations that will get you in a bunch of trouble."

Matt stood up and confronted the man, who although a few years older than Matt, was about an inch shorter and much thinner. Matt didn't say anything, but was clearly not intimidated. Although the other guys stood up and moved closer, he was definitely willing to take them all on.

"Can we stop all the macho stuff and get Luke some help here?" Brad intervened.

At that moment, several men, including Sammy Dornburg, hurriedly entered the room, alerted to the problem at hand. Matt was now being harassed by the group standing around him. The scene was about to get ugly, when Sammy asked, "What is the problem here? Are these intruders causing some trouble?"

Brad looked up, still kneeling beside Luke who was now stirring a bit. "Luke needs a doctor, Sammy!" Brad exclaimed. "I think maybe he has overdosed on something."

Sammy bent down and studied Luke, and took his thumb and pulled up one eyelid. Then he announced, "He'll be alright, nothing that a little sleep won't fix. He's probably just exhausted. He was up really late. Crazy kid gets too keyed up after our service—I mean concert, and can't get to sleep."

Matt turned on Sammy and insisted firmly, "We need to call 911. Who knows what he has taken."

Sammy was clearly not happy with this challenge to his authority, but controlled himself, bearing in mind who Matt's father was. "Look, guys, I'm sure Luke will be OK, but just to make you feel better, I will call for my personal physician, and we'll take Luke in for examination. I sure wouldn't like for anything to happen to my star drummer." He flipped out his cell phone and started dialing.

About this time Brittany came rushing in with a small pillow and a plastic first aid kit. As she bent down to try to offer assistance to Luke, Brad noticed tears in her eyes.

"In the mean time," Sammy continued, "since our establishment is not open until six this evening, you fellows are actually trespassing. But I will not press charges if you will leave peaceably. Pete, Lumas, please show these gentlemen to the door." Two large thug types stepped forward and motioned Brad and Matt toward the exit.

"What about Luke?" Brad asked.

"Yeah, how will we know he's alright?" Matt added.

"Well, why don't you come back for the concert tonight? It's only five bucks to get in. Then you can see that there's no problem."

"Someone should contact his parents." Brad stated emphatically.

"Don't worry. I'll take care of it. Now get going." Sammy replied, his irritation growing. As the boys started to leave, one of the band members came up to Sammy and whispered something in his ear. Sammy's expression changed to a pondering type of scowl. Before they left the room Brad looked back. Sammy's eyes were fixed on them, as he talked on his cell phone in a very serious tone.

The man known as Pete walked in front of them. A six inch long, graying braid trailing down his back, was framed by his black shirt. The guys followed him back through the menagerie of magical symbols to the front entry. He opened one of the large wood paneled entry doors and stepped outside, holding the door for the others to exit. He smiled broadly, revealing a shimmer of gold edging from one of his front teeth that seemed to be balanced by a similar reflection coming from a small ring gripping his left earlobe. "I hope you boys will join us one evening. I'm sure you'll never forget it," he remarked, his eyes flashing with sarcasm.

As Matt and Brad walked across the parking lot, Matt spoke to Brad nervously, "Do you know who that was?"

"No. Who?" Brad wondered.

"It's Rattlesnake Pete. He must be working for Sammy now." The guys jumped in the car, and Matt started the motor.

"Did you hear what Luke asked me?" Brad asked, as he rolled down the window.

"I couldn't really make it out," Matt replied.

"He asked if I had the pouch. He must have been talking about the one he took out of his drum."

"What do you mean; he took it out of his drum? I thought you said he left it in that shed," Matt questioned, trying to remember.

"That's what happened last night, but earlier in the day I actually saw Luke at his house. He had hidden it in the bass drum in his room. I saw him take it out and put it into a gray satchel," Brad explained. "What could be in that thing? He's obviously lost it. Whatever's in it must be very important."

Matt backed Ruby up, pulled out of the parking lot and headed down the road back toward town.

As they both sat thinking, Matt asked," Why did Luke ask you if you had the pouch? Did he ever give it to you?"

Brad thought a few seconds. "No, it's weird. He didn't know that I saw him take it out of the drum—I don't think. It's almost like the dream was real because in the dream he showed it to me. He asked me to deliver it to your dad, if anything happened to him."

"But that was just a dream, wasn't it?" Matt wondered.

"Yeah. But, I don't know why he would think that I would have it. Maybe he was just talking out of his mind. He was totally delirious."

"Well," Matt glanced repeatedly at his rearview mirror, "I don't think he did you a favor by asking you about that pouch in front of those guys."

"What do you mean?"

"That black Hummer that was in the parking lot is behind us. I think he might be following us," Matt announced as he sped up a little.

Brad's excitement rose, "Really? Well, floor it. Let's show them what this baby can do."

Matt shook his head. "Bra-d, this is serious, not some TV action series. I think we should pretend not to see them and find out what they are up to.

Brad looked back at the black monster following them in the distance. "Yeah, right. That's like David pretending not to see Goliath." He paused, thinking. "You know, one of the band members did come over and whisper something in Sammy's ear right before he kicked us out. I bet that rat told him what Luke said. I bet they're all in on it." Brad felt a shudder of fear as he understood the danger. "Matt, they think I have it! And I don't even know what's in it. This could be a real problem. What am I going to do?"

Matt thought a second, "First, I'm going to make sure they're following us." Ruby turned down a side street, then onto another. Matt drove down the street a few blocks and went past the high school and continued for about a mile past their church and then into town.

Finally, Brad looked back and confirmed, "They are definitely following us. Where are you going anyway?"

Matt nodded, "Somewhere they surely won't follow." At that point, he wheeled onto a back street in town, through a narrow alley, turning left, then right. Brad smiled with relief when they pulled into a parking lot where several police cruisers were sitting.

Matt looked at him with a grin. "Just thought I might see how late Dad's working this evening." They sat there for a minute and watched as the Hummer stopped at the corner and then turned in the opposite direction and disappeared down the road.

Brad and Matt got out of the car and walked into the police station. "Is your Dad here?" Brad asked.

"He should be. His car is out there."

They walked down a hall and came to a door with a little placard on the wall beside it which read: Sgt. Shackleton, Investigative Unit. They could hear a man's voice coming from inside. The door was open, so they went inside. Matt's dad looked up from his desk and smiled. He motioned for them to have a seat while he finished up his phone conversation. He hung up the phone, scribbling some notes on a pad. "How's it going, guys?" he greeted them, with a big smile below his dark but graying mustache. Standing up to shake their hands, it was easy to see where Matt got his size from. "What are you two up to on this beautiful Sunday evening?"

This prompted Brad to glance at his watch. It was almost five-thirty. They only had an hour before the G-Man Bible study. Matt noticed Brad looking at his watch, "Hi Dad, we're on our way to the G-Men meeting, and I wanted to stop in and let you know about someone that might be in trouble."

Sgt. Shackleton sat back down and responded with a laugh, "I see. So this is an official visit. Here I was thinking that you just missed dear ol' Dad and wanted to come by and tell him how much you loved him."

He winked at Brad and frowned in jest.

"Da-ad," Matt responded, fighting a smile, "Listen; we don't have a lot of time. We were just over at the Snake Pit and . . . ."

"You were where?" Sgt. Shackleton questioned, his joviality turning to concern.

"Let me explain, Dad. We're concerned that a friend of ours might be in some sort of trouble. His name is Luke Hunter, and he plays the drums for a band called The Slammers. He hasn't been home for a while, and we were concerned that he is hanging with the wrong crowd."

His dad, seated behind his desk, listened intently, squinting one eye, in thought. "That name rings a bell. Have his parents reported him missing?"

"No, I don't think so. They're out of town," Brad volunteered.

"How old is this boy?" Sgt. Shackleton asked as he flipped over a page in his yellow pad and started writing.

"He's only fifteen, Dad, and he's playing the drums at that Snake Pit bar."

"I was talking to Henson this morning about a kid who was accused of taking some money from that establishment, but the charges were dropped. If he hasn't been reported as missing, there's not a whole lot we can do. He can work with the band, with his parent's permission since he's fifteen. So long as he's not drinking alcohol or taking some illegal substance, he can play with the band there. The place has new owners, and they are trying to change its image some. But, I will certainly check it out," the sergeant affirmed with a concerned look.

"Dad," Matt spoke soberly, "there is one other thing. While we were there talking to Luke, he had some sort of seizure or something and fell right off of the drum stool. His eyes were rolling back in his head and everything."

"Really?" Sgt. Shackleton remarked, with a serious look. "Did they call for medical assistance?"

"It was so strange Dad. They acted like it was no big deal, and said that it was probably exhaustion. Sammy came in and said that he would take him to be checked out by his personal doctor, but then they asked us to leave."

Sgt. Shackleton shook his head and asked, "Was that Sammy Dornburg?"

"Yeah, Dad. He's one of the new owners of the place," Matt said excitedly.

"I wasn't aware of that, but I'll check all of this out. I don't trust Mr. Dornburg as far as I could throw him."

Brad punched Matt and insisted, "Tell him about the Hummer following us."

"Oh, yeah. When we left the Snake Pit a black hummer started following us, so we came right here."

"Smart move. You should keep your cell phone with you and let me know if that happens again. I think it would be a good idea to stay away from the Snake Pit," his dad advised as he continued to scribble notes.

"But what about Luke, Dad? How will we know that he's alright?"

"I'll contact his parents and look into it, OK? Don't worry about him, just pray for him. It sounds to me like he's making some pretty bad choices in his friends right now."

Sgt. Shackleton was involved with the youth group in their church, and served as a deacon. Growing up as a problem kid who was on the wrong path himself, he had a real heart for wayward kids. When he was eighteen, Jesus had intervened in his life following a tragic incident. It involved a car accident and the death of a close friend while they were drunk and up to no good. While he was recovering in the hospital, a nurse explained that Jesus would forgive any sin and change any life, no matter how bad it had been. He gave his heart to Jesus and allowed God to totally change his life. Instead of a life of committing crime, he felt God was calling him to fight crime. He and Matt were very close. Matt's dad had actually come up with the idea of starting a young men's fellowship in the church. This brotherhood would hold each other accountable for taking the word of God seriously; applying it daily to the difficult life of a teenager. The G-Men were born from that idea.

"We better get going if we want anything to eat before G-Men," Matt announced.

"Tell you what," Matt's Dad suggested, "why don't you meet me at the Burger Palace? I'll buy you guys a couple of burgers, and you can be on your way."

Matt's eyes lit up. "That's a plan, Dad!"

After thanking his dad for the burgers, Matt and Brad jumped into Ruby and started toward the church. Brad reached for the sumptuous smelling bag of burgers and fries. He started to pull out a juicy cheese deluxe.

Matt contested, "Whoa, nuh-uh."

Brad asked, "What?" Knowing full well that Matt had a thing about eating in his car, he declared, "Man, I'm hungry."

"You can wait five minutes, and we can eat at church," Matt stated firmly.

"Eat in front of all the guys who may not have anything; how rude," Brad debated, trying to guilt him into submission. Matt just shook his head and held onto the bag. He knew that a lot of the guys brought burgers or pizza and ate it before the meeting.

"How 'bout just a fry?" Brad pleaded.

Unwavering, Matt replied, "We're almost there."

Brad frowned, "Anybody ever tell you that you act like an old lady?"

"Ay-ah. Watch your mouth there, sonny boy." Matt mimicked in a high raspy voice, while turning into the parking lot.

Brad and Matt walked into the Refuge amid the chatter and laughter of a dozen boys ranging in age from fourteen to eighteen, who were standing around in the room. Several other guys greeted them as they proceeded to discuss various sports scores, movies worth seeing, computer game facts, as well as debate the best Christian bands. Matt and Brad sat down and devoured their dinner, along with two other guys doing the same.

Jason Stewart, who sported an iPod with head phones came up to Brad. "Brad, listen to this. It's Oh Sleeper's latest album."

Brad put on the ear phone and was immediately transported into a realm of exhilarating drums and wild guitars that sent his head bouncing into the rhythm. "Cool" he declared a little too loudly, because he couldn't hear himself. He took the earphones off and handed them back to his friend. Several of the older boys started arranging the chairs in a circle and they all began to sit down. Pulling out their Bibles, the meeting followed the usual routine. One of the older boys gave a brief teaching of a lesson from the Bible followed by discussion on how it might affect their individual lives.

At the end of the meeting there was a time of prayer. Brad spoke up and asked for prayer for his friend Luke. He limited the details to the fact that he was hanging around with wrong people and needed Jesus to intervene in his life before he made some major mistakes. The young men all agreed in prayer, asking God to snatch Luke from the jaws of the enemy. The meeting ended and dispersed with the usual Go for God, huddle. Each boy gathered around in a circle and placed one hand on top of another's as they shouted: "Go, for God! Hu-ah!"

Chapter 9

Curiosity Killed the Cat

On the way out the door, Matt pulled out his cell phone, which he had turned off before the meeting. As he looked at the tiny screen, he said to Brad, "I think you better call home."

"Oh man, I forgot to let them know I wouldn't be there for dinner." Brad smacked the side of his head and gritted his teeth a little. "Can I borrow your phone?"

"Sure," Matt replied, handing it to him. "They shouldn't be worried. They know you're with me," he boasted jokingly, with a cockeyed smile.

Brad's mother answered the phone. "We missed you at dinner, dear. We were getting a little worried until Matt's dad called and told us that he had taken you out to the Burger Palace. He said you had stopped by his office and were running late for the meeting."

"I'm sorry, Mom. But everything was going so fast, I totally forgot to call and let you know what was going on. I'll fill you in when I get home. We need to run an errand first, though. I should be home by nine. Is that OK?"

There was a brief pause before his Mom reluctantly replied, "That's fine, son. But, no later. You do have school tomorrow."

"Thanks for understanding, Mom. I love you, too. Bye." Brad closed the cell phone and noticed the time on the screen, 7:32.

As they walked across the parking lot, Matt asked, "So, what's this errand you told your mom about?"

"We have to go back and make sure Luke is alright. I don't trust that Sammy guy any more than your dad does."

Matt looked concerned, but was quiet until they reached the car. Pulling out the keys, he turned to Brad, "I don't know that we should go back over there. We certainly weren't very welcome and Dad said we should stay away from the place."

Brad walked around to open the car door. Looking over the glossy red, vented hood, he responded, "Matt, we have to find out if Luke's OK. He could die if it was a drug overdose. Haven't you heard the stories about people going missing from that place? Besides, your Dad didn't tell you that you had to stay away from that place. His exact words were that it would be a good idea to stay away from it. Don't you care about what happens to Luke?"

Brad's frustration at his cautious attitude irked Matt. "Certainly I do." Matt exclaimed, testy at his friend's insinuation. "But Dad said he would check it out, and I am sure he will." He paused, seeing the disappointment on Brad's face. "Well," Matt admitted, letting out a quick sigh, "I guess we would both sleep better tonight if we knew he was OK."

Brad's face lit up, "Thanks, man, we don't need to stay long, just long enough to see if he's alive and kicking. Besides, Rattlesnake Pete practically gave us a personal invitation."

"I hope I don't regret this," Matt muttered as he started up the engine with a roar. He pulled out of the church parking lot heading back toward the lair of "The Dragon" with some feeling of trepidation. The two boys didn't notice the dark green sedan which pulled out from a gas station across the street from the church. It followed them, discreetly.

Matt pulled into the now familiar parking lot. There were more cars than before, although the lot was still less than half full. Brad was amazed how the lighting around the building gave it an ancient feel. The gothic lamps flanking the entry flickered, giving the eerie impression that the place had been there for centuries.

"I guess Sunday nights are a bit slow," Brad suggested, surveying the area.

"It's still early for a place like this," Matt said, looking down at his watch. "Dad says these places don't usually get cranked up until about nine or so." Matt turned off the ignition and turned to Brad, "You're sure you want to do this?"

Brad nodded uneasily and grabbed the door latch, then stopped. "Let's pray first." He bowed his head, letting out a deep nervous sigh. "Lord Jesus, please protect us from harm, and help us to find Luke. Let him be conscious and willing to talk."

Matt agreed, "Yes, Lord. Please give us wisdom in dealing with this situation. Amen."

They got out of the car and walked to the door. Brad asked, "Have you got any money on you?"

Matt opened his wallet and declared, "Three dollars."

"Three dollars! Brad exclaimed, "How are we going to get in? It costs five bucks apiece."

Matt was indignant. "I wouldn't pay five of my hard earned dollars to get into this place even if I had it. I haven't lost a thing in there."

Brad frowned at his cheapskate friend, and remarked, "I guess we'll have to go to plan B."

"And just what is that?" Matt asked, arms folded, skeptical.

Brad smiled with all of the charm he could exude, "I will just have to sweet talk the hostess."

Matt rolled his eyes and let out a "Ha!"

Brad took hold of the heavy metal handle and pulled the large door open. The place looked even darker now with no light coming through the few windows which dotted the stucco walls. A hazy smoke wafted through the air. The posters and gothic paintings adorning the walls now glowed from tiny spot lights carefully positioned over them. There was no one at the hostess station and only one couple seated at one of the tables toward the back of the room. Over the hard rock background music, laughter and talking could be heard coming from the bar area. Brad noticed a little bell sitting atop the wooden podium near the entry. He was considering tapping the top to alert the hostess. Suddenly, from the doorway of a little office just behind the podium, appeared a huge man with slick black hair and a black goatee. He was dressed in a black T-shirt with a black sports coat, and was adorned with a heavy silver chain around his neck. "May I help you gentlemen?" he asked in a very deep voice.

Brad, unnerved by the unexpected appearance of this giant, lost all of his charm. Clearing his throat, he stammered, "I—I— ahm was hoping to speak to the ah… ahm, hostess about your seating arrangements." The man forced a smile and replied, "Our hostess is busy at the moment with other guests. I am Raymond, and I will act as your host this evening. There is a five dollar cover charge for any seat in the house. Also, you must be twenty-one to order any alcoholic beverages. Would you prefer a table or a booth?"

Torn between wanting to laugh out loud and absolute curiosity, Matt wondered how in the world Brad would pull this off. Noticing a stack of business cards, Matt took one and slipped it into his pocket.

Brad, realizing the situation was hopeless, asked with a half smile, "I guess you don't have a non-smoking section?" The man just looked at him with a frown. "Perhaps we'll try someplace else. My friend here has allergies," Brad said trying to lighten the tension.

As the guys shuffled out the door into the parking lot, Matt chuckled, "That was really smooth. The best sweet talking I've ever heard. You had him eating right out of your hand."

"Would you just stop it?" Brad grumbled, clearly frustrated.

"So—what are we going to do now?" Matt asked. Then, reaching into his pocket, he pulled out the business card. "Plan C, perhaps?" he added, holding up the card.

"What's that?" Brad asked.

"It's a card from in there. I'll just call from my cell phone and ask for Brit. I think she'll help us. She was clearly disturbed about what happened to Luke this afternoon."

They walked over to the car. Matt pulled out his cell phone, called the number and asked for Brittany. A few seconds later the familiar feminine voice answered, "Hello."

"Hi, Brit, this is Matt." He could barely hear her over the din in the background of laughter and music.

"Matt. Matt who?" She said, confused.

"Matt Shackleton. Brad and I were there today to see Luke," he reminded, raising his voice in attempt to talk over the crowd in the background.

"Oh, Ma-tt. Hi. Hold on a minute," She requested, followed by some rattles, and bumps, and then silence. "Is this better, Matt? I could hardly hear you, besides the fact that some people like to listen in, if you know what I mean."

Matt asked, "Are you safe? Can you talk? Where are you?"

"I hope I am. I'm in the ladies room and I'm alone." She confided, obviously nervous.

"How's Luke? Have you seen him?" Matt inquired.

"Yes, he's OK. He's going to play tonight, although he was out of it most of the day. I am concerned about him," her voice softened. "He seems so young."

"Do you think we can talk to him, Brit?" . . . There was silence on the phone. "Brit, are you there?"

"Yes, I'm here. I don't know if you should see him. Sammy will be furious if he finds out. But, let me think." There was a brief pause. "There's a stage door in the back of the building by the dumpsters. They don't start playing until nine. I'll see if I can get to Luke and ask him to take some trash out to the dumpster for me or something. You can talk to him then. Just wait out back by the dumpsters. What's your cell number in case I can't get to him?"

Matt gave her the number, thanked her for her help, and ended the call by saying, "Brit, be careful, I'll be praying for you."

There was a brief pause and she responded, "Thank you, Matt." Matt closed the phone and motioned for Brad to follow him. About that time, a car pulled into the parking lot and four guys got out and headed toward the entry of the building. Brad and Matt ducked down behind a car to wait for the guys to go inside.

"What are we doing?" Brad asked, peering over the hood of parked car.

"Hopefully, we're going to talk to Luke. We've got to get over to those dumpsters without attracting any attention."

"Cool," Brad exclaimed. "Just like playing army around the neighborhood at night."

"Not quite," Matt cautioned, looking around nervously. "This enemy has real bullets."

Brad swallowed hard as a chill ran up his spine. He hadn't thought of that.

"The coast is clear, let's go." Matt motioned. They both took off toward the large dark square silhouettes about one hundred feet away. They stood in a narrow space between the two dumpsters and waited. An eternity seemed to pass.

Finally, Brad asked, "What time is it?"

Matt pressed a button on his digital watch, and the small screen glowed. "8:22," Matt announced.

"I hope he comes soon. I can't be late; I told Mom I'd be home by nine."

Matt agreed, then asked, "Are you sure we should be doing this?"

"Aren't you curious about what happened to Luke?"

"Yeah, but my mom always said that curiosity killed the cat," Matt replied.

"Well, my mom adds: 'but satisfaction brought him back'."

Matt just shook his head. "How can I argue with that?" He laughed nervously. They heard the sound of a door open.

Brad whispered, "What if it's not him?"

"Sh-h!" Matt responded and ignored the question.

Matt peeked around the corner and could see the outline of their skinny friend holding a small trash can, talking to himself nervously. Luke grumbled, "I don't know why this stupid trash couldn't wait 'til tomorrow. . . .but no-o. . . has to be done right now." Luke opened the sliding metal door and began emptying the contents into the dumpster. Luke stopped to look inside the plastic trash can to make sure it was empty then turned over again and banged the bottom with one hand.

Matt stepped out of the darkness and spoke just above a whisper, "Luke!"

Luke jumped back, startled and held up the trash receptacle as a weapon. "Who's that?"

Brad stepped out into view, "It's me, Brad."

"And Matt," Matt chimed in.

"What are you guys trying to do, make me mess up my pants? Geez! What are you doing out here?"

"We just came to see if you're all right." Matt replied defensively.

"Yeah. When we saw you earlier this afternoon you weren't in very good shape. How are you feeling now?" Brad added.

Luke held his hand up to his right eyebrow and massaged it. "I've certainly felt better. My head feels like a cement block is sitting on it." He stopped and spoke slowly as he thought, "Wait a minute. When did you see me today? I haven't seen you today." Luke wondered, perplexed. "What kind of mind game are you guys playing? I've been right here most of the day."

"Luke, don't you remember? Matt and I came by here earlier today to talk to you. It was about three thirty or so. Right before you passed out."

"Passed out?" Luke exclaimed.

"Didn't they tell you what happened to you? You were testing out your drums and just fell over— you know, collapsed," Matt recounted.

"Has anyone been feeding you some sort of illegal drugs?" Brad asked.

"No!" Luke asserted defensively, his tone growing angry. " You guys don't know what you're talking about. I've just not been getting enough sleep, that's all. No need to make a big deal out of it."

"Luke, what we saw this afternoon was a reaction to something. Are you sure no one's giving you some sort of pills?" Matt queried.

"Look, I have trouble getting to sleep so Tommy gives me some of his sleeping pills. They're harmless."

"How can you be sure?" Brad refuted.

"Why would they be trying to poison me? How could I play the drums for them then?" Luke reasoned.

"Well, what about that black bag or pouch?" Brad asked.

"How do you know about that?" Luke responded, in a serious tone.

"I saw you take it out of your drum when I was at your house, and then when you were delirious today you asked me if I had it."

"No! When did I say that?—Did anyone else hear me say anything about a black bag?" Luke asked with a worried look in his eyes.

Brad thought a moment, "That guy Tommy was standing very close. I'm pretty sure he did." Brad noticed a nervous faraway look in Luke's eyes. "What's in that bag that's so important? Is it stolen money or drugs or something?"

"Nothing! Nothing you need to know about," Luke stated defiantly.

"Well I do, if they think that I might have it," Brad responded.

"I'll take care of that. You guys just need to stay away from this place."

"Luke, don't you remember anything about this afternoon?" Matt asked.

Luke put his hands over his ears, his face wrought with pain and fear. "I don't know," he whined. "I wish this ringing would stop." Luke squatted down on the pavement. Brad remembered what Luke had told him, how the aliens would do something to the people that they captured to make them forget. He began to wonder if this was happening to Luke. *Was the lead singer Tommy giving Luke something that would fry his brain so that he would mindlessly follow the group? Or maybe Sammy? Even worse, was this guy Dragon creating some sort of cult-like following in these young people?*

Suddenly, they heard the back door from the club open. Brad and Matt ducked back into the space between the dumpsters. Sammy's sleazy voice called out, "Luke, you out here?"

"Yeah, I'm over here." Luke called back.

"What you doing out there?" About that time Luke heaved. A loud barfing sound like he was losing his entire lunch, interrupted an awkward silence. Sammy who had started toward him, let out some choice four letter words and headed back toward the bar. Finally, Luke responded, "I'm sick. What do you think I'm doing?"

Sammy called back, "You need to get it together, you're on in fifteen minutes." He then closed the door behind him.

Brad reappeared, "Luke, are you all right?"

"Sure, I always blow groceries before I go on stage." Luke grumbled, holding his stomach.

"Man you can't stay here like this. Come back to my house, and stay until your parents get back in town."

Luke moaned a little. "I can't leave now. The show must go on, you know. You guys need to go. Chances are someone's already seen you."

"We're not leaving without you," Brad declared as he grabbed Luke's arm and started to pull him toward the car. Luke jerked free and raced toward the door. Brad started after him but a strong arm reached out and held him back. Matt insisted, "Face it, he's not going to come with us, and we've got to go. It's almost nine o'clock. Your parents will be worried." Just before Luke closed the door, he turned and looked back, wishing he could be free of all this mess he was involved in. But for now, it seemed, he was trapped. He lifted his hand and waved to his friends and went back inside the building.

Brad waved back and hung his head.

"It's hard to help someone who doesn't want to be helped. We just need to pray for God to open his eyes to his true state. Luke has to realize he needs help." Matt whispered.

As they walked back to the car Matt and Brad began to pray for their friend's safety. Once inside the car, Brad phoned his parents to tell them he was on his way home. As they drove home the two G-men continued calling out to God on behalf of their friend. They asked God to show him the way and open his eyes to the devices of the enemy who was trying to keep him ensnared.

Matt pulled into the driveway of the Johnson home and let Brad out.

"See you in class tomorrow," Brad said as he closed the door of the car.

"Yeah, bright-eyed and bushy-tailed." Matt responded.

Brad thought, *Wow, it will be Monday tomorrow. Where has the weekend gone?*

CHAPTER 10

OPENING LEVEL 66

WALKING THROUGH THE GARAGE TOWARD the kitchen door, Brad massaged his temples lightly. He entered the house and greeted his parents, who were still in the kitchen.

"Boy, am I beat." Brad kissed his mom, gave his dad a hug around the shoulders and said good night.

As he was heading for the stairs, his mom asked, "Brad, if I invite the Finney's over for a cookout next Sunday afternoon, will you see if Luke can come?"

Brad looked at her and smiled, "I'll do my best, Mom, but Luke seems sort of mixed up right now." He turned and headed up the stairs praying that God would speak to Luke's heart in a very real way. Brad entered his room and went through the nightly routine, getting ready for bed. He finished brushing his teeth and re-entered his room. As he sat down on his bed, he reached over to reset his alarm for six o'clock. This would give him just enough time for his twenty minute morning devotion and breakfast before he was out the door for school.

He turned out the light and lay down on his back, pondering the events of the weekend. As he lay there, deep in thought, Brad realized his room was illumined with a bluish hue. *What now?* he thought as he sat up. He saw that it was coming from his computer screen. He had apparently left it on. Curious, he walked across the room to his desk and clicked the mouse. Up popped The Draegonian Invasion game. "Dare to enter the world of Draegon," the deep voice of the game taunted. *That's weird,* he thought, *it's been two days since I played that last.* He felt sure he had turned off.

Oh well, I'm not really that tired; it's only 9:40. So he clicked, "continue," and the game came to life. Brad sat down and began to assail the forces of evil across the galaxy. His mind was partially on Luke and the strongholds which held him in their grip. He tore into the various villains that appeared in the maze of scenarios with amazing skill and ferocity, using the different weapons of his futuristic arsenal. Before he knew it, the game was opening up into a new realm in which he had never been. All of a sudden, the screen went totally black. Crawling up from the bottom was a message in an eerie elongated, glowing, green script. It read, "CONGRATULATIONS WARRIOR, YOU HAVE REACHED LEVEL 66. PREPARE TO MEET DRAEGON . . . . AND DIE!" *Yeah right,* Brad thought. Instantly, the screen was engulfed in the most realistic-looking flames that Brad had ever seen. He drew back as he could almost feel the heat from the screen.

"Whoa," he marveled, watching the screen blaze. He forced himself to reach out and touch it. About the time he did, the flames began to change. Within the flames, something silvery in color began to form. Two tiny brilliant red beads of light appeared, about two inches apart, just above the central point of the flames. The object seemed to grow in size as if it were getting closer. The image became clearer as the flames dissipated. The two red beads of light grew larger, and two black vertical slits formed inside them. Brad realized he was now staring into the glaring, serpent-like eyes of some great beast. Watching, mesmerized, Brad heard a low, deep, almost growling voice, "You cannot defeat me, you must follow me."

Brad shook his head, and drew back from the screen. *Did I really hear that?* He wondered. The hypnotic eyes continued to stare at him in silence, except for the sound of low rhythmic breathing. Irritated, he clicked the mouse. Slowly the head pulled back, revealing a fang laden snout whose nostrils flared golden red. As Brad watched, the scaly head recoiled to reveal the entire body of a muscular, yet mechanical looking creature, very similar to the huge dragon Brad had seen earlier at The Snake Pit. The intimidating monstrosity writhed and contorted, oozing a greenish-black liquid from its joints, spewing flames from the mouth beneath its swirling nostrils. Abruptly, it began to spin into a tornado of fire which grew until it covered the entire screen. In the middle of the spinning mass of flames, a face began to appear. As the flames faded away, the pale features became more and more clear. It was a man with piercing green eyes, like a cat, and a black goatee with streaks of gray, his head shrouded in a pointed black hood. The figure then began to morph into a field of background graphics depicting an ancient castle retro-fitted with futuristic weaponry. The villain Draegon moved back into a hallway lit by the golden blaze of torches on the stone walls. He beckoned with his hand, and spoke, "Follow, if you dare."

Suddenly, dual red lasers flashed from his eyes causing an explosion of fire near Brad's character, who had now appeared on a stone bridge. He was a young man in his mid teens with shining black hair. Brad was amazed at how much he resembled Luke.

That's interesting, Brad thought as he quickly read the scenario description which appeared on the screen:

> Greetings, warrior. In the caverns, beneath Draegon's ancient fortress, souls are imprisoned. Your quest is to fight through the maze of evil forces to retrieve "The Great Key" which is hidden in a small wooden box. Use the key to free the imprisoned, and return with it to open the door of eternal power. If you are successful, you will know which is the correct door. If you are not, YOU will become Draegon's captive. Press "enter" if you are willing to take up the challenge.

Brad studied the two large doors in the room where his character now stood. He guessed that along the way there would be clues as to which door was the right one. Brad couldn't help but see the parallels in his life as well as Luke's. He pressed "enter." Before continuing, the screen directed him to choose his weapon. A display case lit up about ten steps away. Brad pressed the button on the controls, and his character started toward the case. Without warning, Draegon appeared in an arched doorway. Flames shot from Draegon's mouth, exploding some large canisters stacked near the weapons case. Brad's character paused briefly as the distraction dissipated. Above the case Brad read the words: "CHOOSE WISELY" written in an ancient-looking script. Peering inside the lit case he discovered daggers, double-sided axes, and grenades, as well as a variety of laser cannons and pistols. Deliberating over the assortment of weaponry, Brad looked again at the words. He wondered if some of these weapons, as powerful as they seemed, weren't adequate to defeat this enemy. He remembered the dragon at the beginning of the game. Brad realized that the dragon had become the man with the goatee, who was now pitted against him. *What is the classic weapon for the destruction of a dragon?* he reasoned, perusing the array. Shimmering on one side of the case was a large, silver, double-edged sword with gold framing the handle.

Brad studied it. He remembered Hebrews 4:12, which likened the Word of God to a two edged sword, able to separate what was of the flesh from that of the Spirit. As Brad reached for the shining symbol of God's word, flames again shot out of the mouth of his evil foe. Instead of grabbing the sword, Brad reached to the left of it and brought up a sparkling red and gold shield just in time to protect himself from the flames. Quickly, he maneuvered the shield into his left hand while grasping the handle of the brilliant sword in his right. As he brought the sword out of the case he squinted as a white-blue flash of lightning crackled from the tip of the sword. Amazed, Brad pointed the blade in the direction of his nemesis. Instantly, a bolt of lightning shot out of the tip, striking the very place where Draegon stood less than a second before. With a quick leap, the agile devil eluded the strike. Flipping into the air and landing on his feet, he disappeared down a dimly lit hallway. Feeling confident of victory, Brad raced down the corridor after him.

He entered a new room of glowing machinery, gauges and lit control panels. Cables, metal pipes and large round exhaust vents stretched above him and disappeared into a distant ceiling. Behind nearly every piece of machinery, and from every corner, an assortment of enemies opened fire on him. Holding tightly onto his shield he pressed forward. Pointing his sword toward each hidden enemy, he reveled as they were incinerated before him. The clamor died down, and as quickly as it started, all was quiet.

Brad noticed an opening to another room. A wonderfully warm, sparkling light drew him into it. Inside were all manner of treasures: gleaming jewels and crowns, gold coins, beautiful swords, paintings, and statues. "Wow," Brad exclaimed, pondering the wealth displayed before him. He saw a large wooden chest and dropped his shield to open it. It was full of shimmering gold coins. He reached down and picked up a handful of them. *Man! This would certainly pay for any type of cool ride I could imagine.* He was about to fill his pockets with the glittering treasure, when he sensed movement. Looking around, he caught a glimpse of Draegon and realized his shield was at his side. Instantly, a bright red laser shot forth from Draegon's eyes, striking him in the shoulder as he leapt for cover. The pain was hot. It burned as if a red hot knife had sliced his skin. How stupid he had been to let all those treasures sidetrack him from his mission. None of that was as valuable as the "Great Key." He had let down his shield, and the flaming arrows of the enemy had stung him viciously. *But why did it hurt so? Isn't this just a computer game? How is it that I am actually fighting with my own hands?* Before he could think more about it, he noticed Draegon maneuvering into position. He reached out and took hold of the shield. Suddenly, another burst of energy struck the now uplifted shield. Brad quickly thrust the sword in the direction of his opponent. A brilliant streak hit the black caped villain in the shoulder and sent him reeling backward into a heap.

"I got him!" Brad said to himself as he looked admiringly at the gleaming sword he was holding. "Cool!" But as Brad was picking himself up, the dark figure jumped to his feet and again disappeared down another dark corridor. *I wonder how many times I have to hit him in order to end the game,* Brad thought, as he staggered across the room in pursuit. *Man, my shoulder and neck hurt. This game is way too realistic.* Brad wondered how long he would be able to hold up the sword.

Stealthily, he traversed until he came to another large room. Before going into it, he noticed his reflection in some sort of large, glass, display case. He was dressed in what looked like a gray or khaki flight suit like air force pilots would wear. *It's me,* Brad thought, in amazement. *What happened to the character that looked like Luke at the start of the game? What is going on?* "This is totally weird." He said, as he drew closer to the large case. Looking past his own reflection he could see shapes moving in the reflection. Large heads and slender bodies of beings he had seen before, but this time he could make out large pointed ears. Realizing that they were coming up behind him, Brad turned quickly. Nothing was there. The beings had vanished.

A light from behind sent him spinning around again, this time to face a six-foot tall glass case, which had lit up to reveal its contents. As Brad's eyes adjusted to the light, he saw that a person was inside. Clothed in rags, was an emaciated man who appeared to be in his eighties. His sad eyes peered forward, a hopeless tormented expression on his face. He stood with gnarled, boney hands flat against the glass as if he couldn't see out, like a specimen trapped in a cage. Brad wondered if he was alive. The pitiful man never moved, but stood motionless, as if in some type of comatose state.

Abruptly, Brad was jolted out of his thoughts by a loud mechanical "clunk," followed by hissing and the whine of hydraulics. He turned, noticing a large metal door opening upward in the hallway behind him. Rising to a height of about twelve feet, the door stopped with a "clank." Green, glowing steam billowed from inside the massive doorway, through which a creature as tall as the opening emerged. It was the shape of a giant man, but it appeared to be part mechanical and part flesh. Its huge head was covered in a silvery helmet that came down over his nose and the sides of his face, like a mask. The vital areas of his hulk-like body bore a pewter-colored metal which gave him a mechanical appearance. Its powerful thighs and legs were completely machine. Shiny steel rods, wires, and hydraulics worked in sync as it stepped out of the holding bay. Fixing its golden cat-like eyes on Brad, it began moving straight toward him, at the same time flinging something round in his direction. As the spiky ball-shaped object hit close to Brad, it exploded; sending metal spikes in all directions, pelting Brad's shield with such force that it knocked him to the ground. He instantly scrambled around the corner of the stone wall and into the next room.

Where is my sword? He wondered, realizing it had been knocked from his hand when the Goliathoid had opened fire on him. Brad sat there a moment and prayed, *Lord, if you know what's going on, please help me.* Brad peered around the corner and could see a silver glint on the stone floor only about fifteen feet from where he was. He considered a run for it when a familiar verse came to mind:

"Lift up the shield of faith, for it will protect you from the fiery darts of the enemy."

Brad grasped the smoldering shield firmly, braced it with his arm. Then he crouched and began moving toward the sword. He was almost there when the metallic ogre hurled another spiked bomb. It exploded about twenty feet away. Brad felt the force of spikes pelting his shield. He instinctively ducked, hearing metal whizzing by inches from his head and then crashing into the walls around him. Before the smoke cleared and his opponent could see the results, Brad dove for his precious weapon. He took hold, rolled over and wielded it toward the glaring hulk. A blue-white flash burst forth, hitting the strange being in the shoulder, tearing the right arm from its body. The appendage sparked and popped as it crashed to the stone floor. Instantly, it raised the other arm and a pointed weapon rose from an inside compartment on its forearm. Brad quickly pointed the sword again. Another burst met the target square in the chest. With a huge fireball, it exploded, sending parts flying through the air. The foe fell forward, crashing onto the stone floor, in a quivering mass of smoking junk.

Brad sat there a minute amidst the buzzing and hissing of the wreckage, wondering what he should do next. An ominous pitiful moan drew him back toward the glass case. It hadn't come from the case, but echoed as it if it had come from afar. Brad realized that the case was actually sitting in a large stone entryway to another room. He cautiously entered and had taken about six steps into the dimly lit chamber when it began to brighten. Brad could see that it was an enormous space with soaring ceilings of stone that made it feel more like a giant cavern. The light came from hundreds, maybe thousands of those glass cases, which Brad could now see were stacked on five or six levels above him, connected by a maze of rusty, metal catwalks. As Brad walked forward, cases on either side of him illuminated, revealing the mournful, pathetic figures inside. Row after row, each one different, varying in age; but they all had the same, solemn expression of lonesome agony, as they gazed hopelessly from inside the cases.

Brad continued down the large central passage trying not to look at the depressing figures. A few feet from him, one illuminated, that seemed, somehow, familiar. He forced himself over to it. He studied the face of a teenage girl dressed in ragged black clothes. Her eyes were bright blue, but bloodshot with heavy dark circles surrounding them. Her ashen complexion was stained with mascara from what seemed to be an endless flow of tears. Brad knew this person. It was Brittany, Matt's old girlfriend, who had helped them get in to see Luke. He stood there a second, wondering if he should take his sword and break the glass like some story book hero rescuing the damsel in distress. Brad realized that his cheeks were wet, as a horrific feeling of sadness and despair overtook him. His legs became weak as he fell to his knees and began to cry out to God. It was as if he was experiencing the burden of agony felt by those who were in bondage to the enemy. Lost, lonely and hopeless, they had no clue as to how to get free.

Suddenly, he heard the eerie sound again, a pain-filled moan coming from far down the expanse of this huge dark cavern. Brad picked himself up and continued past the multitude of the doomed, until finally he could see a faint light exposing a figure. This individual seemed to be standing with his arms spread, upon a stone platform. As he got closer Brad could see that the person's arms and legs were shackled to a pair of large wooden posts which protruded from the platform. The head of the imprisoned was hanging limply down, facing the debris-strewn, stone floor.

By the dim light of torch lamps along the wall, Brad saw disturbing movement on the floor of the platform. A shudder ran through his body as he understood what it was. Large rats were meandering around the raised area right around the captive's feet. *I hate rats,* he thought. *I guess that Chuck-E- Cheese incident when I was a kid really did have an effect on me. Rats just totally creep me out.*

As he surveyed the area, keeping his shield before him, he saw movement from the slim victim. With another soulful moan the dark head lifted briefly, then, collapsed back onto his chest. Slimy drool dripped from his mouth onto his dark, ragged shirt. When he raised his head, Brad immediately recognized the face. "Luke?" Brad called out just above a whisper. *It can't be.* He looked so much older and haggard. His hair was covered in dust, and his skin was ashen. The wavering head of the enslaved slowly lifted, squinted one eye as if trying to comprehend what was going on and then fell down again. It was definitely Luke. Brad reacted to the sight of his friend in such a condition by running up the half dozen steps to the top of the platform. Tossing his weapons down, he grabbed the shackles holding Luke. The rusty, but sturdy bonds were clamped tight to his wrists and ankles, which were bloody and raw. The collar of each had a heavy padlock which required a key.

Where is the key? Brad cupped his friend's barely recognizable face and turned it toward his and asked, "Luke, do you know where the keys are?" Brad repeated his inquiry, but it was no use, Luke just stared at him incoherently. In frustration, Brad picked up the sword and tried striking the chains that went from Luke's feet to the post. Sparks flew, and Luke flinched and cried out in pain, but to no avail. The chains held fast. At a loss to know what to do next, Brad began to pray and think through the situation.

A snarling growl rumbled from deep within an arched cavern nearby, unnerving Brad. The cavern, to the left of the raised platform, was about twenty feet in height. The snarl grew louder and louder until it became a deafening roar. Suddenly, the cavern brightened with a brilliant orange light followed by an enormous fireball which exploded from the entry. Through the smoke and flames appeared the enormous, silver gleaming head of a dragon, green slime oozing from his nostrils. Fiery red eyes searched for prey above glistening pointed teeth. The head was followed by a long snake-like neck of silvery-green scales and then a streamlined body with smaller front limbs (like small arms) and hands with sickle-like claws. Huge powerful legs and a long tail, tipped with knife blade-like appendages, stabilized the beast. The dragon entered the room with such quickness and ferocity that Brad stumbled backward and fell, losing his grip on his powerful blade. Paralyzed with fear, he lay on his back helpless without either shield or sword. He came to his senses only to realize that the rat-like creatures were dragging away his weapons.

The huge dragon, seeing that Brad was disarmed, took one giant step right over to Brad, flinging his large, dripping snout down toward Brad, stopping right in his face. Nose to nose with the trembling boy, evil red eyes glared directly into Brad's. Its forked tongue flicked from between the pointed teeth inches from Brad's face. Overwhelmed by a putrid stench, Brad's hand went immediately to his mouth. He gagged and turned away, muttering, "Augh, dude, don't you ever brush your teeth?" As he turned to the side, Brad noticed a heavy piece of chain on the floor beside him. He instantly rolled over and grabbed the chain. Rolling back, he flung the chain up as hard as he could, slapping the repulsive reptile in the mouth with the metal ring attached to it. The beast reared back in anger, as Brad continued to roll right off the edge of the platform. Falling about five feet and hitting the floor hard, he landed next to the stone wall of the platform in front of a two foot tall arched opening underneath it. Ignoring the pain, he quickly scurried through it. A huge fire ball burst around the opening behind Brad, as the dragon vented its anger. The dark, dank space beneath the stone platform reeked. The foul smell nauseated him, but he persevered. Unable to stand because of the low ceiling, Brad crawled toward the light from a similar opening on the other side of the stone platform. Suddenly, his vision blurred as he felt the sticky mat of a spider web on his face. Frustrated, he quickly wiped it away. He flinched, as he felt the tickle of prickly legs running down the side of his face onto his neck. In a frenzy, he slapped at the eight legged menace to get the dreaded thing off of him. His body broke out into a cold sweat, as he moved away from the web. Trying to get his bearings, he stopped and sat still for a moment. Then, he moved closer to the light from the little archway, and noticed a round object, like a hard ball, lying a few feet from him. *Perhaps I could use that as a weapon.* He reached out and picked it up, only to drop it immediately as he realized what he was holding. *A human skull!* A shiver shot through his body. *Had this person crawled in here and never escaped?* Brad moved away from the ominous object, toward the light, the only exit on this side of his small chamber.

Brad's heart jumped with excitement. He could see, lying on the stone floor directly in front of the opening, the glint of his sword. Crawling over to the wall next to the arch, he reached out and grabbed hold of the handle. At once, pain shot through his hand as a large black boot crushed his hopes of regaining the weapon he had lost earlier. He jerked his bleeding, throbbing hand back into the alcove. Then, Brad heard a deep, sly, articulate voice.

"It is pointless to resist my power, Brad. You are in my world now. I am lord here. There is no one who can help you now, so you might as well admit that you have lost. It would go much easier for you if you just follow me, like most people do. Following me, you will have nothing to fear, and I will give you all of the pleasures you could ever want."

Brad could hear the sound of tiny feet, scratching around in the darkness near him. He pulled his knees up to his chest and sat in a ball as fear, like he had never experienced, threatened to overtake him.

"Jesus where are you? How do I get out of this place? I can't do this," Brad confessed in a trembling whisper. After a moment, a gentle breeze blew across his sticky, grimy cheeks, and a sweet aroma displaced the rankness around him.

A peaceful, comforting voice spoke softly to him, "You have said correctly, you cannot do this. But I can."

Brad's heart leapt within him. "Lord, please help me. Are you here?"

"I am right next to you. Even if you go down to the depths of the earth, I am with you. Be strong and courageous."

Brad could feel the power of God strengthening him. An overwhelming urge to worship Jesus flooded his heart. He leaned forward on his hands and knees, thanking Jesus for His encouraging power. In this position of absolute humility, Brad realized that this situation with Luke was indeed beyond his ability to solve. The only one who could truly save Luke was Jesus. There was no way to free him from the chains that held him without the power of Jesus. Brad moved his hands to sit up. Something hard jabbed his palm. Moving away some loose stones, he felt an object that appeared to be rectangular in shape, a small box about the size of a Bible. It seemed to be carved out of wood. Feeling around the edges, his fingers passed over metal hinges on one side.

"Sure wish I had that little flashlight of Luke's right now," Brad muttered to himself. Finally his finger hit upon a small latch, which moved and the box slowly opened. "Whoa!" Brad exclaimed in astonishment as he shielded his eyes. Brilliant golden light radiated from the inside of the box, breaking through the morbid darkness of Brad's temporary tomb. The light illuminated his small prison and sent the encroaching wretched rodents into quick retreat. Inside the box was a shimmering gold key, about five inches in length, from which the light emanated. Brad reached into the box cautiously; passing his fingers within a half inch of the glimmering key to make sure it wasn't glowing hot.

Then he heard the still small voice say, "Don't fear. Pick it up."

Brad picked up the remarkable object and began to examine it. It seemed like metal but was transparent like glass. Brad remembered reading in his Bible about the streets of gold. It described them as being transparent. *Could this be the same stuff?* It was then that Brad realized the top of the key was in the shape of a cross.

As his eyes got used to the light, they came more into focus, and he could see letters engraved down the middle of the key. "THE TRUTH," Brad read out loud. He thought a second. "A key with The Truth written on it," Brad marveled. "'The truth will set you free.' It's from the Bible, John chapter 8 verse 32. Man, those memory verses do come in handy sometimes." Brad's mind raced, remembering the large padlocks which held his friend Luke. He stuck the key into his pocket and looked out of the arched opening. The sword was still lying there, right where it was before.

"You don't want me to come in there and get you, boy." A deep foreboding voice again sent shivers through Brad.

He remembered one of the phrases of the G-men. *Feel the fear and do it anyway.* Brad prayed, "Lord, guide me." Then he picked up the empty wooden box and hurled it back toward the way he came in, sending rats scurrying out of the opening. Listening, Brad heard foot falls moving away. He burst out of the little archway, and caught hold of the sword with one hand. He rolled up onto his feet, pointing the blade at his adversary who was reeling from being caught off-guard by Brad's diversion. Instantly, a lightning bolt flew from the sword, striking the evil figure in the shoulder, sending him flying through the air into some metal drums stacked nearby. The menace lay perfectly still in a black heap, smoldering as electrical current crackled through his body.

Secure that he was rid of Draegon for the moment, Brad leapt to the platform and pulled the key from his pocket. Gazing at it briefly, he turned to Luke, who seemed a little more coherent. Brad held the shimmering object up for Luke to see, and quoted the scripture: "You shall know the Truth and the Truth will set you free." He then shoved the key into one of the padlocks and turned it. With a loud, echoing "click" it popped open. Keeping an eye on his steaming adversary, Brad opened each lock. Luke collapsed onto the floor. Brad gave him a couple of light slaps on his face to help revive him. As he did, Brad looked over and realized that Draegon was gone. Vanished!

"Luke, we've got to get out of here!" Brad announced excitedly as he pulled Luke up and placed an arm around him. The two stood as Luke began to comprehend and move forward. Grappling with the sword in one hand, they made it down the steps. "You sure are heavy for a skinny guy," Brad quipped with a smile, trying to disarm his fears.

Through his delirium, Luke responded, "Yeah—I been working out."

Brad laughed. They continued down the central passageway past the glass cells of the imprisoned. Brad stopped as the case which held the young woman, whom Brad thought to be Brittany, illuminated. Propping his friend on a stone pillar beside the case, Brad got an idea. He pulled out the key and looked for a lock on the glass encasement. There was none to be found. Finally, Brad noticed a small knob about mid-way on the right side of the case. He grabbed it and gave it a pull. It opened.

"It's not locked!" Brad declared, as he opened it all the way. "Brittany?" She didn't respond but stared directly in front of her. It was then that Brad realized all of the walls inside of it were mirrored. Although he could see her, she could see nothing but her own reflection. "Brittany!" Brad called again, louder. "Come on out. You can be free, but we have to go." Brad reached in and pulled her to the outside of the cage. She stumbled. Brad caught her.

She looked up at him with confusion, and then insisted angrily, "Just leave me alone." She pulled away from him and stumbled back into the case, again gazing at her reflection. She reached up, stroking her hair.

Dumbfounded, Brad stood speechless. "Why would someone not want to be free of this?" He wondered aloud.

"A person must accept freedom. They must see the Truth as the Truth," A soft voice behind him explained. Brad turned with a start to see the man in the long white coat, who Brad knew to be Emmanuel.

"Most people spend their lives in prisons of their own creation. They are content to focus only on themselves. They are enslaved by their own selfishness, their version of the truth. It's so sad that they never discover the meaningful life for which they were created. Always remember, Brad, you were created to lay down your life for others."

Brad heard a sound in the distance: A low howl got louder and louder. Suddenly, a fireball burst into the air near the platform and the red-eyed head of the familiar silvery beast rose into the air, searching the cavernous room for its prey. At least thirty five-feet in height, reaching almost to the ceiling, its eyes focused on Luke, who was scrambling behind the column he'd been leaning on. Amid a tumultuous fury of roars and bellows of fire, the dragon, in a tyrannical rage, stomped forward to devour his victim. Brad looked toward Luke and his sword propped up against the column. He turned to the figure dressed in white.

"I'll take care of this," Emmanuel remarked calmly, smiling. Fearlessly, he stepped right out into the path of the obnoxious approaching reptile and just stood there. As soon as the dragon saw Him, it came to a dead halt and began to moan and wail in terrible distress. As it began to back away, green smoke began to ooze from between its scales. Soon it was completely engulfed in a green cloud. With a sweep of Emmanuel's hand the cloud dissipated. The giant creature was gone. Cowering in its place was the black-hooded, green-eyed villain from the start of the game.

"Leave us!" was all the Man in white said. The scrawny figure sneered and disappeared into the dark shadows of the hall. With that Emmanuel was gone as well. Brad could hear Luke calling his name and pulling on his shoulder. Looking confused, Luke asked, “Brad, how do we get out of here?”

Chapter 11

What Is Going On At West Lake High?

"Brad! Brad, you need to go to bed, Son." Brad lifted his head which was throbbing from lying on his desk. His mom was shaking him gently, trying to wake him enough to lead him to bed. "It's past one o'clock," she stated as she rubbed his back. "I can't believe you fell asleep playing this silly computer game again. You've got school tomorrow." She helped him up and over to his bed, shaking her head in dismay. Brad sat down on the bed in a daze.

"Mom, you won't believe the dream I just had."

"Well, Son, it's a little late to hear your tales of spaceships kidnapping people in the neighborhood," she replied as she walked to the door.

"No Mom, this time Draegon became a huge dragon, and Emmanuel helped me defeat him and free Luke. I mean, actually, I helped Him, a little. He did the real work."

She turned to Brad, with a smile, and affirmed, "Emmanuel is the only one who can truly set anyone free from the chains that hold them."

"Yeah," Brad agreed. Then, with a puzzled look, asked, "How'd you know Luke was in chains?"

"Oh, it just popped into my head. Maybe it was the Spirit of God. Good night."

Brad turned off the light and lay back on his bed. He began to talk to Jesus and thank Him for all that his dreams were teaching him about overcoming fear, and for giving him a burden for those who lived in a cage of selfishness. Without warning, his computer screen lit up in a blaze of digital fire and Brad sat straight up in bed. He gazed at the burning screen as two beady, red eyes appeared followed by the entire head of the dragon. Snarling, it glared at Brad as if daring him to enter his world again. Incensed, Brad jumped up and walked over to the computer, "I'll fix you." He grabbed the mouse and declared, "Be gone, devil." Then, with a click, the beast was gone. He started toward the bed, paused, then turned and reached down. Yanking the plug out of the wall socket, he muttered, "Now, I can get a decent night sleep," and fell back into bed.

The next day Brad overslept. He quickly got dressed and ran down the stairs to gobble down a bowl of cereal. Glancing at his watch, he got up, kissed his mom, hugged his dad, and darted out the door to meet Matt at the curb.

The sleek crimson ride had just pulled up. Brad jumped in as Matt greeted, "Good morning, Bradford," mimicking Brad's Mom. "Dare I ask, how you slept?" Matt inquired with a wary look.

Brad rubbed his eyes, still in a bit of a fog. "I slept well once I got in bed, but I fell asleep playing the Draegonian Invasion game."

Matt laughed and interrupted, "You did that again? I guess that‘s why your hair looks like that."

"Yes," Brad admitted a little irritated, "I'm sure I'm not the only person who has fallen asleep at the computer. What‘s wrong with my hair?" he asked, self consciously looking at the little mirror on the sun visor.

"Yeah, maybe some hardworking college student doing homework or something like that, but playing a computer game and dozing off, is a little crazy. Maybe you need to set an alarm clock at your desk." Matt shook his head, with a cockeyed grin.

"Seriously, man, what's wrong with my hair?"

"Didn't you look in the mirror this morning?" Matt asked, laughing to himself. He knew that Brad was sensitive about his hair. Brad had always fought with it. His hair was the stubborn type that seemed to have a mind of its own. In reality, Matt didn't think Brad's hair looked all that funny, but now that he had the boy going he couldn't resist continuing to mess with his mind. Chuckling, he watched as Brad was now trying to flatten out his hair, which was sticking up just a little in one place.

"I overslept. I had trouble getting back to sleep after this dream I had."

"What, another dream? Did Darth Vader try to kidnap your sister or something?" Matt chided, still laughing at Brad's attempt to fix his hair.

"Be serious, Matt. I got to level 66 playing the Draegonian Invaision game, but I fell asleep at some point. The evil Lord of Draegos, Draegon, is able to transform into this huge metallic dragon."

"That's crazy!" Matt laughed, "You have the wildest dreams, man. I didn't even know that game had a level 66. I suppose Luke was in this dream, too."

"Yeah, he was," Brad replied defensively. "But, there was also someone else in this dream that you know." Brad feigned smugness.

"OK, I'm sorry. Who else was in this dream?" Matt's curiosity was now in gear.

"Brittany." Brad stated matter-of-factly.

With a serious tone Matt repeated, "Brittany?" Matt's deep fondness for his old girlfriend was apparent. He regularly wrestled with a feeling of guilt for their somewhat hostile parting of ways. Back then he was struggling with the battle between the emotional and physical attraction he had for her versus obeying God and being pure in heart. He had done what he felt was right, but Brittany couldn't see anything but hurt and abandonment. He always wondered if he could have done something more to ease the pain of it. Brad could tell that Matt still cared about what happened to her. He knew that his kind-hearted friend had spent many hours praying for her to truly understand the truth of the Bible and what it meant to really follow Jesus.

As they traveled down the road toward West Lake High, Brad related the escapades of the night's excursion, and they discussed what it all meant. The boys reached their destination, grabbed their backpacks, and began walking across the school parking lot.

"Wow," Matt remarked, thinking about the picture Brad was painting in his mind. "That's quite a vision that the enemy keeps so many people caged up in their own self-centered behavior. I know Brittany was always looking for a life of fun and fantasy, so much so that she could never see what God might have been calling her to do."

"Yeah, and we have to be careful of that, too. Remember Jesus' parable of the farmer sowing the seeds, the last part of it describes people who heard God's word and began act to on it, but later on were neutralized by the selfish pursuits and worries of this life. It's not hard at all to fall into the trap of thinking that we are god, and everything should revolve around us."

"Man, that's good preaching," Matt affirmed as he slapped Brad on the shoulder.

Walking through the parking lot, Brad noticed a couple of guys in his class who were pointing and snickering at them. The guys were dressed in black, and heavy silver chains dangled from their pockets. Their arms were clad with black and silver riveted wrist bands. One of them had on a t-shirt with "The Slammers Band" emblazoned on it.

Annoyed, Brad glanced at Matt and asked, "Wonder what their problem is?"

Matt looked over at the guys, then back at Brad and responded with a smirk, "They probably just like what you've done with your hair."

Brad's hand immediately went up to the crown of his head pressing down the rebellious locks. Matt laughed, which evoked a friendly jab in the arm from Brad.

"There's really nothing wrong with your hair, man. I was just messing with you," Matt joked. "I guess it goes to show that we do need to look into a mirror every once in a while, like the Bible tells us to."

"Yeah," Brad laughed. The two friends parted ways and headed to different classes.

At lunch time Brad found some of his friends in the cafeteria and sat down with his tray. Looking around the room he wondered, *Is it my imagination, or is black attire becoming the height of fashion?* Almost half of the kids were wearing all black.

"Hey Brad, what's up?" he heard a familiar voice approaching from the side.

He turned to see a tall, lanky fellow, about seventeen, in black jeans and t-shirt with dyed black hair extending from reddish roots. "Jared?" Brad asked in astonishment, "Is that you?" He was sporting a small reddish square of hair between his lip and chin. "What's going on with you, friend? You look kind of different." Brad had known Jared Spain practically all of his life. He had been in Boy Scouts for a while and they had gone to the same school as long as Brad could remember. Jared had always been a pretty straight laced guy who was in Brad's Sunday School class until Jared started having baseball practices on Sundays and got out of the habit of coming. "What's with the black get-up?" Brad queried.

"Oh, I just like it. Looks cool, doesn't it?" Jared boasted, displaying his confidence. "All the kids who are really into black metal are dressing like this. It's really awesome that we have a great group like "The Slammers" right here in town. D' you know that they are planning to cut a CD next month? They are going to be in the big-time soon, and a bunch of us plan to follow them right to the top."

"Right," Brad remarked, trying to control his sarcasm."

"Brad, you should really come to the new Dragon's Den this weekend and hear them. They're jam-min'. Luke Hunter, from right here in our class is incredible on those drums."

"I'll agree with you there: Luke is an amazing drummer. By the way, have you seen Luke at school today?"

"No, I haven't." Jared replied with a come-to-think-of-it look about him.

Brad observed the cheerful, smiling face of his friend and wondered how he could so easily substitute following this band for following God. "I haven't seen you at youth group in quite a while. We sure miss you there." Brad smiled and looked him in the eyes.

"Well, during baseball season it's sort of hard to get there," he admitted sheepishly, as if he knew that he ought to be there.

What Brad wanted to ask was, "Is baseball going to save you from hell?" But instead he said, "The guys all miss seeing you there."

The young man's face lit up, "Really, they miss me?" Jared was one of the boys the G-Men had been praying for, who had seemingly been drifting onto a path that led away from God. Brad could tell that Jared was indeed searching for acceptance in other groups and was struggling with what the world had to offer.

"Some of the guys are meeting at the church gym to shoot some hoops Saturday. Then, we're going out for pizza. It would be great if you'd come."

He was about to answer when, "Jared, dude, how's it going?" Then—whack! A punch thrust into Jared's arm. "What are you doing hanging out with Mr. Goodie Two-Shoes here? "

"Oh, hi, Blane," Jared laughed rubbing his arm.

Brad was immensely annoyed, but kept his cool.

"Has Deacon Johnson been trying to keep you on the holy path? Did you tell him how much fun we had bashing mailboxes the other evening. I think you had a little too much fun, Jared, my boy. A few beers and you're a crazy man." Blane Stevens regularly boasted that he had never darkened the doors of any church, and he didn't need that "religious bull" in his life. Brad thought it amazing that at the ripe old age of seventeen, Blane, in his infinite wisdom, had discovered that God didn't exist. He had conveniently decided he was an atheist. If there was no God, then there was no sin to deal with, and he could do anything he wanted, so long as it didn't really hurt anyone. I guess that didn't count with mailboxes. Brad and some of the G-Men had spent many hours fixing some of the mailboxes these guys had destroyed, which belonged to some of the older folks in the community.

"How's it going, Blane?" Brad asked with a cheerful smile, squelching the desire just to punch the guy in the nose. "How'd you like to go out with some of my friends this weekend and repair some of those mailboxes? I've often wondered why some people hate mailboxes so. Is it revenge against government authority, or do you just like making people's lives miserable?"

Blane, with a smirk, replied, "You Christians are the ones always making people's lives miserable. You guys don't want anybody to have any fun."

"No, we like having fun. It's just that our definition of fun is different from yours. We believe our actions have consequences and we're responsible for them. I was just inviting Jared here to come out for pizza and basketball Saturday evening. Why don't you come? We have a lot of fun and nobody has to fix anything afterward." Brad looked directly at Blane and smiled, sincerely hoping Blane would come.

"You've got to be kidding me. You don't want me there." Then a devious grin spread across Blane's face. "Can I bring a couple of six packs?"

"Sure, the guys like Seven-up or Mountain Dew."

Blane rolled his eyes, "You guys are so lame." Then Blane turned to Jared, who was standing there struggling within himself, and stated, "Well, I'm afraid my friend Jared and I have other plans on Saturday."

A stunned Jared stammered, "W-we do?"

"Yeah man, a bunch of us are going over to the old house in the country to listen to Luke's band practice. It'll be a blast and a lot more fun than some cheesy basketball session with a bunch of holier- than-thou types. Plus, I'll bring the beer. OK, dude?"

Jared laughed, and looked nervously at Brad. He punched Blane in the arm and affirmed, "Sounds great, dude." The two guys started off. Jared looked back at Brad, "Sorry. Maybe some other time, OK?"

Brad nodded, "Sure man." Blane and Brad had been friends at one time. But as Blane seemed to be more and more interested in drinking and then drugs, their friendship became strained. When Brad tried to explain why he didn't go in for that sort of "fun," Blane became angry and defensive, calling Brad out on some hypocrisy in his past. Blane had witnessed Brad lose his temper on the basketball court a while back and always seemed to be trying to stir up that temper again.

Brad's thoughts were suddenly interrupted by a sweet familiar voice. "Hi, Brad. How are things going?"

Brad looked up to the cheerful face of his sister and replied, "Hi, Sis. OK, I guess."

"I saw you talking to Jared and Blane. It looked a little intense. It seems like Jared is getting hooked into that black metal stuff, too."

"Yeah, and Blane is always trying to get me to lose my cool. He sure knows how to tick me off. I can't help imagining what it would be like to. . ." Brad struck his fist into his palm and shook his head in dismay. "Oh Lord, I repent. Help me see past the schemes of the enemy," Brad prayed, as he lowered his head.

"I'll be praying for self-control and that God will give you a burden to see Blane saved," she consoled, putting a hand on his shoulder.

"That would be a miracle," replied Brad, "but God could certainly do it." Brad's eyes drifted around the room, looking for someone.

"Who are you looking for? Are you expecting some nice young lady?" Mandy asked jokingly.

"Yeah, right," Brad frowned. "Have you seen Luke at school today?"

"No, I haven't, Brad. You don't think something is seriously wrong with him, do you?"

Brad glanced at Mandy's concerned expression. "I don't know, but I sure wish I could talk with him and see how he's doing."

"Well, I've got to get to class. See ya later." She exclaimed, picking up her backpack. She waved goodbye and at the same time greeted Matt who was just walking up to where Brad was sitting.

"Don't rush off on account of me," Matt kidded.

"Got a class," Mandy called, as she hurried out of the room.

"What's up?" Matt asked cheerfully. He could see that Brad was deep in thought.

"All this stuff that's going on with Luke and the band—I can't get my mind off of it. Look around this lunch room at how many kids are wearing black. It's amazing how quickly so many of them have gotten into this black metal thing." Brad shook his head.

"It's that "herd" mentality," Matt replied. "They are sheep looking for a shepherd. If we aren't diligent to point them to the real Shepherd, then they'll follow another one."

"Why is it so hard for them to see the truth of who Jesus is?" Brad wondered aloud.

"The Bible says that Satan has blinded the eyes of those who don't believe. Black metal music is just another lure he uses to keep them blinded by so-called "fun." It seems to be part of our flesh nature to desire fun over doing what's right. Fun has become the god of this age."

"Why does it seem like God hates fun?" Brad asked, in serious thought.

"I think it's because most people let the devil define fun. They listen to what he says is fun rather than what God says. There are many things which are fun to do that are totally innocent, but many people today don't think something is fun unless it has some edge that gives them a rush. Their rebellious nature has made sin fun just because it's something that they are not supposed to do."

Brad sat there considering Matt's words. Seeing that Brad was still wrestling with his thoughts,

Matt asked, "Which is more fun, going to a concert or walking across the water with Jesus?"

Brad did a double take. "Walking across the water. What are you talking about? We can't walk on water."

Matt laughed at his friend's reaction. "Peter did. You know, when Jesus came to the disciples in the boat. Who says we can't? Maybe we are too sidetracked by worldly fun to ever really experience true fun with Jesus. I think God created the whole world so that He could show us all the fun stuff He created for us. Perhaps the problem is that our own selfishness traps us into never really experiencing God's fun. We listen to the world and adopt their idea of fun."

Brad, thinking about Matt's words, spoke up. "Yeah, why is dressing in black, getting drunk, and going out bashing in a bunch of mailboxes fun? It's certainly not fun to the mailbox owners. Why don't we consider laying hands on the sick and seeing them healed fun?"

"Or telling someone about Jesus, there's nothing more exciting than to see someone accept Jesus," Matt added. As Brad thought, he looked around the lunchroom at all the lost souls laughing, talking, and going through life without knowing God. "Why doesn't it seem like fun? It seems scary to share the gospel. I've tried it, and I'm afraid I just make Blane Stevens angry at me, not to mention Luke. It's fun to talk to them about Jesus; but the rejection, if they don't like what you tell them, isn't fun."

Matt nodded in agreement, "I guess just having fun is not really what life is all about. There's something greater than fun. Jesus didn't go to the cross because it was fun. Most great accomplishments aren't made because they are fun."

"Yeah," Brad replied. "So often, pursuit of fun just causes people to waste their lives doing nothing truly worthwhile."

"Well, whether it's fun or a challenge, I'm not going to let the enemy dictate what's fun and take all these kids captive. We've just got to show them the love of Jesus and let them see His truth in our lives, right?" Matt acknowledged emphatically.

"Right!" Brad heartily agreed.

"By the way, are we still on for cleaning up Mr. Guthrey's fallen tree tomorrow?" Matt asked.

"You bet. I told him we'd be there around three-thirty. I'm dying to get a look inside that shed and figure out what this mysterious pouch is all about."

The electronic bell sounded, and the entire room went into action as everyone headed back to their classes. "Oh, got to go," Brad said.

"See you later, man," and they were off to class. As the two walked away, the boy who was sitting behind Brad appearing to do homework pulled out a cell phone and called someone. Watching them, his eyes followed them out into the hall.

Chapter 12

Exploring the Shed

At the end of the school day, Brad met Matt in the parking lot. The mystery of the black pouch had dogged him all day. Brad was ready to get to work and find out if it was real or just a dream.

When Matt hit the button to unlock Ruby, Brad opened the door and hopped in. "You ready to do some serious yard work?"

"Yep," Matt replied. "Dad said that I could use the chain saw. It's in the trunk."

"Great, that should speed things along. I called Mr. Guthrey last night, and he mentioned he had all the tools we should need. They are right there in the shed. Now we have every right to explore it and find that illusive pouch. What if it contains a bunch of money, or drugs, or something? What do we do with it if it does?" Brad asked, pensive.

"We have to turn it over to the police," Matt replied, dogmatically.

"But, what if they ask us how we found it? They'll think I'm crazy if I tell them I saw it in a dream."

"Yeah, they'll know the truth about you," Matt joked, with a smirk.

"I'm serious, man. What if this gets Luke into some kind of trouble with the law?"

Matt thought seriously about Brad's words. "I'm afraid Luke might already be in some trouble with the law, but I'm more concerned about what Sammy and Mr. Dragon might do if he is holding out on them in some way."

"Why do you say that?

"Dad told me that we should be very careful how we get involved in this whole thing. He says that Mr. Dragon and his lot are an extremely dangerous bunch. Although they have yet to pin anything on them, except for a drug trafficking charge on Sammy a few years ago; they are implicated with several missing persons and at least one homicide."

"Murder? You mean your Dad thinks they actually killed someone?" Brad gasped. "We've got to get Luke away from those guys."

Matt turned onto Morning Star Way. Just before Brad's house, he pulled into a narrow drive that wound into the woods. As Ruby disappeared down the path, her powerful engine rumbling deeply, a black SUV curiously pulled up and parked on the side of the road about fifty feet away. Undetected by the boys, two figures in dark clothing jumped out and went into the woods near the path.

Matt drove past the rambling ranch-style house of the Guthrey's, alongside a row of fruit trees and a small garden. He rounded a bend, and the little shed came into sight. Mr. Guthrey was standing in front it unlocking the padlock. He turned, taking the pipe he was smoking from his mouth. Smiling, he waved at the boys.

They hopped out of the car and greeted the friendly gentleman. "Beautiful afternoon for working outside," Matt announced cheerfully. The afternoon was indeed wonderful. It was about seventy-nine degrees with a gentle breeze rustling through the trees, a perfect early May afternoon. Matt opened up the trunk, and pulled out the chain saw, a gas can, and some work gloves.

"I see you boys came prepared," Mr. Guthrey exclaimed, as he came over and shook their hands. "The shed's unlocked, and the tools are inside. You should have everything you need. I have to take Mrs. Guthrey to a doctor's appointment, but should be back before you finish."

"I hope it's nothing serious with Mrs. Guthrey," Brad responded with genuine concern.

"Well, she's had some trouble with her heart for a few years now, and we are hoping that she won't have to have surgery."

"We'll surely pray for her." Matt affirmed, "She's a special lady. She taught me in Sunday school in third and fourth grade."

"She did?" Mr. Guthrey beamed, "Well, I'm sure that it would bless her so much to know that you boys are praying for her. I'll be back in about an hour." He turned and slowly walked back toward the house. Matt carried the chainsaw over to the fallen tree and set it down. Brad started toward the shed, then turned, "Why don't we pray for the Guthrey's right now?"

"Sure, that'd be great," Matt replied laying down the work gloves. The guys prayed for Mrs. Guthrey's heart condition, as well as the elderly couple's health in general, and then got to work. Brad walked over to the shed door. With anticipation, he removed the unlocked padlock and opened the door. The tools were all neatly arranged and hanging from rusty nails on carefully placed boards. Although obviously put there years ago, it was apparent Mr. Guthrey was the type of person who believed that everything had its place. The shed was not exactly like Brad remembered it from the dream. There were a couple of old boxes with a variety of old magazines and some empty jars. Aside from the yard tools, there was not much else in the shed. Brad searched everywhere in the shed to no avail. There was simply no black pouch to be found.

Finally, Matt came in, "No luck, huh?"

"I've searched everywhere. There's no pouch here. I'm kind of glad. I don't know what I'd have done if we found something incriminating in it. Now, we don't have to deal with that."

"Yep, you're right," Matt agreed, as he nosed around a bit himself, just to make sure Brad hadn't overlooked something.

"Well, I guess we should get to work." Brad suggested. He grabbed a rake and an ax and headed out the door. Matt followed him out, cranked up the chainsaw, and they soon had the tree cut into manageable pieces. Mr. Guthrey had instructed Brad to pile the branches in a certain area at the edge of the woods. Brad had just dragged a bunch of branches over to the pile of debris and was heading back to the shed when he heard a sharp "snap" in the woods behind him. He looked back instinctively, his eyes searched through the woods. He couldn't be sure, but it was as if someone had been there. Brad had the eerie feeling of being watched, but shrugged it off as heightened imagination. *After all, there was no pouch in the shed. It was all just a dream, wasn't it?* He headed back over to the shed, picked up a rake and started raking some of the small branches and dried leaves. As he pulled the rake back, he noticed something silvery tumbling amongst the leaves and branches. He bent over and picked the object up, about the same time realizing what it was. "Oh Man!" he exclaimed. "Matt! Look at this.

Matt put down the ax he was wielding and rushed over. "What is it?"

"Maybe it wasn't just a dream."

"What did you find?" Matt queried curiously. Brad held out a metal flashlight about eight inches long.

Matt looked puzzled. "What's so special about that? A lot of people have flashlights like that."

"Really." Brad said looking at the base then unscrewing the cap. "How many of the have L. H. etched into the cap? Plus, it has this special compartment for extra batteries."

Not only did Luke have it in the dream, but he had it before that, when I saw him at his house after the storm. It proves that he has been here," Brad stated confidently, shoving it into his coat pocket for safe keeping.

"Maybe," Matt admitted. "Although, someone could have borrowed it or something."

"I believe Luke was here. And, the pouch was here too," Brad affirmed. "But what could have happened to it?"

"It's possible. I guess someone could have gotten to it before Mr. Guthrey locked it up," Matt hypothesized.

"Yeah, I wish we could just talk to Luke and find out. This whole thing is about to fry my brain." Brad took the flashlight, reassembled it and stuck it into his pocket. Matt walked back over and picked up the ax, and the boys resumed the task at hand. As they did, Brad's eyes, drifted toward the woods. He seemed to sense the eyes that were watching their every move, and listening to their discussions. As the boys finished up, the mysterious men in black made their way back to the parked SUV and slipped down the road.

Brad and Matt were putting away the tools when Mr. Guthrey walked gingerly down the path to the shed. "Mighty fine job you boys did. How much do I owe you?"

"Nothing, Mr. Guthrey. We were glad to be of service to you," Brad responded.

Mr. Guthrey, quite taken aback, objected, "Now, I can't let you boys do that. I insist on paying you for the work you've done here."

Matt spoke up, "Well sir, if you would like to, you can just make a donation to the youth missions program at church. It will help some of the young people pay for the upcoming mission trip to Haiti."

Mr. Guthrey's face beamed, "That is a fine thing to do. I'll send them a check this week." He shook the boys' hands and thanked them again. "Just leave the shed unlocked, I want to tidy up in there a bit," he instructed, and started back to the house.

Brad called back to him, "Mr. Guthrey, how'd the appointment go?"

He turned and affirmed with a smile, "It went just fine. The doctors say that she is doing much better. The test results were good, and they don't think that she will need the surgery after all."

"Great," Brad exclaimed, "that's a real answer to prayer."

Matt loaded up the chainsaw, and the two boys got into Ruby. Brad glanced again through the woods. He pulled the seat belt over as Matt started the car. "Did you get the feeling that we were being watched?"

"Watched?" Matt exclaimed. "Why would you think a thing like that? Did you see someone?"

"I can't be sure. It was more of a feeling," Brad conceded, continuing to scan the woods.

"Would you stop it? You're creeping me out." Matt frowned as he wound through the wooded path and turned right onto the road. Ruby came to a stop in Brad's driveway.

Brad gathered up his back-pack, "See-ya tomorrow."

"Yeah, man. Have a good night," came the reply, as Matt revved the motor gently and eased out of the driveway. Brad stood there a minute, watching longingly as the shiny muscle car glided down the street. He was turning to go into the house when he caught a glimpse of a black Hummer dart by the house. His mind quickly traveled back to that night at the Dragon's Den and the black Hummer with Dragon 1 on the license plate. Was it just a coincidence? He knew of no one in the neighborhood with that type of vehicle. Brad dropped his backpack, picked up the phone and dialed Matt's cell phone.

Matt answered.

"Matt, it's Brad."

"Hey, man, what did you forget?" Matt asked, since on more than one occasion he had returned to Brad's house because of something left in his car.

"Nothing, listen! Is there a black hummer following you?"

Matt glanced in the rear view mirror. "No. Why?" Matt responded a little nervously.

"Right after you left, one sped by the house. It looked just like the one that was at the Dragon's Den that night."

"Are you sure?" Matt questioned.

"No. But, no one in our neighborhood has one of those things. Just keep an eye out and be careful. OK?"

"Believe me," Matt conceded, "you've got me so keyed up, I'll watch every big black thing that moves. See you later."

Brad hung up the phone, "Oh, Lord, please keep Matt safe from the schemes of the enemy. This is all a little too exciting. Please help me be able to talk to Luke." Continuing to pray silently, he headed upstairs to start on his homework.

As he walked by Mandy's room, she called, "Brad, is that you? Mom called and said that she and Dad will be home in about fifteen minutes. They are at the store getting some stuff for the cookout on Sunday. Did you see Luke today? His family is coming over on Sunday, you know."

Brad stuck his head into her room, "Thanks for the update. Mom told me they were coming over, but I haven't seen Luke. I didn't see him at school. Did you?"

"No. Myra Burk, his old girlfriend, says he's staying at that old house in the country with the guys in the band."

Brad shook his head. "I don't know why his parents let him. He's only fifteen, and those guys party all the time."

They were interrupted by the sound of the phone ringing. Brad darted into his parents' room and answered, "Hello. Johnson's residence."

"Is this Brad?" a young lady's voice asked.

"It's Brad. Who's this?"

"Brittany Erickson," a timid voice replied.

"Brittany. Hi. How's it going?" Brad asked cordially.

"Not very well, I'm afraid," she lamented, her voice breaking up.

"What's wrong, Brit?" Brad pressed.

"Everything," she whimpered with a sniff. "I really called to talk to your sister, Mandy. Is she at home?"

"Yes, she is."

He was about to call his sister when she interrupted, "But— I need to tell you about Luke. He's missing again, and Sammy and Mr. Dragon seem real upset about it. I think that he has something that belongs to them, and they're after him," she added, with a hint of desperation in her voice.

"Do you know where Luke is?" Brad asked calmly.

"No, I don't. He was staying out at the old house, but last night there was some sort of problem, and during the night Luke disappeared. I know that Sammy doesn't have him because he's got people looking for him. I'm really afraid for Luke. Those guys are mean. They'll stop at nothing to get what they want." Brittany's voice was trembling with fear.

"Where are you, Brit? Are you safe?"

"Yes, I'm at my Mom's house. Oh, Brad, I'm in such a fix, I don't know what to do. My Mom said that she's been praying for me to come home, but I don't know if I can stay here. When she finds out how messed up I am, she'll probably ask me to leave. She knows your sister Mandy really well from helping out at the crisis center at church, and she suggested that I give her a call. You know, to talk. Brad, I don't know what else to do," she sobbed.

"I-It's alright Brit. I'm sure Mandy would be glad to talk to you. Hold on; don't go anywhere." Brad put his hand over the receiver and called, "Man-n. . .!" Then stopped as he realized she had been standing right behind him, listening, sensing that something was wrong.

"Brad, who is it? What's wrong?"

"You remember Matt's old girlfriend, Brittany Erickson? She's in some kind of trouble and wants to talk to you. She said you have worked with her mother at the crisis center."

"Yes, I know her mom, I'd be happy to talk with her." Brad handed her the phone, and the girls began to talk. Mandy went into her room, and Brad knew that he should pray for Brittany. He understood now that she needed deliverance from that prison of self-centeredness, which plagued every human. Brad's mind returned to his dream and the mirrored cage that held her captive. Her expression of painful hopelessness haunted him. He realized the only way anyone could truly be freed from that cage of selfishness was through a relationship with Jesus. Nothing but the life-changing power of the Holy Spirit living inside of her could do that. While he was calling out to God to speak to her heart, his mother came into the room and asked for whom he was praying so earnestly. Brad explained. Soon they were all praying, as Dad also joined in.

Mandy stepped out of her room, in serious thought. "Well, that was an amazing conversation. She has a lot of things she's dealing with, but she knows that she's going down a wrong path and wants to change. She has been so hurt by many people. I asked her if I could tell you all about it, so we could all pray for her. She said that would be OK. She has been doing a couple of different drugs as well as drinking alcohol regularly. The thing that most concerns her is that she has just found out she's pregnant, and the baby's father is pushing her to have an abortion."

"Oh, no! She can't do that. How could a father want to do that to his own child?" Mom exclaimed.

"It just shows how cold and callous our society has become," Dad added.

"What did you tell her, Sis?"

"For the most part I just listened as she poured out her heart. I was amazed at how open she was with me. She is so bound up in fear and shame, and really needed to get it out. I told her she could come over and that I would pray for her. I hope you don't mind, Mom. She'll be here at eight."

"Oh, sweetie, that's fine. Dinner is on the table, and we can go down and be done before she gets here," Mom suggested, giving her a reassuring hug.

At ten after eight the doorbell rang. Mandy greeted Brittany and gave her a warm hug. Mandy and Brittany went up to her room and talked until almost ten o'clock. The two of them came down, and Brittany thanked her with tears in her eyes. They agreed to meet again later in the week. Brittany wanted to hear more about the Bible; admitting that it had been a long time since she had even read it.

Brad met them near the front door, "Brit, I just want you to know that I care about what happens to you, and I'm praying for you."

A grateful smile appeared amid tear-streaked cheeks as she tried to express her feelings. "I really want what you have in your life, but I don't know if I can do it. I know Tommy hates anything to do with God and the Bible."

"Tommy?" Brad asked.

"Tommy Warwick. You know, the lead singer of The Slammers Band," She replied, her eyes welling up again.

Mandy interrupted Brad by placing a hand on his arm and slightly shaking her head. He took the hint.

"It's OK," Brittany acknowledged. You should know that Tommy is the father. I was such a fool, thinking I was the only one, or that he might be interested in marriage and a family one day. But, he informed me that he didn't really believe in marriage, and that he wouldn't be tied down to just one woman. He said that I should have an abortion and get on with my life. How could I have been so blinded by my own wishful thinking?"

Moved by the deepness of her hurt, Brad put his hand gently on her shoulder. "Brit, believe me, we all have that problem. That's why we so desperately need Jesus. He's the only one who can set us free from that."

She lowered her head and nodded in agreement. Brittany and Mandy walked to the door. Suddenly, as if remembering something she needed to say, Brittany turned back to Brad and pleaded, "Brad, Luke really needs your help too. I think he's in a lot of trouble and wants out, but doesn't know how."

Brad nodded, "I know. I'm trying to hear from God on how to help him."

She seemed relieved and smiled. Then, the fearful look returned, "Be careful. Those guys are dangerous."

Brad glanced over at his mom's concerned face and declared, "Believe me, I will."

Mandy walked her to her car and came back into the house. The entire family discussed the night's events. "Brad, I don't like you taking on these dangerous people. I think we should have a talk with Matt's dad and get the police involved," his mom cautioned.

Brad agreed, "Matt keeps his dad informed of what's going on, and his department is investigating all of the characters involved with the Dragon's Den. Besides Mom, after all of these dreams I'm learning that God is in control and will protect us."

Dad spoke up, "Son, I agree with that completely, but make sure that you are in His will and not overstepping the authority God has placed in your life. You don't want to get outside of His will; that's when we get into trouble. Make sure you run anything that might be dangerous, by us, OK?" His dad put his arm on his shoulder, squeezed it firmly and smiled. Brad smiled back. He was grateful to know that both his earthly father and his Heavenly Father, were looking after him.

Mandy and Brad said goodnight and headed up to their rooms. Brad stopped at her door and asked, "Did Brittany ask Jesus into her heart?"

Mandy thought a second then replied, "No, but I think that she will soon. She's so afraid that she won't be able to turn away from all the stuff she used to think was such fun, even though it has caused her so much pain. She really loved Tommy, but to him she is just one of many loves. He used her. He says that he loves her, but it's obvious that it's just her body he loves and not her."

"Why is it that some things, that are really such obvious truths, we still have to learn the hard way?" Brad wondered aloud. "Good night, Sis."

CHAPTER 13

CONFRONTATION IN THE SCHOOL PARKING LOT

FOLLOWING BREAKFAST THE NEXT MORNING, Brad headed out the door as Matt pulled into the driveway. During the ride to school, Brad excitedly told Matt of Brittany's phone call and her subsequent visit to the house. "She and Mandy talked for almost two hours in her room."

"Wow. Praise God! Did she give her heart to Jesus?" Matt asked with excitement.

"No, she didn't, but Mandy says she's close."

"Well, I know if there's one person in the whole school who knows Jesus and can lead someone to Him, it's your sister," Matt declared confidently.

"I can't deny it. It was her dedication to God's word, and how seriously she put it into practice in her life that got me out of my dead religion," Brad agreed gratefully.

There were a few moments of silence, then Matt asked, "What do you think brought on Brit's sudden desire to talk to Mandy? She seemed pretty cold to us a few days ago at that Snake Pit, or Dragon's Den place. Is she in some sort of trouble?"

"Well," Brad hesitated, "I guess you'll find out soon enough. Brit's . . . pregnant, as well as having some problems with drugs and drinking."

Matt's head dropped, and he shook it slightly, "Who's the father? That Tommy guy with the Band?"

"How'd you know that?" Brad recoiled.

"It wasn't hard to tell by the way she acted all ga-ga around him the other day. Besides, Tommy has quite a reputation."

Matt was quiet for a few minutes. Brad could tell that deep down Matt was hoping that one day Brit would come to know Christ. Then, she would truly understand why he had made the decision to break off their relationship, before it led to sin. He hadn't wanted it to happen this way. As they pulled into the school parking lot, Matt finally spoke, "We should seriously pray for her because it sounds like she's in a real crunch time in her life. It would be so wonderful if she really knew Jesus."

Brad smiled and nodded in agreement. As they exited the car and grabbed their stuff Matt asked, "Have you heard anything about Luke?"

"Oh, man. I've been so caught up in Brit's troubles I completely forgot to tell you. Brit said that Luke's in some kind of trouble with Sammy and Mr. Dragon. He's missing, and they're looking for him. Maybe we need to talk to your Dad and get him on the case. Brit said that those guys are very dangerous and will stop at nothing to get what they want."

"Whoa, calm down. I'm one step ahead of you. Dad knows about it, because Luke's parents reported him missing. They haven't made a big deal about it because of Luke's habit of not staying home, and apart from being sort of weird, they haven't been able to pin anything on "Mr. D.", as they call him. Dad also told me that over two hundred high school kids are following "Mr. D. They say he captivates his audience with unusual feats of, what he calls, 'the ancient magical arts.' Dad's agents tell him that it makes quite a show, mixed in with that black metal music. It's easy to capture the imagination of that age group. It seems as though he's trying to establish himself as some kind of black metal guru. Did you know that he has three other places like the Dragon's Den in other cities?"

Brad was astounded and laughed, "You mean we could own our own Dragon's Den franchise. Instead of Micky D's, it would be Mr. D's."

"Yeah," Matt laughed. "And you get a free magic trick in every happy meal along with a little plastic dragon that plays black metal music."

"That's pretty scary," Brad remarked more seriously. "This Dragon's Den thing may or may not be a new movement, but it is definitely big business. I'm afraid Luke has gotten himself into something way over his head. These guys aren't going to let one little teenager get in the way of their empire building. How in the world are we going to get him out of this mess?" Brad asked, thinking hard.

"We?" Matt asked with an are-you-crazy look on his face. "My Dad says that we should be very careful not to do anything real heroic because these guys are suspected in quite a few disappearances and seem to be very good at covering their tracks."

Walking through the parking lot, they became keenly aware that a group of guys seemed to be surrounding them. As they approached the edge of the parking lot, Blane Stevens confronted them. "Can we help you, Blane?" Brad asked curiously, ignoring the typical sneer on Blane's face.

"No, but you can help yourself, if you know what's good for you."

"What do you mean, Blane? What's your problem, anyway?" Matt asked, obviously a little annoyed by Blane's cocky attitude.

Blane laughed, looked down and shook his head, "You preacher-boys like to poke your nose into everybody else's business, always trying to keep others from having any fun."

Matt interrupted, "What's your point, man? We need to get to class."

Blane looked at him with a sly smile and taunted, "I'm just giving you a friendly reminder that not everybody appreciates a busybody. You best stay away from Jared and Luke, unless you just like asking for trouble."

Matt, who stood a good head taller than Blane, stepped forward so that Blane had to step backward. He looked Blane square in the eyes, with a smile, "What kind of trouble, Blane? I guess I'm just supposed to shut up and not speak what I know is the truth, because it interferes with your agenda."

Blane clearly didn't expect this kind of response, being used to people bowing to his verbal intimidation. He backed up a step and looked behind him at some of the guys in the background, but before he could speak, Matt turned to the crowd and spoke. "Do all of you guys agree with Blane, here? Have you made him your leader? Why are you so threatened by us? We aren't forcing anything on you. We aren't getting a group around you threatening you, are we? All we do is explain that the God who created you loves you, and wants to have a relationship with you simply because He loves you."

Blane shouted, "That's ridiculous. There is no God. You Christians just use that nonsense to keep people from experiencing the fun in life. Can you prove there is a God?"

Matt looked past Blane into the growing crowd, gathering around to see what all the commotion was about. "The bigger problem for all of you is to prove that God doesn't exist. Are you willing to stake your eternal destiny on what Blane, here, thinks? He says that God wants to take away all of your fun. Keep in mind, that's *fun* the way Blane defines it. Usually, his type of fun involves someone else's pain. How much fun is it to kick a drug habit that incidentally, guys like him are making money off of? Or perhaps you think it's fun to get drunk and drive around and do crazy things. How many young people have been buried after doing that. Why does having fun have to involve doing something that's wrong? Is this the kind of leader that you want to follow? The One I have chosen to follow died on a cross to forgive us of our sins. He teaches us how to live according to what is right. He teaches us how to love each other, not use others for our own selfish idea of fun."

Blane was now infuriated, standing on his toes, his reddening face right in Matt's, "You will regret this!" Cursing under his breath, Blane marched away, followed by several of the boys standing around.

Brad, amazed at what had just taken place, marveled, "Man, that was intense! I was afraid you were going to punch him or something."

"I can't say that I didn't think about it, but the Spirit of God stopped me. What good would it have done to deck him. It would have just shown that we're exactly what they thought, hypocrites. When I saw all the people that gathered around I was certainly not going to give them a fight to watch. My heart went out to them. I saw the nervousness in their faces, at the challenges Blane was throwing out against God. I didn't want to let God down by allowing my pride to ruin the situation."

About that time a dark-skinned boy who was in the tenth grade came up to Matt. Donning a contagious smile, beneath big brown eyes and short cropped curly hair, the excited fellow grasped Matt's hand in a firm hand shake. With a glowing face, the boy exclaimed, "Man, I appreciated what you said. It made a lot of sense. I've seen how things seem to be changing around school, and a lot of my friends are getting into the black metal stuff. I was afraid that I was going to be a nerd or something if I didn't get into it too, but I now realize that was stupid thinking. I recently became a Christian, and I want to follow Jesus no matter what my friends do."

Matt looked down at him, blinking back tears and replied, "That takes a lot of courage, but with the power of God's Spirit and the support of other believers, I know you'll do it. We have a group of guys who meet at church on Sunday nights called the G-Men whose purpose is to help each other stand in this difficult time. Would you be interested in checking it out?"

The boy's face lit up, "That sounds great! By the way my name is Bart, Bart Graham."

Matt held out his hand. "I'm Matt Shackleton, and this is Brad Johnson."

"Good to meet you Bart." Brad held out his hand. Bart shook it eagerly. Brad looked at his watch and exclaimed, "Wow! We better get to class or we'll be late." As they walked into the building Brad noticed a black hummer driving out of the parking lot and wondered, *how many of those things are there in this town?*

The bell rang ending forth period, and Brad made his way through the halls. Along the way he met faces of young people: some he knew, most he didn't. Few had smiles. Most had a forlorn sort of look, as if wondering; Why am I here? Why do I exist? Brad had never really noticed this before. His heart began to ache for them. He realized that an existence without experiencing God was hopeless misery and pain. He made a conscious effort to smile at them. *I'm going to try to get to know more of them,* he decided, hoping for a chance to give them the truth they needed to face the harsh world around them. Brad entered the lunchroom, got his lunch and looked around. He saw a couple of guys, he didn't know, dressed in black with heavy silver chains dangling from the hip pockets. He gathered up his courage and went over to the table to sit down.

"Is anyone sitting here?" Brad asked.

The two looked at each other, then back at Brad curiously. "If they are, they're really small," one of them muttered, as they both snickered.

Brad laughed, trying to cover his nervousness. "Do you mind if I sit here, then?"

The boys looked at him again, now with suspicion, as Brad sat down with his tray. Finally, the other one mumbled, "No, man, we were just leaving anyway." They looked around to see who might be watching and gathered up their trays.

Why were they so nervous? Brad wondered, feeling as though he had some type of dreaded disease. He turned to watch them leave, noticing a pair of cold steely eyes fixed on him. Like a hawk, Blane Stevens watched. His smug expression made Brad uneasy. Brad could feel discouragement literally creeping into his heart. A voice whispered hauntingly in his head, "This is my territory. You have no right to them." Brad was stunned. He looked back at Blane who was still glaring at him. Brad shuddered with fear.

Then another voice, this time in his heart, encouraged, "I have overcome the world and have come to set the captives free."

Yeah, Brad thought, *you get behind me Satan, I believe Jesus.* He looked back at Blane and smiled. Blane turned away. Just past him, Brad noticed a familiar face in line for lunch. Seeing Matt lifted his spirit. Brad raised his hand and waved. Matt acknowledged with a thumbs up. Brad saw a second person waving right behind Matt. He recognized the beaming countenance of their new friend, Bart. *That's cool,* Brad thought. *We need to support each other and it's obvious this young believer needs a friend.* Brad was discovering firsthand the difficulty of swimming against the tide of worldly peer pressure. He was seeing more and more how important it was not to take others for granted. *We are indeed our brother's keepers,* Brad pondered as Matt and Bart came over and sat down.

Bart talked a lot. He was excited about coming to the G-Men meeting. "Since I got saved six months ago at a youth retreat, I've struggled to find other kids who really seem to take the Bible seriously. I read stuff in the Bible and don't see others, who say they are Christians, living it. I've been so confused. Your speech out there was the first time I've seen anyone our age really stand up for God outside of church."

"In that case you might like to come tonight to 180. That's what we call our Wednesday Bible study for high school students. You're certainly welcome to come. A lot of the G-Men come to it and you can meet some of them," Matt proposed, as he twirled spaghetti onto his fork.

"Really?" Bart proclaimed. "That sounds great."

He had barely finished responding to Matt when, suddenly, CR-A-SH! A whole tray of refuse came toppling onto the table, including a half full cup of red bug juice which spread across the table and into Matt's lap. Matt instantly jumped up, trying to avoid the inevitable catastrophe. But it was too late to avoid the red wet staining blotch right in the most embarrassing area of his jeans. Matt turned almost as red as the juice, a mix of confusion and anger on his face. He glared right into the smiling face of Blane Stevens.

Amid a chorus of laughter, Blane began a mock apology: "Oh, how clumsy of me," He raved as he picked up the trash and put it back on the tray. "But accidents do happen." His voice deepened, issuing a veiled threat, "Don't they?" Standing over the table with a defiant gaze at Matt, Blane was hoping that Matt would lose it and blow up at him.

Brad prayed for his friend. Suddenly, Bart jumped up and got in between Matt and Blane. "Man, you know you did that on purpose. That was so lame."

Matt put a hand on Bart's shoulder and stated calmly, "Blane, it's OK. You're right, things do happen." Then with a look of genuine compassion Matt added, "I forgive you." Blane's smirk faded as his jaw tightened. He walked off in the anger of another defeat. His groupies followed behind him, glancing contemptuously at the G-men.

Matt sat down blotting his jeans with some napkins. "Well, I guess this problem is not, just going to go away."

"You were awesome," Bart declared excitedly. "I thought you were going to take his head off. I kind of wanted you to, but I know that isn't what Jesus would have wanted."

"You're right man, but I don't know if I can keep being pushed and not react," Matt conceded, shaking his head. Everyone in the lunch room knew Matt because he was one of the largest and strongest guys in school. They had all witnessed his fearlessness on the football field and knew that he was no coward. Many of them had the greatest respect for his self-control and genuine concern for others.

"The Bible says that God will not allow us to be tempted beyond what we can take, but will provide a way of escape. I guess God knows you can take it. It must be hard to take that from a guy you could easily shut up with one blow," Brad remarked, wiping red bug juice from the table with his napkin.

Matt nodded in agreement. "You know, I really have a burden for his soul. He is so lost, and is desperately clinging to his illusions."

"Speaking of illusions, did you hear that Mr. Dragon is meeting with school officials to plan some kind of magic program? It's going to be like—an assembly or something in a few weeks?" Bart reported. "Some of my friends have seen him perform. They say he's pretty incredible. The stuff he does on stage is unreal. Levitation, making things disappear then reappear, even turning water into beer are all part of his act. He even can hypnotize people and get them to do all kinds of crazy things, and they don't remember a thing. He always dresses in black and has these red dragon and dagger designs on his clothes. What do you guys think of all that stuff? Do you think he has sold his soul to the devil and that's where he gets his power?"

Brad shook his head in disbelief, "That sounds pretty wild. Did you say he turned water into beer? That sure sounds like a spiritual copycat or even a mocking of Jesus."

Matt, picking through his tray, attempting to salvage his juice-laden lunch, added, "Most of that stuff is illusion and slight-of-hand, you know, done with mirrors. But some of those guys like Mr. Dragon seem to move into the black magic and do things that may be even satanic or demonic. Mostly, it seems that Mr. Dragon is in it for the money, but I'm not too sure that it's his only motive. Some of the artwork we saw at The Dragon's Den certainly seemed spiritual in nature. Either way, he's not leading these young people to God, but away from Him."

"Yeah, it seems that the enemy doesn't care so much that a person consciously follows him, he just doesn't want them to follow God." Brad added, remembering some of the things he'd learned in his dreams. "Most people simply follow their own selfishness and spend most of their lives focused on things that have nothing to do with seeking God's kingdom. They become totally distracted by worldly stuff."

Matt agreed, "All the devil wants to do is neutralize us, and make us completely ineffective for God. If he can get us all bound up in the desire for sin and meaningless mind games, then he's won. We waste our lives doing nothing for God, never impacting a single soul with the truth of the gospel."

"How can people live like that and think that they're Christians?" Bart asked.

"Well," Brad admitted, "we grow up religious, seeing a lot of hypocrites and then wind up living as one ourselves. I know this from personal experience. We tend to take advantage of God's grace, until one day we fall flat on our face. Thank God for true believers who will challenge us and bring us to our senses before it's too late."

Brad smiled at Matt who added, "It seems that all of us find ourselves in that boat at one time or another. But, we must realize we've fallen short, and admit it. It's essential that we're willing to do whatever it takes to change and then stick with it. It's not easy, but it is certainly worth it."

"It sounds to me like it's not the easy way, but it is the only way." Bart concluded.

"Well put. I guess they'll be calling you preacher boy, too, pretty soon."

Bart beamed and asked, "You think so?"

Brad marveled at his fearless attitude. Bart wasn't a big kid, just kind of average build, but he was tough. His dad owned a yard care service, and Bart explained that he had worked with his dad a lot.

"Bra-ad!" Mandy's familiar voice echoed from across the cafeteria as she came running over to him, her friend Sherrie Baxter right behind her. "Have you seen him?" she panted, almost out of breath with excitement.

"Whoa. Slow down girl. Seen who?" Brad replied with a start.

"Luke Hunter," Sherrie chimed in. Sherrie smiled sweetly at Brad. Brad had known for a while through his sister that Sherrie was somewhat smitten with him. She was a very thoughtful girl with dark hair and sparkling green eyes and was devoted to God. She knew and completely respected Brad's decision not to get entangled in a relationship at this stage of his life. That caused her to admire him even more.

Brad smiled politely, "Hi, Sherrie. Did you see Luke somewhere?"

"Yes, Mandy and I both saw him earlier today when we arrived at school. He was coming out of the bathroom. He still acts totally out of it. We said "hello," but he acted like he didn't even know who we were."

Brad thought a second and asked, "Was there anyone with him—you know, any of those guys in black?"

She shook her head, "No, he was alone."

"I wonder why he's not in the lunch room and why he wasn't in first period class," Matt questioned aloud.

Mandy seemed to be fixated on Matt's messy tray and asked, "Matt, did you have a little accident or something?"

Matt smiled, "Yeah, I guess you could say that."

"Hey guys! Wha's happening?" an excited voice from behind Brad asked.

Brad turned and greeted Shad Reiner who was in their G-Men group. Jared Spain was also with him, dressed in his new black jeans and t-shirt with a silver studded belt.

Matt greeted them, "There's plenty of room here. You guys have a seat."

Shad pulled out a chair, "Great. How's it going?" He greeted the girls and was introduced to Bart. Jared, however, stood there as if wondering what he should do. Brad noticed that he glanced across the lunchroom and his eyes caught the stares of several guys, also dressed in the dark clothes of what had become the black metal uniform dress code. It was as if they were watching to see whose side Jared was on.

Brad, seeing his indecision, spoke up, "Jared, how's it going? Have a seat, and tell us what's going on, man." Jared smiled and glanced over again nervously at the steely-eyed group who conjured up ideas of black vultures waiting for fresh prey. Brad saw Blane give a quick nod.

Jared replied, hesitantly, "That's OK, man, maybe later, I see some friends I need to talk to. See ya around." He hurried off toward Blane and his friends. As he sat down to high fives and punches, Blane looked over at Brad with a smug grin as if he had won a victory of some sort. Brad's heart could feel the struggle going on inside of Jared, torn between what he knew was right and wickedness cloaked in fun. In his heart, Brad cried out to God for Jared.

As Mandy and Sherrie said goodbye and left for the library, Matt quizzed Shad, "What's up with Jared? Why's he so interested in the Slammer's groupies?"

Shad looked a little sad, "Well, gentlemen, it appears Jared has been seduced by the dark side. He just really likes that kind of music and says that he doesn't care about the lyrics. To him all that stuff about dragons, death, and drugs is just hype to sell more records. And the black clothes and silver studs are cool." Then Shad leaned sort of close to them and whispered, "But the truth is, I think is that he's scared. I get the idea they have something on him and are holding it over his head. It has something to do with drinking and going for a late night car ride a few weeks ago."

Shad and Jared were close friends, and Jared had been coming to youth group. He even raised his hand in a meeting last year to receive Christ, but lately seemed to be going in another direction. Shad confided, "I don't know what to do. I've tried to talk to him about his walk with Jesus, but he seems to think that he's not doing anything wrong. And, he's not interested in doing anything that involves learning more about God."

"It's so like the enemy to get someone trapped in the guilt of some sin, and then hold it over their head until hopelessness sets in," Matt suggested, with a disgusted frown.

Brad's mind drifted back to the vision of Luke shackled to those two huge posts in his dream and wondered if they had something on Luke. His thoughts returned to something Bart had said earlier about hypnosis. He began to wonder if Mr. Dragon had used that on Luke, in order to get him to do what he wanted. Luke seemed so different, and he was so out of it when they had spoken at the Dragon's Den. Was someone doing things with his mind, like Luke had mentioned in the dreams?

Chapter 14

The Bathroom Incident

The sound of the bell snapped Brad out of the spell, cast by his deep thoughts. The guys said their see-you-laters, and went their separate ways. As Brad headed off to class, he suddenly realized he needed to make a pit stop in the men's room. Waiting for two guys to come out of the door, he entered the bathroom. Setting his backpack down on the floor by the wall, he entered a stall and closed the door. Brad was about to flush the toilet when he heard the bathroom door open and several sets of feet shuffling around. He waited, listening. He heard whispering. Standing there, with an uneasy feeling that something wasn't right. He asked, "Who's there?" No answer. Brad started to push the door of the stall open when abruptly, the lights went out. Fear gripped him as he stood in total darkness. The stall door was slammed back with a BANG! He pushed on the door, but it wouldn't budge. He was trapped. Someone was holding it shut. His heart pounded loudly, and he could feel panic overtaking him. Suddenly, he felt someone grab his foot from underneath the stall door, yanking it forward. Losing his balance, he fell backwards clutching the wall as his shoe was torn from his foot. This, he knew was no dream. Trembling helplessly in the pitch-black stall, Brad began to pray in his heart asking, *Jesus protect me.* He backed up and listened again.

He heard malicious snickering, followed by someone whispering, "Hurry up." Movement in the stall next to him and caused him to back away until he felt the cold concrete wall on his back. A muffled voice, trying to hide their identity threatened, "OK, preacher boy, you scared yet? This is your last chance. Keep your mouth shut, and stay away from our guys, or the next time you come in here you won't come out. Got it?" Then Brad heard the feet shuffling out the door.

Brad burst out of the stall toward the door, but his foot hit something. Before he could stop himself, he was sprawled out and sliding across the tile floor. Lying on the floor in the dark, he realized that his chin was stinging from the impact. Slowly, he picked himself up, staggered to the wall and found the light switch. He looked back toward the stalls and realized that somehow he had tripped over his backpack. Brad glanced in the mirror and saw that his chin was dripping blood from a nasty scrape with the bathroom floor. Hurriedly, he washed it off and dabbed it with a paper towel; then he grabbed his backpack.

Brad looked down at his mismatched feet, and the lone foot missing a sneaker. He had a sinking feeling where it might be. He opened the stall door next to the one he had just broken out of. Sure enough, drowned in a pool of nasty, yellow urine was his sneaker. He flushed the toilet a couple of times before he pulled out the soggy black shoe. He took it over to the sink and washed it again and then tried to dry it a bit with the wall-mounted hand dryer. Brad was now racing against the impending ring of the dreaded tardy bell. Quickly, he stuck the damp Converse back onto his foot, grabbed his backpack, and dashed hurriedly out the door, squeaking all the way down the hall. Thankful to reach class just as the tardy bell was sounding, he walked by Shad who sat a few seats up from him.

"Dude, what happened to you?" Shad whispered excitedly. "Did somebody slug you?"

Brad was holding a slightly bloody paper towel under his chin. His biology teacher, Mr. Roper, noticed that Brad was having a problem and came over to ask him if he was all right.

"Yes sir, I'm fine. I just seem to be a little clumsy today.

"If you need to go to the rest room or the school nurse, you have my permission."

The thought of going back into the bathroom made Brad cringe. "No sir, I'll be fine. It's just a little scrape."

"Well, OK." Mr. Roper conceded, with some apprehension. Brad tried to keep his mind on the class, however, he couldn't seem to shake a feeling of impending doom. Finally, he prayed and placed all of the events of the day in God's hands. He felt better, but still uneasy about what had happened in the bathroom. He knew something was just not right. *Why didn't they beat me up or something?*

The class was almost over when there was a knock on the door. The school security guard came into the room, spoke to Mr. Roper, while handing him a piece of paper. The bell rang, and students began to file out of the classroom.

"Brad Johnson," Mr. Roper stopped him. "Mr. Dunphey needs for you to go to the office with him."

Brad's heart sank. *What in the world is happening now,* he wondered. Mr. Dunphey had retired after twenty-five years on a neighboring police force and was very suspicious by nature. Brad didn't know the man, but had seen him often enough walking the halls around school. *Too bad he wasn't walking past the bathroom an hour ago,* Brad thought to himself.

"Sir, what is this all about?" Brad asked respectfully.

Mr. Dunphy gave Brad a scrutinizing look and responded coldly, "Just come with me to the office, please. We have a little matter we need to clear up."

Brad walked quietly down the halls, catching stares from people as he went along. Everyone knew someone walking beside Mr. Dunphey was in some sort of trouble. *How could this be?* Brad went through every scenario in his mind. *Either this is a mistake—or maybe Mandy! Something happened to Mandy! Lord, if those guys did something to my sister I don't know if I could . . .*

"Right in here, please." Mr. Dunphey pointed to the administrative office.

As he was about to enter the office, Bart Graham caught sight of him and shouted, "Hey Brad, what's going on?"

Brad looked at his new friend, frowned, and raised his shoulders. Bart sensed the fear on Brad's face and his expression changed. Bart acted as if he had something important to tell Brad, but Mr. Dunphey abruptly closed the office door. Bart was left gazing through the glass, dumbfounded.

Brad was directed into a small room where the principal, Mr. Farnell, and a guidance counselor were seated at a conference table. "Hello Brad," Mrs. Cherry, the guidance counselor, greeted.

"Hello," Brad responded cordially, feeling nervous. His stomach was crawling. *Why am I so nervous?* Brad wondered to himself. *I've done nothing wrong.*

The principal, a no-nonsense type of fellow, spoke professionally. "Mr. Johnson, will you please place your backpack on the table and empty out the contents. Brad hesitated a second wondering why he was being asked to do this.

"Yes, sir," Brad replied respectfully, "but may I ask what you are looking for?"

Mr. Farnell smiled pleasantly, caught off guard by Brad's genuinely respectful attitude. He cordially responded, "Mr. Johnson, we will know that, when we find it." Brad had a sinking feeling. He nervously unzipped the bag and began to take out various books, pens, paper, as well as a month-old Hot Rod Magazine. Then, he unzipped the smaller compartment. As he was pulling out a little pocket Bible he always carried, he realized that there was something else in there. It was a black zippered pouch about eight inches long. It looked exactly like the pouch that he had seen Luke remove from inside the drum that night. Brad studied it with disbelief.

"And what is that, Mr. Johnson?" Mr. Farnell asked with an air of suspicion in his voice.

Brad stared at it in amazement and fear, not knowing what it contained. "I—I don't know. It's not mine, and I have no idea how it got into my backpack." He could see officer Dunphey roll his eyes and frown as if to say, *Sure, a likely story.*

"Would you please open it and show us the contents," Mr. Farnell instructed, now sitting up and leaning closer to the black object of potential doom.

"But, it's not mine. How can I open something that's not mine?" Brad contested, completely at a loss as to what to do.

"Mr. Johnson, is this your backpack? Mr. Farnell demanded.

"Yes. But—I—I," Brad stammered.

"If it is in your possession on school grounds, we have a right to know what it is. The police will be here momentarily. Things will go far better with you if you voluntarily show us what this is. Please, just open the pouch."

Brad picked up the pouch and unzipped it. Inside was a roll of cash and four plastic sandwich bags containing what looked like crumbled up leaves.

Mr. Dunphey frowned and remarked, "I suppose you don't have any idea what that is either."

Brad had never seen any before, but he supposed it was marijuana. Mrs. Cherry, who had been quietly watching, knew Brad was a good student who had never been in any trouble. She spoke up and asked, "Brad, are you sure you don't have any idea where that stuff came from?" Brad could see a mother's compassion in her eyes.

Confused, he thought about Luke, but he didn't really know if it was the same bag. Then, he remembered, *the bathroom incident.* That's why he tripped over his backpack. Someone had messed with it. "Actually, I think I do know. I think it may have happened in the bathroom earlier today."

"What do you mean?" she continued.

"I believe someone put it in there while I was going to the bathroom."

Alarmed, Mrs. Cherry asked, "Why would someone do that?"

"I'm not sure, but I think someone's trying to get me into trouble."

"Well, they are doing a pretty good job of it," snarled Mr. Farnell. "I'm afraid this is a matter for the police to solve. They'll be here any minute." As he stood up, there was a knock on the door.

A secretary poked her head in the door and affirmed, "The officers are here."

"Send them in, Mrs. Peachtree. Let's get this over with."

Brad sat there in a daze. An officer dressed in black, with badge shining and side arm gleaming on his belt, entered the room. The middle-aged man looked at him with suspicion. Henson was the name on his badge. To Brad's relief, another man entered the room. It was Sgt. Shackleton, Matt's dad. Tears began to well up in his eyes as he saw that perhaps some element of sanity was returning to this crazy situation. God was still in control. Sgt. Shackleton spoke quietly to the principal and the security guard. Then, he looked over and smiled at Brad reassuringly. Brad was thankful that Sgt. Shackleton knew him and would believe him.

Sgt. Shackleton sat down with Brad. Seeing Brad's distress at the situation, he asked, "Brad, do you have any enemies who might be trying to discredit you or get you into trouble?"

Brad didn't have to think hard about that. Blane's threat earlier in the lunch room came to mind. "Yes, I think so. This guy named Blane Stevens has been giving Matt and me grief for several days now."

"What on earth for?" the sergeant asked.

"If you can believe it, he doesn't like us sharing Jesus with the students."

"Is he associated in any way with a man named, Alister Griswald?" Brad looked confused. "He's better known as The Dragon. He, along with a Sammy Dornburg, recently bought the old Snake Pit bar out on highway ninety-eight."

"Blane is a follower of The Slammers Band. I know he regularly hangs out with them," Brad explained. "Sgt. Shackleton, you don't think that this stuff is mine do you?"

"Professionally, I have to gather all of the facts, but the school officials agreed that you have a perfect record here, and that it's not likely you would do something like this."

Brad breathed a sigh of relief.

"But, we still have to deal with the issue of where this stuff came from and how it got in your bag?"

"It had to happen here at school. I know that it wasn't in there this morning. I put my books in my bag every morning, and I would have seen that pouch."

The sergeant pondered, "Think carefully, was your bag out of your sight for even a few minutes at any time today?"

Brad nodded, "Yes. I'm pretty sure it happened in the bathroom about an hour and a half ago, during second lunch shift. I set my backpack down outside the stall when I went into the bathroom." Brad proceeded to tell Sgt. Shakleton about the bizarre incident of intimidation in the bathroom. *What a clever cover up,* Brad thought. That had to be why it wasn't against the wall where he had originally placed it.

Sgt. Shackleton looked concerned, "Brad, you guys need to be very careful. These guys are serious. Whoever planted this on you didn't mind blowing almost two hundred dollars, plus several hundred in marijuana, just to try to set you up. We have a good idea that Sammy and Mr. Dragon are behind this stuff, but so far, we can't pin anything on them. I want you to keep me informed about any other problems you have. Keep your ears open. Perhaps someone saw the kids coming out of the rest room. We need some hard evidence. Do you think you could identify the voice?"

Brad thought hard a few seconds, "I'm sorry sir. They distorted it, so that I couldn't tell."

"OK Brad, if you think of anything else let me know. I'll give your parents a call tonight and explain the situation to them, but I think you should tell them first."

Sgt. Shackleton turned to Officer Henson and directed him to gather up the evidence, and file a report. The officer pulled out a plastic bag. Carefully, he slid the pouch and its contents into the bag and sealed it. "I'll take care of it, sir," Henson replied, still glaring at Brad as if he were guilty of something. He placed the bag of evidence in a black brief case and exited the room.

Mr. Farnell stood and thanked Sgt. Shackleton. Then, he spoke quietly to Mrs. Cherry as the two of them, along with Mr. Dunphey, left the room.

"Sgt. Shackleton." Brad asked, puzzled. "How did they know it was in my backpack?"

"An anonymous tip—a phone call to the principal's office, from outside the school. Someone said you were selling pot from a black bag in your backpack. So keep your guard up. These guys are ruthless."

"Yes, sir. Thank you, sir. Is it all right if I leave now?" Brad inquired.

"I'm not sure. Just hang out here until I talk with the office folks and make sure. They may have some more questions. I know they'd like to find out who did as much as we would." Sgt. Shackleton and Officer Henson exited, leaving Brad sitting alone at the large conference table.

Brad pulled out a notebook thinking that he might study while he waited. Before he knew it he was engrossed in a drawing. Looking down at his sketch, he considered his experience of the night before when he'd reached level 66. He erased a section and redrew the giant android he'd named Goliathoid. He studied his creation and decided it was a keeper. He would add it to his collection when he got home. His drawings had become like a visual diary of events in his life.

About thirty minutes later, Mrs. Peachtree appeared in the doorway and announced that he was free to go. Brad collected his books and repacked them. He was about to leave when Mrs. Cherry came up to him with a reassuring smile. "Let us know if you have any more problems. I tried to tell them that you would never do something like this. You are a fine, upstanding, young man, and I'm sorry you had to go through this."

Brad returned the smile, "Thank you, Mrs. Cherry. I appreciate your vote of confidence." He hurried down the hall, and out the door to try to find Matt in the parking lot. The three o'clock bell had just rung. He had been in the office for almost two hours, and now the school day was over.

"Brad! Brad!" A voice shouted from behind him. Brad turned to see Bart running toward him. "Are you alright? Whoa, what happened to your chin? Did somebody punch you? I saw the security guard taking you into the office. What's going on?" Bart quizzed in rapid fire.

Brad, amused at his excitement, chuckled, "Hold your horses, man. It was just a bit of a misunderstanding in the office, and my own clumsiness landing me face first on the floor." Brad decided not to tell him the whole story just yet, afraid that Bart in his zeal might get himself into trouble. Bart was obviously a loyal person, and might say something to put himself at risk with these unscrupulous characters. He turned to Bart and replied, "Thanks for your concern, Bart. I really appreciate it, but I need to take off, or I'll miss my ride. I'll see you tomorrow, OK?"

"Sure, OK. See you later, dude." Bart replied, still wondering.

Brad started out the door toward the parking lot. As he got nearer to the back side of the lot where Matt' s car was parked, he saw about a dozen kids standing around in front of the car. One tall dark haired figure, Matt, stood in the center. Brad's heart jumped, wondering. *Oh no, not again.* Was this another of Blane's mobs threatening Matt? He picked up the pace and sprinted over to the group. As he approached, he realized that the kids weren't hostile. They were just onlookers, standing there while Matt talked on his cell phone. Brad came up behind him and looked over Matt's shoulder to see what was going on. His heart sank and then burned with anger as a disgusting sight met his eyes. Emblazoned on Ruby's hood, in bright orange spray paint were the words, "BACK OFF P BOY!" There were also streaks and crosses all over the car, in addition to at least a dozen broken eggs literally frying in the hot sun.

Matt was clearly trying to control his emotions. He closed the cell phone. Biting his lip, he looked at Brad and forced a smile. "Well, friend, we might be a few minutes late getting home. They're sending a unit over in a cruiser to investigate."

"How could someone do this without being noticed? Someone had to see this." Brad shook his head as anger overtook him, clinching his teeth. "I bet it was that stupid Blane. I'm going to . . ."

Matt turned to him and put his hand on his shoulder. "No. Don't go there. This car is just a thing. A thing that I'm afraid I've made a god in my life. It may be His way of showing me to keep it in the right perspective."

"But, Matt, no one has a right to get away with something like this." Brad contested, trying to control his frustration.

"You're right, and they won't. But the Bible says that we are not to seek vengeance. He is the one who deals with that. Besides we don't even know who did this. The police will conduct an investigation, and if they find out who did this, the guilty party will pay for it according to the law."

A police cruiser pulled up. An officer got out and came over to Matt. "Hi, Matt." The officer half smiled, and then looked sadly at the once immaculate muscle car. "It looks like you've run into a bit of trouble here."

Matt reached out his hand. "Hi, Officer Brent."

Officer Brent inspected the car. "Now, why would someone want to do a thing like that? This is carrying a prank way too far," He lamented, gazing at the mess made of the previously perfect candy- apple paint job. Matt's dad had been on the force for twenty years, so almost every officer had known Matt since the day he was born. Many of the officers attended Bible study with Sgt. Shackleton, or played golf with him regularly. "I'm sure sorry this had to happen to your car, Matt," Officer Brent added. "Do you have any enemies or someone that you have upset lately?"

Before Matt could answer, Brad blurted out, "Blane Stevens practically threatened him in the cafeteria today."

"Oh?" Officer Brent pulled out a little note book and asked, "Is that true?"

Matt looked at Brad with a frown. "Well, I don't think he really meant any harm, but we did have a little problem in the lunchroom."

Brad was dumbfounded, "Why are you sticking up for him after what he did?"

"Were you a witness to what took place?" Officer Brent inquired.

"I sure was." Brad began to recount the incident to the officer.

"And, may I have your name, please?"

"Brad Johnson."

"Brad Johnson?" The officer looked at him with some puzzlement. "Did you also have some trouble today?"

Brad was startled that he knew about it. "Yes, sir. I did. I believe the same group of guys that did this tried to set me up today, too."

"Why do these guys dislike you so?"

"They don't like the fact that we stand up for Jesus. They think we're trying to keep them from their fun," Matt replied finally getting a word in.

"Who is P BOY? That doesn't sound very flattering."

"That would be me," Matt admitted humbly.

"Blane calls him "preacher boy." He has some sort of chip on his shoulder about the gospel of Jesus. For some reason, he hates it."

"Speaking confidentially," Officer Brent added, "I'm afraid a lot of people are like that these days. The whole idea of God scares them because that means that they might be held accountable for what they do wrong. If more people believed and lived according to God's commandments, it sure would make my job easier. People can be so cruel to each other." He paused, shook his head and continued. "I'm going to check the area for any evidence. Then, you guys can go. You might see if any of your fellow classmates might have seen or heard something. Pranksters like this usually boast about it to others. If we get lucky, someone will brag about it to the right person who will come forward."

"Officer, what seems to be the trouble now?" A man's voice from behind them asked. They turned to face the principal, Mr. Farnell, who looked at Brad as if to say, *Oh, it's you again*. Officer Brent detailed the situation. Mr. Farnell expressed his deep regret that this had occurred, and said he would do everything in his power to find out who was responsible.

Officer Brent walked past Ruby, which was on the last row of the parking lot away from the school buildings. He was looking through some tall grass near the woods, when he stooped down and picked something up. He motioned to the boys who headed over to check out his discovery. Holding a half empty can of neon orange spray paint, he explained, "Boys, anyone could have sneaked through the tall grass here, and done this. It could have been someone from off campus. Until all this trouble dies down, I suggest that you park closer to the school buildings, where your car won't be such an easy target."

Matt nodded in agreement and laughed at the irony, "I park back here because there are fewer cars, thinking there wouldn't be as many door dings. I guess, once again, my vanity has been dealt with."

As he was getting into his cruiser, Officer Brent paused and confided, "Boys, I just want you to know that I will be praying for you. Sounds like you've been counted worthy to suffer some persecution for the sake of Christ. Be strong, and be careful, OK?"

They both smiled and agreed with a, "Yes sir."

The boys got into the car and pulled out of the parking lot, amid a group of about twenty or thirty gossiping onlookers. They were silent for a couple of minutes when finally Matt asked, "So, exactly what happened to you today. How'd you get that nasty scrape on your chin?" As Brad recounted the day's events, Matt's expression got more and more sober.

"Brad, they could have really hurt you in there."

Brad thought a moment. "I believe the Lord protected me. Through these wild dreams I've been having, God has shown me that He is truly with us and will keep us safe."

Matt nodded. "You're right. God doesn't want us to walk around in fear of doing His will. He said in His word that we would encounter persecution; although, in this country we haven't really experienced it."

Brad's heart was heavy. "I can't believe how mean some of the kids are getting. Evil has become some sort of joke, and isn't taken seriously. I guess they see so much wickedness on TV and computer games that they consider it to be like a game and not real."

Matt, trying to clearly think through all that had transpired, cautioned, "I think that we ought not take any chances. We need to call around to the other G-Men and get together to explain what's going on. It's crucial that we stand together, and watch each other's backs."

"That's a great idea. Better yet, I'll e-mail them when I get home to let them know what's going on. You know, I think that God will use this to bring us together as a spiritual army like we've never seen before. It seems as though the enemies of the gospel are gathering for an organized battle in our school. We can't sit by and let it happen. Maybe we can get together at the Refuge tonight after Bible study to pray for all of this."

Matt's serious tone was now turning to excitement, "Brother, I think I see a plan emerging here. God is doing something big in our midst. He doesn't want to see our school delivered over to the kingdom of darkness."

Matt dropped Brad at his house, and Brad headed inside where his family greeted him with concern. The school office, as well as Sgt. Shackleton, had called and informed Brad's mom of the events in the office. Later that day, Brad's parents expressed their deep concern over what had gone on at school. Dad sat down beside Brad and stated sincerely, "Son, we have no doubts about your innocence. I know you would never try any drugs, much less deal them. We are concerned that someone would attempt to get you into such serious trouble."

"I can't believe you were ambushed in the bathroom, that's scary. And then they trashed Matt's beautiful car. That was so mean, and just hateful," Mandy declared indignantly.

"They could have seriously injured you," Mom agreed. "Their methods seem so sinister and sneaky. No one even seems to know who's really involved."

"Guys, it's like this." Brad explained, "I know that there is some majorly bad stuff going on around school. I believe all these crazy dreams I've been having are God's way of preparing me for this spiritual battle. I know He will protect me and help me get through all of this—and see Luke delivered in the process. The enemy would love to scare me off. Believe me, he's doing a pretty good job. But, I'm going to persevere no matter what. We're e-mailing the G-Men for a special prayer time tonight after the 180 Bible study tonight."

"I think that's a great idea," Dad affirmed, "just as long as you keep in mind that this is a spiritual battle. As much as you hate what these guys are doing, you must not hate them. Remember, you aren't in a Christian gang. God can teach us all a lot through this ordeal if we stay in the Spirit. Also, if anything happens that is at all dangerous, you are to report it to Sgt. Shackleton. He has a full-scale investigation going on involving the fellows at The Dragon's Den, including Sammy Dornburg, and that band Luke's involved in."

Brad nodded, "Yes, sir. I'll be very careful. Sgt. Shackleton and I had a great talk today. I'm thankful that he showed up when he did."

"Also, Son, Luke is still missing. Sgt. Shackleton thinks that he's hiding something of value to Sammy and that Dragon fellow. If you see him, try to convince him to talk to Sgt. Shackleton about what he knows."

"OK, Dad, I'll try my best; but Luke is rather hard to figure out these days. By the way, are the Finney's still planning to come over this Sunday?"

"So far, they haven't changed anything, but with all that's going on I wouldn't be surprised if they postponed it. I'll call in a couple of days to make sure it's still on," Mom replied.

Brad started up the stairs to do his homework since they would be heading to church right after dinner. When he walked into his room he thought he heard noises coming from his computer and walked over to it. He clicked the mouse and nothing happened. He assumed that it was his imagination and sat down at his desk and started work on his homework.

Later that night, when Brad and Mandy walked into the large room at church, where the youth group met, known as the Refuge, it was abuzz with chatter about the day's events.

Shad Reiner ran up to Brad almost in hysterics. "Brad, Brad! There's a rumor going around that you were busted today for drugs. Is that true?"

Mandy, decidedly irritated that Shad would even ask such a question, spoke up. "Shad! How can you even consider such a dumb thing? How long have you known Brad?"

Shad, somewhat embarrassed by the rebuke, replied, "A bunch of people saw you walking down the hall with Mr. Dunphy."

Brad wondered a second, then asked, "Shad, who told you it was about drugs?"

Shad stopped, an eyebrow furrowed as he tried to remember. "It was that strange-looking kid with the red streak in his hair that calls himself Dagger. He hangs out with Blane Stevens and some of the guys in the Dark Legion gang."

"Dark Legion, what's that?" Brad asked with a frown.

"Those guys who follow the Slammers have kind of started this gang or club. They're trying to get a bunch of kids to join with them, just to hang out and listen to those types of bands. Sammy Dornburg throws these parties on the weekends and buys them pizza and stuff."

Brad's mind was racing. "So, this Dagger told you I was busted for drugs."

"Yeah," Shad responded. "I didn't believe it, but when some other guys asked me if I saw you being escorted down the hall by the security officer, I didn't know what to think. So, what's the deal? Why were you taken to the office?"

"Shad, it was just a little mix up involving my backpack in the bathroom." Brad had just finished his explanation, when another voice called, "Hey Brad!" Brad turned to see Bart hurrying toward him.

"Bart! Glad you could make it." Brad held out his hand. Bart shook it excitedly.

"Matt told me what happened to you today." Brad shot him a look. Bart understood and took the hint, quickly changing the subject. "Thanks for inviting me tonight. I'm looking forward to jumping into God's word for some answers to my questions."

Brad smiled, "We can talk more about those questions afterwards." Brad enjoyed the thrill of feeling like they were talking in code.

Josh, the youth intern, got up and started the meeting with prayer. The discussion for the night centered on being lights in the midst of a corrupt generation. It was a great strategy session on how to make a difference in the lives of those we see every day, who are oblivious to the ways of God, or even hostile toward the Bible.

Right after the meeting, a seventeen-year-old named Stacy, remarked to Matt that he didn't think that it was such a big deal to just listen to dark metal music as long as you didn't pay attention to the words. "I just like the cool feel of the music," he added, justifying himself. "I think all that stuff they sing about is just hype to sell more CDs."

Matt replied with a look of concern, "It may be true that most musicians and promoters are just after making a buck. But, spiritually speaking, who's really guiding them if they don't know Christ? If it's not Jesus, they are open to any spiritual force that can influence them, many times without their even knowing it. The enemy of God simply entices them to seek their own desires."

While listening to Matt, Brad's mind was drawn back to one of the dreams. He remembered how Luke had explained that the demonic looking beings didn't care so much that people wittingly worshiped them, but that they would follow their own selfish desires. In doing this, they were in essence serving the enemy. Brad was beginning to truly understand the reality of the spiritual battle being waged by Satan and his demonic cohort, against mankind. "It's like they're hypnotized by the enemy into thinking that they are free to do whatever pleases them. But in reality, they are just enslaved by those same desires to do the enemy's bidding," Brad interjected.

"But, it's just music. Is it a sin to just listen to music? I'm not hurting anyone by just listening to some good guitar," Stacy retorted.

"Well, would you say that eating a piece of fruit was a major sin?" Matt asked.

"No," Stacy replied, but then suddenly realized Matt's point and added, "not usually."

"Think about it," Matt continued. "The sin that caused the fall of all mankind was eating a piece of fruit. It isn't the particular act that is the sin, but the fact that it was done in rebellion against God's will. Or, maybe it's that we don't really care enough about the will of God to ask Him what we should or shouldn't do. Either way we are following our own will and not seeking God. We just ignore Him. That's when we get into trouble."

"It's also important to remember that, according to the Bible, Satan seems to have been involved in music, along with praise and worship in heaven, before he was cast out. He would certainly understand that you can preach anything you want right into a person's spirit, if you just distract them with cool music or an awesome beat," Brad added.

Stacy replied, "I see your point, but I still think the sound is cool. I believe I'm mature enough to tune out the lyrics. But, I'll keep this in mind. If I start to be swayed, I'll be sure to stop listening, OK? Look guys, I've got to take off. I'll see you later."

"Stacy, if you'd like to come, some of us are sticking around to pray for Luke and some stuff that's going on around school." Brad had been inviting Stacy to get involved with the G-Men group for over a year.

"That sounds great, but I've got a project due Friday, and I really need to get busy with it. Maybe next time."

Brad smiled and held out his fist, "Sure man, see you on Sunday." Brad couldn't help but wonder why Stacy never appeared to have any interest in the G-Men group. He didn't seem to like to pray, at least in a group. He enjoyed the fellowship and knew all the right answers, especially about the idea of grace and forgiveness, but always questioned getting serious about living a holy life. *Why is it some people want to try to live on the edge of sin, as if to see what they can get away with?* Brad thought, *That's such dangerous ground. It's like they want to live in both kingdoms.* Brad remembered the verse where Jesus talked about the two different paths a person could take in life. *One is wide and easy, but it leads to destruction in the end. The other is narrow and difficult, but leads to eternal life.*

When the meeting was over, about fifteen of the guys, who formed the core group of the G-Men met for prayer in an adjacent room. Matt introduced Bart to the group. Then, he and Brad shared some of the things that had been going on in school, and how the enemy was using intimidations and threats to hinder God's word from being spread. They prayed that God's Spirit would keep them strong and give them wisdom and self-control when dealing with these struggles.

Bart spoke up at the end and thanked Brad and Matt for inviting him. "I think it would be a good idea to have sort of a buddy system with guys watching each other's backs at school. These dudes are sneaky and dangerous, and I think that we would be wise to not go places alone."

Brad jumped in, "I agree. The bathroom can be a very dangerous place these days. We shouldn't take it for granted."

Mark Franklin, whose dad was a retired army ranger, joked, "OK who's signing up for potty patrol?" They all laughed, and then got down to the serious business of making a plan to be their brother's keeper.

Brad got home from the meeting with his fellow G-Men about nine-thirty. Totally drained from the day's events, he said good night to his parents and went up to get ready for bed. He stopped by Mandy's room and saw her sitting in front of the mirror doing something funky with her hair. He stuck his head in the doorway and said, "If you don't quit messing with your hair so much, you'll probably wind up bald before you're thirty. I saw that one time on the internet, you know."

"Brad, you can also find out where Elvis currently resides on the internet," she quipped.

He started to leave, but stopped to ask. "Have you heard anything else from Brittany?"

"Yes, I actually talked to her on the phone last night. She's really struggling about the baby. She's afraid having it will ruin her life. I tried to explain that it would be a major commitment to go through with a pregnancy. But, once the baby was born, and she saw how much joy it would bring the adoptive family, she would know that she made the most loving choice. I told her about the Whitmans from church, who so want to have children but can't. They desired to adopt but have been on a waiting list for two years. Brad, I'm praying that she might even choose them."

Brad thought a second, "I know them. They are the couple who teach children's choir on Wednesday nights. They sure seem to be fine people, and would make great parents."

"You know what's strange, Brad? She said that she was scared that if she had the baby, she wouldn't be able to place it for adoption. Her emotions are running so wild right now."

"Is she still seeing the father, Tommy?" Brad asked with a bit of a frown.

"I think that she has pretty much had it with him. He's really upset at her and is pressuring her to have an abortion. It's like he doesn't want any feeling of responsibility in the matter. If the baby is gone, then so is his guilt. It seems as though he has no conscience at all."

"That's really sad. Maybe we should be praying for him. Although he seems to have set himself on a particular course in life, it's still not too late for him to change," Brad suggested.

"You're right, Brad. I'll certainly join you in that prayer."

"Good night, sis," he said, as he continued to his room. He prayed for a miracle to take place in the situation between Tommy and Brittany. *Wouldn't it be cool to see Tommy leading praise and worship to God rather than glorifying the kingdom of darkness?*

As Brad went through his nightly routine of getting ready for bed, he began to wonder who could have put the black pouch in his backpack. *It looked exactly like the one he had seen at Luke's house that night. Could Luke have been involved? Or could someone have planted it on Luke, like they did with me? But, he'd discovered it, and was hiding it?* Brad had seen black zippered pouches like that many times when he had worked in the office at school, or volunteering for the basketball camp program. They were commonly used for any money which had been collected. There were probably hundreds of those same bags around the town.

With a big yawn, Brad stretched out on his bed and began to pray for all the things on his heart. Suddenly, lightning flickered outside his window. Brad's emotions were mixed. He had always enjoyed lying on his bed watching the flashes crackle through the night sky, excited by the awesome display of the power of God's creation. *This is the time of the year when the weather is constantly changing. Lightning is an almost nightly event*, Brad thought as he yawned again. *But, lately, lightning is like a doorway into some fantastic journey with a spiritual lesson on standing firm against the onslaught of the forces of darkness.* Brad was almost afraid to close his eyes. He fought the fear, and closed them anyway, trusting God.

Chapter 15

Brad's Drawings

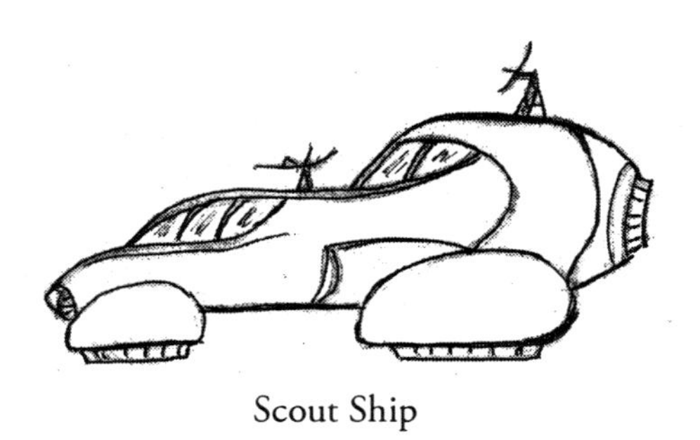

Scout Ship

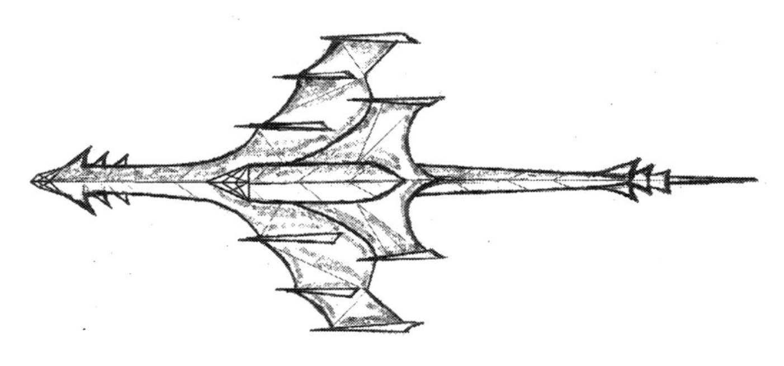

Draegonian Battle Cruizer

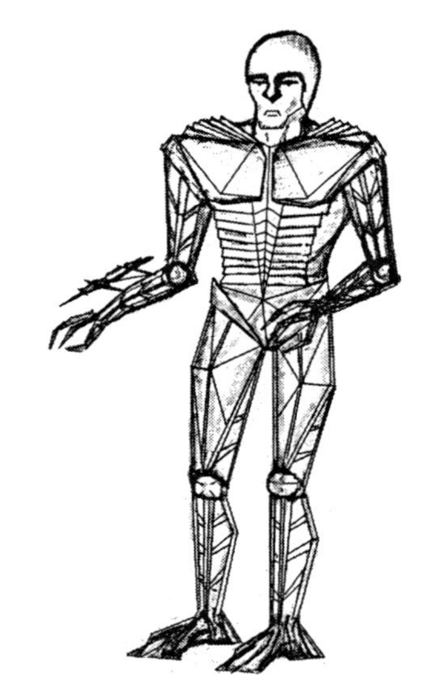

Goliathoid

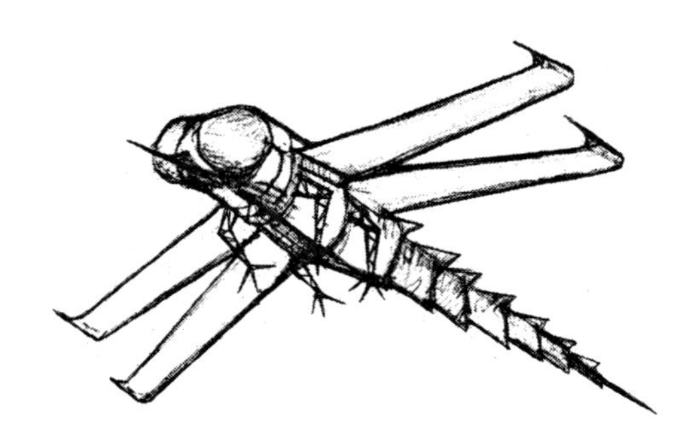

Dragonfly Droid

Alien head

Guardian of the Abyss

Ruby

Chapter 16

Mr. Dragon Goes To School

BEEP! BEEP! BEEP! The annoying sound of Brad's alarm clock droned on. Finally, Brad became coherent enough to turn it off. He opened one eye to see a green glare a few feet from his eyes. As his eyes focused, the glare became clearer. 6:15 stared back at him. His body, as usual, was sluggish from the paralysis of la-la land. A hint of blue, introducing the morning light, was beginning to brighten the blinds covering the windows of his room. He blinked a few times and couldn't believe that he had made it through a night without battling some evil being.

Following breakfast, Matt arrived to pick Brad up at the usual time. Brad's heart sickened as he walked up to the defiled Ruby. The bright orange reminder scripted across the two wide, black stripes which raced from the front of the hood to the trunk, screamed viciously at Brad's spirit. Brad felt the heat of anger and disgust rising from the pit of his stomach. Opening the car door, his whole mood changed, however, when a surprisingly chipper Matt greeted him.

"Good morning, friend. Isn't it a great day to serve God?"

Wow, Brad thought as he looked over at Matt who was beaming like he had just swallowed a two hundred-watt light bulb. "How can you be so happy?" Brad asked. "Aren't you still irritated at what they did to your car?"

"Nope," Matt replied glibly. "I got up and had a great time with the Lord this morning. I let go all of my anger. I forgave whoever did it, because Jesus has forgiven me of all my sins. He, in turn gave me a real peace in my heart about it. He also said that He would redeem the situation."

As the boys made their way across town and pulled into the parking lot, it was quite evident that yesterday's incident had made its way through the school gossip chain, commonly known as the web.

E-mails had been flying all night. Groups huddled, pointing fingers. Some laughed while others were disturbed by such a spiteful and destructive act.

Matt parked his humbled ride in a spot closer to the building. As he and Brad got out of the car and walked over toward the building, a tall gangly fellow came up to them.

"Whas-up?" he said in a friendly tone.

Matt recognized the boy, who was a senior at their school. He was the son of the mechanic from whom Matt had purchased the car less than a year ago. "Hi, Zeke. How's it going?" Matt smiled, as he held out his hand.

Returning the smile, Zeke grasped Matt's hand with his somewhat stained mechanics hands. "I'm doin' ar-right," he replied as he walked past them toward Ruby. He just stood there shaking his head. "Darn shame," he muttered.

Though he couldn't be sure, Brad thought for a minute that Zeke's eyes were glassing up as if he was about to shed a tear.

"Man, this is wrong. I can't believe someone would do this to her. If you find out who did it, and want to exact some pain. Let me know. I'll stand with you." To say that Zeke was a car enthusiast was a gross understatement. To him, cars were great works of art. He was into auto body work, and he had personally painted the black stripes on Ruby. He had a 1969 Shelby Mustang of his own, that he had inherited from his father, which he kept in immaculate condition. Seeing the heartfelt emotion in the eyes of his friend, Matt was torn between wanting to laugh out loud at such loyalty to a machine and the need for calming Zeke's desire for revenge.

"Zeke, it's alright. I don't want to get even. I want to do what Jesus did and forgive them."

It took few seconds for what Matt said to sink in. Then, Zeke looked at Matt like he'd just slapped his grandmother or something. "Forgive them? Are you kidding?"

"Zeke, do you know Jesus?" Matt continued.

Zeke, startled by the question, replied. "Yes, I do."

"What would Jesus do, then?" Zeke looked down at his grimy sneakers and thought. Matt knew he was a Christian and that his father, Big Zeke, was in the Bible study group with Matt's father. Matt and Zeke had played together growing up.

"Well, I guess you're right. We have to forgive 'em."

Matt, added, "But, if they're caught, I will make sure that they're prosecuted so that they will think twice about doing it to someone else."

"I just wanted to let you know that I'll fix her for you. I can paint her and make her look just like she did before." Zeke declared as he ran his hand across the blemished hood.

"I appreciate that, Zeke. As soon as I save the money, you'll be the one to do it."

"You don't have to save the money, just bring it on over. I won't take a penny for the labor, and we'll just charge you cost for the paint. You can pay for that when you have it."

Matt was speechless, and totally blown away by the kindness of his friend. "I—I don't know how to thank you, Zeke."

"It's nothing. You just keep preaching. Don't you let anybody shut you up, man."

Matt, looked at him, beginning to feel the power of God's Spirit welling up inside. "Thanks, man. You don't know how . . ."

Zeke stopped him, "I get you. It's cool, dude. Besides, we can't let God's man drive around in this abomination." The boys laughed, Zeke started off, and then, called back, "Just call me, and let me know when you can bring her in." Matt gave him a thumbs-up sign.

Brad exclaimed, "Man, that was amazing! It's like God took care of that before you even asked."

As soon as first period class started, the intercom system crackled. Mr. Farnell cleared his throat, and announced, "We have had some problems involving malicious pranks on campus. These actions will not be tolerated at all. Anyone participating in these types of harassments will be suspended and dealt with by the local authorities." Everyone knew he meant the police. He didn't go into specifics, but every student knew about the incident with Matt's car. Brad hoped the guys who had ambushed him in the bathroom had gotten the message also.

As soon as class was over, Jackson Boyer, a fellow G-Man, met him at the door. They walked down the hall together, part of their newly devised buddy system. Jackson was also in the tenth grade, and had many of the same classes as Brad. Strolling down the hallway, Jackson pointed to a bulletin board and exclaimed, "Brad, check out that flyer on the board."

Brad looked to see what had animated him so. He was shocked to see bold letters beckoning, "COME SEE THE DRAGON." The bug-eyed boys were drawn like a magnet to the poster. It advertised a special demonstration of the magical arts by "master illusionist, The Dragon," along with a concert by the "popular local band, The Slammers." It was all going to happen in the school auditorium and was being sponsored by a local group promoting diversity and the arts. Admission was a canned food item for the local food bank.

"Just warms your heart, doesn't it? That sleazy Dragon dude is trying to promote himself as a dark Mother Teresa, or something," Jackson chided.

"It's amazing the lengths they go to, to appease their consciences."

"Friday, the sixteenth. That's only about two weeks away," Brad confirmed, as he glanced at his watch. "Man, that guy will be right here in the school, dazzling everyone with his wild magical show. I wonder if he'll demonstrate hypnosis and make people bark like dogs or cluck like chickens."

"I heard that he can levitate people, too," Jackson remarked intensely. "I wonder how he does it."

Brad studied the photo in the middle of poster. It was a friendly looking face with a perfectly trimmed goatee. He noticed the hand, carefully posed with a finger resting just under his chin. On it he wore a gold and black ring decorated with a religious symbol. It looked like a cross, with a loop on the top of it. Brad had seen it before in a book on the occult, but wasn't sure what it meant. As he studied it he began to wonder if Mr. Dragon was merely gifted at slight- of-hand, or perhaps there was a deeper source of his power. Either way, he was looking to make quite an impression on the vulnerable minds of the young people in this school.

"Pretty impressive, huh," came a familiar, unnerving voice from behind him.

"Blane. I guess you're involved in this little gimmick." Brad turned to face his nemesis.

"Gimmick! You just show up. You'll be amazed at what The Dragon can do. It'll blow your mind, dude. Plus, you can rock out with the Slammers. It'll be nothing short of awesome, unless you guys think that God might strike you down dead if you come or something."

Jackson, clearly annoyed, asked, "So, Blane, are you going up on the stage when he asks for volunteers to be hypnotized?"

A smirk crept across Blane's face. "I think I'll leave that for you simple-minded types," he snarled as he brushed Jackson's shoulder with his and walked away.

"Man, you stuck him with that one," Brad chuckled with a smile. "Just be careful when you go to the bathroom, it can get awfully crowded in there."

Jackson half frowned and then smiled, glancing at Brad, "You've got my back, right?"

"We better get going," Brad reminded as they took off down the hall.

Brad, Matt, Bart and several other G-Men met at lunch period to check on how the day was going. The main topic of discussion was the whereabouts of Luke Hunter, along with the big show that The Dragon and the Slammers were to perform in the school auditorium in a couple of weeks.

"How is it the school will allow such a seedy group on campus? Don't they know of all the junk that goes on at Mr. Dragon's establishments?" Bart asked, incredulously.

"Matt, what do the police think about allowing these guys on campus?" Brad wondered.

"I know that they have conducted some investigations and Mr. Dragon has tried to comply with everything that they've requested. He says that he just wants to provide a safe place for kids to have fun. To date, he hasn't been directly tied to any crimes; although some of those around him like, Sammy Dornburg, have. Mr. Dragon says he's is trying to reform some of these wayward young people by giving them an outlet for their wild oats."

"That sounds all well and good, but just last week several of the guys that hang out at the Dragon's Den were picked up for illegal drug use," Jackson added.

"What are we going to do about this big show they're putting on? Are we going to just sit around and let the school sanction this stuff?" Bart questioned.

Matt was thinking hard, quietly listening to the concerns of all the guys. Finally, he commented, "I don't think that we could make any headway if we just came out in opposition to their little benefit concert. It would make us look like the bad guys. I think we should put together a benefit concert of our own, but since the school year is almost over, we should plan it for next fall with the praise band from church. In the mean time, what we need to do is pray. We can meet in the parking lot a couple of hours before the event and bind every evil spirit that might be influencing the minds of the audience. The Bible talks about pulling down strongholds and demonic forces. That's exactly what we need to do here," Matt stated confidently.

Bart added, "Ephesians 6:12 says that our battle is not against flesh and blood, but against powers and principalities in heavenly places."

"Can we really do all that? We're just a bunch of kids," asked Thomas Dowdy, who was fairly new to the G-Men group.

"There's also a scripture that tells us not to say that we are just youths, and do nothing. If we have the Spirit of God, we can do all things through Him. This is our school. It's the place where God has put us to be lights in a dark world. He's given us the responsibility for those around us. If we don't do something, who will?" Matt responded, like the warrior so apparent in his character.

"Maybe that should be the topic of Sunday night's G-Men meeting. We can all look for scriptures on spiritual warfare and discuss them so that we will be able to stand firm on God's word," Brad suggested. He could see heads nodding in agreement all around as each of them caught the vision of the battle set before them.

"That's a great idea, Brad," exclaimed an excited Bart. "We won't let the enemy of God take over our school." The group soon parted ways as they headed to afternoon classes. The rest of the day passed without any problems.

"I guess those Dark Legion guys are sort of laying low after the principal's announcement this morning," Brad commented to Matt, as they wound their way along the usual route home from school.

"Yeah, they wouldn't want to do anything right now to jeopardize that concert. They must have been given orders to walk a tight rope for the next week or so," Matt replied.

"I bet Blane is about to bust. If anyone messes up, I'm sure it will be him. He doesn't seem to like anyone holding him back." Brad laughed, as he glanced in the rear view mirror, noticing a black hummer in the distance.

"Matt, I think someone might be following us again."

Studying the rear-view mirror, Matt retorted, "If they are going to tail us, they should really get a less conspicuous vehicle." He paused. "Unless—maybe, they want us to know they're there." Matt turned onto Morningstar Way and slowly made his way to Brad's house. The Hummer slowed but did not turn to follow them. Instead, it sped away. "I think they're just trying to scare us," Matt affirmed, looking nervously down the street.

The next day was Friday, and the school day was without incident. After school Brad said goodbye to Matt, who dropped him off at home. Matt was heading out to work on his grandfather's farm for the weekend. Brad envied him. Matt had invited Brad to come out and help on the farm several times. Brad enjoyed the work and the animals, as well as the fellowship of Matt's grandparents. Brad's closest grandparents were five hours away. The others were even farther, so he didn't see them as often as Matt saw his.

This weekend Brad had chores to get done and some chemistry to catch up on. Brad unlocked the back door and entered the kitchen. Mandy was rambling away on the phone. He waved as he headed up to his room. Sitting down at his computer, he went through his e-mails before starting his school work.

Shortly, Mandy, was off the phone and came up to her room. "How'd everything go today?" she called. Her head appeared in his doorway.

"Smooth as glass, today," he replied. "We figure everything will be pretty calm before the storm of their big concert. We're getting a bunch of guys together to pray for all the kids during next week. How was your day?" he asked cordially, looking up from his desk.

"It was OK. Brittany and I are becoming good friends. She's really counting the cost of following Jesus. She understands that her life will change, and she wants to get all the facts. I admire her for that. But, I hope it doesn't just turn into putting it off, like, forever. At some point you have to stop trying to figure it out and just go for it."

"Yeah, some of it you can't really grasp until you commit yourself to Jesus and let Him explain it," Brad agreed.

"I think she's very close, though; if she will just let go of her emotional ties to Tommy, and put it all in God's hands. Tommy called her and left a message that he wanted to talk, but she's afraid he'll just try to talk her into aborting the fetus, as he calls it. I don't know why people delude themselves with that term, as if it wasn't a human being but a tissue mass, like some kind of tumor."

"Anybody home?" A call pierced the air from downstairs.

"Yes, mother dear, we're here," Mandy returned jovially.

"Dinner will be ready in about twenty minutes. Dad's on his way with Chinese."

"Chinese! Yum. I hope he got some crab rangoons," Brad called back.

"We'll see," replied the voice from below.

Mandy disappeared down the stairs to help set the table. Brad soon followed. He opened the door for his dad, laden with brown paper bags full of delectable oriental-style morsels. Soon the kitchen island was spread with the feast of several types of entrees, as well as egg rolls, and the treasured crab rangoons. Each one served himself buffet style. They all sat down, and Dad thanked God for His provision in their lives, and asked God's blessing on the meal. Everyone then began to feast on the tasty morsels.

"I called Marcia Finney today, and we decided to reschedule their visit. Their house is still being repaired, and with Luke's whereabouts still uncertain, they felt it would be better to wait. I told them that we were praying for Luke and their family, and invited Marcia to church on Sunday."

"What did she say?" Mandy asked enthusiastically.

"Well, she said that she would talk to David and see."

"That sounds encouraging," responded Dad.

"Boy, that would be great if they would really come to know God. Maybe that's why all of this is happening. God is using this to affect their entire family," Brad added.

Dad looked at his watch and announced, "Dear, we'd better get a move on if we are going to make that eight o'clock show."

"Show?" Brad questioned, puzzled.

"Where are you guys going?" asked Mandy.

"We have a date," Mom declared, glancing at Richard with a smile.

"Yep, we're off to a movie. Then, to spare no expense, we thought we'd hit Chick-Fil-A for a milk shake. So don't wait up for us," Dad beamed.

Brad, trying to look as stern as possible replied, "OK, but don't be out past twelve."

"OK, Pop." Dad laughed and grabbed the back of Brad's neck with a squeeze.

"Can I catch a ride over to Wren's house? We're working on a project for World Civ. tonight. Her Dad will bring me home." Mandy inquired.

"Sure, but we need to leave in ten minutes," Mom stressed, as she jumped up and began putting the leftover food away. Following her lead, the entire family soon had the table cleaned. Brad volunteered to finish loading the dishwasher so that they wouldn't be late. With a flurry of hugs and kisses they were out the door, and Brad was all alone.

Chapter 17

A Stranger In The Dark

The kitchen was quiet except for the clinking of silverware as Brad finished up the dishes. He headed out of the kitchen and noticed the bird clock on the wall. *Seven thirty-two. I hope they get there on time*, he thought to himself, trudging up the stairs to his room. He grabbed his backpack and searched for his chemistry book. His room brightened for a second and in a moment he heard the familiar, but now ominous, distant rumble of thunder. *Great,* he thought sarcastically, *another stormy night. Where is that book?* It wasn't in his backpack. "Rats!" he declared out loud. Remembering that he couldn't fit it in his backpack, he had carried it under his arm when he got into Matt's car that afternoon. *What could I have done with it?* He sat down on the bed and thought hard. Suddenly, lightning flickered outside his window. Brad felt a chill run up his spine. He wondered if every time a storm arose he would feel a bit nervous, concerned what might be about to happen. Brad's attention turned toward the window. The sky was dark, almost pitch black in between the scattered brightness of distant lightening. He turned and glanced at the clock, *seven forty-one.* He was about to get up to go down to the kitchen to look for his book, when suddenly the lights went out totally. Brad sat there a moment in the quiet darkness. "Oh great," He muttered, breaking the silence. He stared at the window, paralyzed momentarily by a surreal feeling of de'ja`vu.

Strangely, there was a different type of light coming into his room from the window. It was not as bright as the lightning. *What is that?* He shuddered. *Do I really want to get up and look out of the window?* "That's silly. It was all just a dream," he said to himself, looking toward the window, remembering how real the dreams had seemed. *But, I'm certainly not asleep now,* he thought, *or am I?* He shook off the crazy mind game going through his brain and boldly stood up. He hesitated as he pondered the strange light. "This is too weird," he admitted to himself. The light had a sort of pattern as if someone were trying to get his attention. He walked over to the window and cautiously stood near the curtains, peeking out through the mini-blinds. The sky was still flickering with lightning in the distance. As another beam of light passed back and forth across his window, Brad could see someone standing in his yard. The person was holding a flashlight and shining it up to Brad's window.

The hooded figure walked closer to the house and Brad raised the window. He heard a quiet voice calling, "Brad! Is that you?"

Brad called back, "Yeah, who wants to know?"

Luke turned the light from Brad's face and shined it on his own. "It's me, Luke. Can I talk to you?"

"Luke!" Brad replied excitedly as he recognized the voice of his friend. "Is it really you? I'll be right down."

"I'll meet you at the back door, OK?" Luke called back nervously.

"OK, I'll be right there." Brad turned and moved quickly across the dark room running into his desk chair in the darkness. He let out a quick, "Ouo-o," as he shoved the chair out of the way. He was kind of relieved to feel pain. Hopefully, that meant he was not sleeping and that this encounter with Luke wasn't a dream. After all, he had done a very similar thing before, only to wake up and find that it had only occurred in the thought world of dreamland. Brad continued to carefully make his way down the dark hallway to the stairs, and then quickly to the backdoor which led onto the wooden deck. Out of reflex he flipped the light switch. He laughed at his dumbness, and unlocked the door.

"Is anyone else home?" the quiet voice asked.

"No," Brad responded. "Everyone's out for the evening."

The medium-sized, thin figure stepped inside the house, pulled off the hood and asked, "What happened to the lights?"

"I don't know. The electricity died right before I noticed your light. I figure it was the lightning. Come on in, man. Have a seat. Somewhere around here we have some candles." Brad walked over to the kitchen and, after a few seconds of rummaging in a cabinet, found some matches. He lit a scented candle in a jar his mom kept near the stove. Brad placed it on the coffee table and sat down. He couldn't help staring at the condition of his long lost friend. In the dim light of the candle he could see a pitiful face. Luke's big, once sparkling brown eyes now seemed cold and sunken into dark circles. His face was dirty, and he had scabby wounds on his lip and over his eye. Luke had been so confident before. He had been living for fame and fortune. But now, at the young age of fifteen, he had been used and abused by the world. He appeared to be in a desperate state.

Luke's situation reminded Brad of the story in the Bible of the prodigal son. He wondered if Luke, like the prodigal son would come to his senses and return to the Father. Brad remembered, however, that Luke had been abandoned by his father. The thought of returning to a loving father, waiting with open arms, would be hard for Luke to understand. Brad's heart went out to his battered friend.

"Luke, it's so good to see you, man. We've been looking for you for a week. Where have you been?"

Luke was a little dumbfounded. "You've been looking for me? He asked with a look of skepticism. "Why?"

Brad was a little taken aback, "I'm concerned about you. If you want to know the truth, I think God put you on my heart because I've had several dreams about you this past week."

Luke just stared at him, as if trying to comprehend what he was saying. At that moment the lights flickered, the computer beeped, and they were no longer in the dark. As Brad's eyes adjusted, and he got a good look at Luke, he realized his truly sad state. His clothes were filthy and ragged in places. Brad understood that Luke must have been living in the woods or somewhere. "Luke, when is the last time you've eaten?"

"Yesterday. I used up the last of my money on a bag of chips." Brad jumped up and went into the kitchen. Grabbing some granola bars and a bag of pretzels, he brought them to his friend. "Here. Eat this for now. Hey, do you like Chinese?"

"Right now, I'd eat broccoli if you offered it to me."

Brad laughed. "You must be starving." He knew how much Luke hated broccoli. "I'll warm up some leftover Chinese we had for dinner." As Luke devoured the snacks, Brad went back into the kitchen and got a glass of apple juice and set it on the coffee table. "Where have you been living?"

"Different places. An old shed mostly. I spent one night in the bathroom at school. I don't recommend it. Those are the hardest floors."

Brad shook his head, amazed that he had done such a thing. He knew personally how hard those floors were. "Luke, why are you hiding? Or who are you hiding from?"

"They think I know too much. I think that they want to kill me or something. But they haven't, because I have something that belongs to them. They think I stole it, but I didn't. I got it by accident and hid it in a black pouch. I think it belongs to Sammy Dornberg. I'm not sure why he had it, unless he might be holding it over The Dragon's head—you know, just in case of trouble. But, I'm not sure."

"What is it?" Brad asked.

"I'll take you to see it. I have it hidden not far from here."

Brad looked wonderingly at him as a strange thought passed through his head. "It's not, by chance, hidden inside the little wooden shed just through the woods, is it?"

Luke returned the peculiar look with a pause. "No-o." Just as Brad was about to breathe a sigh of relief, he added, "It's not—in the shed. It's more like, behind it"

"Behind it? Where behind it?"

"It's hidden on top of a cement block underneath the back side of the shed."

"That is too weird!" Brad exclaimed. "I had a dream last week that you and I were trapped in a shed and you showed me a black pouch. You told me that a bunch of alien creatures were after you, who used mind control to get people to do their bidding."

Luke's whole body shivered suddenly, and a petrified look overtook him.

"Luke, what are you so afraid of?" Brad asked, seeing the effect of his words.

"Brad, have you seen them, too?"

"What do you mean have I seen them? Seen who?"

"Alien creatures, the thin dudes with the big heads," Luke declared, his eyes wide with excitement.

Brad wondered at Luke's intensity. "It was just a dream, or actually a couple of dreams."

Luke shook his head adamantly, " Uh-uh. You might think it was just a dream. That's what they want you to think, but they are real. I've seen them, and so have many others. Aliens do exist. Do you know that one out of four people have had some kind of encounter with alien beings, whether it was seeing a UFO or even being abducted? There are many web sites that monitor this type of stuff. The air force has many documented cases of fighters chasing UFO's. Some aircraft have even disappeared. There have also been sightings where hundreds of people have seen them at one time." Luke rattled on almost as if he had been programmed to repeat this stuff.

Brad was amazed at how sincerely Luke believed it all. "You say that you've actually seen these alien beings? When?"

Luke shuddered again, and Brad watched him as Luke's mind began to replay a very frightening experience. "One night about two months ago, I was staying out at the house the guys are renting in the country. I was asleep and was awakened by a strange noise—a throbbing, humming sound from outside. There was a bright greenish-yellow light streaming in through the window. I got up and sneaked out of the room I was in. I made my way down the stairs and could see that the light was coming in through the first story windows as well. We'd practiced late that night and everyone else was asleep. The greenish glow intensified around the front door, and I got really scared, so I hid under the computer desk. The front door opened slowly."

Brad wanted to crack a joke about little green men saying, "Take me to your leader," but didn't dare. Luke was opening up about something obviously very serious to him.

Luke paused, and Brad could see he was physically shaking. "I know this sounds crazy, but it did happen." Luke looked Brad right in the eyes, searching for trust. No matter what Brad believed about aliens from outer space, he could see this was a very real experience for Luke. He wanted someone to know what happened to him.

Brad attempted to reassure his skittish friend, "I have had some pretty wild experiences lately myself. What happened next?"

Luke swallowed hard and continued. "Through the glaring light of the open door, five dark shapes appeared, although when they got into the room they weren't dark. They were almost florescent and stood about my height, very slender, but not bony. Their large heads and eyes were just like the drawings I've seen of aliens that many people have experienced. The beings just stood there for a moment inside the doorway, and I could smell this foul smell—like rotten eggs. Suddenly, one of the guys who was sleeping on the sofa in the living room was startled and woke up. He turned on the floor lamp next to him. One of the beings raised a hand, and instantly with a bright spark and pop, the light bulb exploded, sending glass flying everywhere. It was as if the guy on the sofa was struck dumb with fear or something. He just sat there, staring at them. One of them raised his long fingered hand, and I could hear it say, 'Come, it is time.' It was weird, though, because their mouths didn't move. It was like he wasn't speaking with an audible voice, but I could hear it in my mind. Well, I wasn't going anywhere, so I didn't move. But, all of a sudden, all of the other seven guys who had been staying in the house were now coming out of their rooms. The aliens parted, and the guys filed out of the house, some of them in their underwear, like they were in some sort of trance. I thought about trying to stop them, but I was just too scared. When all of the guys were outside, the five strange figures stepped back out of the house and the light was gone. I sat there for hours, too afraid to move. Finally, I guess I was so exhausted I must have fallen back to sleep."

Brad sat motionless, thinking through the amazing tale he had just heard. Remembering his own vivid dream, he asked, "Don't you think that you might have just dreamed it?"

Luke frowned, "I didn't think you would believe me."

"No, I believe something very real happened to you. Did the guys ever return?"

"Well, I awoke the next morning, and I was really sore from sleeping under the desk. By the way, if it was all a dream, how did I get under the desk? Anyway,

I awoke to the snoring of that guy, Benny, who was asleep on the sofa. I went upstairs, and all the guys were fast asleep. I thought maybe I did dream it all. I went back downstairs somewhat relieved, and as I walked across the room I felt a sharp pain in my foot. That's when I realized that it wasn't a dream. There were pieces of glass all over the floor. I carefully went over to the floor lamp and saw that the shade was partially scorched. The metal socket inside, where the bulb screwed in, looked as if it had melted. I knew that it was not a dream."

Brad's mind was racing. He was battling a myriad of thoughts that were now crowding into his head. *It can't be true. God is real, not aliens.* However, Brad could see that something very strange had happened to his friend. How could this be?

Then a thought popped into his mind. "Ask him about hypnosis," Brad heard in his spirit.

"Luke, I want you to know that I totally believe you. There are strange forces at work on the earth. But they aren't always what they make themselves out to be."

A skeptical look spread across Luke's face. "What do you mean?"

"Have you ever been hypnotized?"

Luke folded his arms in defiance, and thought. "Well," Luke paused, musing over the question. "Yes, I have. It's part of Dragon's act. He likes to practice on people in the band. He uses it to help calm us down and take away the jitters of performing.

"Does Mr. Dragon ever talk about aliens?" Brad asked curiously.

"Well, he's never said much about them, but I know that he believes they exist. One of the guys in the band told me about some web sites Dragon had recommended on the subject of extra-terrestrials. Those guys are into all sorts of wild stuff. They like to explore all kinds of religions, supernatural phenomenon and stuff that's hard to explain. They get on these highs and sit around for hours discussing it. Sometimes it's the inspiration for a new song."

"Do you think Mr. Dragon uses hypnosis to get people to do things they might not ordinarily do?"

Brad's question caught Luke a little of guard. Brad could see that Luke was sincerely considering the idea. "I don't know. But, the Dragon does have a way of getting people to follow him and do what he wants, almost like he's some kind of god or something. Yeah, I think that hypnosis stuff really seems to work. It's not just a gag. I've seen some pretty amazing things happen when people where under: like grown men terrified because they thought they were covered in nonexistent snakes, or that they were being attacked by a dog that wasn't there. I guess that sort of power does evoke a certain amount of fear in a person's mind."

Brad nodded in agreement."Fear is a powerful thing." He paused and then asked seriously, "Luke, do they use some kind of drug with that?"

"I don't know for sure, but they do use a variety of drugs. I did try a few of them for my nerves, but they made me feel so weird afterward—like—I felt, I was losing control. You know—like I wasn't really me, and my mind was in such a fog afterward. It took a while for the effects to wear off—before I could think more clearly again. I can see how that stuff can fry someone's brain over time, so I told them I didn't need them. They harassed me about it, so that I just pretended to do the drugs and waited until they were all out of it to slip away."

"How'd they ever get you into it in the first place? You know how miserable people are who are addicted to drugs?" Brad asked curiously.

"Everybody was doing it. They said that it made you more creative as an artist. I figured out, though, that's all just a lie to you get you hooked so they can make money off you. It was kind of fun at first, but I always felt so terrible afterwards. Tommy kept telling me it was the guilt trip that you and the other religious types had forced on me and that I needed to just forget all that stuff. But you know, one night I had a dream, too. I was trapped in this old warehouse, one like the one where I was hiding. The Dragon and Sammy had locked me in and were setting fire to it. I couldn't find a way out and figured I was going to die. Then, this man dressed in a white robe-like coat, appeared through the smoke and showed me a way out. As I followed Him through the maze of danger, He brought me through the flames, only to be attacked by these metallic android-looking dudes. I began to realize who it was. I heard about Him when I went to church with you when I was a kid. I know that it was just a dream. But, I believe He was telling me that I was in over my head with this group—and that we were leading people in the wrong direction."

Brad couldn't believe his ears. He sat there with his mouth open.

Luke looked at him and asked, "Do you think I'm just crazy? I don't know what to believe anymore. Aliens—Jesus—Is any of it real?"

That's when it hit Brad like a lightning bolt what all of this was really about. *Confusion. Satan is trying to get people so confused that they will never figure out the truth in the midst of all the wild and crazy things in the world.* "No, no. I don't think you're crazy at all. That's what the enemy wants you to think. I believe Jesus is trying to get your attention. He wants you to follow Him, instead of this bunch of thugs, or fame and fortune, or aliens, or any other wild and crazy thing that tries to capture your imagination. Jesus is the only thing in all of this that's real. He's let you see all this to open your eyes to the truth. The truth is: He's calling you to follow Him."

Luke shook his head slowly. "I don't think that I can do that. I'm so involved in this group, that I don't think they would let me live if I got out. These guys will not let anyone screw up their plans."

Brad could see Luke's eyes beginning to water as he pondered his dire situation. "Luke," Brad grabbed his arm firmly, "God is bigger and stronger than all those guys. Just like in the dream you had, Jesus wants to show you the way out. In the dream I had about you this week, God delivered you from the shackles of a dragon. I have no doubt that God will deliver you from this situation if you just turn to Him."

Luke nodded as he listened. "I believe what you say, but my life is such a mess right now. I don't see how I'll ever get straight."

"Man, God knows every problem you have. His word says that while we were still sinners He died for us. He opens His arms to us even while we're still in a mess. If we're willing to come to Him, He gives us His Spirit to live in us, to clean us up. It's impossible for us to clean ourselves up, but His power is fully able to change us."

Luke stared down at the floor, and then back up at Brad. "I know I need something to get me out of this trap. Brad, can you pray for me? I don't know what to do."

Brad looked at him, "I can pray with you, but I can't pray you into God's kingdom. You must talk to God yourself. You need to admit that you have sinned against Him and ask for forgiveness. Then, be willing to turn away from those sins and follow His words written in the Bible. Is that what you want to do?"

Luke thought a few seconds, "I—I don't know if I can. But—I," He paused again. Then his tone changed. "Yes, I really want to. I would like to ask Jesus to help me. I don't believe anyone else could."

Brad was fighting back his own tears of joy for his friend and said, "Then you just need to tell God that. Tell Him what you are wanting to do."

Luke looked puzzled, "Right now? Will He hear me?"

Brad laughed. "Of course He will. He's right here with us. Just talk to Him."

"What do I call Him? Sir—Father—God?"

Brad laughed again, "Yes, His name is Jesus, remember? But He goes by those names, too." Luke was now smiling. He bowed his head and said, "Jesus, my life is such a mess, please help me. I have sinned against You and many others. Please forgive me. Help me to follow You and do what is right. Thank you for Brad caring and being home tonight." Then he looked up and asked, "Was that right? Oh, wait, I forgot the amen, didn't I?"

Wiping tears from his eyes, Brad replied, "That was perfect." Then he prayed for his friend and agreed with his prayers. Brad looked up at him and explained, "You know, Luke, this is the start of a new life for you. It starts right now and will continue everyday for the rest of your life, as long as you continue to follow Him. It's a constant battle, and it may intensify now that you changed your path. The world and your old nature will be at war with you, but you have to persevere, and always remember that you are not doing this alone. Jesus says that He will always be with you no matter what happens. He will see you through."

Brad noticed a look of concern in Luke's dark glistening eyes. "What's wrong?"

"I don't know how much more I can take, the battle is pretty bad right now."

"Don't worry, the Bible says that God will not give us more than we can bear, but with every temptation provides an escape route. We just have to always look for it, and take the escape route."

Luke's countenance brightened, and a smile spread across his motley face. "Yeah, just like the dream I had. He showed me the escape route. All I have to do is follow Him through it."

"There's so much that you need to learn from the Bible. It's the key to our freedom because it shows us the truth. It's our instruction manual on how to live every day. Knowing what it says can mean the difference between standing and falling." Brad explained with concern.

"Will you help me?" Luke asked.

"Certainly, I will. And not just me, but Matt and all the other guys in our group will, too. We can study the Bible together, and you'll see God's plan for you become real. It'll be a blast."

Luke smiled, and Brad could see a glimmer of hope in his dazed eyes.

"Right now, though, we need to get some food in you. I'll throw some of that Chinese in the micro- wave. Why don't you go upstairs and take a shower. I've got some clothes from a couple of years ago that should fit you, and maybe we can wash these. Brad took him upstairs to get cleaned up. While Luke was in the shower, he found a pair of jeans and an old NC State sweatshirt, along with a towel, and laid them on the counter in the bathroom. Then he went down to the kitchen and prepared a big plate of leftover Chinese takeout.

Luke was soon downstairs, hair still wet. He commented, "These things fit pretty well, even though I have to wear this State thing. But, it is warm and clean."

Brad remembered all the banter they'd had over the years, as to which was the best school. Luke's mom was a graduate of UNC Chapel Hill and Brad's dad, NC State. So, there was an ongoing battle stemming from the intense rivalry of the schools. "State red looks good on you," Brad ribbed.

Luke shook his head with a smile, "Wow, this is quite a feast." Luke gazed down at the glistening plate of sesame chicken and lo mien.

"Dig in." Brad pulled out the chair as Luke sat down and started to eat. Brad sat across from him with a crab rangoon. "I still want to know about that pouch. What's in it that's so important to those guys. Is it money, or drugs, or what?"

Luke slurped a noodle into his mouth and replied, "I'll just have to show you. The pouch was supposed to have just money and drugs. They're used to make drops to drug dealers. They're really just money bags with a false lining that has Velcro at the top. The drugs are stuffed into the lining."

"So, they are in the business of dealing drugs. Is The Dragon the ringleader?" Brad wondered aloud.

"The best I can tell, he is. Although, he has associates in other cities, Sammy Dornberg was sort of his right hand man, here."

"What do you mean, was? Isn't he still running things around here?"

"Well, yes, but he had some sort of screw up and almost blew the whole operation, because he wanted to be more heavy-handed in dealing with you guys. The police are watching them carefully, looking for someone to nail for some disappearances and drug crimes. The relationship between Sammy and Dragon is strained, and I don't think either one of them trusts the other. I think that the Dragon might be looking for a way to get rid of Sammy. Sammy is just trying to protect his butt."

Brad thought a minute, "What does Blane Stevens have to do with them?"

Luke looked up and replied, "Blane Stevens—now, that is a wicked dude. How do you know him?"

"Let's just say that Matt and I have had a bit of a run-in with him at school."

Luke shook his head, "That guy almost seems to worship The Dragon. It's like Dragon has kind of adopted him as his son or something, which really irritates Sammy. Blane will do anything for him, and he's smart about it. He doesn't do it himself, but gets all of those brainless groupies that follow the Slammers to carry out his pranks. This makes everyone in on the act, guilty. He then holds this stuff over their heads in case they get cold feet or something."

Brad frowned and retorted, "That's all we need around here is a Dragon Junior. Why did you say that he's wicked?"

"I don't know. It just seems to fit him. It's like he enjoys getting people into trouble and then having control over them. Isn't that what the devil does?"

Brad pondered Luke's statement and agreed, "Yeah, I guess you're right." Brad was amazed at Luke's spiritual perception.

"The Dragon is even teaching Blane some of his magic stuff, and how to hypnotize people. He can be really weird sometimes, too. It's definitely not just illusion, but almost like a religion to them. I don't want any part of that stuff."

"What stuff?" Brad pressed.

"All those chants and quoting the ancient texts—Dragon calls them. And he's always talking about allowing your inner self to be free. It's just too weird for me. I always just nodded and tuned it out. They even have séances where they try to get in touch with dead people. I've seen some pretty strange things, although, I don't know how much was drug induced. That stuff really messes with your mind."

Brad nodded in agreement, then asked, "Do you think the drugs really have something to do with the hold The Dragon has over all the kids at school. Are they all on drugs?"

"Not all of them, but most of them are. They start off with certain prescription painkiller-type drugs. Once they get kids used to taking them, they can give them whatever, and they're hooked. Then they sell them one pill for a ridiculous price. Once they're hooked, someone will do almost anything to get them—stealing, hustling, and so-called personal favors from the girls. It's really sad, and nothing less than human slavery. It's incredible how we can get ourselves into such bondage to others, all because of a temporary high."

Brad's mind was suddenly transported back to the dream where he had seen Luke shackled to the huge posts, as well as, all the others (including Brittany) in their mirrored cells.

"Brad, we've got to do something to help them, to wake them up." Luke's words jolted Brad out of his thought world.

"The only way they can break free is through the power of Jesus. He's the only One who can set us free from the prison of selfishness and sin."

Luke agreed, "He sure rescued me." As Luke finished the last of his lo mien, he glanced at his watch and exclaimed, "I can't believe that it's past eight-thirty. Let's go over to the shed, I want to make a copy of what's in the pouch, and give it to you for safe-keeping."

"Great, just leave the dishes on the table. I'll clean them up when we get back."

Chapter 18

I Hate Snakes!

The boys started out of the house into the cool night. "Sure is dark," Luke remarked, pulling a cheap plastic flashlight from his pocket. It flickered as he tried to switch it on. He gave it a smack and lamented, "I wish I hadn't lost my old flashlight. It had been a faithful friend through the years. I dropped somewhere in the woods one night last week."

"Wait a minute," Brad exclaimed. He dashed through the house and up the stairs, returning with the small metallic cylinder in his hand. "Is this what you're missing?"

Luke's eyes lit up. "Where'd you find it?"

"Near the shed, when we were cleaning up, for Mr. Guthrey, after the storm.

Luke clicked it on, and a bright beam of light shot forth from the little beacon. "As faithful as ever," Luke affirmed.

Brad laughed, "Linus has his blanket and you have your flashlight."

On the horizon, the flicker of lightning momentarily brightened the night sky, as they headed out the door. "I hope it doesn't rain again," Luke muttered. "I'm so tired of being wet, cold, and stinky."

"I don't know about cold, but the stinky part was pretty bad." Brad laughed and jabbed him in the side as they walked across the yard.

"Hey-y," Luke responded, "at least I had a good reason for it, what's yours? You don't smell like a petunia yourself."

Brad laughed and then thought. *I guess I haven't had a shower in a couple of days,* and out of reflex he sniffed under his arms. "Shew-wy." Luke punched him in the arm, and they both laughed as they entered the edge of the woods.

Luke pointed his trusty flashlight into the woods, shining the bright beam through the leaves and branches onto a narrow path between the trees and brush. The path widened into a clearing where the trees' canopy opened. Stars peeked through a hole in the clouds as the moon shone through a thin veil nearby. The boys made their way down the embankment of the small creek which ran down and under Morningstar Drive. As they carefully hopped across the stones, a rumble of thunder rolled in the distance. Brad thought back to the night when he and Luke followed the creek to the pipe under the street and watched the invading force menace the neighborhood. He kept telling himself it was only a dream, although somehow he felt it was more than a dream. If he hadn't had that dream, he would have never gone to see Luke and found out about the pouch. God used that crazy dream to open his eyes to Luke's plight. None-the-less, Brad couldn't help feeling that he was reliving that night, and that the danger of that invading force was still all around him. As they stood on the other side of the creek, Luke pointed his light down the path. A branch snapped in the woods and Brad exclaimed nervously, "What was that?"

Luke shined the light in the direction of the sound. As they stood frozen in their tracks, Luke remarked, shrugging off his own jitters, "Don't do that, you're creeping me out. It was probably just a raccoon or something. Let's go." It appeared Luke had grown more fearless out in the woods. It was as if he knew the area and felt comfortable when he couldn't be seen. They continued to wind through the menagerie of branches and vines as the pathway narrowed. Finally, they reached the clearing where the beam of the flashlight exposed the familiar outline of the little rustic shed. Brad followed Luke along the side of the small structure. Parting the honeysuckle vines growing on saplings which had sprung up around the structure, they made their way to the back of it. Luke held the light, revealing six or seven logs of old firewood piled near the side of the shed.

"Here, shine the light down here, while I move the wood," Luke instructed as he handed the light to Brad. Brad took the flashlight and held it as Luke pushed back the logs. When he moved the last log both boys gasped, then jumped back almost in unison. A very healthy brown colored snake lay coiled in the dry leaves. It raised its glistening head up, ready to strike. Brad almost dropped the flashlight, but managed to hold on to it. Blinded by the light, the reptile quickly slithered through an eight-inch gap in the wooden siding near the concrete block foundation underneath the shed.

"This place is giving me the creeps. Let's get this thing and get out of here," Brad insisted.

Luke looked up at Brad, his mouth agape. Brad realized that Luke was shaking nervously. "Wait, where is the pouch?" Brad asked, knowing the answer. Luke pointed to the gap in the siding that was now the home of the unknown type of snake. "Well, we have to get it, don't we?" Brad said swallowing hard. Luke nodded, still speechless and staring at the small dark space. "I'm pretty sure it's not poisonous," Brad declared trying to encourage his friend.

"Pretty sure?" Luke finally spoke.

"Look. All we have to do is scare it away." Brad picked up a stick and got down close to the small opening. As he pointed the flashlight into the dark space, it suddenly dimmed and went out. "Oh great," Brad grumbled.

"Just give it a smack," Luke advised. Brad slapped the light and it came back on. He proceeded to jab the stick into the space in an attempt to send the slithery foe packing. As he sat there on his hands and knees, Luke instructed, "Just reach inside and up to the right. There's a cement block. It's sitting on top of that."

Brad looked up at him as if he were crazy. "Yeah, right." Brad turned back to the ominous rectangular hole and let out a deep breath. He reached into the unknown and felt for the cement block. Suddenly, he let out a cry and jerked his arm out of the hole. Luke jumped back with a yelp, then grabbed Brad and exclaimed, "Are you OK?"

Brad chuckled, "Gotcha!"

Luke smacked him on the back of the head. "Man, are you trying to make me mess up my pants or something? Will you just get the thing?" Brad laughed and pulled out the elusive prize. He handed the black pouch to Luke, examining it to make sure that there was no viper hanging from it. Nerves still on edge, Brad stood up.

"Let me have the flashlight?" Luke requested. Brad handed him the light, and Luke started through the thicket around the edge of the shed. Holding the light under his arm, he began to check the pouch. He pulled out a couple of zip-lock plastic bags, one with pills in them, and one with a stash of cash.

"Luke, we should turn this over to the police and explain the whole thing."

"Do you think that they would believe me?" Luke asked with a pensive look. Then Luke felt between the lining and said aloud nervously, "Where is it?" His hand finally felt something. "Here it is." He pulled out a small black rectangle about two and a half inches long and an inch wide.

"What is that?" Brad asked as he started to lean closer to get a better look.

Suddenly, Brad heard movement in the brush behind him. Luke immediately dropped to the ground, and the flashlight went out. Brad turned and cried out, "Who's there?" There was silence. "Luke, shine the light over here! Something's out there!"

"Just a minute," Luke was doing something with the flashlight. "There," Luke finally whispered, and the light flickered on.

At that exact moment, a bright light from the brush ahead of him, flashed in Brad's face. Brad held his hand over his eyes. As he did, he felt a searing pain in his stomach. He doubled over and felt a second blow to the back of his head. The next thing he knew his face was buried in leaves. Brad turned and looked up. The bright light was now spinning, and he could hear Luke yelling something.

"You take your hands off of me! I'm not going—"

The rest was a blur. Brad tried to get up but everything was still spinning. He heard rustling and a man's deep voice. "You got it?"

"Yo," came the response. "Get him, and let's get back."

Brad could hear Luke struggling as they carried him off, then silence. Brad was finally with it enough to raise his head. The light of the assailants moved away through the woods toward the street. Now up on hands and knees, dizzy, Brad saw the dim beam of Luke's flashlight shining up though the dry leaves of the woods' floor. He crawled over to it. He felt something warm running down the side of his face. Reaching up, he rubbed it off and looked at the bright red stain on his hand in the beam of the light. *I'm bleeding,* he thought as he felt the painful knot forming on his head. It didn't seem too bad, a small cut, but boy it stung. He reached out and grabbed hold of Luke's flashlight, and got up. Brad staggered through the woods in the direction of the bushwhackers. He came to the path which led to Morningstar Way. Brad looked down the path and heard the sound of a motor starting up. Around a curve in the path he could see bright headlights moving away as the vehicle was backing up. Summoning all of the energy from his battered body, he began to run toward the street. He stumbled, hitting the gravel hard. Picking himself up he jogged toward the street, amazed at how far away it seemed. Getting closer to the street he could hear the car racing off. Finally reaching the pavement, all he could make out were the red glowing tail-lights of the large, dark beast which had swallowed up his friend Luke, disappearing in the distance.

In despair, Brad collapsed onto his hands and knees, the pavement cold and unforgiving. His body ached, and despair attacked his thoughts. Darkness ruled, accept for the faint glow of a distant street light, and an occasional flicker of lightning. Brad cried out, "Jesus, please help me. Don't let the enemy steal Luke! Please, I just can't help him." Sitting there helpless and dazed, he wondered what he could do. Suddenly everything started getting brighter, literally. He turned to see two bright lights coming toward him. Holding his arm over his face, suddenly it dawned on him that he was sitting in the middle of the street. Brad tried to stand and move, but stumbled, hitting the rigid pavement still clutching Luke's flashlight. The car slowed and stopped right in front of him.

The car door opened. He heard a familiar voice. "Brad!" called the strong comforting tone. "Are you all right?" Matt asked, as he bent down to try to help. Brad was so relieved that he wanted to give his big friend a bear hug, but all of a sudden, he remembered Luke and cried out, "Please, help me up. They've got Luke, and we've got to go after them." Matt helped Brad to his feet and into the car.

Matt jumped into the driver seat and asked, "What are you talking about? Who's got Luke?" Noticing the blood on the side of his head, Matt exclaimed, "Man, you're bleeding! Are you OK? Do you need to go to the emergency room?"

"No!" Brad grimaced in pain, and exclaimed, "I'll explain later, just go! Follow that car!" Brad thought how surreal this all seemed, just like in the old movies. He'd always wanted to say that.

Matt handed Brad some napkins he had in stuck in a compartment for spot cleaning and asked, confused, "What car?" Brad took the napkin and dabbed the side of his head. The blood was already sticky. He fumbled for the seat belt and replied in frustration, "Just trust me. A big black vehicle like a hummer took off down the street with Luke in it—just go!"

Seeing the intensity in his friend's eyes and grasping a sense of urgency, Matt hit the accelerator and Ruby screeched off. Their heads jerked back as the power surged from the huge engine. "I still don't see any big black car," Matt protested. They came to the intersection of Morningstar Way and Highway 1010 and could see tail-lights gleaming in both directions. Matt stopped as a small sedan drove by. "What do we do now?"

Brad's heart was racing as his mind tried to sort through the menagerie of thoughts crowding his battered brain. His head still throbbed from the blow he had sustained earlier. He just had to figure out where they were taking Luke. He was afraid that Luke might just disappear like the others he'd heard about. Luke had been so irresponsible lately. People would just think he took off or something, never to be heard of again. Finally Brad surmised, "If it was Dragon's dudes, we pretty much know where they are heading. Turn left."

Matt shook his head. "Don't you think we should let the police handle this?"

Brad nodded, "Yes, but we don't have time. Luke was terrified of these guys. He really believed they might kill him or something. We at least need to find out where he is, and then we can call the police."

Matt nodded in agreement and darted onto the highway in the direction of the dubious destination. He looked over at Brad, who was holding the napkin against the side of his head. "How are you doing? Are you sure you don't need to see a doctor?" Matt asked with real concern.

"I'm fine," Brad responded, not being totally honest. His head did feel a little better. Although still aching, things at least had stopped spinning.

"OK, but let me know if you're going to pass out or something," Matt declared smiling at his abused friend. "And try not to get blood all over the upholstery, OK."

Brad, with a frowning smile replied, "I'll be very careful," knowing that Matt was trying to lighten the situation.

"Are you sure that's where they are taking him, to the Dragon's Den? If they plan to do him in, they could be taking him anywhere."

Brad didn't want to think of that possibility. "I just have a feeling that they're taking him there."

"Did you recognize someone, hear anything or get a look at their vehicle?" Matt queried.

Brad thought, then remembered hearing one of the goons say they needed to get back. "Not really, but I'm pretty sure that's where they are heading."

"Well, just to make sure, I should call my dad and let him know what's going on. He could put out a watch for that vehicle. I sure wish we had a better description." Matt flipped open his phone, brought up his dad's number and hit "send." After three rings Matt heard his Dad's voice.

"Sergeant Shackleton." The low, firm tone comforted Matt's heart.

"Hi, Dad. We've got a bit of a situation here. It seems that Luke has been kidnapped. I'm wondering if you can put out a bulletin on a large dark SUV." Matt paused to hear his dad's response. Nothing. There was a cold silence. "Dad? Dad!" Matt looked down at the dark cell phone. "Oh blast it!" He threw the phone down in disgust. "I knew I should have charged that thing yesterday."

"Don't you have a charger for the car?" Brad asked as he picked up the dead phone.

"No, I've been meaning to get one. I guess we'll just head over to the Dragon's Den and see if they are there." Matt sighed uneasily.

"Don't worry, Matt. God will take care of us. I pray that He is watching over Luke, too. You know, he prayed to receive Jesus tonight."

"Really, when?" Matt asked excitedly.

"He showed up at my house, and we got to talking. He knew that his life needed to change but didn't believe he could do it. I told him that Jesus would be there right by his side to help him. That was right before we went over to the shed to look for the pouch."

"The pouch?" Matt exclaimed, "Did you find it?"

"Yes, but I guess Dragon's goons have it now," Brad lamented.

"Did you ever find out what was in it?"

"Well, sort of. It was dark, but I know there was some money and bags of illegal drugs. That wasn't all. There was something small and rectangular." A light bulb went on in Brad's head. "Wait, I know what it was. A flash drive, you know a USB drive like you store stuff on for a computer. Some people call it a thumb drive. That's what his protection was. It must have had some kind of proof of all the illegal stuff Dragon is involved in."

"Man, that might be just the evidence that would shut down Dragon and send him to prison," Matt interrupted. "What happened to it?"

Brad thought and shook his head, "I don't really know. Luke had it in his hand about the time we were ambushed. Perhaps he dropped it, or those guys might have it. But, I'm sure that Luke would not have just handed it over to them."

"I wonder how Luke got something that valuable."

"I think he got it sort of by mistake from Sammy Dornberg. Evidently, Sammy and Dragon aren't getting along, and Sammy was holding on to this for protection in case Dragon decided to try to get rid of him."

Matt laughed dryly, "Sounds like a real loving little family, doesn't it?"

Brad smirked and retorted, "Not!"

Matt turned down Highway 42, which would lead them to their dreaded destination. Brad was thinking about the night's events and wondered why Matt just happened to be on Morningstar Way so late at night. "Matt, tell me something. Why aren't you out at your granddad's farm? How'd you just happen to be driving down my street at the very time I was in need of help?"

"Chemistry!" Matt replied,

"Chemistry?" Brad repeated. "You mean that you and I have known each other so long that you know when I need help before I ask?"

Matt laughed, "That could be true. I guess I could take credit for being so perceptive, but no, not that type of chemistry. You left your chemistry book in my car and I knew that you'd need it to study this weekend."

"That's right! I was looking for it right before Luke showed up. Man, it is amazing how God does work all things for good according to His plan, just like the Bible says."

"Yeah," Matt agreed, "that's a great verse. I hope it holds up the rest of this night. I can't help wondering if we should be doing this. We might wind up in over our heads."

"I think God will keep us safe. We can't just sit around and do nothing when a brother in the Lord is in trouble."

Matt cocked a suspicious-looking half smile and remarked, "Well, we could just pray for him."

Brad laughed and shook his head. "Yeah, right." This was a longstanding joke amongst the G-Men group. It was code for Christian cop out; saying that you would pray for someone when you had it in your power to do something as well, but didn't want to lay down your life and be inconvenienced. "The fact that you showed up just at the moment I needed help to follow these guys indicates that God wants us to do something."

Matt looked at Brad and nodded, "I think that you're right, and I appreciate your faithfulness to do the right thing even in the midst of possible danger. Loyalty is one of the basic Christian character traits we've been trying to learn with the G-Men. I'm totally with you. I just want to make sure we keep in mind another basic truth: don't do anything stupid."

Brad laughed nervously, "I'm with you there." As they neared the night club, the new neon sign came into view. The sky glimmered, with the blazing red, green, and gold monstrosity. Standing twenty-five feet tall, the display featured a Dragon with its tail coiling behind into a spear-tipped point and golden flames spewing from its fang-laden mouth. "Man, it's amazing what they can do with neon these days," Brad exclaimed.

Driving by the packed parking lot, Matt slowed to scope out the situation. The place was in full swing. "There's the black Hummer near the back. No, wait. There's another black SUV, too. I think it's one of those Cadillac things. I'm not sure. It could have been either one of them, but I'm sure they brought Luke here." Brad insisted.

A car honked behind them, and Matt pulled ahead to let the car full of rowdy teenagers turn into the parking lot. Matt slowly continued down highway 42 past the parking lot. "Well, what do we do now?" Matt wondered out loud.

"We've got to go in and see if Luke's there," Brad exclaimed.

"Are you crazy? They'll never let us in," Matt replied.

"Why didn't you turn in? We have to find out if Luke's in there!" Brad shouted.

"Calm down, dude," Matt responded in frustration. "They're not just going to let us waltz in there and talk to Luke. They probably have him hidden somewhere. Remember, we're not exactly welcome around here, and I'm sure they're watching the parking lot."

Brad nodded, "I'm sorry. You're right. I guess Ruby is an easily recognizable ride."

Matt noticed an old logging trail going off to the right and pulled onto it. Ruby bounced and bumped down the old path until it made a slight turn and Ruby was out of sight from the road. Matt turned the motor off and Brad reached for the door latch. "Wait!" Matt declared seriously. "We should pray. These are dangerous people we are dealing with."

Brad agreed and bowed his head. Matt prayed, "Oh Lord, we don't exactly know what's going on here, but our friend Luke needs help, Your help. I pray that You would watch over him and protect him from harm. Help us to find him. I ask that You would keep us safe, too, and help us not to act foolishly but with Your wisdom."

Brad added, "Yes, Lord, we need Your guidance. I pray that You make us invisible to these goons."

Matt looked up at his friend, somewhat amused by his prayer request.

"What?" Brad responded, noticing Matt's reaction.

"Invisible? That's pretty bold."

"Lord, I mean, that they won't recognize us in the crowd and we won't be noticed," Brad continued. "We place our trust in You, Lord. In Jesus' name, Amen."

Matt nodded his head in agreement and repeated, "Amen. Sorry, when you said invisible, I got this picture in my mind of an old sci-fi flick, and us wandering around trying to find each other."

Brad laughed, "Well, the Bible does say that all things are possible through Christ, and tonight I'll take all of God's protection I can get."

Brad reached for the handle to open the door and was about to get out when Matt asked, "Do you still have that flashlight?"

Brad fumbled around in the seat and finally found it on the floor. "Here it is. I'm not sure it still works, though." He clicked it on and a beam of light shot right into Matt's eyes.

Reacting to the painful brightness, Matt squinted and held his hand over the light. "Are you trying to blind me or what? What type of batteries does he have in that thing?"

"Sorry," Brad responded, snickering under his breath. Brad clicked it again, and the beam weakened. "Wow, it appears to have two settings, I guess I should keep it on low beam." Brad marveled.

"Well, I don't think we want the flood-light setting, this isn't a Hollywood premiere night. We should take it in case we need it, but don't turn it on again as we approach the building. I think a floodlight shining through the woods might be a bit conspicuous." Matt chided.

Chapter 19

Return To The Dragon's Den

The boys exited the car and made their way along the edge of the woods, ducking as headlights illuminated the night. A lonesome dog barked in the distance as they traversed the thickets at the edge of the woods along the rural road. "Ow-oo," Brad exclaimed as a vine of briars grabbed his pants leg.

"Sh-h-h," Matt responded. Brad managed to untangle himself, and the two boys continued slowly until the woods opened to the gravel parking lot. A slight mist hung in the air, giving the lights in the parking lot a glowing halo. They ducked behind a car as laughter echoed across the lot. Three guys were raucously making their way toward the building. Brad looked up into the sky and couldn't help noticing a patch of stars through a hole in the clouds, as lightning still flickered in the distance.

Brad's mind flashed back to that first dream. He recalled the image of the ominous outline of the craft which would take people away and alter their minds, enslaving them with their selfish desires to serve the seductive evil lord of the air, Draegon. Consigning them to go through life blindly following the dictates of their own selfish desires; they would serve a master of the addictions and cravings of their bodies. *Isn't that what happens to all of us who aren't freed from the bondage of sin,* Brad thought. *We blindly follow an enemy that we don't even understand.* As Brad stared at the outline of the building, he noticed the similar wedge-shape formed by the addition of the new auditorium. The shape reminded him of the eerie battle cruiser in his dreams. His body shuddered at the revelation. He scanned the sky nervously and then laughed at himself for thinking he might actually see the pulsating lights that had seemed to initiate this great adventure. Those dreams, wild as they were, had opened his eyes to the plight of his friend, Luke. Now, life itself had suddenly taken a wild and crazy turn. Here he was, crouching at the den of a dangerous enemy, trying to rescue Luke from his clutches. Who would have thought. . .

Matt's voice arrested his imagination. "The coast is clear. They've gone inside. Let's move closer." The boys stooped and crept between the parked cars until they could see the front door. A very tall, heavily built man in a black jacket was standing outside the door smoking a cigar. The muffled frenzied sound of heavy metal music, laced with the sputtering of drums filtered through peaceful night air like the sound of a distant invading force. Matt's mind raced, trying to figure out how in the world they would be able to get into this den of craziness.

"Ok-ay-y, what do we do now?" Matt wondered.

Eyes fixed on the obstacle in front of them, Brad declared, "Lord, what we need here is a miracle." As they watched, wondering what to do, one of the massive wooden doors opened and a young woman stepped outside and spoke to the hulking attendant. Brad grabbed Matt's arm and whispered, "There's our miracle."

"That's amazing!" Matt couldn't believe it. Brittany had come out of the door and was walking in their direction.

"It's Brittany," Matt exclaimed. "What's she doing here? I thought you said she had quit working here."

"Mandy told me that she'd given her two week's notice. I guess she has another week left." Brad replied just above a whisper. "Praise God, she can find out what's going on with Luke."

Brittany stopped at a car about three spaces over from where they were hiding. They moved in that direction. "Careful. We don't want to freak her out. She might scream or something," Matt whispered. Brittany unlocked the door of her car, sat in the driver's seat, and began rummaging through a large handbag. The door still open, Matt and Brad were now close enough to get her attention.

Matt called out in a quiet voice, "Brittany."

She instantly froze. "Who's there?" She asked, clearly nervous.

"It's Matt," he called back as he crouched around the car.

"And me, Brad Johnson." She turned and leaned out of the open door toward the back of the car. Brad came into view and waved at her.

She gave a confused smile and waved back. "What are you guys doing out here?"

"We were wondering the same about you. We thought you'd quit this job," Matt responded.

"I have given my notice, but they wanted me to work through the end of the week. I really need the money, so I agreed."

"I'm sure glad you did," Brad replied with a hopeful smile. "We could use your help, if you can. Luke was abducted by some thugs tonight, and we believe they brought him here. Have you seen him?"

"Luke?" She pondered aloud, "Well, I have been working in the bar area. Wait a minute. I did see Lumas and Sammy come in through the side door and go straight into Mr. Dragon's office. They may have had someone with them, but I didn't get a good look at him. It could have been Luke, I guess. I got the idea that they didn't want any spectators."

"What time was this? Brad inquired.

"It was, maybe, twenty minutes ago."

Excited, Brad exclaimed, "It has to be him. We've got to get in there to find out."

"Are you crazy?" Brit rebuffed. "They'll never let you guys in there."

"There must be a way. What about a back entrance?" Brad asked, refusing to give up on his friend.

Brittany thought, and then, agreed, "OK—OK." She stammered nervously. "Are you sure you guys want to do this? They could kill you and say that you were breaking and entering if they catch you."

Brad looked at Matt, who had for the most part been silent, wondering if they were doing the right thing.

Matt affirmed, "I believe that God will keep us safe. We have to do something to stop all this. There are so many kids being swept up in the Dragon's wicked ways."

Brittany looked at Matt and smiled, the infatuation of their former relationship giving way to deep respect for his desire to do the right thing, even when facing great danger. After a brief pause to think, she spoke, "You remember that back door by the dumpsters, where you met Luke the last time you were here?" They nodded in unison. "Be there in ten minutes. I'll get one of the hand-stampers and meet you at the door. That way if anyone challenges you, you'll look legit. Once you're inside, you're on your own. I won't be able to help you if you get into trouble. You have to be very careful. If anyone recognizes you, it probably won't go well with you. They don't like disturbances of any kind and will throw you out in a heartbeat."

"We'll be careful," Brad assured her. Then a scary thought struck him and he asked, "Is Blane Stevens, by chance, here tonight?"

Brittany's brows furrowed a bit as she tried to remember. "I don't think I've seen him tonight, but you never know when he might show up. He's usually here."

"He's the one person who might really cause us trouble," Brad cautioned.

"You guys be careful." Brittany whispered.

"You too, Brit. And, please pray for Luke. I'm afraid he's in real danger." Brad whispered back. "He asked Jesus into his heart tonight, and I'm afraid the enemy is trying to steal him back."

"God won't let that happen, I'm sure of it. He's really been helping me lately," Brit replied and squeezed his arm. "I'll pray for him and you too." The group cautiously parted ways.

The teenage dynamic duo made their way back toward the outer edge of the parking lot, away from the lights that were nearer the building. Brittany disappeared through the front door. A gust of wind blew across their faces. Lightning flashed on the horizon and seemed to be moving closer. "I think we're in for another storm," Matt whispered.

Brad looked up, concerned, "I hope it holds off until we get inside." They entered a wooded area on the outer edge of the parking lot toward the back of the building. Matt scanned the building for surveillance cameras. Seeing none, they made their way to the dumpsters and waited. Another five minutes passed. A bright flash lit up the western sky, followed by the muffled rumbling of thunder.

"What is keeping her? I hope she didn't get into trouble or something. I hate to get her mixed up in this dangerous quest," Matt lamented, a definite feeling of concern in his voice. A few seconds later the door opened, and Brittany cautiously peered out. "There she is. Let's go." Matt carefully started toward the door, scoping out the terrain as he went. Brittany saw them and motioned with her hand for them to hurry up, obviously nervous. The boys entered a dark space which smelled of musty cloth. Brit closed the door, and the light from the street lamps in the parking lot disappeared. The room was almost pitch black. Brad clicked on the flashlight making sure to point it toward the floor. The light revealed a room obviously used for storage. Shelves stacked with boxes and electrical equipment lined the walls.

"You might want to cover that light with something. It's too bright." Brad clicked on the low beam. "That's better." She fumbled with opening the little ink pad, and proceeded to stamp the top of each of their hands. Brad glanced at the red stain on his skin. He felt a dull pain in the pit of his stomach as he recognized that he had just been marked on his hand with the image of a small red dragon. *The mark of the beast*? he wondered. All the Bible verses he had heard and read about the mark of the beast came rushing into his mind. He resisted an urge to wipe the abominable blemish off of his hand.

Matt was also staring down at the glaring symbol of the devil that marked his own hand. "It's OK. We're not in the end times yet. Besides, we are under cover for God."

Brittany studied their clothes, shaking her head. Brad's bright Carolina-blue shirt blazed even in the dim light. "That'll never do." She made her way down the center of the narrow room, past all the shelves. "How about shining that light over here so that I can see what I'm looking for?" Brad shined the narrow beam of light in the direction of her voice. "Here they are," she said, under her breath, as she began rummaging through a clothing rack full of black shirts. She pulled two of them down. "Here. Put these on. These are used by stage hands when they move props during the show. Everybody wears black in here, so these will make you less conspicuous." She handed one to each of the guys.

Brad laid the flashlight on top of some boxes so that it would shine on them, as they quickly put on the large black shirts over the ones they were wearing.

Brittany inspected them and acknowledged, "There. That's better. Just stay in the dim light and maybe you'll get away with this scheme." Brad was still trying to button the shirt when she added. "I've got to get back to work, so let me show you where to go." She walked over to a doorway and stopped. The guys followed and saw that the door led into a stairwell. At the bottom of the stairs was another door which was slightly open. Dim light filtered through the six-inch space, and illuminated the stairs enough to descend them safely. "Follow these stairs to the hallway on the other side of the door. Turn right and follow the corridor until it turns. You'll see the bathrooms on the right. A little further down are the swinging doors that lead into the auditorium. You'll have to make your way to the back of the auditorium to the far left. There is a hallway there with bathrooms on the left. Follow that hallway until it turns. Mr. Dragon's office is the third door on the right. But be careful. He has guys everywhere watching for trouble."

Matt and Brad nodded and watched as she descended the flight of about ten steps. She opened the door at the bottom of the stairwell a little further. Brit peered into the hallway for a few seconds. She turned. A pretty, reassuring smile lit up her face as she looked up to Brad and Matt who were holding onto the railing at the top of the stairs. Giving a thumbs-up, she disappeared through the doorway. The two nervously stood and watched the somber yellow glow which dimly lit the bottom of the empty stairwell for a few seconds, listening for any sound of trouble.

Matt began buttoning up the front of the black shirt Brit had given him and Brad quickly followed suit. Having a thing about looking "squared-away" as he called it, Matt tucked in the tail of the shirt. Brad credited this characteristic to Sgt. Shackleton's Army Ranger background. Brad preferred to let his tails hang out.

"I think the coast is clear. We can get started," Brad whispered to Matt.

"Are we sure we want to do this?" Matt responded.

"No, but we're committed now," Brad retorted and started toward the stairs.

Abruptly, Matt grabbed his arm. Brad turned quickly, about to say something, but noticed that Matt had a finger to his lips. Matt then put a finger behind his ear. In the background they could hear the muffled sound of music from the auditorium. The thump of the bass guitar rumbled in his chest. Listening carefully, Brad could hear it. First the metal clinking sound of a door closing, then some type of shoes or maybe boots on the concrete floor of the hallway below. As the boys listened intently, they quietly backed up into the doorway of the stairwell. Matt noticed the flashlight still burning. Quickly he clicked it off. Then he turned back watching the stairwell from the doorway. The clud, clud, clud got louder and moved ever closer to the open door. The boys were now motionless, silent. It was dark enough that they wouldn't be seen in the threshold at the top of the stairs, if only the intruder wouldn't switch on the light at the base of the stairs. Ominously the light from the hall below began to darken as the tall, dark shadow of a very large man loomed in the doorway. Hearts pounding, the guys were practically holding their breath for fear of making any sound. Brad and Matt, grasping the danger, were silently and simultaneously calling out to God to somehow intervene and make them invisible.

The oversized hand of the man dressed all in black reached inside the doorway toward the light switch, when suddenly, the jingling sound of electronic music erupted from the man's pocket. Brad couldn't help chuckling inside as he recognized the familiar tune as the theme song from the old Adam's Family TV series. The stranger stopped and turned, pulling the ringing cell phone from his trousers. He glanced at the screen. Then, he flipped it open and put it up to his ear. Hearing the deep voice of the creepy fellow Brad had come to know as Lumas, he got a very real picture in his mind: *Lurch. He could be his twin brother.* Brad held back a nervous chuckle. Apparently, the always serious man had a streak of humor buried deep down inside of him.

"Lumas here," the low voice grumbled and moved back into the hallway away from the door. There was a pause. The gruff voice with a Jersey-style accent reported, "It's quiet; no kids down here. I'm down near the backstage storage area." Another pause, then, "Sure, I'll take care of it. I'm on my way." The voice, along with the cludding of the boots, started moving back down the hall. Matt and Brad looked at each other and simultaneously exhaled in relief.

After several minutes—waiting—listening. Brad spoke softly, "I think we're in the clear." Nervously, they started down the stairs. Matt grabbed his shoulder. Brad jumped. "Don't do that!" Brad snapped, in a whisper. "What?"

"I don't know if we are doing the right thing. Maybe we should go find my dad," He whispered intensely.

Brad's mind went through the possibility. "That would take forever. What if that Lumas guy was being called to get rid of Luke. He looks like just the type to do it. We're wasting time. If you think you should try to find your dad, then maybe you should go ahead; but I'm staying to try to keep an eye on Luke," Brad replied just as intensely.

"We don't even know for sure he's here," Matt retorted. "But, I'm not leaving you alone. Crazy or not, I guess this plan is the only one we have at the moment."

Brad half smiled, nodding his head in gratitude. Matt followed Brad as they slowly and cautiously made their way to the bottom of the stairs, both wondering how they would ever find Luke without being noticed by Dragon's thugs. "Oh Lord, please guide us and loose angels around us to protect us," Matt prayed under his breath.

Brad was now peering into a gray hallway dimly lit by bare light bulbs protruding from the unpainted ceiling. As they moved down the hall the music grew steadily louder. They walked about twenty feet and the hallway turned to the left.

Matt asked, "How do we find him? We can't just waltz into Dragon's office and say, 'Hi, have you seen Luke?'"

Brad was wondering the same thing. "Maybe we can find Brit, hopefully by now she's found out something." Matt nodded. As they rounded the corner they noticed that the paint was a different color and newly applied. On the right were the rest rooms, just as Brittany had said. The music was now much louder, and the screams of electric guitars overpowered the muffled thumps of the bass. They could hear talking, then the higher-pitched tone of feminine laughter coming from behind the bathroom door. Brad noticed a partially open door, which seemed to be a closet. Motioning to Matt, the two ducked inside.

"What do we do now?" Matt asked, feeling foolish for cowering in a closet. "Look," he continued, "if we're going to make this work we can't be trying to hide every time we see someone. It just makes us look suspicious. We've got to keep going and act like we're supposed to be here."

Brad agreed and boldly opened the door, re-entering the hallway. The nervous duo started toward the sound of the music. They had taken about six steps when the bathroom door burst open. Out walked three chattering and laughing teenage girls, dressed all in black. Their unnaturally darkened hair shimmered as they passed. One, clinging to her individuality, sported bright green steaks running through shoulder-length, straight locks. The luster of silver metal piercings glinted from various parts of the faces on two of them. Brad's eyes met those of the third young lady, along with sense of uneasiness. She was slightly older, and looked very familiar to Brad. He wondered by her reaction if she knew him. Although she smiled, she looked away, and kept going. The other girls glanced, giggled, and proceeded through the double doors which led into the auditorium.

Matt whispered, "I'm glad we didn't know any of 'em." Noticing Brad's look of concern, he asked. "What? Did you know them?"

Brad bit his bottom lip and said, "I'm not sure. One of them looked so familiar. She didn't really act like she knew me, though. At least, she didn't say anything. But, I feel like I know her."

"Well, let's go in." Matt sighed and then paused, noticing that Brad was staring up above the doorway. Over the door was the twisting turning silhouette of a Dragon painted in black, surrounding the ominous, gothic script which read, "The Abyss." "Are you having second thoughts?" Matt asked his wondering partner.

"No," Brad replied emphatically. Determined to proceed, he pressed forward through the double doors, entering the world of The Dragon.

CHAPTER 20

THE SPELL OF THE DRAGON

THE ROOM WAS PACKED WITH about eight hundred young people, their arms waving with the excitement created by the performance on stage. The band was really rocking at a frenzied pitch. Trying to blend in, the boys made their way around the edge of the crowd. Overhead, a smoky haze wafted through the large room, creating a medieval feel with the flickering glow of the wall-mounted torch-type lights.

Once in the crowd, the boys turned to face the stage and were instantly mesmerized by the awesomeness of the stage set. The effect of columns, fire, and smoke gave Brad the feeling that he had stepped back in time to some ancient pagan temple. A greenish light emanated from the back of the room through the haze. It formed the shape of a giant writhing green dragon on the black, sheer backdrop behind the band. The haze gave it almost a 3-D effect. It would rise up, and slowly spread its wings, and lunge forward to display its large pointed teeth and forked tongue. This continued for a few minutes as the music intensified. With one final lunge, its mouth opened wide, and a bright light (which gave the appearance of flames) shot forth from its mouth onto the stage. At that exact moment, a series of pyrotechnics erupted on stage. Then, everything stopped. Suddenly, in the middle of the stage, as if spewed out of the dragon's mouth, a lone hooded and caped figure appeared, silhouetted by the lights and surrounded by the creeping fog. He stood with his back toward the audience, which was now going wild with applause, whistles, and screams of delight. As he stood there facing backstage, he slowly began raising both arms out from his sides (which seemed to cause the stage lights to go up) revealing a gleaming, shiny-red silk dragon sewn onto the back of his cape. It was trimmed in red sequins and had a ruby-like gemstone for an eye. As he stood there frozen for a few seconds the audience began to chant quietly: DRA-GON, DRA-GON, DRA-GON. Getting louder and louder, the entire throng was soon shouting it, and clapping at the same time.

As the crowd began to die down, a deep, professional-sounding voice announced: "The Dragon's Den is proud to present the master of the magical arts, and lord of the world of illusion. The one and only," the announcer paused for another outburst of praise from the audience and then said, in the tone of a prize fight announcer, "Th-e –e Dragon!" At which the band began a fevered pace of music. The Dragon threw off his robe and began almost dancing across the stage performing various acts of illusion making things disappear then reappear.

Dragon was still dressed totally in black. He wore the same type of button down black shirt as Matt and Brad with the exception that his had two red silk daggers sewn onto the chest area.

Finally, the energy of the music began to slow. Various youthful helpers appeared, bringing props on stage to assist in the illusions. They were both male and female, and clad in black tank tops, black military-style pants and army boots.

Brad and Matt stood there, completely engrossed in what they were seeing and the reactions of the crowd. It was apparent that this man had total control of this group of young people, including Brad and Matt who had utterly forgotten why they were there. In a few moments, the music began to soften, and The Dragon stepped forward and addressed the audience. Motioning with his hands for them to quiet, he called for a volunteer from the audience. Hands shot up all across the room. He chose an attractive, giggly, blond teenage girl who seemed to be just dying to get on stage. He asked her name, and she responded, "Sandra Morrison."

A light bulb went on in Brad's head jolting him out of his trance-like fixation on the performance. *Sandie,* he thought. The older girl he had seen coming out of the bathroom earlier was Sandie Hunter, Luke's sister. *What is she doing in a place like this? And, why was she made up like that?* He wondered. Brad knew she never went in for this kind of stuff. Mandy had told him she had become a believer in Christ. *Had the seed withered away like in the parable Jesus told in Matthew about the seed which fell on stony ground?* Instantly, Brad responded, arguing with himself, *but you're here. Maybe she's doing the same thing, trying to find her brother.* She had always been a bit protective of him and was not happy at all with his joining this "crazy band full of crack heads," as she called it. Brad began scanning the room, hoping to get a glimpse of her.

Matt, noticing Brad's fidgeting, asked, "Who are you looking for?"

"Sandie Hunter!" Brad said in a whisper.

Matt's brow wrinkled as he pondered the name. "Luke's sister?" he whispered back.

"Yeah, she was one of the girls who came out of the bathroom." About that time, some strange music began flowing from the speakers on stage. Dragon announced he was now attempting, "to put this young lady into a hypnotic state which would allow her to do amazing things." Raising his hands, he quieted everyone again. Reassuring, soothing words poured from his mouth: calming her—controlling—until finally she was standing perfectly still, repeating only what he told her to repeat. "You will feel nothing," he spoke to her gently. Then, he had her lie down, face, up on the floor. "You are as stiff as a board. You are a wooden board."

The Dragon motioned, and three male assistants brought out three wooden chairs and placed them in a row across the stage in front of her. About eighteen inches apart, the seats all faced stage right. The three helpers, one of whom Brad immediately recognized, moved behind the motionless young girl. Blane Stevens, Brad's antagonist at school and the one person Brad knew would likely cause them trouble, stood smiling in the center. A tinge of nervousness shook Brad's body. Then he realized that there was no way that Blane could possibly see them through the blinding stage lighting. Nevertheless, they would need to watch out for him later.

The young girl had become as stiff as a board, literally. The trio of bare-armed young men scooped her up, one at her feet, one at her mid section and the third holding her head. To everyone's amazement they laid her, facing up, on the tops of the backs of the three chairs lined up in front of them. "Man, that looks painful," a thin kid with a buzz cut, standing next to Brad, marveled.

Brad nodded in agreement. "How could she stand that?" Brad asked. He looked at Matt, who just shook his head and shrugged, equally dumbfounded by what he saw. As the three helpers stepped back and stood, arms folded, The Dragon came up behind the girl who was precariously balanced on the backs of the chairs. Waving one hand through the air, and slowly bringing it up to his lips, the murmurings of the crowd died down. With a sly smile, and a quick motion, he tipped the middle chair back and slid it out from under the young girl. Through the gasps of the stunned audience, she remained perfectly still, straight as the board she was supposed to be. She was now held up solely by the backs of the two wooden chairs under her, one at her shoulder blades, and the other at her calves near her heels. Brad looked at Matt who returned a look of total astonishment.

With a theatrical flair, Dragon handed the chair to Blane, the middle helper who then moved off-stage. Next, The Dragon began whirling his hands over and then under the girl's stiff body, as the canned orchestral music, which reminded Brad of "Darth Vader's March," bellowed from the speakers. Dragon whirled and moved in time with the music, creating an interpretive dance akin to a light saber battle. He ended up at the feet of the young girl, who was still stretched across the two chair backs. The booming music in full surround sound, reached a crescendo and then abruptly stopped. In utter silence, with every eye totally focused on him and before anyone could take a breath, he snatched the chair from under the feet of the girl, leaving most of her body suspended in mid air. Her only visible means of support was the chair under her shoulder blades. After a brief pause, the gasps of the stunned crowd turned to applause and cheers, as The Dragon made his way to the front of the stage, and bowed. After a few seconds, with a devilish smile, he held a finger to his lips. The crowd quieted, and the music started up. Again the dark figure began whirling his hands above and beneath the girl's motionless body.

"I can understand why he has such a following," Matt leaned over and whispered in Brad's ear. "That is pretty amazing."

"How can he do it? Do you think it‘s demonic?" Brad whispered back.

"They don't call it the 'black arts' for nothing," Matt speculated.

With the music coming to another pause, The Dragon was now standing at the girl's head. He looked down at her and caressed her hair as if it were slightly out of place. Playfully, he stepped back and looked out into the audience as if to ask, "What next?" Placing both hands on the seat of the chair which was facing him, once again he looked into the audience, smiled and waited. The crowd began to clap, and cheer. Next, a chant started: "DRA-GON, DRA-GON, DRA-GON." Dragon straightened up, facing the audience and struck a pose of meditation. Placing his finger tips together to form a triangle in front of his chest, he closed his eyes, as if summoning all the power at his disposal. The crowd quieted. He turned suddenly, raising his hands above his head with a flourish. Then, reaching down, he grasped the seat of the last chair, and tipped it backwards. He slowly pulled it from under the girl's neck. She was now suspended in mid-air. The crowd went wild, cheering as he bowed before them. He bowed again as the three young men ran back on stage, stopping side-by-side behind the girl who appeared to be floating in mid air. The three held out their arms beneath her. The Dragon turned, held up his arms, then said something which Brad couldn't understand, and clapped his hands. The weight of the stunned girl dropped into the arms of the three strong assistants. Lowering her feet to the floor, the young girl instantly giggled and looked around in astonishment, wondering what was going on.

As she was helped off the stage, The Dragon started speaking to the crowd, "If you want to experience absolute peace in your life, you should focus on the light and throw off all inhibitions and trappings of this world."

Brad whispered to Matt, "Wow, sounds like he's going to preach the gospel."

"Hardly," Matt replied in disgust.

"If you would be free," Dragon continued, "focus on the light." He raised his hands over his head where a bright light had formed over him. As it dimmed Brad noticed that the image of the light had once again formed the shape of a Dragon's head which seemed to be pulsating, growing larger, and then shrinking in rapid motions. Brad noticed that the crowd was gazing at it in absolute silence.

Matt turned to Brad, "Don't look at it. Let's bow and pray."

Brad lowered his head, focusing on Jesus. "Lord, protect us from this evil influence. Keep us safe, and help us find Luke."

Brad could hear the soothing words coming from the speakers around the stage. "You will see exactly what I speak, believe all that I say and act according to my words; for what I say is truth to you."

Brad could hardly believe his ears. Dragon was attempting to hypnotize everyone in the room at one time. *Is that possible?* He wondered.

"Now, awake and believe," he commanded, as he clapped his hands and continued to clap as the band now began to rock. The entire crowd was now cheering and clapping as if nothing had happened, oblivious to the spell that had been cast. The Dragon strutted across the stage and danced around with all of the bravado of some kind of rock star.

As the band continued to play, six assistants appeared from the wings with wooden poles about six feet long, in their hands. Legs spread apart; they stood three on each side of The Dragon, holding the staffs in front of them. The music of the Slammers band stopped, and The Dragon remained center stage with his head down. Misty clouds began to waft upward on each side of him from the rear of the stage. The music changed. A definite middle-eastern tone floated through the air.

"In the great days of old," Dragon began. "When the magicians were called before Pharaoh to perform great feats of the magical arts, to show the power of their gods, they would call on the powers of the great unknown to demonstrate the wonders of a different world. Today, you, too, can witness these amazing wonders." Dragon then took a staff from the hand of the assistant next to him and laid it on the ground and moved back. "Behold the powers of the great unknown, as the staff becomes. . . . . . the serpent."

Immediately, everyone in the front row began to scream and draw back. Dragon began to take each rod from the hands of the helpers, and toss them on the stage floor. Each time the response was wild elation mingled with an awesome fear from the crowd. Brad and Matt looked at each other in amazement, as they watched the stage and the reaction from the crowd. Although Matt and Brad saw nothing but black poles lying on the stage floor, the crowd obviously saw something entirely different. Brad turned to the awestruck kid standing next to him, "What's going on? What do you see?" he asked curiously.

"Can't you see the snakes? There," he pointed. "It's a python and there—that looks like a cobra—and a rattlesnake. Oh, no—It looks like they are coming into the audience." The entire front rows were now trying to move back.

Dragon calmed them, "Fear not, my pets will not harm you." He motioned, and the assistants moved forward and each picked up one of the poles. Gradually, the crowd settled down.

"Did you see that?" the kid next to Brad pointed again. Brad shook his head in the negative. "Boy, you must need some serious glasses or something. All the snakes— when they picked them up, they turned back into staffs again."

"Wow, really?" Brad feigned excitement. Turning to Matt who was still praying under his breath, astounded at the ridiculous spectacle of deception, Brad declared, "This is way too weird."

"We need to find Luke and get out of this hell hole." Matt responded with a frown.

The band was again playing, and Dragon was now taking very theatrical bows. The guys began making their way through the crowd, moving again toward the rear of the room away from the stage. Brad could occasionally hear another strange noise, a deep rumble coming from outside. He realized that the storm which was approaching when they came in, must be upon them; although it was hardly noticeable over the cacophony of the show. Matt and Brad waded sideways through the crowd across the room, down the row of chairs toward the aisle next to the wall. Moving toward the back of the room, they continued slowly, up the slight incline of the auditorium. They pushed past people standing in the aisle, some moving with the beat of the music, some laughing and others in the la-la land of some type of high.

Suddenly, Brad was surprised to find himself almost face-to-face with someone who obviously knew him. The young woman whom he had seen coming out of the bathroom was now standing right in front of him. "Sandie, is that you?" Brad asked with a puzzled look. She looked at him gravely and motioned for them to follow her. They weaved through the crowd and came to the back of the auditorium. When they arrived at a set of double doors, Sandie held one open and glanced around. All eyes were still glued to the antics on stage. They entered a short, dimly lit hallway with bathroom doors on each side. When the door closed behind them, it was quiet enough for conversation. They could keep an eye on the auditorium through the small, square, shoulder height, windows in the doors.

"You guys are about the last two I would have expected to see in this place," She announced with sort of a half smile, half frown.

"I was just thinking the same about you," Brad said, his eyes narrowing as he thought. Matt, who had not yet recognized her, stood there wondering what this was all about. Brad could see the confusion in his eyes, "Matt, don't you know who she is?"

Sandie responded in Matt's defense, "Brad, it has been several years since he's seen me and, I do look a little different with this black mop." She fingered her once blond hair.

"Man, you look so different," Matt finally stated, still unsure. The truth is that he'd only seen her a few times when he was younger. She was several years older than Matt and had graduated high school two years earlier.

"Yeah, it's me," she confirmed, finally breaking into a nervous smile.

Matt smiled back. "We're here looking for your brother," he said with concern.

"We're afraid he's in some serious trouble," Brad added.

"I know he's in trouble," she agreed, her eyes welling up. "He hasn't been home in a week, and my family is so worried about him. This is the second time I've come here trying to find him. I saw them escort him in earlier and take him into a room off the bar area."

"You shouldn't be here alone. This place is dangerous," Matt asserted.

"Well, I felt I had to do something, and try to find out why he was so drawn to this place. Besides," she paused, "I'm not here alone."

"Really, who else is here with you?" Matt asked excitedly.

"Jesus," she stated confidently.

The guys' mouths gaped open as they realized the word she had just uttered. A smile spread across their faces at her faith.

"My sister, Mandy, told me that she'd heard you had become a Christian," Brad affirmed, beaming at her.

She smiled and nodded, "It happened about a year ago. A friend at school, involved with Campus Crusade, began sharing with me what Jesus had done in her life. He has truly changed my life, and now I pray He will change Luke's."

"He will," Brad declared, full of faith. "If we can find him and get him out of this place." All at once the double doors burst open. A couple of young girls bustled past them into the rest room, glancing back at the trio standing in the hallway with suspicious curiosity.

"I think we'd better get about the business at hand. I'm afraid we're attracting attention," Matt advised, trying not to stare through the windows in the doors.

"Sandie, when we get out of this, we'd love to hear all about how Jesus changed your life."

"That would be great. Right now, I'm going to keep a watch out for Luke," she said with determination.

"Promise me that you will just watch and let us know if you see him. We'll take it from there," Brad replied.

"What will you do if you find him?"

"I don't know, but we'll think of something, or rather, the Holy Spirit will. If you see that we're in trouble, get out of here and phone the police. Ask for my dad, Sgt. Shackleton. Tell him where we are and he'll know what to do."

"OK," she nodded, just as the door burst open again, and a dark-haired teenage boy shuffled past them.

Sandie exited the hallway. Waiting about thirty seconds, in order not to be seen with her, the boys moved back out into the crowd. Brad and Matt had decided to check out the hallway behind the bar area. They were moving in that direction when they heard another eruption of applause and turned to see The Dragon on stage taking another grand bow. Abruptly, a different voice boomed from the stage, this one familiar. The obviously patronizing, smooth tones sent chills down Brad's spine. In the heart of the south, the strong Bronx-style accent was easily recognizable as that of none other than Sammy Dornberg. "Wasn't that truly amazing? Give it up for the one and only, The Amazing Dragon, and his incredible talent in the world of the magical arts," Sammy boasted, as he walked out onto the corner of the stage. Cheers and applause again erupted from the fawning crowd. "And, now we have a very special treat for all you committed faithful, who have braved this stormy night. Back from his brief vacation, our own incredible master of the tom-toms: give it up for the talented Luke Hunter."

Brad and Matt did a double-take and immediately began to make their way around the outside aisle of the auditorium toward the stage area. Moving up to the second row, Brad watched the stage and saw a glassy-eyed Luke step out onto the floor from the right, into the glaring spot light. As the audience erupted again with wild enthusiasm, Luke appeared to be oblivious to them, as he took a few steps across the stage. The Dragon stood stage right, applauding. Luke seemed to have his eyes fixed on Dragon, who was smiling and nodding with an almost fatherly expression of warmth that turned Brad's stomach. Matt and Brad were now right at the front row, both wondering what, if anything, they should do. Brad thought, *surely Luke isn't just going to return to all of this after his emotional response to Jesus earlier in the evening. Is he like the seed in Jesus' parable of the sower, who heard and received the truth, but immediately the enemy came and took it away.* Brad felt a pain in his heart, as disappointment began to overtake him.

Meanwhile, Luke, who was still watching Dragon, pulled his hand out of his pocket. Brad noticed that Luke held something shiny in it. Luke looked down at it, then back up at The Dragon. That's when Brad realized what it was, a handgun. "Where in the world did he get that?" Brad muttered, as thoughts raced through his mind.

Matt grabbed Brad's shoulder and exclaimed in his ear, "Luke's got a gun! What's he doing with a gun? Do you think it's part of an act?"

The audience had now noticed the gun and Luke's somber, confused expression. Murmuring spread through the crowd like a roaring wave as people's curiosity got the best of them. Sammy Dornberg, still on stage, sensed the awkwardness of the moment. Apparently not seeing the gun, he turned to the crowd and asked, "Who in here would like to hear Luke jam tonight?" The confused crowd began a spattering of applause, with a few catcalls and whistles intermingled. Luke, however, just stood there looking at Sammy. Luke's facial expression started with fear, and then turned to anger. Brad knew that Luke seemed to distrust Sammy. Brad believed that it was Sammy who had roughed Luke up over a week ago, leaving him battered and bruised.

Slowly, Luke raised the gleaming weapon and pointed it at Sammy, who was now facing the audience. The crowd grew totally silent, followed by murmurs and whispers. Brad's heart was pounding so hard, it was almost deafening.

"I know who you are, you alien demon. You won't take me," Luke cried, eyes wild with fear. Holding the pistol with both hands, he stood shaking, sweat beading on his face.

"What is he doing?" Matt whispered intensely in Brad's ear.

Sammy now turned and faced his accuser, a look of confusion turned to fear, as he noticed Dragon's eyes trained on them both. Sammy slowly backed up, and said calmly, "Luke, it's me, your buddy Sammy," clearly trying to lighten the situation. Brad was amazed that Dragon was doing nothing to stop this, but rather, seemed to have a devious smirk on his face. It was as if Dragon really wanted Luke to shoot Sammy Dornberg.

Brad turned to Matt and grabbed his hand, "We've got to pray." Matt followed his lead and bowed his head. Brad began, "No, Satan. In the name of Jesus Christ, you may not have Luke. He has asked Jesus to change his life, and I say that you have no authority over him." Brad's voice got louder and more fervent, shouting now to the point that all of those around him were listening. Even Dragon turned to see what was going on.

Matt was shouting too, "Yes, Lord Jesus. Holy Spirit, break the power of the enemy and loose Luke from his grip." Realizing that everyone was staring, Brad looked up on stage and saw Luke standing there looking at them. Luke blinked a couple of times, and then looked down at the gun with an expression of complete astonishment. His eyes appeared totally different now. It was as if he had been freed from some drug-induced hallucination and just had come to his senses. His whole body started shaking as he stood before this sea of gawking faces, who were trying to understand what they were witnessing. Luke gazed at the gun he was holding, and then back up at the crowd. As white as a sheet, he looked as if he could collapse at any moment. Finally, he slowly shook his head and laid the gun on the floor. Dragon's eyes flashed angrily, and he lunged across the stage toward Luke.

Suddenly, there was a loud CR-A-A-C-K, along with the brightest light Brad had ever seen that flashed right through the room and across the stage. It was followed by a deafening boom of thunder that shook the entire building. Stage lights flickered as sparks flew from the top of the silver metal framework surrounding the stage, and showered down onto the stage. At the same time, an electrical panel near the stage blew, sending forth another blaze of sparks. The room was plunged into blackness, as the circuit breakers cut the electricity. Everyone in the room immediately crouched on the floor.

Abruptly, a loud "POP-POP," with corresponding flashes from the stage broke the murmur of the crowd. It was followed by a cry and a deep groan. A second later, the emergency lights flickered on. In the dim light that filtered onto the stage, Brad could see Dragon holding Luke. The gun was still on the floor, but in a different place right next to Luke who was trying to free himself from Dragon's grasp. Then Brad noticed that Sammy was on his knees, holding his stomach. "I think Sammy's been shot," Brad informed Matt, as they stood up to get a better look. Sammy wobbled and then collapsed onto the floor with a thud. Screams erupted from some of the girls near the front, as blood could be seen in a pool on the stage floor. Dragon released Luke and stood up facing the crowd, now deathly silent except for an occasional whimper.

"Everyone, remain calm. It appears that Luke has shot Mr. Dornberg. We need for everyone to calmly exit the building," Dragon announced, still holding Luke by the arm. Ushers began moving down the aisles, trying to calm the restless group. There were now cries of "FIRE," and smoke appeared to be thickening. A small flame seemed to be growing near the blown control panel and young people were now on the verge of panic as they began to fear for their lives.

Chapter 21

Taken Captive By The Enemy

An usher with a bull horn was now shouting, "Please remain calm. Move to the nearest exit!" Emergency doors on all sides of the building were opened, revealing the torrent going on outside, as the thunderstorm raged. Luke struggled to get free of the Dragon's hold.

Matt and Brad jumped onto the stage. "Let him go, Dragon," Brad insisted.

"This boy is a killer. Who are you to demand that I let him go? Didn't you see what he did?" Dragon retorted, glaring at them.

"We're not under your spell Dragon. Luke didn't have the gun. Everyone saw Luke put the gun down. He didn't shoot Sammy," Matt chimed in.

Sammy! Brad remembered. *He's been shot!* Brad walked quickly over to Sammy who was crumpled on the floor groaning in pain. Brad bent over him, a pool of blood slowly spreading from his waist. "He needs help. Don't you even care? Someone call a paramedic!"

Several of Dragon's men appeared on stage. Dragon whispered something to one of them, who turned and looked at the boys. The thug, Lumas from the close encounter earlier in the hallway, spoke, "You boys need to come with me."

"We're not going anywhere without Luke," Brad asserted.

Luke, who was kneeling with his hands over his face, finally spoke, "You stay away from them, Lumas."

Lumas scowled at Luke, as if to say, *You'll regret that, boy.*

"Luke, my friend," Dragon responded soothingly, "I don't believe that you're in any position to demand anything. My security people here will hold you, all of you, until the police arrive to arrest you for attempted murder." He bent down and with a black glove on his hand, picked up the tainted firearm.

"Someone needs to call an ambulance for Sammy. Don't you even care if he dies?" Brad repeated.

Dragon shook his head with a frown. "It has already been taken care of. I have the utmost concern for my business partner and friend." A weak groan emanated from Sammy, who was now being attended to by one of the men.

Yeah, I bet, Brad thought, as he kept his gaze fixed on the cold, dark eyes, and menacing grin of the face of utter deception. One of Dragon's men came over to the stage area with a fire extinguisher and sprayed the area of the wall where the electrical outlets were beginning to burn the wall. When he finished, he opened a door which had a plaque on it that read: "Power Room, Authorized Personnel Only." When he did, smoke poured out of the top of the door, which he quickly shut and moved back. "I hope somebody has called the fire department. This place is on fire."

Most of the audience had now departed into the night, and were sitting in a traffic jam trying to leave the filled-to-capacity parking lot. Lumas ordered Matt and Brad off the stage. They moved past the still groaning Sammy Dornburg. As they passed, Brad looked down into his pale face. Beads of sweat were trickling from his forehead down to his cheeks. Sammy's eyes opened briefly and met Brad's. Brad had never seen such fear and anguish on anyone's face. It was as if he knew he was going to die, and that no one cared.

Brad's heart went out to him, and he knelt down, "Sammy, it doesn't matter what you've done. Jesus can save you and change you. Just cry out to Him. He will forgive you. I'll be praying for you." Sammy looked at him, totally silent, fear transformed to complete astonishment, as if he had never heard anything like that. But before he could utter another word, Brad felt something cold and hard strike the side of his face followed by a searing hot pain. As he reeled backward onto the floor, he saw the bottom of Dragon's black boot ready to strike again.

Dragon stood over him enraged, "You stay away from him with those phony, pie-in-the-sky lies."

Matt, reacted, lunging forward at Dragon, and almost had him, when a huge arm from another of Dragon's men, clothes-lined him. Holding Matt with one arm around the neck, he then brought Matt's arm around and up his back in a way that caused Matt's face to grimace in pain. The pain sent him to his knees. Determined not to cry out, Matt was clinching his teeth so tightly that his face literally twitched. The burly man then grabbed Matt's shirt by the shoulder, picked him up off the floor and growled, "Now, shut up and move!"

Brad squinted as the bright beam of a flashlight was now directed at his face. His head was still ringing from the blow of the hard black boot, and he could feel warm blood again flowing from the reopened wound he had suffered earlier.

"What'll we do wid-em, boss?"

"Take them to Sammy's office for now," Dragon ordered. Then, looking up at the thickening smoke on the ceiling, Dragon advised. "On second thought, we better get out of here. Just take 'em out to the Hummer for now, and sit tight until I call you." The big man grabbed Brad's shoulder and lifted him to his feet. Brad dizzily stepped forward. As he did, he caught a glance of Luke; his face torn between a look of shame, for having gotten mixed up with these people, and anger, at the treatment of perhaps his only true friends.

"Get going, punk," Lumas' gruff voice bellowed.

Luke sat there, almost delirious. "You can't make me go. I've got proof that'll send you all up for years, unless you let us go right now."

Lumas looked him with a smug expression. "Kid, you don't have nothing that will hurt me. But I've got something that will hurt you, or these buddies of yours. I bet I can make a case for breaking and entering charges against them." He reached inside his black jacket and pulled out a cold, black handgun, and motioned with it in the direction he wanted them to go. Dragon grabbed Luke by his hair and pulled him up. As Luke started to stand, Dragon lifted one foot and planted his boot in Luke's back, thrusting forward, pushing him across the stage. Luke stumbled into a couple of metal chairs, landing face first on the stage floor. Brad never wanted to punch someone in the face so badly in his life, but his body would not cooperate. All he could do was stagger over and help Luke down the steps of the stage. Brad and Matt took hold of Luke's arms and helped him walk.

Another of Dragon's associates followed them off the stage. But Dragon stopped him, and ordered, "Frankie, come help us with Sammy. Lumas, you deal with these intruders." The ogre motioned for the boys to move. Matt was in the lead; then Brad, and Luke who were followed by their captor, Lumas. They continued up the slight incline of the auditorium until they reached the hallway.

"Turn left," Lumas ordered.

Following his direction, the reluctant group started through the office area, behind the now deserted bar. Walking slowly through the dark hallway, the flashlight Lumas was holding behind them cast huge eerie shadows on the bare, gray walls ahead. At the end of the hall, a red exit sign glowed, obviously powered by the emergency lighting system. Walking past an open door of one of the offices, Brad sensed movement inside, but kept on going. Behind him, Luke slowed, becoming totally disoriented. His whole body began to shake violently as he stumbled onto the hard, tile floor. Brad and Matt turned to see Luke suffering from what appeared to be a seizure.

"What have you guys done to him?" Brad accused Lumas.

"Don't worry, the punk will live." He laughed and added sarcastically, "Maybe." He motioned, using the dark weapon as a pointer. "Keep going!" Lumas sneered. As he bent down to again yank Luke up, Brad was startled by a thin figure darting out of the office door right behind Lumas, a large cylinder shaped object in his hands raised above his head. With a loud DON-N-G, the obviously metal object made sharp contact with the back of Lumas' thick skull. Brad could almost see the stars encircling his head like a cartoon character. Amazingly, Lumas reared up and turned toward the brazen figure who promptly gonged him again, right in the forehead, this time sending the huge man back and into the wall.

The gun went flying from his hand, and Matt was quick to retrieve it. His father's training and years of hunting had schooled Matt in the proper use of a firearm, but he had never been faced with the prospect of training a gun on a man before. *How could I pull the trigger on a human being, one made in God's own image?* Matt's thoughts raced, and he decided he would aim for a leg if the need arose. Thankfully, Lumas didn't get up. He was out cold.

Brad scooped up the flashlight, which had fallen from Lumas' hand and pointed it up to the mysterious attacker. Peering from behind a bright red fire extinguisher was a determined, wide-eyed face. "Sandie?" Brad exclaimed, astounded by the brass and boldness of this young woman.

"You better lay there if you know what's good for you," she threatened the fallen giant as she again reared back her unusual weapon.

"Where'd you learn to handle that thing like that?" Matt asked in amazement.

"I guess those ladies' defense classes finally paid off." She replied. Then, seeing Luke rocking on the floor, she put down the extinguisher and bent down to help her little brother. "Lukey," she consoled quietly, "Are you OK?" He didn't respond. "H-he's shaking," she stammered, looking up at Brad. Matt shined the light down onto Luke's face. "What's the matter with him?" Sandie cried. Luke's eyes where rolling back in his head, revealing only the whites.

"He's going into some sort of shock," Matt exclaimed. They could hear the muffled sounds of sirens in the distance. "We've got to get him outside. I'm sure there will be paramedics along with the fire crew." Matt said, handing Brad the flashlight. Then, he scooped up the limp body and headed toward the door.

Without warning, two dark shapes appeared, looming in the hallway in front of them. Matt stopped dead in his tracks and stared at the figures. A deathly quiet filled the hallway as they all seemed to hold their collective breath. Matt could feel Luke twitch and convulse occasionally in his arms. Finally, emotionally spent, he shouted, "Get out of the way. This boy may die if we don't get him to a doctor."

A familiar, comforting voice spoke, "Matt, is that you?" A flashlight shone in his face.

"Dad?" Matt's voice quivered in disbelief.

"It's me, son. Are you all right?"

"Yes, sir but Luke's in some type of shock. We think that it may be drug-related."

"Bring him this way." Sgt. Shackleton turned and opened the door behind him, at the same time raising a walkie-talkie to his mouth giving directions: "We need a paramedic at the south side of the building."

As the group made their way out into the fresh air, Brad realized how smoky it had been in there. It was no longer raining, although lightning flashed in the distance, and the thunder rumbled. The winds had died down, but water from the torrent stood in deep puddles and still ran in the gutters. They followed the men around toward the front of the building. A sea of red and blue flashing lights, from a half dozen emergency vehicles, lit up the darkness. Several men came running over with a stretcher and helped Matt lay Luke's still body on the stretcher. The men began to work on him right there, pulling equipment out and checking vital signs. Brad and Matt stood there for a minute watching, praying. Sgt. Shackleton, who continued giving directions on his walkie-talkie, came over and placed his arm around his son. Finally, one of the men turned to the group huddled around them and asked, "Anyone know what this kid has been taking?"

Brad spoke up, "We don't, but you might ask Mr. Dragon. We think they might have drugged him."

"Will he be all right?" A very emotional Sandie asked.

"We think so, Miss, but we need to get him to the emergency room and find out what he's on. His heart rate is quite elevated, and he appears to be having some type of allergic reaction." An ambulance pulled up close to them. The men transferred Luke to another stretcher on wheels.

A loud, irate voice erupted from behind the group. "I want those boys arrested," the dark cloaked figured stormed, addressing the officer.

"What seems to be the problem, Mr. Dragon?" Sgt. Shackleton responded in a very professional manner.

Dragon turned and studied the man who was dressed in plain clothes. Realizing who Sgt. Shackleton was, he took on a more subdued tone. "I have reason to believe that these two boys were trespassing on my property and may have been involved in starting the fire. They may also have been accomplices in a shooting."

Brad couldn't believe what he was hearing. "You are insane!" he blurted out, before he realized it.

"Hold on just a minute," Sgt. Shackleton intervened. "These are some very serious charges. Are you saying that you saw one of these boys shoot someone?"

"The whole audience saw the boy pull out a gun on stage and threaten my partner."

Sgt. Shackleton was astounded. "Really? Who was it that you saw pull a gun, Mr. Dragon?"

"It was Luke Hunter, a boy whom I had given a chance in our band and tried to help. But, I guess some kids are just beyond help."

Brad felt sick in his stomach at the drivel Dragon was spewing. "That's a lie. Luke never shot anyone. He put the gun down. It wasn't even in his hands when the lights went out." Brad shouted. He was livid at the ridiculous accusations.

Feeling a hand on his shoulder, Brad turned as Matt leaned over and whispered, "Be cool, dude. Let Dad handle it."

Brad began to realize that his emotions were getting the best of him. From behind him, he heard a groan, and some slurred words.

"Oh, Luke!" Sandie cried, responding to her brother's distress.

Dragon, hearing Luke's name, quickly followed the groans over to the stretcher. "That's him. He's the one, officer. We all saw this boy pointing a gun at my partner, Sammy. The next thing we knew, Sammy was shot." Luke was now more conscious and began to squirm nervously. Dragon's voice seemed to have a troubling effect on him.

"Well, Mr. Dragon, I assure you that there will be a full investigation," Sgt. Shackleton interjected. "By the way, where were you, when the lights went out?"

Dragon turned, and glared at Matt's dad. "I'm not the one under investigation here, that boy is."

"I'll be the judge of that," Sgt. Shackleton stated calmly.

It was as if Luke had suddenly awakened into a state of total confusion. Brad noticed that he was trying to sit up as if he wanted to get off of the stretcher. Sandie, seeing Luke's struggle, moved closer to him. Brad followed. Luke was wild-eyed, frantic and trying to say something. "I've— got to—find it." Two paramedics who were attempting to move him into the ambulance tried to get him to lie back down but Luke sluggishly resisted them.

"It's all right, Luke," Sandie whispered, trying to comfort him. "These men are just trying to help you."

Luke's eyes finally caught sight of who was speaking. He stopped momentarily, trying to figure out how he knew this person. Tears formed in his eyes, and it was apparent he was fighting for reality. Luke studied Brad's face and then glanced back at Sandie. With a confused look, he stammered, "San—die?" His speech was thick and slow. He blinked hard a couple of times, trying to focus. Looking back at Brad, "Br-ad!" he said more clearly. "Brad—where is it? Do you have it?" he asked intensely.

Brad, somewhat startled at his dramatic turn-around, tried to calm him. "Luke, it's OK,"

"All right, son. We need for you to lay back down," one of the men insisted.

"No!— No!" Luke was almost shouting, glaring at Brad. "You have to find it, Brad!" The men tried to force Luke to lie back, attempting to restrain him.

"Don't hurt him." Sandie pleaded, overcome by her little brother's distress.

Brad put his arm on her shoulder, trying to comfort her, at the same time keeping his eyes on Luke, who was focused intensely on him. Finally, Brad leaned over to him. "Luke, I will find it for you, but what are you looking for?"

Luke stopped, as if in deep thought for a second, as if trying to pull it from his memory. Then, in exhaustion whispered, "The light—I need it."

The light, Brad wondered? *Is he crying out for Jesus?*

Then Luke repeated, "You must get it. Please! What happened to it?" Luke sat up again, with one foot hanging off the stretcher, trying to overpower the attendants. It took one of these full-grown men to hold his small, thin frame onto the stretcher. Quickly, the other man got a syringe into Luke's thigh. Within a minute, Luke was calmer. He stopped struggling, and his eyelids began to get heavy. One last time, he looked up at Brad, breathing heavily and repeated, "The light—B-Brad—in the light."

Brad nodded, wondering what in the world Luke could be talking about, "You rest, Luke. It'll be OK." Luke closed his eyes, nodding slowly, peacefully, as he drifted off into the la-la-land of the sedative. Brad held on to Sandie and prayed for Luke and then for Sandie, whose face was streaked with mascara. The men loaded the stretcher into the ambulance and the doors were closed.

Brad spoke to the attendant, "Sir, this is Luke's sister, Sandra. Are you taking him to the emergency room?"

"Yes. Can you notify your parents so that they can meet us there?" Sandie nodded her head in agreement and started walking away. Brad followed her over to her car.

"Sandie, are you all right?" Brad asked, responding to her continued distress.

She wiped her eyes. "Yes, I know I look terrible, but I'm just so concerned about Lukey. I hope he can kick whatever he's been on."

Brad nodded in agreement. "I really believe that he will. He has asked Jesus to help him, and what is impossible for a person to do on his own is totally possible with Jesus."

Sandie's eyes brightened but looked confused, "What do you mean?"

Brad beamed and explained excitedly, "Sandie, Luke repented of his sin and asked Jesus to come into his heart earlier this evening, before all this happened.

"Really?" she wondered, wiping away fresh tears. "Mom and I have been praying so hard for him. Oh! I've got to call them and let them know what's going on." She unlocked the car door reached inside pulling a cell phone out of a handbag and began pressing buttons.

Parents! Brad thought as he looked down at his watch. *It's 10:40. They're surely home by now, he thought. I'd better call them and let them know where I am.* "Sandie, do you think I can use your phone to call my parents when you're done?"

"Oh, sure." She smiled slightly. Brad could see that her despair had given way to hope. *Jesus makes all the difference,* he thought to himself.

"Bra-ad!"

Brad turned to see who was yelling across the parking lot. Brad strained and could see someone waving a hand, and running toward him, in the glow of the parking lot lights. As the young fellow got closer, he realized it was Bart. *What's he doing out here at this time of the night?* Brad wondered. "Bart, what's going on, man." Brad asked as he held out his fist to his new friend.

"Hey, man. I saw Matt over there, and he said you were out here. He filled me in on your wild night."

"Yeah, it was pretty crazy. But what are you doing way out here?"

"Oh, I'm involved with the Scout Rescue Explorers and came out on call with the fire department. We come to learn and help out with support jobs."

"That's cool." Brad replied.

Sandie ended her phone call, wiped a tear from her eye and handed the phone to Brad. "I didn't get an answer. I left her a message for her to call me as soon as she could."

"Sandie, this is Bart. Bart, this is Luke's sister, Sandie."

Bart smiled shyly, "It's good to meet you, Sandie." She smiled back politely and greeted him.

Brad took the phone and called home. His mom answered, and he explained the situation. "Mom, I know it's late but tomorrow is Saturday, and I'd like to go to the hospital with Matt and check on Luke before I come home. Is that OK?"

"I think that would be great, but try not to be too late," she responded in her wonderfully comforting way. "And son, we will be praying for Luke."

He thanked her. "Good night, Mom. I love you." He closed the phone and turned to Sandie who was looking for her car keys. "Will you be all right?" Brad asked, concerned about her driving alone.

"Oh, yes. I'm sure Mom and Dad will meet me at the hospital. I'll be fine."

"O-Ok," Brad affirmed, hesitantly, not feeling right about her going alone. "Well, we'll see you as soon as we can get there," Brad assured her.

Sandie turned and began to search for her keys in her purse. "What did I do with those keys? I just had them," she muttered in frustration. At that time her cell phone rang. She stopped looking for her keys and answered the call. "Hi, Mom," she smiled and gave a little wave to the boys as they left.

Brad and Bart walked back to the crowd of rescue workers and investigators. Bart leaned over and spoke softly. "Brad, it shouldn't be long before we can leave, but the police would like to ask you a few questions about what happened here, since there was a shooting." He paused and studied Brad's head. "Man, I think you should see a paramedic. Do you know you have a glob of dried blood on the side of your head?" Brad's hand instantly went up to the side of his head and wiped the stain.

Matt and his father were coming out of the front door, now roped off with yellow caution tape. The fire men were in the mopping-up phase and busy putting equipment away. "Oh man," Bart declared excitedly, "I'm supposed to be helping those guys." He started off and then turned back to Brad. "Do you think I could ride over to the hospital with you and Matt when we're done? It shouldn't be more than about twenty minutes."

Brad smiled, "No problem, I'm sure Matt won't mind."

Matt and Sgt. Shackleton were now close enough to overhear them. "Mind what?" Matt asked suspiciously.

"You don't mind if Bart comes to the hospital with us to check on Luke, do you?"

"No, not at all. That'll be great. Dad would like to ask you some questions about tonight. It seems that Mr. Dragon is accusing us of sabotaging his show. Now he says that Luke was part of the act, and that there were supposed to be blanks in the gun. But someone, he believes Luke, put real bullets in the gun."

"That's ridiculous," Brad reacted.

"Why do you say that, Brad?" Sgt. Shackleton asked.

"Well, I know Luke would not have wanted to kill Sammy. He just wouldn't. If those bullets were replaced, I believe Dragon did it. Luke told me earlier today that Dragon wanted to get rid of Sammy because of some problems they were having."

"Did you see Luke pointing the gun at Sammy?" Sgt. Shackleton queried.

Brad thought a second, and reluctantly continued, "Yes, but he seemed to be under The Dragon's influence."

"The Dragon's influence—what do you mean by that?" Sgt. Shackleton raised an eyebrow.

"Hypnosis is a big part of The Dragon's show. I believe Luke was under hypnosis when he pointed the gun at Sammy. He seemed to think that Sammy was an alien being from another planet. Luke told me earlier that he had seen aliens while staying out at the house with the band. I believe that Dragon hypnotized him, and made him think these strange beings existed and that Sammy was one of them."

"That's a pretty wild story. Do you have any proof of that?" Sgt. Shackleton responded.

Brad thought, then shook his head, wishing he did.

"Dad, do you think there's anything to all this hypnosis stuff, or is it just an act?" Matt questioned.

"There are plenty of studies that show that the mind can be strongly influenced by the power of suggestion through hypnosis. People will actually begin to pet a cat they only imagine is in their lap. It's pretty amazing stuff. Proving it in court is the questionable part."

"Dad, it was incredible," Matt explained. "It was like Dragon had hypnotized the entire audience into thinking the place was crawling with snakes."

"Yeah. Is that possible?" Brad questioned.

"I don't know." Sgt. Shackleton scratched his head. "I'll have to do some research on this. Did you guys see any snakes?"

Brad shook his head, "I didn't see anything but the long sticks rolling around on the stage."

Matt agreed and added, "But everybody else was going crazy, thinking they were about to be bitten by all the snakes."

"Getting back to the gun, you did see Luke holding it, right? Then what happened?" Sgt. Shackleton asked.

"Well," Brad thought a moment, "You might find this hard to believe, but I could see Dragon. His eyes were fixed on Luke. He appeared to be wanting Luke to pull the trigger. Luke was literally shaking, and his eyes were wild. He kept glancing at Dragon and then back at Sammy. That's when Matt and I began to pray and bind the power of the enemy."

"Really!" Sgt. Shacketon grinned at Matt.

"Yeah," Brad continued. "We prayed together, and when I looked up, Luke seemed to kind of wake up and come out of it. It was like he didn't even know where he was. He looked at the gun as if he wondered where it had come from. Then, he noticed the audience. Trembling, he laid the gun on the floor and began to back away."

Sgt. Shackleton nodded. "Then what happened?"

"That's when the lightning struck, shorted out the lights, and everything went dark. People started to scream and cry out. There was a loud popping sound. A few seconds later the emergency lights came on. We could see Dragon had hold of Luke, but Luke did not have the gun."

"Where was the gun?" Sgt. Shackleton asked, puzzled.

"It was still laying on the floor, but not in the same place."

"Are you sure it had been moved?"

Brad mused for a second, "I'm pretty sure it had been moved at least a foot."

Sgt. Shackleton turned to Matt, "Son, do you think it had been moved?"

Matt, shook his head, "It all happened so fast that I can't be sure, but I do believe the gun was in a different position when the emergency lights came on.

An officer came up to Sgt. Shackleton and whispered something in his ear. "Guys, I might have a few more questions later, but I need to handle something that's come up right now."

"Dad, we're going to the hospital to see Luke. After that, I guess I'll head back out to Grandpa's, OK?"

Sgt. Shackleton nodded. "Just stay out of trouble," he cautioned, smiling at his son. Sgt. Shackleton turned and walked away, talking with the officer.

"Don't forget. Bart would like a ride to the hospital." Brad reminded, looking across the parking lot.

"Do you think he's about ready? If he's about done with his duties here, we need to head out. It's almost eleven o'clock." Matt noticed Brad scanning the parking lot. "Who are you looking for?"

"I was thinking," Brad replied, "I might ride over with Sandie. She's by herself, and Bart can ride with you, if that's OK."

"Sure, it's fine with me. Is she still here?"

"Yeah, she's still talking on the phone, I think. Her car is still here."

"I'll go get my car and then come back and pick up Bart. Will you find him and tell him?"

"Sure, there he is." Brad said as he pointed in the direction of the fire trucks. "That's right; Ruby is still parked down the road in the woods. I hope she hasn't gotten too lonely out there, "Brad chided.

Matt smiled, turned and walked toward the dark road.

Too bad we don't still have that flashlight, Brad thought as he watched his friend disappear out of view, past the lights of the parking lot. "You be careful," Brad called. He then turned and walked toward the fire trucks, which were getting ready to pull out.

Bart was now running over to him. "Hey, man. I'm all done. Where's Matt?"

"His car is parked down the road," Brad explained that he would ride with Sandie while Bart went with Matt. "He just started down the road to get it. You can catch him if you hurry." Brad pointed toward the road. Bart ran off calling out for Matt, who answered from the darkness. *Boy, they sure need a flashlight.* Brad thought. I *wonder what happened to the one we had earlier.*

As Brad stood there thinking, he couldn't shake the feeling he was missing something—as if the Spirit of God was prompting him. *What is it, Lord?* he wondered. Luke's flashlight stuck in his mind. He could see in his mind's eye Luke doing something with it at the shed, when they were in the woods. He thought back to what Luke said in his state of delirium, right before the ambulance had taken him away. "Find the light—in the light." Brad walked around the building toward the side parking lot still thinking. *Could Luke have been talking about his old flashlight? He did have it at the shed, when he pulled the pouch from underneath.* Then a light bulb went on in Brad's head. That old flashlight had a compartment for storing extra batteries that Luke used to call his secret compartment. He would hide stuff there when they played spy games, when they were kids. It would be the perfect place to hide a little flash drive device. A sense of urgency overtook Brad. *What happened to that light?* He thought hard. *I had it when they came through the back door by the dumpsters. Brittany gave us the shirts.* He remembered he had put the light down on top of a box on a shelf while he got into the black shirt. Then, he got distracted when Lumas appeared in the hallway. *It must be still on that shelf.* If the thumb drive was indeed hidden inside it, he knew he had to retrieve it before one of Dragon's men discovered it. Brad studied the ominous dark façade of the building as he realized that meant going back inside the dreaded den of The Dragon.

Chapter 22

Trapped!

Walking by the side door of the Dragon's Den where they had exited the building earlier, Brad was deep in thought. *I've just got to go back and get that flashlight.* Luke seemed to think that it was crucial to the case against the Dragon. But what about Sandie? He looked up and realized that the parking lot was now empty. Sandie had already gone. Brad turned back and looked at the door. *I could just run in and explain to the officers about the light, show them where it is and be back outside in time to catch Matt as he drives by.* He pulled on the metal side door. To his surprise, no one had locked it, and it came open. The place was still dark from the power outage. He entered and closed the door quietly. Lumas was gone, and there was an eerie silence. Brad cautiously crept through the dark hallway past the offices. Hearing a sound, he stopped to listen. A door opened, followed by muffled talking ahead. It was the voice of Dragon speaking to one of his guys on a cell phone.

"Bring her in here, when the cops have left." Brad heard a car pulling up to the door through which he had just come. He dashed through the doorway which led into the bar area, now dimly lit by a few glowing candles. Brad's mind raced as he tried to figure out from which direction the voices had come. He hid behind the massive bar and closed the little swinging half-door behind him. Sitting down with his back against the shelves filled with various bottled beverages, his knees folded up against his chin, he quickly surveyed the surroundings. The bar was about fifteen feet long with swinging doors on each end which were about four feet high, from the floor to the height of the bar surface. As Brad pondered what he should do next, the exterior door, through which he had entered the building, opened. He could hear muffled whimpering and the shuffling of shoes across the tile floor. Brad held his breath as fear gripped him.

"Secure that door," one of the men ordered.

"I'll take care of it," A familiar gruff voice replied.

Lumas, Brad thought. *If he finds me, I'm dead meat.* He heard the metal tinkling of keys on a key ring. *Oh, great. Now I'm locked in with these guys.* He fought to get a grip on his fear. *Why in the world did I come in here all alone?* He asked himself. *The guys have left by now.* He began to pray, "Lord, strengthen me. Give me wisdom, and set Your angels around me to protect me from the hand of the enemy." Brad felt like he had been in this situation before. He was facing the same fear he had experienced in the dream when he was hiding under the platform where Luke was chained. But Luke wasn't here. A question entered his mind. *Who was it the goons had brought in?* From what he heard Dragon say, he knew that it was a female. It couldn't be Sandie. Her car was gone.

"Bring her in here, and lay her down." Brad heard the voice of the Dragon, now standing in the bar room where Brad was hiding. Brad pushed his body up as close to the bar as he could and steadied his breathing. He could hear the thugs struggling to bring her into the room. With a thud, her body hit the floor. A faint cry broke through the quietness.

"She'll be out for a while," Lumas stated, with a sly chuckle.

"It's a pity. She's such a pretty thing, too. I thought she was with us, but it appears that something or someone has messed up her thinking over the last couple of weeks. That careless Tommy got her pregnant, and she started talking about wanting to keep the baby. I'm sure she must have been talking to some of our local Christian fanatics. What a pity," Dragon feigned a lament.

"She must have been the one who let those guys in tonight," Lumas added.

"I know they didn't come in through the front door. I was stationed there all night," replied the other goon.

Brad's heart sank within him, as he realized that they had Brittany. A glimpse of Brittany's face appeared in Brad's mind as he remembered the expression of sadness and despair on her face in his dream. Imprisoned in that mirrored cage, held by her own vanity and selfishness. However, things in her life had just begun to change. She was beginning to crawl out of that prison, thanks to Jesus. As she spent time with Mandy, reading and discussing the Bible, Brittany was coming to understand the truth of God's Word how it could change her life. But, now she was held captive by another evil force. A righteous anger began to rise up in Brad. He understood that it was for more than one reason that God had led him into this situation. But, what could he do? *I am just one kid against these huge guys.* As soon as he thought this, a verse popped in his mind: "If God be for you, who can be against you."

"Well, gentleman, it seems that we're in a bit of a dilemma," Dragon declared, sarcastically. "Unfortunately, she heard our plans earlier, thanks to her eavesdropping, trying to find out about Luke. So she will have to be eliminated."

"Do you want us to dump her in the river?" Lumas' compassionless voice asked.

"No, I think we may use her to slay more than one bird with a single stone. Sammy is another problem. If he lives, I think that he may betray us and cut some sort of deal with the D. A. who desires to get to the bigger fish, so to speak."

"We did find his flash drive, full of damaging information," Lumas responded.

"Do you know how easy it is to use one of those things? Knowing Sammy, he likely had several of them." Dragon fumed.

Brad almost gasped out loud, but stopped himself. *They know about the flash drive. I've got to find that flashlight. But, what about Brittany?* He wrestled with himself about how to deal with both issues at hand.

"I still believe that little trouble-maker, Luke, got his hands on one of them. It would be better if he didn't live through the night, either. Wouldn't it be interesting if my dear partner, Mr. Dornberg, would turn up suffocated while our little friend Luke, was in the room? Do you gentlemen think that might be arranged later this evening?

"Yeah, I know just the guy. He'd be great at impersonating a doctor or male nurse," Lumas advised.

"See too it," Dragon ordered. "We don't have much time before he gets well enough to sing, especially if he figures out who really shot him. You guys get on it ASAP."

"What about her?"

"She will unfortunately succumb to looting, and in her haste to steal the money in the till to support her drug habit, she will knock over a burning candle and—poof. She and this place will be gone. It is a shame. It was going so well here. But it's a liability to me right now. Besides, it's well insured, and I will build an even better place once all the flack has died down. I'll take care of this end. You guys just take care of things at the hospital. I need to get some things out of the office first."

"Why don't I fix us a drink, and then we'll all head out." The other man suggested.

Oh, Lord. Please, no, Brad prayed as his heart sank hearing the nameless thug approaching the other end of the bar. Brad stared at the half-sized swinging door at the opposite end of the bar. If the man opened it, Brad wondered if he should make a dash for it on his end. While considering his options, he noticed a tiny object moving toward the crack under the door. *A mouse,* Brad thought.

Too coincidentally, just as the man touched the door, the little mouse darted underneath the door, disappeared from Brad's view, and scurried right between the man's feet. It is amazing how a grown man can be so traumatized by something so small. Apparently, the huge man shared Brad's fear of rats. Brad would have to reconsider his fear of them, now that one had literally saved his life. The frantic man jumped back, startled. Cursing, he stumbled over a chair in his effort to escape the loathsome creature.

As laughter burst from the other men who witnessed this open display of fear, Brad saw his opportunity. Amid the commotion and distraction, he darted out of the swinging door on the other end and around the corner into the hallway, completely unobserved by his would be assailants. In the darkness, he paused, listening to hear if he had been noticed. Brad could still hear the men laughing.

"It's just a stupid mouse," Lumas ribbed.

The Dragon's voice intervened. "Enough foolishness—we need to get going. You guys know what you need to do. Bring some light so that we can get what we need out of the office."

Brad took that as his cue and quietly moved from the hallway into the empty auditorium. The emergency lights still dimly lit all of the exits. Quickly, he made his way to the front of the auditorium. Moving across in front of the stage, he headed toward the double doors through which he and Matt had entered earlier that evening. He wondered, *The electricity is out. How in the world will I find the light in the darkness. What a profound question,* he thought. *Isn't that what the whole world struggles with? We are all born into darkness in this fallen world. People groping in darkness— we wander aimlessly in vain pursuits, with no hope of finding the truth unless God lights the path. The only way we can find the light in the darkness, spiritually, is if Jesus shows us the way.* The same was true for him now, in a literal sense. Brad was amazed that even at this intense moment, the Holy Spirit could show him such a basic truth.

He reached the doors and pushed them open. Just as he had feared, the hallway was totally dark. He moved over toward the wall and began feeling his way along. He came to the turn and moved over to the opposite wall because he knew that the door to the stairwell was on the left. Brad felt a door which was closed, and remembered the closet into which he and Matt had ducked earlier. He continued along, praying, knowing time was short. As soon as Dragon was finished in the office, the fire would be set. "Oh Lord, watch over Brittany. Keep her safe from harm, and help me find Luke's light quickly."

He came to another doorway, and felt inside. The door was partially opened, just as they had left it. He entered the pitch black stairwell. Brad moved to the right, holding out his hands until he felt the cold, smooth metal railing. He carefully followed it up each step, until he reached the top. Entering the storage room, he began feeling around the shelves near the rack of black shirts. His hand hit something cold, metal and round. Excited, he grabbed it up. Cold liquid sloshed over his hand and onto his arm. The pungent odor of beer invaded his nostrils. "Oh blast," he muttered in disgust, as he sat the half-full can of beer back on the shelf.

He continued his quest, becoming more and more impatient. He could now feel heat rising in his head as frustration began to overtake him. "Lord, where is it? I know that I laid it down here on top of a box somewhere on this shelf. I need to find it quickly and get out of here. Please help me!" A feeling of desperation drove him almost to the point of tears. Suddenly, a bright light from behind and above him lit up the entire shelf area. Amazed, Brad turned to see how this light had suddenly appeared. Was it an angel? Up toward the ceiling there were a couple of elongated narrow windows used for ventilation. Brad could see that the thick clouds had broken, and at that moment a full moon was blazing forth from between them. "Thank you, Lord," Brad proclaimed out loud as he turned back to the shelf, expecting to see the silver metal cylinder totally illuminated. The light was bright enough to see everything on the shelves as well as around them. Brad knew he had put it right there, but where was it? Perhaps it had fallen off. Desperately, he began looking around on the floor. However, it was nowhere to be found.

Just as suddenly, like the switch had been flipped, the light was gone. The brightness of the moon was again hidden in the clouds. Crushed, Brad began to pull himself together. He felt a compelling force driving him back down the stairs. In the darkness, he lost his bearings. Not realizing that he was at the bottom of the stairs, he stumbled. His knees hit the concrete floor with a thud. Pain shot through his legs, right up to his teeth. He rolled over on his side, groaning, but knew that he must keep going. Reaching out, he felt the door frame leading into the hallway and pulled himself up. Momentarily rubbing his knees, he continued back down the pitch black corridor. Again, he was feeling his way along the wall. Soon, he could see a dim light shining through the small square windows of the swinging doors leading back into the auditorium. As he approached them he remembered the words painted above them. In his mind's eye, he could see the decorative scrollwork and the gothic black lettering spelling the word ABYSS.

Brad knew that word was found in the book of Revelation. He wondered if it was the same as "the pit," the place where the devil and all of his demons were cast at the end of the age. *Why would anyone name an auditorium that?* Brad pondered. *The Devil is surely a master of deception to get people to want to go to a place like that.* Brad remembered another scripture where Jesus cast a whole bunch of demons out of some guy. The demons begged Him not to send them into the Abyss. *If demons didn't even want to go there, it must be a really terrible place.*

He reached the doors, then stopped and peered through the windows to see if there was any movement. *Boy, how long do those emergency lights last?* Brad wondered nervously. *What time is it anyway?* He pressed the button on his watch and read 11:29. *Wow, it seems much later than that.* He felt that he had been trapped in this place for hours, but it had only been about thirty minutes. The back of the huge room was dark, but the doors through which he was entering were lit by the emergency lights. He would have to take his chances that no one was out there, watching. Just to be sure he crouched down and slowly entered, then scurried over next to the first row of chairs. He waited, listened. No one shouted, nor did he hear footsteps.

Abruptly, the thought of Dragon's plan re-entered Brad's mind. He didn't smell smoke, so he knew that no fire had been started, yet. But, time was fleeting. He had to get to Brittany. As he moved closer to the hallway which led to the offices, he could hear movement and voices. *Good,* Brad thought. *They are still moving things out of the office.* Crouching in the darkness, watching and thinking, Brad needed to move. The pain from his right knee seemed to be getting worse. Since Dragon and his men were working in the office, Brad decided to sneak around to the other exit into the main entry, which led through the dining area. Brad moved between the next to the last row of chairs, hidden from their view. Reaching the end of the row he studied the hallway. Shadows danced in the dim lantern light filtering through the open door of the office, but he saw no one in the hall. Light also shone inside the large open doorway to the dining area, indicating an emergency light was mounted on the wall in that area. Glancing back toward the office to see if the coast was still clear, Brad darted across the aisle through the large opening. As he did, he tripped over something, stumbled and then rolled. Brad found himself grabbing his inflamed knee with both hands. Now on his back, eyes closed, rocking in pain, he prayed that no one had heard him. He knew he must keep going. Opening his eyes, fear shot through his mind like a fiery dart. Staring down at him were the two gleaming, red and gold eyes of a dragon. Shaking off the fear, Brad came to his senses. He'd met this slimy behemoth before. The nine foot tall, brilliantly colored reptilian sentry greeted everyone who entered the ABYSS. The emergency lighting was trained right on the dragon, so that no matter what happened, it would be lit.

Its long curling neck arched in such a way that the head now appeared to be looking Brad right in the eyes. He could almost smell its putrid, hot breath and briefly wondered if it was about to come to life. Brad's mind flew back to one of his most vivid dreams, when he had fallen asleep playing the Draegonian Invasion game. This was indeed the same dragon he had battled when he was trying to save Luke. *Will it suddenly begin to grow to twenty feet tall like it did in the dream?* Then, he remembered how Jesus had come to his rescue, and that it had all been just a dream. A door slamming jolted him back into reality. It meant

Dragon and his men were still busy loading stuff into the Hummer. This was no dream, and he knew that he desperately needed Jesus' help, to deliver him from the hands of a very real enemy, a human Dragon. "Help me, Jesus. What should I do?" he prayed.

As his focus returned to trying to save Brittany, the pain in his knee seemed to subside. He got to his feet and began to move through the dining area. Although they were hidden in the darkness, Brad could see, in his mind, the pictures on the wall of the evil characters that he had first seen with Matt a week ago. He particularly remembered the one showing the dragon slaying a lion, with a crown lying on the ground as if they were fighting for control of some kingdom. Brad began to really understand. *That's probably what Satan thought when Jesus was crucified on the cross.* He remembered one of the titles for Jesus in the Bible was the Lion Of The Tribe Of Judah. *Satan must have actually thought that he had defeated God. Could he still really believe that? How dumb is that?* Brad wondered. He took great comfort in the thought that one day soon Jesus would return in all His power and might. *Satan and all of his demonic kingdom will be crushed, and Jesus will reign victorious on the earth. That will be cool. There will be no doubt about who Jesus is, and the whole world will know that the Bible is totally true.*

A low moan broke the silence, and Brad turned away from the darkened picture. Dim light flickered through the darkness from the candles in the bar area. Brad moved forward and could see the outline of Brittany's body, lying on her side, facing away from him. He listened and heard nothing. *They must all be outside*, he thought. He crept over to her motionless body and then looked at the front door. Brad had to get her out of the building somehow. He reached out, grasped her wrists and began to try to pick her up. She flinched, and squirmed. In a state of fear and delirium, she began to whimper.

"Sh-sh-sh!" Brad whispered. "Britt, it's me, Brad. I'm here to help you. We've got to get out of here." Brad heard a car door slam outside, and he knew didn't have much time. He again reached out, grabbed her wrists and summoning all of his strength, pulled her up. To his surprise, she was able get to her knees. Somehow he the managed to get her frail body in his arms and up off the floor. Some might call it adrenaline, but Brad knew it was the power of the Holy Spirit strengthening him. He began to move out of the bar and toward the two large wooden entry doors. He was able to grip the black metal latch and push, but it didn't move. His heart sank as he realized it was a dead bolt that required a key to unlock. A car door slammed and Brad heard the muffled sound of a motor starting. He turned and started back through the dining area. Hearing the side door open and shut, it dawned on him that the two henchmen had left, and now it was just him and Dragon.

Brittany's limp body was getting heavier, and Brad's arms already ached, not to mention the pain shooting from his injured knee. Brad's thoughts raced back to the door by the dumpsters. His only hope was that they had overlooked locking that door in all the confusion of the night.

Suddenly, from out of the silence, he heard a sickening voice coming from around the corner in the bar. "Now, where did she get off too?"

Who is he talking to? Brad wondered. Then he realized that Dragon was talking to himself. *Dragon needs to find her, but not me. That would ruin any chance of escape.* Brad was in no condition to challenge The Dragon, especially if he had a gun. Carefully, he laid Brittany on the floor, and then he moved around the corner to hide, and watch. Turning the corner, he flinched, again. He just couldn't get used to the sight of that tall scaly beast leering down at him, amid the strange shadows cast by the dimming emergency lights.

"Oh Brittan-y, my dear," the sicky-sweet voice cooed in mock concern. "Where are you? You know there's nowhere to hide from me." Brad waited breathlessly for Dragon to round the corner. He heard a different, more serious tone to his voice. This time Dragon was actually talking to someone.

"Hey, it's me, Dragon. You guys head back here. The girl is missing. She must have come to enough to crawl off. You guys have my flashlight, and I don't have time to search the whole place. I don't want to take a chance that she gets away. OK?"

Oh, great, why did he have to do that? Brad thought to himself. He was hoping that he had seen the last of those guys for the evening. He stood a much better chance facing the Dragon alone.

Brad could see the glimmer of flickering light coming toward the entry from the bar into the dining area. A moment later a dark figure rounded the corner holding a kerosene lamp in front of him. As he moved closer, his face was eerily illuminated by the glow of the old glass lamp. Dragon raised the lamp, searching. An evil smile spread across Dragon's face as he found his prey. He knelt down beside Brittany and held the lamp over her. "Well, my dear, I see that you didn't get very far. Don't worry. It will all be over soon," he said, reaching down to stroke her flowing hair. "It's a shame. You are a pretty, little thing."

Suddenly, Brad heard a scratching sound about four feet from where he was standing. He could see that Dragon heard it too. Dragon looked up suspiciously in the direction of the noise. Then stood up and pulled a gun from his chest. Fearing that he would be discovered, Brad moved back behind the statue of the overgrown lizard guarding the Abyss. Suddenly, the little culprit making the scratching noise darted across the floor toward Dragon.

"Cursed mice," Dragon muttered. "I'll be glad to get rid of the rat-infested place." Dragon then backed up and tossed the kerosene lamp into the bar area and watched as the flames slowly began ignite the dry wood of the bar. Dragon quickly walked forward and stopped right in front of the statue behind which Brad was hiding. The sight of Dragon suddenly appearing right in front of him caused Brad to jerk back out of sight, but not before Dragon sensed the movement.

"Who's there?" Dragon shouted, pointing the gun toward the statue. Brad could now smell the smoke from the fire in the bar and knew he didn't have much time. Trapped between the wall and the statue, a desperate thought came to him. Brad braced himself on the wall and placed his feet against the scaly backside of the beast. He then pushed it with all of his might. To his surprise the thing gave way. It was evidently just sitting on top of the square ornate base and had never been bolted down. Dragon let out a cry as the huge monster, the symbol of his fallen world, toppled and pinned him to the floor. Brad raced over to Brittany, who was coughing as thickening smoke began to fill her lungs. He lifted her up, this time over his shoulder and moved past the fallen dragon statue. Dragon, the man, was screaming obscenities and reaching desperately for the gun that had been knocked from his hand. Brad kicked the gun down the hall into the darkness and made his way to the entry of the auditorium.

"Don't leave me." He cursed. "I'll get you, boy!" he yelled. Brad heard his now pleading voice saying, "Someone help me," as Dragon now faced the possibility of coming to grips with his wicked lifestyle. Brad looked back at Dragon and could see the light of the flames behind him. Dark thick smoke clouded the ceiling, and Brad knew that he could do nothing for him. Mr. Dragon was reaping the fruit of the many years of bad seed he'd sown. Yet Brad couldn't help feeling sadness, and a compassionate desire to help him.

Suddenly, Brad heard the door from the side entrance open. He realized that Dragon's goons had returned. With the weight of the young girl on his shoulders he moved quickly through the auditorium. He could hear Dragon yelling, "Lumas, get this thing off of me!"

Brad knew it was only a matter of time before they would be after him. Reaching the double doors that had become so familiar, he went through them into the darkness of the corridor which led, he hoped, to freedom. "Lord, please let that door still be unlocked," he prayed as he felt along the right hand wall, searching for the turn. He rounded the turn and moved over to the other wall feeling for the threshold into the stairwell. His whole body screamed with pain. The weight of Brit's body over his shoulder added to the the pain, emanating from his swollen knee. It was becoming excruciating, and he felt dizzy. Finally, he found the open doorway. He entered the stairwell and could see the faintest glimmer of light coming through the doorway at the top of the stairs. Brad remembered how the moonlight shone through the narrow windows earlier and was thankful once again for some light in this dark situation. His knee was throbbing, and he felt like he was burning up; sweat pouring from his face. Brad could see the metal railing of the stairs and staggered toward it. As he reached out to grab it, his legs suddenly gave way. He sank to the floor trying to soften the blow as much as possible for Brittany, who was still incapacitated. He looked at her and then up to the top of the seemingly endless staircase. In his condition it might as well have been Mount Everest.

CHAPTER 23

THE WILD ESCAPE ATTEMPT

BRAD LOOKED BACK INTO THE darkness behind him, wondering how in the world he would ever get out of this situation. "Lord, please strengthen me." He spoke to Brittany, as he tried to sit her up against the cold concrete wall. "Britt, wake up!" He smacked her face lighlty. She moaned and whimpered, but remained unable to respond and slumped over to the floor. *What in the world have they given her,* he wondered in despair. Gazing helplessly up the mountain of stairs, Brad knew that nothing short of a miracle would enable him to get her up those stairs. He had to try. Dragon and his men would be there any minute. Brad took hold of Brittany's wrists. He began to slowly pull her up the stairs. Crawling up each step, his knee screamed with pain. About the fifth step he thought he heard voices. He stopped, listened, but heard nothing. Brad continued to pull and struggle with the dead weight. Brittany moaned and began to cry. *That,* he thought, *was a good sign. Maybe she's coming out of it.*

At last, he was at the very top of the stairs. He crawled over to look into the storage room. Unexpectedly, he heard a motor outside—a vehicle driving up. Motionless, he listened. *Dragon must have figured out where we were heading.* His heart sank as realized that Dragon would catch them on the very threshold of freedom. *God, how could you let this happen?* He looked back at Brit's motionless body lying in a heap on the stairs. *We almost made it.* His head was spinning, and he just didn't have the strength, no matter how hard he tried. "Lord, I just can't do it." he whispered, as emotion overtook him.

At that moment, he realized another truth from the Holy Spirit. *No matter how hard we try, it is impossible to follow God in our own strength.* He understood that as desperate as he felt right now, he should be just as desperate for the Holy Spirit to help Him follow God every day. A still small voice brought to his memory a verse that made him smile in the midst of this, his midnight hour: "I will never leave you nor forsake you."

"I am not alone," Brad whispered. "Jesus is right here to help."

With that Brad took courage and began to move behind the doorway. As he did, he heard a noise that seemed to come from down the stairs, out in the auditorium, someone shouting something. *Could they be coming from both directions?* Brad wondered. With a loud THUD, the back door burst open, hitting the wall. Two dark figures stood there silhouetted in the brightness of an automobile's headlights. Brads heart raced as the two human outlines walked closer. *At least they're human and not that huge metallic android thing from the first dream.* This thought seemed to give him strength. Brad decided his only hope was the element of surprise. Hiding behind the doorway, he crouched low, ready to leap at just the right moment. His goal was to take them off their feet, and get hold of a weapon. He waited, holding his breath as the sound of the footsteps got closer and closer. Just as he saw a foot enter the threshold, he leapt with all of the strength he had left. Grabbing his foe with both arms above the knees, he caused both of the attackers to topple backward onto the floor.

Brad quickly maneuvered atop the larger one. To his surprise, he heard a familiar voice, "Brad! What on earth are you doing?" It was Matt. Brad gazed down at his stunned friend, and could hardly believe his eyes.

He looked over at the other equally surprised character. "Bart," Brad smiled. Tears of elation, and relief, filled his eyes at seeing his friends, rather than the henchmen wanting to take his life. A feeling of amazement overtook him briefly, as Brad realized he had been able to take Matt down and was in the victor's position. "Matt. Boy, am I glad to see you."

"Well, you sure have a funny way of showing it. Do you mind letting me up now?"

Brad wanted to be funny and say no, to make his friend squirm a bit, but the reality of the situation hit him with a sense of urgency. He could smell the smoke of the fire at the other end of the building. He was barely able to stand and grasped Bart's hand to help him up.

Bart sniffed and asked, "Does it seem smoky in here to you?"

"Well, the place was on fire earlier, remember?" Matt replied.

"We've got to get out of here!" Brad exclaimed. "Dragon and his goons have reset a fire in the bar, trying to kill Brittany and cover all the evidence. We've got to get her and get out of here."

"Brittany!" Matt exclaimed. "Where is she?" Brad moved over to the doorway. "She's right here on the stairs. I managed to get her this far, only by the grace of God."

Matt quickly got to the stairs. He carefully lifted her up and began to move toward the door. A pitiful whimper bubbled from her quivering lips, touching a soft spot in Matt's heart. "What has happened to her?" Matt asked, gazing at her pale complexion.

As he raised the question, voices from below shouted, "Hey, you. Stop!"

Just as Matt darted through the stairwell doorway with Brittany in his arms, an ear splitting BA-NG shattered the darkness.

"Go! Go!" Matt shouted. Brad hobbled out of the door into the damp mist of the night air, followed by Matt, carrying the still comatose Brittany. Brad stumbled but continued to limp forward. "Where's Bart?" he shouted. Looking back, he could see that Bart was still inside. Bart was pulling over the metal shelving units, causing them to crash in front of the doorway from the stairwell. Boxes, bottles, cans and all kinds of stored stuff spilled everywhere, making it impossible for Dragon's goons to follow them easily. Seeing this, a deep feeling of loss overtook Brad, his thoughts returned to that illusive but so important flashlight and the treasure of information hidden inside.

"Bart! Come on—get out of there!" Matt shouted.

Bart, came running out of the doorway. Again a loud BA-NG—BA-NG was heard from inside. As he exited the building, Bart grabbed the handle of the door and flung it shut with a loud SLAM!

"Little help here," Matt called out, as he was trying to get the passenger door open with Brittany in his arms. Bart ran over to open the door, as Brad made his way to the other side. Matt gently set Brittany into the seat, and belted her in, while Bart ran around and got into the back seat with Brad. Matt jumped into the front and started Ruby's powerful engine. With a loud, comforting roar, the motor came to life.

Brad couldn't contain a feeling that he was finally free and this nightmare would soon be over. Tears clouded his eyes and his entire body shook as the strain of the past few hours sunk in. Matt hit the accelerator, and their bodies were hurled forward as the car shot backward away from the building. He turned slightly, and came to a stop beside the dumpsters. Reaching down, he quickly shifted into drive, throwing gravel as the tires spun through rocky area. Matt slowed, as the car began to fishtail a bit and bounce with the uneven terrain. In a moment, however, he rounded the corner of the building. The tires screeched as they hit pavement, and he gunned the motor.

Without warning, the black hummer shot out right in front of them. Matt slammed hard on the brakes at the same time turning the steering wheel slightly to the right. Ruby was now sliding sideways right into the side of the monster machine. The Mustang came to a stop with a loud CLUNK! It stopped just as it had come into contact with the side of the Hummer.

"That crazy fool!" Matt shouted, as frustration and fear got the better of him. Through the rear window, Brad could see a trail of smoke billowing up from the end of the building. "Hold on, I'm going for it," Matt yelled, realizing they couldn't just sit there. He pressed down on the accelerator. With some slight scraping of metal and a couple of jolts, the car moved forward minus the rear bumper. It was dangling from the rear fender of the opposing force. Brad could see the grimace on Matt's face, as he experienced vicariously Ruby's pain.

The side-doors of the building flew open. Lumas and the other seedy fellow were now barreling toward them, guns waving in hand.

"They're coming!" Bart shouted, as he stared back at the smoking building. "Wow, look at that. This time it will have more than a little smoke damage. Why in the world would Dragon set it on fire?"

Brad was about to explain, when Matt floored the accelerator, and the embattled Ruby leaped forward, tires screaming on the pavement. Racing across the parking lot, Matt slowed suddenly to make a slight turn to exit the parking lot, throwing everyone to the right side of the car. Brad's head caught the side of the car with a bump, as Bart, who hadn't remembered to affix his seat belt, was now virtually on top of him. Brad helped him right himself.

"Sorry, man. I hope I didn't hurt you."

Brad had let out a groan as he rubbed his throbbing noggin. As he did, he felt the scabby wound from his first struggle earlier that evening. *Was that this evening,* he wondered. *Man, so much has happened in such a short time.* He was getting totally confused about the chronology of all that had happened.

Matt wheeled out of the parking lot and onto the road, throwing their bodies in the opposite direction. The tires again peeled, as they spun faster than the car moved. Hitting a slight dip in the pavement, which allowed rain water to drain between the road and the parking lot entrance, Ruby seemed for a split second, to take to the air. The car bounced as it landed, and sparks flew from the rear as the tail pipes came into contact with the road.

Brad turned to see the two villains pile into the Hummer, which had been driven by an unseen daredevil. Although not clearly visible, Brad knew who it had to be. Mr. Dragon was the only other person there. The Hummer immediately tore out of the parking lot and down the road behind them. Brad took comfort in the fact that there was no way that huge, heavy SUV could outrun Ruby. She was fast as lightning.

"They're behind us," Bart stated the obvious.

"They'll never catch us in that tank," Brad retorted.

"You'd be surprised at how fast those things are," Matt responded, glancing at the speedometer. He was doing almost seventy. He slowed as he came to a slight curve, but not quite enough, and the car began to bounce and shake as the passenger side tires left the road for a few seconds. The force of rounding the curve pushed everyone to the passenger side of the car. Brittany rolled to one side and muttered some incoherent gibberish. Looking over at her, Matt realized all this would be moot if they were all killed in an accident because of his carelessness.

"They're gaining on us," Bart announced, the intensity rising in his voice.

"I really can't safely go much faster on this old, windy two-lane road." Another turn approached and Matt tried to keep the car more to the center of the road. "I can't believe that these guys are going to follow us once we get into town. We've just got about four miles, and they should back off." The road straightened out. Matt sped up, and so did his pursuers. Matt knew that another turn was ahead. He moved more to the center of the road to compensate for the centripetal force that would cause this fast moving object to resist the turn. As he swerved more toward the center of the road, headlights appeared in front of him from around the bend. He quickly slowed and moved back to his side of the road. When he slowed, the Hummer gained ground. The driver of the Hummer did not correct his course as much, remaining partially on the wrong side of the road. The passing car slammed down on his horn and hit the shoulder, bouncing, swerving and finally spinning around in the middle of the road behind them.

"Man, did you see that? Those guys are crazy!" Brad exclaimed, in frustration.

"I'm sure the guy in that car had a few choice words for that Hummer," Matt replied, shaking his head. The Hummer was now right on their tail. Matt had to slow his speed because the road was not at all straight, turning first one direction and then another like a great serpent on the landscape. Matt didn't remember this particular road having so many curves. But, he had never been in the tense situation of someone on his bumper trying to kill him before. As he rounded the next curve he knew that the road would straighten. Then, he would floor it, and gain some ground.

Looking back, Brad exclaimed, "That Hummer is close enough to spit on."

The sentinel, Bart, intensely announced, "They've got a gun pointed out the window."

Brad looked back at the black monster trailing them and prayed, "God, please deliver us from the hand of this enemy."

Matt could see, in his rearview window, an arm wildly waving from the passenger side of the Hummer. Suddenly, he heard a loud pop and realized a shot had been fired. Matt instinctively hit the brake, and there was a loud CRUNCH, as the Hummer's large, gleaming, metal bumper collided with Ruby's trunk. Matt grimaced with the impact, knowing the wound which would be exacted on his once perfectly-kept baby. Matt held the car steady, while the Hummer weaved and bobbed, leaving the road then back again—dropping behind slightly, as it was forced to slow in order to compensate for the impact. As he rounded the last sharp curve, Matt punched it, and faithful Ruby shot forward, leaving the Hummer behind.

"Oh, no!" Matt cried out. "Hold on!" Two shining red eyes had appeared in the middle of the lane in which he was traveling. He regained his composure and quickly pressed the brakes to slow Ruby. The occupants of the Hummer could not see the slender animal, which stood frozen, mesmerized by the oncoming lights. The SUV gained ground—Lumas' arm again out of the window. Matt turned the steering wheel slightly to the right, and whizzed by the startled doe. What happened next was somewhat of a blur. At about the same time that Matt swerved to miss the deer, a shot rang out from Lumas' weapon. The confused deer leapt right into the path of the speeding Hummer, crashing into the windshield and then rolling over the top of the vehicle. It was flung into the air, coming to rest on the shoulder behind. The poor creature never even knew what hit her.

Matt, trying to compensate for his maneuver, had lost control and was now spinning down the middle of the road. Brad's heart beat like a snare drum, as he tried vainly to make sense out of the chaos outside of the car. The Hummer was also careening out of control, as the driver seemed to have lost his bearings momentarily, struggling to see through the shattered windshield. The driver tried to slow the massive vehicle, but not before it had run off the road, straddling the ditch for a moment, and then crashed through a wooden fence and into a pasture.

Ruby finally came to rest near the right shoulder, her front end facing and partially on the right shoulder. Brad and Bart simultaneously breathed a sigh of relief, thankful that the road was desolate. Few traveled this lonely road so late at night. Brad craned his neck to see the proximity of their enemies. All he could see was the demolished fence and the glow of their headlights in the tall grass of the unkempt pasture. Studying the light and listening for a moment, Brad could hear the sound of a motor revving.

"It sounds like they're stuck," Bart hypothesized.

Brad could see dark shadows moving in the headlights. "I don't think we should wait around and offer them a ride. They're out of the car. I think that we should make like the wind and blow out of here." Matt turned and smiled at Brad's metaphor.

"I'm with you, brother." He carefully backed Ruby up slightly, and turned the wheel to face toward town. Then he hit the accelerator and Ruby roared forward. Matt could see two figures come into view behind them, silhouetted by the lights of the hummer. A feeling of relief came over him as they disappeared in the distance.

Brittany began to moan and cry, and then mutter uncontrollably. Matt turned to her with compassion and spoke softly, "It's okay, Brit. You're safe now."

Brad pondered that. *Are we really, Lord?* At the moment, he was safe from this physical enemy, but Brad realized, this was one of many enemies in the world. God had shown Himself strong and intervened to save both him and Brittany this night. Brad was only beginning to understand how Jesus truly was watching over him in every situation, with every enemy, both physical and spiritual. As his eyes filled, Bart noticed Brad's emotion.

"Brad, are you alright? Are you in pain?"

Brad laughed, realizing he must look terrible. He felt like he'd been hit by a Mack truck, aching all over. He appreciated his new friend's concern. What a blessing Bart was, so faithful. God had brought a real ally to them in the midst of all this turmoil. "I'm fine," Brad finally responded. "I'm just so thankful to God for His being there tonight. He was right there with us, just like He promised in His Word. He will never leave us, nor forsake us."

"Yeah," Matt chimed in, "even when we get in over our heads."

"Especially when we get in over our heads, if we are obeying Him," Brad added. "Sometimes it's hard to know whether it's obedience or our own craziness. But, if we're seriously interested in following Him, I believe that He'll let us know when we're going the wrong direction."

Bart agreed, "Do you think that's what Jesus meant when he said, 'My grace is sufficient for you?' If we're trying to obey Him, and we mess up, He fixes it?"

"I totally agree," Matt acknowledged. "If we are willing to admit it when we do make an error, and seek God to correct it, He will. I really believe God wants us to step out in faith and do something for Him rather than sit around doing nothing, afraid of messing up. That's not faith at all. That's fear."

Brad pondered the conversation, then added, "It's like that parable Jesus told, the one about the guy who was given some money from his master. Instead of using what the Lord had given him for his master's service, he buried it in the ground. When the master rebuked him for that, he responded that he didn't do anything with it because he feared losing it."

"Yeah," Bart interjected, "then he lost it. The master took it from him and gave it to the servant who had made the most of what the master had given him."

Wow, Brad thought, *that's deep.* Brad was glad he hadn't given in to the all of the fearful thoughts he'd had over the past few weeks. The dreams—the persecution at school—and tonight, the very real fear for his life, all seemed overwhelming at the time. But God had strengthened him and given him courage with a simple reminder that He was right there with him in each circumstance. Knowing that he was not alone had made all the difference. Jesus' presence had given Brad the courage he needed to keep going and not give up. For a few moments, Brad felt invincible.

Then hauntingly, Dragon's plan from earlier that night filled his head. The gut wrenching fear that Brad had just stomped under his feet came back to life, and began to attack his mind. The sly deep voice of Dragon echoed in his head, as he remembered Dragon explaining to Lumas how they could get rid of both Luke and Sammy at the hospital. Brad realized that this battle was not over. He was coming to understand that the battle is never really over. *We might have times of rest from the fight, but as long as our enemy, the enemy of God, roams around seeking whom he may devour, the war is never over. Not until Jesus returns and casts him into that pit—that Abyss—will it truly end. Even if we have the victory there are others like Luke and Brittany who have just begun the fight, and many more like Sammy whom we must fight for.*

Chapter 24

The Intense Battle

Brad pondered their situation, sitting in the back seat of the battered Mustang with his friends, his fellow crusaders in the battle for the souls around them. The picture played in Brad's mind of Luke on that stage tonight, physically shaking, under the power of the enemy. He was in such a fragile state. He had given his life over to the Lord just hours before, only to have all of the forces of hell immediately unleashed to destroy him. Fear had once again been trying to overwhelm Brad's mind, but was now being devastated by a righteous anger. The thought of such a ruthless, hate-filled enemy, so focused on destroying a newborn believer in his infancy ignited a passion in Brad's heart. *If this is true with Luke, it must be true with all believers. Man,* Brad thought, *this is real all-out war.* Never before had he so poignantly grasped his responsibility as his brother's keeper. *Lord, I need to take following you seriously, not just for me, but to be there for those struggling around me.*

Brad could hear the Spirit of God speaking to his heart. "That's why I created My church, not just for a social club, but for an army of people committed to watching each other's backs."

Brad looked over at Bart, who was staring out of the rear window and then up at Matt and Brit. He made a decision in his heart. "I will do it, Lord," He stated under his breath. *I will stand with them.*

"I don't see anyone following us," Bart announced.

Brad smiled. *Bart gets it. He's always watching our back—a loyal brother.* Brad was again almost overcome with emotion at the goodness of God.

"I think that those goons are probably still trying to get out of that soft field. You know, it's nothing short of a miracle that a Hummer could get stuck like that." Bart continued, beaming with excitement at the possibility of God's intervention in their situation.

Brad slapped a hand on his shoulder and shared the awesome feeling of victory in watching God's power at work. "God is great, isn't He?" Brad acknowledged.

An excited Bart responded, "All the time!"

At that point, Brittany sat straight up in her seat and asked, "Where are we going?" She was totally oblivious to what had occurred during the last several hours. Brit turned to Matt, looking at him with that deer in the headlights look, as if trying to figure out who he was.

"You're OK, Brit, but you've not been feeling well; so we're going to the hospital. You'll be all right," Matt attempted to comfort her. She continued to stare at him for a few seconds as the words wandered into her confused head, slowly being processed.

Finally she questioned softly, "M-Matt?"

"Yeah, it's me. Everything will be OK when we get to the hospital," he reassured her.

Slowly nodding her head, she lay back on the seat.

Matt's words resounded in Brad's head. "Everything's not all right at the hospital!" Brad blurted out. "They are going to try to kill Sammy and make it look like Luke did it."

"What? How are they going to do that? They're still trying to get out of that field," Matt asked skeptically.

"No, you don't understand. Lumas called some guy who was going to pose as a male nurse and kill Sammy—at the same time, framing Luke for it."

"Why didn't you tell us this before?" Matt asked, pressing the accelerator to speed up.

"I don't know. With all that was going on, I guess I'm—just—kinda out of it," Brad confided, gently massaging his temples.

"Luke! Where is Luke? They took him. We need to find him!" Brittany exclaimed, slowly beginning to remember some of the evening's events, as the effects started wearing off.

"Luke's OK, Brit. He's at the hospital. You can see him tomorrow. Just lay back and rest. We'll be there in about eight or nine minutes." Matt came to the intersection of 42 and the parkway around town and stopped at the traffic light. When the light turned green, Matt continued down the road noticing a dark car behind him. Soon, he got the feeling that the car on his tail was following him. There were no other cars on the four lane road. Why was this one not passing him? The speed limit was 45 and Matt was going about 51. Matt glanced nervously ahead and then into his rearview mirror several times.

"Is that car following us?" Bart asked, right on cue.

Brad, who was almost asleep, roused himself at the possibility of once again being pursued. *Will this never end?* He wondered wearily.

"Well, we don't have far to go now, and he's not going to stop us." Matt was about to hit the accelerator when suddenly a wall of blue lights began flashing behind him. Matt felt so stupid as he realized his stalker was an unmarked police car. "I must be really tired not to have recognized the type of car," Matt remarked, relieved that this wasn't the enemy, but the good guys. Matt pulled onto the shoulder and stopped. He turned off the engine and waited for the officer.

The officer came along the side of the car with flashlight in hand. "Matt Shackleton, is that you in there?"

"Yes, sir. It's me," Matt replied respectfully, as his father had taught him.

"Man, your Dad has been looking all over for you. Where have you been? He thought that you might be in some sort of trouble."

Bart suddenly became extremely agitated and began whispering, "Matt, Matt," while pointing out of the window.

Matt turned to see what he was pointing at. The ominous black Hummer was going by them in the other lane.

"Officer," Matt interrupted, not able to recognize the man, figuring that he must be a newer member of the force. "I'm sorry to interrupt, but we have been in some trouble and that Hummer that just passed us tried to run us off the road earlier," Matt stated excitedly, as he pointed down the road.

The officer turned and saw the Hummer, "Didn't get the license number, did you?"

"No, sir. I'm afraid that we've only seen it from the front, but they also have guns and have taken several shots at us.

"Shots? Are you sure? By the way, I'm officer Gabriel. It's good to finally meet you, Matt. I've heard so many good things about you from your father and the other guys on the force." He reached for the radio, strapped to his shoulder, and called for assistance. "All units in the vicinity of the parkway between 42 and Tryon Ave, be on the lookout for a black Hummer traveling south on the parkway—Believed to be suspects in a hit and run. Said to be armed and dangerous. Over." The dispatcher said something too distorted to understand, but the officer seemed to relate to it and responded, "Roger that. Matt Shackleton is with me, along with two other boys and a young lady."

Brittany tossed and turned in her seat, covering her eyes with one hand, and muttered, "Are we there yet?" It was obvious that she was still out of it.

"I will escort them to the station." Again, the radio squawked to life as the dispatcher asked a question. The officer looked into the car and asked, "Is there a Brad Johnson with you?"

Brad spoke up from his dazed state in the back seat. "I'm back here, sir."

"Your parents will be glad to hear that you are safe." Officer Gabriel pushed up his cap, and started to walk back to his car.

Matt craned his head out of the open window, and called again respectfully, tying to contain a sense of urgency, "Officer Gabriel, we really need to get this young lady to the hospital. She has been drugged by those same guys that are chasing us. We also have reason to believe that Luke Hunter and Sammy Dornberg are in danger at the hospital."

Officer Gabriel, a little dumbfounded, scratched his head as he contemplated all of the trouble that seemed to be brewing. "OK. I'll call all of this in. In the mean time, I will escort you to the hospital." He turned to walk back to his car when Bart started rapping on the window.

"Officer Gabriel! There's one more thing you need to call in."

Backing up, he turned, struggling hard to not to say, *what now*? Exercising great self-control, he simply responded, "Yes?"

"The fire department needs to be sent to that Dragon's Den place out on Highway 42. It's on fire again." Before he had finished speaking, the ominous whine of sirens drifted toward them from farther up the road.

Officer Gabriel turned with a smile, "It sounds like that has already been reported, but I'll make sure." He walked back to his car, and in a moment they were following the patrol car, (blue lights flashing,) heading toward the hospital. Moments later, in the opposing lanes, several fire trucks and emergency vehicles rushed by. Their engines roared as they passed with a flurry of red and gold lights, and deafening sirens.

"I bet this will go down as one of the most eventful nights in town history," Bart announced.

Brad watched the side of the road, mesmerized by the passing signs and street lights. *What time is it anyway? It must be well past midnight. My parents must be worried sick.* Amid the fog in his brain, thoughts swirled. He wondered how Luke was doing and began to pray that Dragon's accomplices hadn't had time to act on his orders. Brad lamented that he'd somehow lost the flashlight with its potentially convicting information about Dragon and his men. He pictured it melting, hidden somewhere in the rubble of the inferno that blazed on Highway 42.

In his fatigued condition, this night had taken on a surreal feeling. Watching the flashing blue lights ahead of them, he drifted into the gray area between consciousness and sleep. He was about to close his eyes when he noticed the large dark vehicle pulling up beside them. It was traveling at about the same speed in the passing lane and was now running parallel with Ruby. A shiver went up the entire length of Brad's body as his blurred vision became crystal clear, recognizing the cracked windshield. He wanted to cry out to the others in the car who hadn't noticed the evil creeping up on them, but the sight of the black metal monster made him totally speechless. He just couldn't get the words out of his mouth.

The Hummer pulled forward slightly, and the passenger side window came down slowly. In the orange glow of the passing street lights, the long somber face of Lumas was leering at Brad. The reflection of the shiny handgun which Brad had seen him brandish earlier that night, served to deepen the fear that now paralyzed him. Lumas pointed the gun right at Matt who still paid no attention to the danger right beside them. Brad tried to say something but could not get the words out. As Lumas was taking deadly aim at his best friend, Brad suddenly leaped forward, reached over the seat and grabbed the steering wheel. He yanked it, just as a shot rang out from the window of the Hummer. The car swerved to the right as a startled Matt hit the brakes and fought to hold onto the wheel. With a jolt that sent their bodies up into the air, Ruby hit the curb—then up and over it. Bouncing around as it traveled on the sidewalk and shoulder, Matt pulled hard to the left and finally regained control. Ruby came to a stop sitting sideways, facing the street—the rear of the car inches from the metal guard rail.

Matt was in the middle of, "What is your problem . . ." when he, along with Bart saw the Hummer now in front of them. It pulled up near the patrol car. Lumas took aim at the tire. The officer evidently saw the gun, and tried to speed up. But, with a flash from the gun, the front tire blew, sending the patrol car spiraling around in the middle of the road. It spun completely around toward the curb. The driver-side tire struck the curb with enough force to send the car flipping over. Brad watched in astonishment as their rescuer's vehicle flipped over the guard rail and disappeared down an embankment. Brad began to pray for Officer Gabriel. *This can't be happening? They were so close to the hospital. How could these guys be so brazen? They must be really desperate to attack a policeman that way.*

Ruby was now sitting on the sidewalk. The Hummer was stopped in the middle of the road about a block away.

Brittany, hands over her face, cried out, "What's happening?"

Bart was just sitting there, mouth agape. "I - I can't believe they just did that. I knew that they were mean, but that was just pure evil—like they have no respect for authority at all."

Suddenly, the Hummer's backup lights flashed, and it began to move in reverse. Whipping around, it stopped, facing them. Matt quickly turned the key to start Ruby up. Usually, the motor roared to life on the first turn of the key. The motor turned over and over, but the car did not start. Matt's frustration grew as he tried again, to no avail. The black beast moved toward them, picking up speed.

Brad looked over at Bart and saw something he had not seen before on Bart's face, the look of excitement had turned to one of sheer terror. He couldn't get over the ruthlessness of what he had just witnessed.

"I think this would be a good time to seriously pray," Brad suggested as the headlights of the Hummer began to blind them. Bart bowed his head as Brad prayed, "Oh Jesus, deliver us from this enemy, who is trying to destroy us. Let no weapon formed against us prosper."

At that moment, Ruby started up. Matt shouted, "Everybody hold on!" He slammed the gear shift into drive and hit the accelerator. The Mustang leaped forward just as the black hulk plowed into the rear side panel of the car. Locked in a sort of a death spiral, the Hummer pushed Ruby's rear around about ninety degrees before the car finally broke free. Ruby jerked and bounced as she hit the curbing. Scraping metal— sparks flying—she tore out down the road. The Hummer spun around, in hot pursuit. Matt suddenly slowed. "Look," he shouted, pointing to the sidewalk.

Beneath a street light stood a man in uniform. Gun drawn, he pointed it in the direction of the Hummer behind them. Brad's stomach soured as the headlights revealed the red shiny glimmer of blood on side of his face.

"Officer Gabriel!" Bart exclaimed, "and he's injured."

Brad watched the headlights behind them as the officer began to unload his firearm into the oncoming juggernaut. Brad could see a brief illumination of fire from the gun each time he pulled the trigger. One, two, three, four times it fired. The bullets meeting their mark with precision, piercing a headlight, then the windshield, and finally the driver's side front tire. The tire blew, sending the mammoth vehicle spinning sideways, tires screaming on the pavement across two lanes and into the grassy median. As it careened sideways, it struck a guard rail in the center of the median with enough force that it flipped up and over the rail. Crashing to the ground with the sound of crunching metal, it came to rest in a heap, upside-down. Steam swirled around the fallen giant as the headlights, which were now unusually dim, emanated a yellowish glow. Matt stopped the car, and for a second everything was still. Everyone in the car stared in disbelief, not knowing exactly what to do next. Brad couldn't help wondering. "Is it really dead?" He finally questioned out loud.

Bart turned to Brad, blinking hard in disbelief. He wiped his face, attempting to cover his emotional display. Then bravely responded, "I hope so," followed by a nervous chuckle. Matt turned to Officer Gabriel, who was walking toward them with a slight limp.

"Is everyone all right?" he called.

Matt got out of the car and met him. "Yes, sir. What about you?"

"I'm OK, just a small cut on my head I think. He pulled out a handkerchief and wiped some of the blood from his face.

Brad got out of the car to check on the situation for himself. He couldn't help noticing a strangeness about the sky. The lightning again flashed intermittently in the distance. Everything seemed to be getting blurry. Brad blinked a few times to clear his vision. As he stood there, trying in vain to hear what Matt and the officer were saying, a hollow feeling seemed to be overtake him. His legs trembled, and the pain in his knee throbbed.

Bart, who was now standing outside of the car, looked over the car roof at Brad. "Man, you look terrible."

"Gee, thanks." Brad muttered, as Bart started around the car. He could see that Brad was as pale as a sheet, his eyes bloodshot and sunken into dark circles.

"Are you alright, man?" When Bart got within a few feet of him, Brad felt his knees buckle, and he clutched the car door to keep from ending up face first on the pavement. Bart immediately caught him and helped into the back seat of the car. For a few seconds the car seemed to spin. Brad closed his eyes briefly, and then opened them.

"Man! What's going on, Bart?" Brad asked, as he lay on his back across the seat. "I feel so bad. Why is it so cold?" Brad shivered.

Bart put his hand on Brad's forehead to check his temperature. "It's exhaustion and a touch of trauma. We need to get you to the hospital, too. I'll tell Matt we need to get going. The hospital's only a few of miles away."

As Bart left and walked over toward Matt, Brad was lying back gazing at the sky. He could hear Brittany, who was still sitting in the front seat. Her face in her hands, she was muttering something he couldn't understand, over and over. He wondered where her mind could be, with all she had been through.

Lightning flickered, diverting his attention toward the horizon. Again, there was an ominous, pinkish glow in the sky. *Are all of the things going on tonight related in some sort of grand scheme of the enemy for this area?* He knew, from reading the Bible, that there were powers and principalities in the kingdom of darkness which controlled certain areas. These forces worked together to hinder the efforts of believers and tried to keep people from knowing the truth.

Brad studied the clouds, as each flash illuminated them. As he did, his heart began to race. *No, it can't be,* he thought. He could see movement and strange bursts of light coming from the sky. Then a reddish-golden brightness burst up from the ground in the distance. Brad sat up, pushed the front seat forward and stumbled out of the car, watching the sky behind him.

Bart returned to the car. Standing beside Brad, he was also intrigued by the unusual sky. "What is that?"

"The kingdom of darkness," Brad replied, as he contemplated the coming destruction.

"What?" Bart asked, confused by his remark. "What are you talking about?"

"God is giving us a picture of what the battle is really like—opening our eyes to see how real and destructive our enemy is."

As the sound of explosions drew closer, Brad could hear the familiar high pitched whining, almost screaming sound of the dragonfly fighters. Suddenly, one streaked right over their heads, gleaming in the night sky. When Brad had seen them earlier, they had appeared more mechanical from a distance. However, up close they looked more like some large flying creatures, silvery in color that seemed to spit some sort of red fire balls from their mouths. Explosions lit up the area behind the overturned Hummer. Both Brad and Bart hit the ground, lying flat, facing the wreckage of the Hummer. Its headlights were still aglow, very dim and golden. There was something peculiar about them. While Brad gazed at them, they turned from gold to a blood red. Unexpectedly, the Hummer started to shake violently. Slowly, the headlights began to rise, like the crushed wreckage was being lifted off of the ground. As it rose, Brad could see that attached to the back of the vehicle was a slender, long, curving mass, like a neck. It was followed by a body covered in gleaming metallic scales. To their astonishment, the cowering boys watched the Hummer morph into the head of a giant serpent. Its massive body was now stretched across the vacant four lanes. Rearing its ominous head, the red headlights had transformed into the creature's darkness piercing eyes.

"Oh, God! Oh, God!" Bart cried out. "Wh-what is that?" Bart, belly-crawled underneath the battered Ruby, peering out next to the rear tire.

Chapter 25

Brittany Faces Her Enemy

Through the open car door Brad saw that Brittany was now aware of what was going on. She was staring wide-eyed at the gleaming, writhing beast, which loomed over them. Her reaction amazed Brad. He wondered why she wasn't screaming her head off. Instead, she was simply staring at the creature with an expression of what appeared to be anger, mixed with determination. She pulled herself up and stepped boldly out of the car. Brad tried to grab her as she walked by. "Brit! What are you doing? Get down! It will see you." Brad cried out.

Brit didn't respond, acting as though she couldn't even hear him. The sound of explosions, the whining of dragonfly fighters, and what seemed like the sound of a rushing wind, made it difficult to hear anything. Brittany walked about ten feet forward, so that she was clearly visible to the giant.

"Is she crazy?" Bart cried out to Brad, "She'll be killed. We've got to stop her!"

Brad tried to get up. But, when he tried to stand, a sharp pain radiating from his injured knee, sent him right back on his face. He closed his eyes in pain. "God, don't you want me to save her?" He prayed.

"You can't save her," he heard that still small voice say. "Only I can save her; but you can help." Brad knew what that meant. He'd learned the value of interceding in prayer for others through the G-man group. They had spent hours praying for each other. Brad knew how many times prayer had gotten him through great struggles in his own life. *When you can't do anything else, you can always pray.* "Jesus, protect her—guide her—save her," he managed to verbalize as he lay immobilized next to Ruby.

Brittany just stood there facing the giant enemy as if to say, "I'm not afraid of you." It was as if she had faced him before. Brad watched in amazement as the dragon, which seemed to be a combination of flesh covered by metal scales, brandished its gleaming pointed teeth. Nostrils flaring, it spewed out its hot greenish-gold breath which filled the air with a putrid smell. The black slit-like pupils focused in on the lone young woman standing below. Peering down on its prey, with its mouth partially opened like a drooling wolf, a stringy glob of thick dark liquid, like oil, fell from one corner of its mouth. It reached the ground with a "splud." After hitting the pavement, it spread like a thick black shiny pancake on the road. As it spread, steam rose from the gooey mass which began to bubble like it was actually eating into the asphalt. The dragon, which stood at least four stories tall, snorted in anger. Its massive head recoiled, and then stopped and for a moment. Cocking its head to one side and then the other— like a dog confused by a high-pitched sound, the beast appeared to study the vulnerable young woman below. Its silvery scales shimmered with a greenish tint, as they reflected the street lights.

Brad was briefly distracted by all the movement in the sky. It was constantly lit by radiant bursts, followed by explosions on the ground, as the area was harassed by what seemed to be an onslaught of hundreds of dragonfly-like flying demons. Brad was agog at the number of them, stunned to see this with his own eyes. He understood God was showing him the seriousness of the battle Christians faced. *This fallen world is filled with spiritual beings that we can't normally see. Their sole mission: to keep people from following Christ. Constantly putting difficulties in people's path, they hope we will either give up in frustration, or begin to blame God for letting it happen.* Even Brad had wondered why so many bad things were allowed to happen. Brad lifted his eyes and surveyed the heavens which were illuminated by multiple explosions. The constant buzzing of the flying menaces, along with the towering evil creature standing before them was an impossible situation. He shook his head in despair. *This is totally hopeless,* he thought. "Lord, how can we possibly win?"

Abruptly, as if it had finally had enough of this cat and mouse game, the reptilian beast before them lifted its huge head and then plunged it forward, right down towards them. Brad threw his arm up over his eyes to shield himself from what he figured was sure annihilation by the crushing force of this great falling object. But, then everything seemed to stop. Brad looked up to see what had happened. Tears blurred his vision. He blinked hard, overwhelmed by the spectacle before him. The dragon's snarling, steaming, slime-dripping head shimmered just a few feet in front of Brit's face; yet she stood there defiantly. Behind her Brad saw the faint radiant outline of the figure he had seen before in his dreams. Brittany couldn't see him, but she obviously felt His presence. Only by His power could she stand up to this overwhelming evil. She understood, in a very real way, the truth of the verses in the Bible that say that Jesus will never leave us nor forsake us. Jesus had truly become her Deliverer from this evil which would try to keep her from Him.

Wow, this is what being a Christian is really all about, Brad thought. *It's facing all of the evil that constantly bombards us with Jesus right by our side strengthening us, demonstrating His great power. Everything in life happens to teach us how Jesus can conquer anything—if, we truly understand that He is literally always with us. "Greater is He who is in me than he who is in the world." "I can do all things through Christ who strengthens me." "If Christ be for me, whom shall I fear?"* The scriptures bombarded Brad's mind as his faith soared.

The great dragon fumed and snarled. The rage that emanated from him turned to complete frustration as the huge head began to back away. Brad could see Brit's mouth was moving. *Is she talking to the thing? No, even better, she's not just talking to it, she's speaking to it.* Brad could hear her saying, "In the name of Jesus, the King of Kings, I bind your power." Brad gasped at the fury with which the Dragon reacted. Its huge head again recoiled and then began to nod back and forth; as a violent hissing sound, along with greenish smoke bellowed from its flaring nostrils. It then lifted its giant oak-tree-trunk sized tail and slammed it to the ground with such force that the earth shook. Ruby literally bounced, sending Bart scurrying out from under it and over next to Brad.

"What a temper tantrum," Brad commented to Bart, who had crawled next to him.

"Yeah, he's just a big baby."

At that moment, the giant beast stopped and looked down, as if it had just recognized who was standing behind Brit. The red, snake-like eyes narrowed then widened, as if startled. Next the wildest thing began to happen. The goliath of a dragon began to get smaller—to literally shrink. Within the space of thirty seconds, the dragon was less than half its original size, about the same height as the street lights. In another thirty seconds, it was smaller than Brittany (all five foot six inches of her). The slimy creature was still as defiant as ever. It sneered in anger and then composed itself, pointing its gnarled clawed finger at her face. Brittany just stood there, somewhat confused by the tenacity of the little creature which was right in her face.

A raspy, wicked voice hissed, "There will be another time. I'll . . ."

At that point, the shimmering figure behind her became more radiant. He stepped forward, raised His hand and pointed. The down-sized beast immediately grew silent, and cowered like a whipped dog. Silenced, it turned, hit the ground, and slithered off; disappearing into the brush, more like a snake than a dragon. Brad realized that that battle around them had stopped. All of the forces fighting in the sky had faded away. Brad marveled at the awesome power of Jesus.

Bart shook his head in disbelief. "That was amazing. I-is that Jesus?" he asked. "I was hoping that He would just kill that dragon."

Brad thought a moment. He had hoped that too. "Someday—Bart—Someday. He will. I guess that time hasn't come. But, for now, He helps us defeat our dragons."

"Yeah," Bart agreed. "What a great day that will be."

The guys looked back over to where Brit was still standing, but now she was all alone. She knelt down exhausted and weeping. Brad's heart went out to her. *She is so young in the Lord, but has already had to fight through so much.* He wanted to go to her and comfort her, but it was as if his body couldn't even move. He was so tired. As he watched, Matt came over and helped Brittany up.

I wonder where he's been all this time? he thought to himself as he lay there. Right now, all he wanted to do was lay there in the grass and sleep. Watching Matt help Brit up, he was thankful for friends that could come along and help.

Bart stood up, looking at his watch. "Boy it's late. I wonder how Luke's doing?"

Like a vision in Brad's mind, Luke's face appeared, pale as a ghost. Luke's eyes were closed. Suddenly, they opened wide, a look of sheer terror in them. Brad blinked hard trying to think. In all the commotion of this wild ride, he had completely forgotten about where they were heading and why. *Typical— this is the whole purpose. The enemy distracted us from our main mission.* He looked up at Bart. "We need to get to the hospital right now!" Brad stated urgently.

"I know. Let's get going," Bart agreed, as he opened the car door and pulled the seat forward. Brad lifted himself slowly, but was so weak he couldn't get up. Bart reached down to help him. He just couldn't seem to move. It was as if his body weighed a thousand pounds. As his friend pulled on him, he felt really dizzy. Then, everything around him began to disappear into a blur.

Brad awakened to Matt's hand on his shoulder, shaking him. "Wake up, sleepy head. We're here." Brad looked up at his friend, who was smiling at him. "Man, you were out of it."

Brad looked around, wondering how they got him into the car. He was the only person left in the car. He rubbed his eyes, "Where is everyone?"

"Brit is in the emergency room being checked out. They say that she'll be fine. Bart went to find out where Luke is."

"Luke!" Brad exclaimed excitedly. "How's he doing? We need to get to him."

"Calm down. Don't worry. Officer Harris radioed ahead and the police are here keeping an eye on things. They've got it under control. With all of the police around here, Dragon's guys would be crazy to try anything."

"OK. Just as long as the police are here. By the way, how is Officer Gabriel?

"Who?" Matt asked, wondering.

"You know the Officer who stopped to help us."

"You mean Officer Harris. He took good care of everything." Matt replied.

"I sure thought he said his name was Gabriel." Brad paused, his memory somewhat blurred. "What time is it?" Brad asked wearily.

Matt looked at his watch, "Almost one in the morning, but don't worry. I've called your parents and told them that you are all right. They're on their way here right now. I'm sorry man. You were sleeping so soundly we decided you needed to rest. But, now the attendants would like to check you out. Can you stand up?"

"I think so." Brad sat forward and swung his left leg out onto the concrete. It wasn't until he tried to move his right leg that the now familiar pain shot up his leg from his knee. "I might need a little help," he admitted as he grimaced, and held up one arm. Matt reached in and pulled him up and out of the car at about the time a nurse came up with a wheelchair. As Brad was lowered into the soft cushion of the chair, the pain began to subside. While being wheeled over to the emergency room entrance, Bart came busting out of the double glass doors, worry painted on his face. Seeing Brad in the wheelchair, he composed himself.

"Brad, whas-up? Nice of you to finally join us."

Brad looked at him with suspicion and cut through the formalities. "How's Luke doing? Did you find out anything?" Bart pensively looked up at Matt as if to question how he should respond. "What? Did we get here too late? What do you know? Is Luke OK?" Brad pressed.

Matt nodded to Bart, letting out a deep breath. "Luke had some sort of allergic reaction to something that was in his system, they call it toxic shock."

"He will be all right though, won't he?" Brad interrupted.

Bart looked up at Matt and then back down at Brad. "He's in a comatose state right now. They aren't sure exactly how to proceed. They're saying it's a drug overdose. Evidently, this is not the first time he's been here for that."

"Are they sure that someone didn't get in there and slip him something?" Brad inquired.

"No, they don't see how that could have happened; he's been so closely monitored since he's been here. Maybe this was all God's way of protecting him from those thugs," Matt added, as they stopped in front of two large swinging doors which lead into the E.R..

"I'm afraid we'll have to part company here. But we'll be praying for you." Bart smiled, holding out his fist.

Brad met it with his. "Thanks, man. Pray for Luke, too. OK?"

Bart nodded.

"Bra-ad," a familiar voice called in controlled distress.

Brad was overwhelmed with emotion as he saw his family hurrying down the hallway toward him. His mom kissed his face several times. Normally, Brad would have said, "M-om," embarrassed at her show of affection in front of the guys, but right now it was what they both needed.

"Where have you been? What took you so long to get here? I've been praying God would keep you safe."

"Well, Mom, I know this is hard to believe, but we were stopped by a huge four-story tall dragon."

"What?" his Mom asked in confusion, while wiping a tear from her eye.

"Yeah, tell-em Bart. He was right there with me. And Brittany, she was amazing. She faced down that monster, and Jesus was right beside her."

Mrs. Johnson glanced up at Bart, who looked back at her. Bart raised his shoulders along with his eyebrows. His expression showed that he didn't understand anything Brad was talking about. Brad wondered at Bart's lack of response. *Why wasn't he telling everyone what we saw? Was he too embarrassed? No, he acted as if he hadn't even been there.* Bart was genuinely clueless as to what Brad was talking about. Brad's frustration grew as he faced their unbelief.

Sensing Brad's struggle, Bart replied, "Well, we did run into some trouble with Dragon's men, on the way here. Is that what you mean, Brad?"

"No, after that, when the dragonfly fighters started flying over, and the Hummer wreckage became this huge dragon's head and—," Brad stopped. The expressions on each of their faces registered real concern that he had just gone off the deep end. Brad looked at Bart, and then at Matt.

After an awkward moment of silence, Matt rescued his friend. "Brad, right after we were stopped by Officer Harris, you fell asleep in the back seat. You were so tired that you slept until we got here."

Brad looked up into his mom's face, his own face hot with embarrassment. Matt again trying to spare his friend added, "Boy, that must have been some dream. I want to hear all about that one. Sounds like God is showing you a lot."

Brad was so tired—trying hard to think. *A dream—It was just another dream.* He felt so stupid. *But it was so real.* Brad turned and looked into his mom's shining face and then up at his dad, who was beaming with gratitude to God for the safe return of his son. Brad's heart swelled with joy as he was suddenly just so glad to see them, that everything else didn't matter. A couple of hours earlier he had really wondered if he would ever have that pleasure again. He could see acceptance and understanding in their eyes, and his feeling of foolishness abated.

His mom smiled and said softly, "I'll sure like to hear what God has been teaching you through all of this."

His sister Mandy came over and grabbed his hand. "Brad, what you said about Brit is so true. She has been so brave, and Jesus has seen her through all of this. It's amazing how God is using your dreams to give you understanding—like

He's bringing the behind-the-scenes workings of his kingdom to life while you sleep."

Wow, Brad thought. *That's true*. Then he asked, "But why? Why am I seeing these things?"

"Brad," he turned, hearing the strong voice of his dad, who simply said, "maybe it's because you are faithful to act on it."

"Sure man," Matt agreed. "If you hadn't pushed us to go over there and find Luke, where would he and Brit be right now?"

Brad's heart was comforted by that thought. Then, he nodded his head, "God has shown me that all of this is like a huge invasion. Powerful forces are trying to take over our whole city, but God wants us to understand what's going on and do something about it. I'm not always sure what to do. But, I know He wants us to pray, listen and then do whatever He says to defeat this very real enemy who is continually trying to brainwash people into following him." He paused and laughed. "The dreams are really kind of cool, but it sure makes it hard to get a good night's sleep." They all laughed with him.

"I'm sorry, folks, but we are ready for Mr. Johnson in the E.R. now," a sweet but assertive African-American voice interrupted. The sturdy woman, dressed in a bright green smock with a name badge that read "Betty," grabbed the handles on the wheelchair. As she did, she leaned down and whispered to Brad, "Don't worry, young man. We're going to take good care of you. God has spoken to me many times in my dreams, too." Brad looked around into her shining face, and returned the smile. He was grateful for her, and felt that God was truly in control now.

The ER doctors cleaned the wound on his head, which wasn't pleasant, but not serious enough for stitches. His knee would need x-rays, but appeared to have a severely bruised kneecap. The doctor believed that there was no major damage, and after an injection, he was free to go.

"Try to keep your knee on ice to alleviate the swelling," the doctor instructed.

Brad wanted to see Luke before he left the hospital, but his dad informed him that Luke was still in ICU, and only family members were allowed in there at this late hour. "Besides, young man, we all could use a few hours of sleep tonight." When Brad finally got home, he drifted off to sleep, praying for Luke, knowing that Luke's battle was just beginning.

Chapter 26

What We Need Is A Miracle

Brad woke up in his own bed, grateful for peaceful sleep. If he had dreamed during the night, he didn't remember it. He could see the Star Ship Enterprise hanging from the ceiling. It swayed back and forth, receiving gentle breezes from the spinning ceiling fan overhead. As his head cleared from the fog of waking up, his eyes focused on the collage of pictures pinned to his bulletin board on the wall, a few feet away. Good times, memories of fun events, as well as crazy things he had done with his friends crowded his mind. The faces of his family—Mom, Dad, and Mandy—of Matt and Luke, one by one, warmed his heart. His mind sprinted to wondering how Luke was doing this morning.

Brad heard someone in the hall outside his room. His sister was evidently monitoring his sleep. He sat up and looked around. The sunlight was peering through all of the slits in the mini-blinds. *What time is it?* he wondered, as he turned over to gaze at the alarm clock. The alarm had obviously been turned off by his Mom. *Eleven fourteen!* He was amazed that it was so late. *What day is it anyway, Saturday?* The night seemed to have been a week long. *What really happened last night?* Questions ran through his foggy mind. *Had it all been a dream?* He thought, trying to comprehend it all.

Brad reached over and pulled his drawing pad from his nightstand. As he thought, he began to doodle feverishly. First, he sketched the outline of a dragonfly fighter from his close-up view in last night's wild dream. Once he had the right shape, Brad added all the detail he could remember. Gazing down at the paper, a tinge of pain throbbed in his forehead. His head still ached a bit. He reached up and felt the bandage. The wound smarted when he touched it.

"Well," he sighed, "Although some of last night was a dream, this is a very real bandage."

Brad cocked his head to one side, hearing whispers in the hall.

"Are you sure he's awake?" Brad heard his Mom ask.

"Yes, I just saw him sitting up."

Brad smirked, and in a heavy booming voice he called out. "Who's that, out there making all of that noise? How's a body going to sleep all day with that racket going on?"

The lurkers in the hall burst into laughter and came into the room smiling. Mom was holding a tray with a couple of pieces of toast, covered in butter and strawberry jam, along with a glass of juice. Brad put down his sketch pad and looked over the inviting treat. He grinned and inquired, "What, no flowers?" His mom faked a big frown. "Just kidding," he added. He poked out his lips as she leaned over and received a kiss. "Thanks, Mom. You sure know how to make a guy feel better."

"Hey, what about me? I made the toast," Mandy asserted.

Brad couldn't resist lifting up one edge of the toast, as if to look it over. "You sure you made this toast?" he asked tauntingly; a subtle reminder of her repeated ability to blacken a piece of bread to the point of causing it to flame up.

She smacked him on the arm. "You're so mean."

"Just kidding, sis. Thank you. You know I love you too." He pulled her over and gave her a peck on the cheek. Then he turned serious and grabbed her hand, "Have you heard anything about Luke?

Mandy looked at her Mom, who nodded, reassuring her. "His condition worsened somewhat over night. He seems to have some sort of infection in his body. They think the combination of drugs he'd been given may have damaged his immune system, and now his body has difficulty in fighting off infection."

"But, he's going to be all right, isn't he?"

With an encouraging look, Mom confided, "Brad, the doctors are doing everything they can to help Luke, but his situation is very serious. They can do only so much; but Jesus can work miracles. I think what Luke needs now is a miracle."

Brad's mind was carried away by that thought. Jesus had done so much for Luke already. He had brought him out of the darkness of the world of Dragon and showed him the truth. Certainly, He wasn't going to take him before he could have the opportunity to serve Him on this earth. "Oh God, I thank You for what You have done for Luke. Please spare his life and give him a chance to serve You in this world," Brad lifted up a spontaneous prayer. He looked up and could see that his Mom and Mandy were agreeing with him. "Mom, can we go to the hospital? I want to get some of the guys together to pray for Luke."

Mom smiled, "I think that's a word from the Lord."

"Whatever you do, don't forget to call Bart." Mandy laughed, "That boy has already called here twice this morning."

Brad gulped down the juice, inhaled the toast and then got on the phone to Matt.

"Brad, how are you doing this morning? Is your knee better?" Matt asked with concern.

"Oh, it's better, but I hear that Luke isn't doing so well."

"Yeah, and I'm afraid that his situation is going to get even more complicated," Matt added.

"What do you mean?"

"Well, the authorities are planning to arrest him, as soon as he's able. They've had a dozen people say that they saw him shoot Sammy Dornberg. The most outspoken being your old friend, Blane Stevens."

"That's a bunch of bull!" Brad blurted out in frustration. "You know that Luke didn't shoot Sammy. We saw him put the gun down before the lights went out."

"I know, but evidently you and I are the only ones who saw it that way. Our testimony is that we couldn't see who did it because the lights went out. Anyway, it's something else we need to pray about."

"Yeah," Brad agreed. "By the way, how is Sammy doing? I wonder if he would testify on Luke's behalf."

Matt hesitated. "Well, I don't know that he could be counted on. He's in pretty bad shape himself, and after all, Luke was pointing a gun at him right before he went down. I also know that Luke had several clashes with him in the last couple of weeks, to the point that Luke was literally hiding from him."

"Man! How can you say that? You sound like you believe Luke did it!" Brad roared over the phone, so loudly that Mandy ducked her head into his doorway to make sure he was alright.

"Take it easy, dude," Matt retorted. "I'm just telling you what it looks like to the authorities. Luke hasn't been hanging with a bunch of angels, you know."

Brad sighed, "Yeah, I'm sorry. I guess I'm a little touchy about Luke right now. He's been through a lot. I just want him to make it and continue to follow Christ. You know the Bible talks about how the Devil roams around, like a roaring lion, seeking people to devour."

"Yeah, but it also says that greater is He who is in us than he who is in the world. So we need to pray for him," Matt reminded.

"We've got a lot to pray about," Brad agreed. "What we need is a miracle. We should see how many of the guys we can get to meet us at the hospital, to pray. I'm shooting to be there at one-thirty. This is an all-points-prayer-bulletin. I'll call all the G-men list through the letter K. You take the rest, OK?"

"No—No. You just get yourself there," Matt insisted. "I'll make sure all the guys know. I'm sure that we can get most of them there, if not they can be praying wherever they are."

Brad huffed, "Oh, all right. But, I'll call Bart. He's already called here twice today."

Matt laughed, "OK. That guy is something else. If you looked up the word "loyal" in the dictionary, I believe his picture would be right there beside the golden retriever."

Brad grinned and agreed. "It sure looks like we have another faithful brother and warrior in the battle. Praise God for him!" Brad said goodbye, and hung up the phone thinking.

The battle—that's sure what life is right now, a battle. He thought of all of the video games he'd played in his lifetime—all of the hours spent moving a joystick, and pushing buttons in an attempt to defeat the enemy and get to another level of the game—only to find more evil enemies to defeat. *Yep, just like life as a Christian. As soon as I get a handle on one problem, another one pops up.* There were several differences in real life, however. The consequences of defeat, he was learning, were much greater in real life. Brad had experienced firsthand the pain of allowing the enemy, sin, to defeat him, and the difficulty of its consequences. Some of the struggles still haunted him through the torment of their memories. The devil was a master at bringing up old memories at his weakest moment. How would Luke make it through all of this? His battle was just beginning, and he had so much to deal with, if he even lives through this. *Perhaps*, he paused, *it would almost be better if he didn't.* Brad stopped himself. *Where did that come from?* He couldn't believe that he had even thought it. "That is a lie from the pit of hell!" he suddenly exclaimed out loud. *That is defeat,* he thought to himself, as he sat up in his bed. "I take that thought captive in the name of Jesus!" he proclaimed out loud. *That's the other difference between real life and video games. Video games merely create an illusion of victory. The real battles of life cannot be won without Jesus. The truth is that every demon in hell is subject to His commands, and they all tremble in fear of Him. Jesus is the only real superhero. It's amazing how society craves, and creates imaginary ones, when Jesus is the only real deal.*

Dad poked his head in the doorway. "Good morning, son. A-are you OK?" he asked, examining him with one eyebrow raised. "Who are you talking to?"

"The devil and all of his demons, Dad," he announced seriously.

Dad nodded slowly and smiled, as if he knew the feeling. "Good, let him have it for me, too.

All right?" Brad grinned at him, as he disappeared down the hall, singing an old praise tune in his deep booming voice, "The captain of the host is Jesus, and we're following in His footsteps . . ."

Looking at the clock, Brad turned and let his feet down onto the floor from the bed. He stood. A dull pain shot from his knee, turning sharp as it ran up his thigh. He winced and instinctively reached down to grab the ace bandage that they had wrapped around his leg the night before. "*O-o-w." I guess I should take things a little more slowly.* As he got dressed, his mind returned to thinking about the battles Luke faced. *I guess fighting battles, and warring in the spirit is a big part of growing as a Christian.* Brad knew he couldn't prevent Luke from having to fight the battles of life, nor would it be good for him if he could. Luke would have to learn to stand up to the enemy on his own. *Well, not really on his own, but with Jesus by his side,* he thought, recalling the vision of Brittany facing down the Dragon. Brad pulled out his sneakers and dropped them on the floor in front of him, staring at them. *If I prevented Luke from facing his battles, it'd be like keeping a newborn in a protective cage or incubator all of his life so that nothing would ever happen to him. What kind of life would that be? He would be weak and totally useless—like a big blob. God hasn't called us into his kingdom to be useless blobs.* Brad thought, still gazing at his sneakers. *He desires to take us, weak as we are and make us bold, brave cadets who are building His kingdom.* Brad was getting excited. He so wanted to be a fearless and faithful follower of his King Jesus; following Him into the great adventures of the Kingdom Of God. *Why doesn't someone make a video game like that,* he wondered? Brad felt convicted that he'd wasted so much time playing video games. It was as if he had allowed the false thrill of a game to steal away the true excitement of life with Jesus. "Oh Lord, help me never again replace the excitement and joy of knowing You with something so foolish."

Finally, Brad bent down to try put on the black and white Converses that stared up at him—mocking the pain in his throbbing knee. He sat up again scowling at his sneakers. The pain eased. *I am such a wimp,* he chided himself. *Perhaps flip-flops are the foot attire for the day.* He thought for a moment and then bent down again, deciding to persevere through the pain. He managed to get one shoe on, and sat up for a breather.

"Hey, man. How's it going?" a cheerful young man's voice interrupted his struggle with his sneakers.

Brad's face brightened at seeing his new buddy. "Bart. Whas-up, man?"

Bart came in and raised his fist for Brad to respond in the modern expression of male greeting. "Hey, I hope you don't mind. I asked your sister to call me when you were awake. So, were you going to sleep all day or what?" Bart joked. "Anyway your mom suggested that if I could get a ride over here, we could all ride over to the hospital together. I hope that's all right with you?"

Mandy now stood in the doorway. "Well," Brad replied, faking a concerned look, "I don't know if I like all this conspiracy stuff going on behind my back."

Mandy rolled her eyes and shook her head, "I think you'll just have to get over it, Mr. Sensitive." She said, throwing a pair rolled up socks she had in her hand, at him. It smacked him on the side of the head, and she continued down the hall to the laundry room.

"Good shot!" Bart exclaimed, as both boys laughed. Brad returned to looking wearily down at his sneaker which still needed to be tied. "We should get a move on, if we're going to get over to the hospital by one-thirty," Bart said. He looked around Brad's room, and then at Brad, who was struggling to tie the shoe lace. Seeing his bandaged knee, Bart responded, "Oh, man. Let me help you." He bent down, and began to tie the laces.

Brad was a little taken aback and almost said no. But a voice inside stopped him. "No, let him help you. Everyone needs help once in a while, and it is a blessing to him."

"God bless you man." Brad felt his eyes welling up. He quickly thought of something else, not wanting his friend to see his emotion. He thought back to last night when they had left the Dragon's Den. Brad didn't know what had actually taken place versus what he had dreamed. "Bart, tell me something," Brad blurted out, watching the top of Bart's dark, curly hair bob as he pulled the laces tight.

"Sure, what?"

"Last night in Matt's car, exactly when did I fall asleep?"

Bart grabbed Brad's other tennis shoe and looked up at him. Squinting with one eye, as he thought, he replied, "I'm not exactly sure. What do you remember?"

Brad looked at him and frowned. "I remember a lot, but I don't think most of it is reality."

"I think," Bart paused, "it was right after the dragon appeared."

Brad was shocked, and then he caught a look in Bart's eye and grew suspicious. "You mean The Dragon, the guy who's the magician?"

"No," he said, "the huge dragon from the Hummer."

"You did see it!" Brad exploded with excitement.

Bart, who had finally gotten Brad's other shoe tied, gave him a look that told Brad he was just egging him on. Realizing that he might be treading on Brad's feelings, Bart apologized. "I'm sorry, man. I thought you were messing with my mind or something. I just heard you mention that last night. I didn't know you seriously thought it happened."

Brad frowned, and laughed. "Yeah, I guess I was totally out of it last night."

"To answer your original question," Bart continued, "I think you fell asleep while we were stopped by Officer Harris."

"So, his name wasn't Officer Gabriel. Was it after his patrol car wrecked?" Brad inquired. He could tell by the dumbfounded look on Bart's face that it must have been sooner.

"A-ahm," Bart started, "I don't—What kind of dreams did you have last night?"

"Never mind," Brad huffed, in frustration.

Bart felt really bad now and started to apologize again.

Brad stopped him and tried to explain, "It's OK. I've just been having these wild dreams lately that are so real I have a hard time figuring out what happened, and what didn't."

"Cool," Bart responded. His eyes flashed, bright with excitement, as he caught sight of the open art tablet lying on the bed. "What's this?" He asked, picking it up to examine it more closely.

"Oh, I like to doodle. It's something I saw in my dream. Drawing helps me remember and figure things out."

"Wow, this is good. You should draw for graphic novels or something."

"You're kidding me, right? I just mess around and draw mostly stuff from video games, but I've been trying to remember the things I see in these dreams. Drawing them helps."

"I can see how," Bart agreed. "Like they say; a picture is worth a thousand words."

"You know, the strange thing about these dreams is, sometimes stuff in the dreams actually happen, making it even more difficult to figure out reality."

"Way cool," Bart added. "Do you think it's God showing you all that stuff?"

"Well, God has definitely shown me some things through all this, although, it has taken some time to understand." Bart finished the laces on the second sneak.

"Man, I would love to hear about some of these dreams. Maybe you should write them down if you really think that they are from God."

"Hm-m, that's an interesting idea, Bart. I might just do that. But, don't spread this around. You seem to understand, but most people would probably think that I'm crazy." Brad stood slowly, and walked forward. The pain was there, but was bearable.

"Can I help you?" Bart asked.

"No, it's OK. They said I needed to walk on it. The kneecap is just bruised." Brad laughed. "Just catch me if I fall."

"I will, if you promise to tell me about those dreams soon," Bart beamed.

"Sure thing. But, right now we need to get to the hospital." Brad got to the doorway, and then turned to Bart, "So nothing happened to Officer Harris' car?"

"Nope, he just escorted us to the hospital. It wasn't eaten by any giant dragon that I know of." Brad appreciated Bart's encouragement that he wasn't crazy.

On the way to the hospital Bart and Brad sat in the back seat discussing the events of the night before, and what had transpired since. "Did the Dragon's Den burn down completely?" Brad asked.

"No, the newer auditorium section had a sprinkler system, so it's still standing, but the bar and dining area were gutted," Bart answered. "I talked to one of my friends on the squad. Who said they were out there all night. It didn't come from the lightning strike. It definitely started just like you said last night, in the front of the building apparently by a kerosene lamp. The back part of the building, where the stage is, was untouched by the fire, although all the stage equipment was ruined by water damage."

"You mean that little back storage room is still there."

"I believe so. Why?" Bart's curiosity was aroused.

"Oh, I think I may have lost something in there."

"I doubt much could have survived between the smoke and the water damage. Although, if it was in the very back of the building, it may be OK."

Brad sighed, "Just a thought." Brad so wished he could have found that flashlight with its precious information. "Dad, have you heard about any change in Luke's condition?" Brad asked hopefully.

His dad, who had stopped for a traffic light, responded, "No, son. I talked to his mom this morning, and it seems that his body is really struggling with a reaction to some of the drugs in his system, as well as the fact that he had lost so much weight."

"Dad, do you think they'll really arrest him when he recovers? I'm concerned he's going to be accused of something that I know he didn't do."

"That is a possibility, but I believe God will take care of him."

Brad stared out the window as they neared the hospital. He shuddered, *what was that*, he thought? A black Hummer was going down a side street. Brad knew that every time he saw one of those things he would wonder if it was Dragon stalking him. *That's silly,* he wasn't even sure if Dragon recognized who he was last night. It was dark in there. "Bart have you heard anything about Dragon's men who were following us last night?" Brad paused then added, "They were following us last night, weren't they?"

Bart snickered, deviously. Brad could tell that it took all of the self-control Bart could muster not to chide him about his current state of sleep confusion. "Yes, they followed us until the deer caused us all to skid. The Hummer ran across the ditch and got stuck in a field; but by the time the police got there, they had gotten it out. Matt gave his dad a full report, and the police are looking for both guys as well as Mr. Dragon for questioning."

Brad could see the hospital coming into view. An ambulance screamed past them. With red lights flashing, it pulled into the emergency entrance. He remembered Luke's face as they were wheeling him into a very similar vehicle. Scared—eyes wild. *How could they even think Luke could have shot Sammy?* But Brad knew the evidence didn't look good. *I need that flashlight. What could have happened to it? Did Lumas find it? Was it destroyed in the fire? That thumb drive has to be the evidence that will prove Luke's innocence. If only we had it back, Lord.* But that, Brad realized, would take a miracle.

Chapter 27

Will Anyone Believe the Truth?

Brad and his family, along with Bart, entered the hospital through the large automated doors which slid open as they approached. They walked across the polished grey marble floors in the large open concourse of the modern facility. Mandy immediately recognized a young woman sitting in a wheelchair near the desk, waiting to be checked out. "Brittany!" Mandy called, as she hurried over to give her a hug. The rest of the group made its way over to see how she was doing. Everyone greeted Brittany and her mom, Jean, who was filing out some paperwork. Brad's mom asked how things were going and if there was any way they could be of any assistance.

Mandy wheeled Brit a few feet away from the adults to talk. "How are you feeling? Did they treat you OK in this place?"

Brit's unusually pale face lit up with a smile, "I'm so glad to see you guys. Things are going OK, although I'm still a bit dizzy. They say that will pass soon enough and we are both fine." She placed a hand on her tummy, and looked up at Brad. "I understand I wouldn't even be here if it weren't for you, Brad." Tears filled her eyes as she continued. "I don't know how I can ever thank you for what you did."

Brad felt uneasy, not knowing exactly how to respond to her flood of gratitude. "I couldn't have done it without God's help," he replied.

"I'm sure glad that you were listening to Him. I don't remember much about last night. I think they put something in my soda. I passed out and woke up at the hospital in Matt's car. Brad, you and Mandy have been so kind to me. I've made so many mistakes in my life, but you both have shown me that it's not too late for Jesus to use me. I want to learn all I can about Him and how to follow Him, so that I can defeat that evil dragon in my life. I can feel Jesus in my heart. For the first time in my life I believe that my life will matter. Mandy, thank you so much for not giving up on me and for telling me the truth even though I really didn't think I wanted to hear it." They hugged again. She held out her hand to Brad. He took it. She smiled and just said, "Thank you."

Brad nodded and asked, "Brit, what did you mean by 'that evil dragon in my life?'"

She thought a moment. "Brad, I know this sounds crazy but I've had a recurring dream about this huge dragon that is trying to steal my baby. I finally understood that it's a demon of death trying to get me to have an abortion. Like, it's trying to convince me that I would be better off just eliminating my troubles. I had a very real vision of Jesus, holding a tiny baby in His arms. He showed me how precious every life is. I finally just stood up to my fears and said, no! Under no circumstances will I abort my baby. There are too many fine couples, who can't have children, who would give him a godly home. There's no reason to make an innocent baby pay the price for my sin. That has already been done."

Brad was awestruck that someone so young in the Lord could be so strong. "Wow! That's powerful, Brit. And no, I don't think you're crazy at all. We all have our dragons to fight." She smiled, nodding in agreement.

"OK, Sweetheart, it's time to get you home," Brit's mom said as they all hugged goodbye. They turned, and watched as she was wheeled toward the door. The two were almost to the door when it slid open, and a group of a half dozen boys walked through, Matt leading the pack. He stopped and spoke to Brit and her mom. Matt continued over to meet Brad and the rest of the prayer group that was forming. The boys high-fived and shook hands with one another, as Brad's parents excused themselves.

"Brad, your mom and I are going to go up to the ICU waiting room to see if there are any new developments. I'm sure Luke's family is still all there. I'll come back down here and let you guys know specifically what you can be praying for. There's a limit to the number of people that waiting room can hold, so maybe you guys can pray down here."

"Dad, I haven't seen Luke at all. Could I come up and see him, and then come back and report to the guys?" Brad quickly asked.

Admiring his son's concern and devotion for his friend, he grasped Brad's shoulder with a little squeeze. His father smiled and agreed, "I think that's an even better plan."

Brad turned to Matt and the guys, "I'll be back as soon as I can."

Brad stood with his family, waiting for the elevator. He could hear the electronic chimes dinging, getting louder as it slowly lowered. He felt nervous about seeing Luke. He knew that Luke was still in a coma, but wondered how much he could understand. He'd read that some people in comas said afterward that they could understand what was going on around them, but their body was like a prison, and they were unable to respond.

The doors opened and Luke's sister, Sandra, was standing there inside the elevator. "He-ey," she smiled, greeting them through tear-stained cheeks. She gave each one a big hug. "Brad, I'm so glad to see you. I was worried last night when they said you were missing. I felt so guilty that you were supposed to be riding with me."

Brad blushed slightly at her unexpected show of affection. "No, no, Sandie. You couldn't have known. I got sidetracked before I ever got to you."

"How are you doing, Sandra?" Mrs. Johnson asked, looking at her with motherly compassion.

"I –I'm OK." Her eyes began to glaze, and she looked down. "I'm afraid for Luke. They don't give him much hope. They're now talking about brain damage, and they're still not sure why he's not responding. It's as if something has a hold on him and won't let go."

As she was talking, out of the corner of his eye, Brad noticed a dark figure walk into the hallway about thirty feet away. His back was facing him as he disappeared down a corridor to the left. Brad felt his body shiver. He'd known that feeling before. *No, it couldn't be. Why would Dragon be here after all he had done?* A sense of urgency to see Luke overtook Brad.

"There's a group gathering in the lobby waiting room to pray for Luke. Maybe you'd like to join them," Mandy said, comforting Sandra. Sandra wiped a tear from her eye, and nodded in the affirmative. "You all go ahead, and I will stay with Sandra," suggested Mandy. Brad was thankful that Mandy was so thoughtful. It was as if she could feel his desire to get to his friend's side.

Brad pressed the elevator button and the door re-opened. Brad and his parents stepped inside and rode up in silence, except for the chime of the elevator. Following the third "ding," the doors opened. They stepped out onto the gleaming white tile floor. A sign on the wall in front of them read "ICU." They turned to the left, amid a flurry of activity. An army of light blue clothed medical staff was swarming around one room. Something was obviously going on. Fear gripped Brad, and he felt a prayer slip from his lips. "Oh, God, please watch over Luke. Don't let him die. There is so much he can do for You." As they walked past the room with all of the activity, Brad held his breath as he came close enough to read the name. Samuel Dornberg. *Sammy,* Brad thought, relieved. Then he felt convicted for being glad that it was someone else. Brad immediately began to pray for Sammy, asking God to spare his life, and save him from his sins as well. Brad remembered how Sammy had fixed his pitiful gaze on him, right after he'd been shot, when Brad had tried to help him.

"What room is Luke in Mom?"

"316," she replied.

"That's a good number," remarked Brad's father. It took Brad a few seconds to realize why he'd said it. John 3:16 was perhaps the most famous scripture in the Bible and described the purpose for Jesus' coming into the world.

Luke's parents greeted them at the door. The two moms exchanged hugs while the men shook hands. Brad looked past them, trying to see Luke. Seeing his anxiety, Mrs. Finney said, "Brad, you can go on in and see him."

The room seemed dark and scary. Brad had never liked hospitals, and this ICU unit was particularly eerie, with multiple gadgets beeping and blinking, along with a variety of tubes running into Luke. He got the feeling that one of the Borg would enter at any minute and try to assimilate him.

As he moved closer, Brad heard his mom ask," How's he doing?"

Mrs. Finney's voice broke as she replied, "Not very well. They just don't seem to know what to do for him."

Brad moved over to get a good look at his motionless friend. A sick feeling knotted his stomach at what he saw. The once bright face was ashen gray with deep dark circles under his eyes. The normally sharp features of his face were now rounded and bloated. Brad could not believe this was Luke. He looked so different. What had happened to the boy with whom he had roamed the woods, played army, and soccer—who was so full of life? Tears trickled down Brad's face. "Why, Lord?" The situation appeared totally hopeless. Luke looked as if he were already dead. Brad questioned, "Why is this happening, Lord?" A desperate feeling of failure attacked Brad. He could feel bitterness trying to take hold.

"See, God isn't real. No one can help this wretched fellow. He's going to die, and there is nothing you or anyone else can do about it." A devious voice spoke cruelly, to his mind.

"No hope," Brad heard a tearful voice echo in the background, as Luke's mom erupted into sobs.

There's no hope. Brad thought in agreement. *Luke is gone.* Brad had never felt such sadness and despair. It overtook him like an engulfing wave.

"Don't give up on him just yet, there is still time." Brad heard the wise, comforting voice of his mom speaking to the Finneys. "The Bible says that all things are possible to those who believe. The Bible has several accounts where Jesus raised people who had died, and He could do it just as well for Luke, right now. We shouldn't give up when we could pray instead. Just last week I read a true story of a man who was killed in a terrible auto crash involving a tractor-trailer truck, and God brought him back to life. If God can do it for him, He can do it for Luke."

Brad felt as if huge chains, which had been wrapped around him, were suddenly broken. The power of the gloom and depression that had overtaken him, instantly vanished. *How could a spirit of doom immobilize me so quickly?* he wondered. He knew all of those stories, and had seen God heal people through prayer before. Why had he so easily given in to the worst case scenario? Why had he so quickly abandoned faith, and allowed the enemy of doubt to win the victory. He could almost hear a demon of death laughing at him. Brad immediately wiped away his tears, and then reached out and grabbed Luke's cold hand. "In the name of Jesus Christ, Son of the Living God, I say, be healed. In the mighty name of Jesus, you spirit of death, you must leave him alone. Luke Hunter is a child of the King, and you may not have him." Brad was trembling, aware that he now had an audience. The parents, who were outside, were now by his side. Brad felt his dad's hand on his shoulder. In his low deep voice, a prayer of agreement for Luke's healing poured forth, followed by his mom.

For a few seconds all was silent, and then the quavering voice of Luke's mother cried out for her son, "Oh Lord, I know that I haven't been faithful to you for a long time, but I ask for your forgiveness. Please, heal my Luke."

Brad looked at Luke, who was still lying there motionless. *OK,* Brad thought. *Any second now he's going to open his eyes and start talking like he used to.* He waited, then, felt nervous again. The feeling of hopelessness began creeping back. *Why isn't he waking up? God, please do this. I need to see You do this. We all want to see You demonstrate Your awesome power. I will not give in to the doubts and lies of the enemy, and I thank You for hearing our prayer.* Brad's eyes were now fixed on Luke. *Come on,* he thought, *wake up*. There was still no response.

Brad lowered his head. He felt another hand on his arm. He turned to see Mrs. Finney's grateful smile. "Don't give up on him, Brad." She encouraged, through tear-filled eyes. Brad smiled back and nodded. He then felt something strange. He was still holding on to Luke's hand. To his amazement it was no longer cold, but hot. Brad looked up at Luke again. He still didn't move, but his face seemed to have more color.

The guys, Brad thought. He turned to Mrs. Finney and his parents, and stated, "God is amazing! I really believe that He's healing Luke. Mom, I think I need to go down and join the guys in prayer. OK?" His mom smiled and nodded in agreement. Brad got up and hurried from the room. In a flash he was on the elevator. Pushing the "L" button, he headed down to the lobby waiting room, filled with excitement about what God was doing.

Suddenly, the elevator stopped, but not at the lobby. The number two was illuminated in bright green as the doors parted, revealing a tall dark-clothed man with the silvering goatee. Brad's excitement was instantly swept away in a flood of fear, as The Dragon himself stepped onto the elevator with him. Brad was paralyzed for a second. *I should get off.* He thought as the doors closed. *Too late!* He was now in the elevator alone with the source of all of his troubles. They stood there in silence as the elevator seemed to be in slow motion as it descended to the next floor. Brad wondered if the doors would open revealing the bowels of the earth and the flames of hell itself. His mind was racing as he stared ahead at the elevator doors. Finally, they opened, and he stepped off with Dragon behind him. As Brad quickly walked away, he looked back nervously. Dragon, who obviously didn't realize who he was, caught the glance, and glared back at him with suspicion.

Brad tried to refocus, getting angry at this obvious attempt by the enemy to sidetrack his faith. As he turned back to face the direction he was actually walking, he stopped suddenly, almost walking right into the huge figure of a man. *Lumas!* Brad stared up at the man's long face looking solemnly down at him, one eye squinting as if he was thinking, wondering. *Maybe he doesn't recognize me either. After all, it was dark in the auditorium last night.* "Excuse me, sir," Brad muttered coolly, pretending not to know him. Brad shuffled by and continued down the hall. Following a sign with an arrow that read "REGISTRATION," he turned right and soon found the group of young people, deep in prayer.

Brad joined in as they prayed for Luke's healing, and complete deliverance from the strongholds that had a grip on his life. After a few minutes, there was a pause in the intercession, and the guys greeted Brad. Mandy gave him a hug and asked how Luke was doing. Brad filled them in on his condition and related what had just happened in Luke's room. He explained that he'd run into Dragon and one of his men, and that he was afraid they were up to no good.

"What in the world are they doing here?" Bart asked in amazement.

"I'm not sure. But, I don't trust them," Brad replied, looking past the group nervously.

"Maybe we should spread out, and watch them," Suggested a tall dark-haired boy named Collin.

Suddenly, Brad's stomach knotted again, as down the hall two familiar figures came into view. "I don't think that will be necessary," Brad remarked, eyeing his nemesis.

"Why not?" Collin asked.

Matt, noticing Brad's wide-eyed gaze, turned and replied, "Because, I think they are watching us."

"What are they doing here?" Bart asked indignantly. "Shouldn't they be in jail after all they've done?"

"You'd think so," Matt agreed, as he also eyed them suspiciously.

Finally, Mandy spoke up, "I wouldn't put it past them if they were just trying to interrupt our prayer time for Luke. The enemy knows how powerful prayer is."

"Yeah, sis," Brad agreed. "Guys, let's just ignore them, and focus on praying for Luke. While we're at it, we will stand against any 'schemes of the evil one', as the Bible says." They all agreed and returned to prayer. "Before we start," he paused. "I would like to add someone to our prayers: Sammy Dornburg. I don't think that he's doing very well, and I really believe God wants to do something in his life."

"He really needs it," Bart added, "One of the nurses, who's a friend of my mother's told me that he had gone into cardiac arrest, and had flat-lined twice, but they brought him back." They all agreed and returned to prayer. Matt prayed too, but kept looking back at their enemy, wondering why he was so bold. *Something isn't right. Why are they here?* Matt had given a full report of what had happened to his father. *Why haven't they been arrested?*

After about fifteen more minutes of prayer. Matt was relieved when he looked up, and saw several officers coming down the corridor. They stopped and began talking to Mr. Dragon. His feeling of relief turned to nervousness when he saw that the conversation was more cordial than he thought it should have been. *Where are the handcuffs?* Matt was stunned to see the entire entourage start walking over to their prayer vigil. He got a sinking feeling and wondered where his Dad could be. The officers were now only a few feet from the group of boys, when one of them, an older man, cleared his throat and asserted, "Excuse me, guys."

Brad, who was in mid-prayer, was startled by the abrupt voice of interruption. He had his back to them and had no idea that the officers had joined the two men in black. *Perhaps it was illegal to gather here and pray.* Wild thoughts began flying through Brad's confused mind. He turned, while still sitting in the lobby chair, to see the three blue uniforms standing a few feet away with Dragon and Lumas in the background. *Could Dragon have called the police just to stop us from praying?* he wondered.

"Is there a Bradford Johnson here?" Brad's heart leapt at the curt manner in which this figure of public authority pronounced his name with such formality. Brad paused a moment, not knowing what he should do. He looked over at Mandy. He could tell by her expression that she, too, was confused by what was going on. *I have nothing to fear*, Brad thought, wondering why he was so nervous. He took courage, stood up and acknowledged calmly, "I'm Bradford Johnson."

The officer smiled politely and continued, "Mr. Johnson, I need to speak with you concerning some events that took place last night."

"Yes sir, I'll be happy to tell you all that I know."

"Matt," the officer turned, "I'll need to talk with you also."

Matt nodded, "Yes, Sir. Captain Fry."

"There was another boy in the car last night. I believe his name was Bart." Captain Fry continued,

"Is he here by chance?"

Bart stood up and respectfully said, "Yes, sir. I'm Bart Graham."

At this, Mr. Dragon came over to the officer in a huff. He protested, his voice tinged with irritation, "I want these vandals arrested immediately."

"Now, now, Mr. Dragon, we have to make a full investigation."

"Look, you have the license number of the red car, and I made a positive I.D. on it in the parking lot. We all know who it belongs to. I demand that you arrest them and take them in. I hope the fact that the owner of the car is the son of a member of your force will have no bearing on your investigation," Dragon fumed.

"I assure you, Mr. Dragon, that all of your charges will be fully investigated," the officer replied calmly.

Brad couldn't believe his ears. He looked over at Matt who was equally stupefied.

"What are they talking about, Matt?" Bart asked tugging on Matt's shirt.

With a look of frustration, Matt retorted, "It seems that Mr. Dragon views the events of last night in a different light than that of the truth."

Mandy, who was listening in silence, came over to her brother and whispered, "I'm going to get Dad." Quickly, she disappeared down the hall.

Two of the officers took Matt over to the side, out of earshot of the others, and began asking him questions. They had talked for about five minutes when Matt's dad arrived. His jaw was set, his gait quick. It was apparent that he was not happy. He strode up to the officers who were questioning Matt. He did not speak, but listened intently. Dragon, who obviously knew Sgt. Shackleton from a previous run in, began to rant at an officer standing near the boys. "Why is he here? He should not be part of this investigation."

The officer could not help rolling his eyes. "Mr. Dragon, since Matt is still a minor, he certainly has the right to have his father present during preliminary questioning. Although you've made some accusations, we must keep in mind that right now, they're only accusations."

Dragon huffed, and one could almost see the steam rising from his ears. "This is ridiculous. It's just department bias. I'm calling my lawyer."

The officer shook his head and smiled at the boys. They marveled at Captain Fry's composure. The officers finished up with questioning Matt, and then called Brad over. "Hi, Brad. I'm Captain Fry and this is Officer Henson." Brad remembered Henson. Brad smiled, trying to contain a feeling of uneasiness. "We would like to ask you some questions about what happened last night, between the hours of eleven and twelve-fifteen, at the establishment known as the Dragon's Den." Sgt. Shackleton, who was talking to Matt a few steps away, came over once again to listen, this time with a small notebook in his hand.

"Sir, my father is upstairs, and my sister went to get him. Could we wait until he gets here to begin?" The officer smiled and nodded, appreciating his respectful tone. At that moment, Brad could see behind the officers. Walking hurriedly down the hall was his father, along with Mandy.

Mr. Johnson came up to the two officers and held out his hand in his usual jovial fashion. After he had shaken hands all around, he asked, "What seems to be the trouble, gentlemen?"

The officers explained that they were conducting preliminary investigations into some allegations made by the owner of The Dragon's Den. "We have some questions for Brad, here."

Richard looked down at his son and smiled. "I'm sure that he will answer them honestly."

"Thank you, sir," Captain Fry replied. "Brad, were you at the Dragon's Den last night between ten and twelve?"

"Yes, sir. I was. Matt and I went there earlier, trying to find a friend of mine who was kidnapped by a couple of goons."

"Kidnapped? Are you sure?" Officer Henson contested.

Brad remembered Officer Henson from the questioning after the bathroom incident. Either he was just naturally skeptical, or he simply did not trust Brad. As the man continued to stare him down, Brad began to wonder about him.

His mind a little foggy because of all the dreams, Brad quickly replayed the incident in his mind. He had been bashed on the head by someone, but he didn't see whom. *Did I actually see Luke being taken?* Brad wondered. He remembered hearing Luke struggle in the darkness. Then, he'd followed the noises through the woods, and saw taillights which drove off at the same time Luke went missing. Finally Brad replied, "Yes, sir. A couple of guys ambushed us in the woods near my house. I saw a large black vehicle leaving the scene. I thought that it belonged to Dragon's men, because we had seen a couple of black Hummers parked at the Dragon's Den. Matt stopped to help me, and I talked him into going there to see if we could find Luke."

"So, you had been to the Dragon's Den before last night?" Officer Henson asked suspiciously.

"Brad, why didn't you phone the police?" queried Captain Fry.

"Well, I guess I wasn't thinking very clearly, and I was afraid for Luke's life. We were going to do it once we got there and saw the Hummer sitting in the parking lot, but Matt's cell phone died." Brad continued to recount the story of the night's events: how Dragon set the place on fire in an attempt to kill Brittany, who had overheard too much of their plan; how Matt arrived just in time to help them get out of there; and how it ended with the scary chase, trying to get away in Ruby. Brad finished the story there because he wasn't actually sure when he had fallen asleep in the back of the car. He decided not to tell them stuff that he had merely dreamt.

"Well now, that is quite a tale. Do you have anyone who can corroborate your story?" Officer Henson interrogated, amused at the wildness of Brad's account.

"I guess, Matt could tell you about before and after, but I was inside the place alone for about forty-five minutes, except for Brittany, who was totally out of it."

"What about this Brittany? Can she attest to the fact that it was Dragon who started the fire?"

"No, sir. I don't think so. She had been drugged, and I don't think she would remember anything." Captain Fry nodded as he scratched on his notebook with his pencil, then asked, "Brad, what were you doing in there after the place was evacuated following the first fire?"

Brad thought a second, *Why was he in there?* "Oh, yeah, the flashlight. I went back because I'd left a flashlight in there when we had come in earlier."

"A flashlight?" Officer Henson asked with a puzzled look.

"Well, not just any flashlight. It had a secret compartment where Luke had hidden some important information that would expose Dragon's criminal activities."

"Really?" Officer Henson asked with a chuckle that made Brad wish he hadn't said it. "And where is this flashlight now?"

Brad hung his head in despair, "I don't know. I didn't find it."

An arrogant, irritated voice cut through the sounds of the room. "Are you going to arrest these boys, or am I going to have to call my lawyer?" Dragon, who was now standing right behind Brad, fumed. Brad turned to look the man in his cold dark eyes. Dragon scowled at him. Brad's heart sank at the possibility of Dragon overhearing what he had just said about the flashlight.

Officer Henson replied calmly, "Mr. Dragon, we're still gathering information. You will be notified as soon as our investigation is complete."

Dragon was not appeased. "Well, make sure it's complete, Henson."

"Oh, you can be sure of that, Mr. Dragon."

Something about the look Officer Henson gave Dragon made Brad nervous. He turned to his dad, and then looked at the officers, "Could we get back to praying for Luke, now?"

Dragon, who had turned to leave, spun around, and pointed at Brad, "You're wasting your time praying for that killer."

"Killer!" Brad cried out, "He's no killer."

"That's what he will be if Sammy dies. Everyone saw him holding that gun. He's going to do time for that, boy."

"If anyone is a killer around here, it's you." Brad exclaimed, no longer able to contain his contempt for the evil liar. "How many people have you killed because they got in the way of your wicked plans? You couldn't control them with your hypnosis so you just did away with them."

Dragon's face turned beet red. He literally began to tremble. Brad wondered if anyone had ever dared to challenge him before. "You little son of. . ." Dragon stopped himself, noticing he was the center of attention. The officers, as well as Mr. Johnson and some of the other boy's parents who were there to pray were all hanging on his next words. In an amazing feat of self-control, his entire countenance changed in a split second. "My boy, I'm afraid that you have let the theatrics of my craft get the better of your imagination. I have never done away with anyone. Unless you want to defend yourself from a slander lawsuit, I suggest that you get a grip on these outrageous accusations. As for your friend, Luke, I tried to be like a father to the poor, lonely boy, and he repaid my kindness by shooting my partner in front of an entire auditorium full of people."

Brad's anger roiled at his continued lies. "That's a lie and you know it. Brad put the gun down on the stage floor before the lights ever went out."

"Look, son," Dragon added with a now sickly sweet, compassionate tone, "I know that Luke is a close friend. I'm sure that's what you want to believe, but hundreds of people saw him do it." A sly smile spread across Dragon's face. Brad was so angry now he could have spit nails. Tears began to form in his eyes. It irritated him that this beast would see such a display of wimpiness. *Oh, God*, Brad thought, *Help me. It all seems so hopeless*. Brad couldn't say anything, turning away in embarrassment.

Finally, Mr. Johnson spoke up, "Well, Mr. Dragon, we know that things aren't always as they appear in the excitement of a traumatic moment. By the way, do you know anything about the drug that the doctors found in Luke's system? They say it's commonly used in the field of hypnosis, to make the subject more susceptible to its influence."

Dragon, clearly irritated by this comment, replied. "No, I would not know all the drugs kids today experiment with."

Sgt. Shackleton, who was also standing there, then asked, "Wasn't Luke in your care right before the incident?"

"Yes, but I don't see why that would have any bearing on what he might have taken before we got him." Dragon stopped suddenly, realizing his poor choice of words.

"Got him? Just how did you get him, Mr. Dragon?" Sgt. Shackleton pressed.

"Look, we just found him wandering the streets, and took him in for his safety. Is this an interrogation? I resent these baseless accusations, especially from the fathers of the boys who fled a crime scene, and attempted to burn down my business. I have nothing else to say to you without my lawyer."

"Very well, Mr. Dragon, but I wonder if we go out and search through the wreckage of that building what kind of drugs we might find, since as you say it is a crime scene."

Dragon glared at him, and without another word, turned and stormed off.

"That man has no shame," lamented Sgt. Shackleton.

"What do you know about him?" Mr. Johnson asked.

"Well, we know that he's from Massachusetts, and has a doctorate in psychiatry. His real name is Alistair Draeggen Grizwald spelled D R A E G G E N. His father was from Romania and died when Alistair was young. His mother evidently dabbled in the religion of Wicken. She also was an admirer of a fellow named Alistair Crawley, an infamous figure of that movement. We think that is where he got the name Alistair. He had a very nice practice in the Boston area, but then got into some trouble prescribing questionable drugs to his patients. He also got into the magical arts gig about ten years ago. Since then he has made a fortune in these "entertainment centers", as he calls them. Although there has been some criminal activity surrounding them, nothing has ever been actually pinned on him. He's very smart and always seems to keep himself out of the picture. There's always a fall guy."

"But, I saw him set the fire. Isn't that arson and attempted murder?" Brad asserted in a frustrated tone.

With a sympathetic smile Sgt. Shackleton continued, "You are the only one who saw it, and you were actually trespassing on the property at the time. It could be argued that your dislike for Mr. Dragon and his establishment caused you to take radical action. Do you know a kid named Blane Stevens?"

"Yes sir," Brad replied, wondering why he had brought up this wretched fellow who had given him so much grief.

"He came into the department this morning, bringing several other boys with him, to say that they saw Luke shoot Sammy Dornberg. They claimed to have been in the audience last night and witnessed the whole thing. The group also said that they believed you set the place on fire, because you were a religious fanatic who thought it was evil, and needed to be destroyed."

"That fellow is the biggest liar in the whole school," Brad exclaimed angrily.

Officer Henson who was taking notes, asked, "Is it true that you were organizing a prayer meeting to stop the proposed performance Mr. Dragon was to give at the high school auditorium?"

Brad bristled at the suspicious tone in his voice. At this point, Matt, who was now listening, spoke up. "It is true that we were organizing a prayer meeting to stop the spiritual forces that were attacking our school and any person that might be bringing in bad influences. But, we would never act illegally, much less burn down a building."

"Uh- huh. Did you and Brad enter the Dragon's Den earlier this evening illegally and try to incite a riot on the premises?" Officer Henson persisted. Brad couldn't help but notice a slight smirk on his face. *This guy is really out to get me,* he thought to himself. Brad was afraid to say anything.

Matt answered, "We didn't break in. We were let in by an employee, who gave us a free pass. It is quite common. Employees are encouraged to give out free passes to new people to drum up business."

"Oh, really?" the officer replied cynically. "I assume that person would be willing to testify to that."

"I'm sure she would," Matt replied, hoping he wasn't getting Brit into trouble. She could get fired. But, since she had already quit, and the place was now closed because of the fire, all that didn't really matter.

"And the name of this employee is?" Henson continued.

Matt didn't like the way he was looking at him. Officer Henson seemed to be pursuing this case with an unusual fervor. At this point Sgt. Shackleton spoke up. "George, I will make sure that the investigator assigned to this case has ample access to my son."

Officer Henson glared at him. "Fine, I will file my report to him." The irritated officer tipped his hat, nodded his head and simply quipped, "Sarge." He turned quickly, and strode off.

Matt spoke to his father, "Dad, what was that all about?"

"Just a little internal problem, son. Maybe he's trying a little too hard for a promotion."

"Seems to me, more like he's in Dragon's back pocket," Brad commented in disgust.

"Brad, we don't know that, and we have to be careful with those types of accusations. They can destroy a man's career. Officer Henson hasn't been with the force all that long, but was a distinguished officer on the DC police force. So far as I know, Henson is an honorable man. I also know that Mr. Dragon has made a lot of friends in high places. It seems that he knows whose campaigns to contribute to," Sgt. Shackleton remarked in dismay.

Chapter 28

We Can Never Give Up

"Well, are you boys going to pray or what? Sounds like you have plenty to pray about," Mr. Johnson encouraged.

"Dad, it appears to be hopeless. Why does it always seem as though the enemies of God have the upper hand? "Brad asked sincerely.

His dad thought for a few seconds. "I believe that God is showing us the truth that there is nowhere else we can place our trust. Only God is righteous and true, and the enemy is constantly attempting to deceive us. Life is hopeless without Him, because we live in a fallen world. Sin ruins everything, and only Jesus can change that. That's why it's so important to pray and stay close to Him. His Word says 'all things are possible to those who believe.' If we keep believing, He will show up in a powerful way and demonstrate what only He can do."

Brad looked into his Dad's kind face and took courage as the faith of his father's inspired words grabbed hold of his heart. He shook off the wet blanket of discouragement the enemy was trying lay on him. Turning to Matt, he announced, "It's time for the G-Men to go into battle."

Matt smiled, "You better not let Officer Henson hear you say that. No telling what he might write in his report on that comment."

Brad frowned and nodded. "Yeah, some people really don't have a clue as to the real battle we fight." Brad and Matt joined the other guys. They continued to pray for Luke and against the accusations that Dragon had made about them. "Lord, I ask that You have mercy on Sammy Dornberg. I pray that You would spare his life and turn his heart toward You. Lord Jesus, open his eyes that he might see Your truth and turn away from his life of crime and sin." As Brad prayed, he couldn't get his mind off of the desperate look on Sammy's face the night before.

Brad, sitting with his eyes closed, still thinking about Sammy, felt a tug on his arm. He looked up to see his sister, Mandy. She motioned for him to follow her, which he did. As they walked away from the group, she whispered, "He's awake."

"What?" Brad asked with astonishment. "Who?" he whispered back, unable to grasp what she was saying.

"Luke, silly. Who else?"

"He's awake?" Suddenly he realized what she was saying. He couldn't get out of his mind his last view of Luke barely an hour ago; bloated and swollen, ashen color, his hand cold and clammy. He felt convicted. In his heart he'd struggled to believe that he would ever see his friend alive again. He had appeared to be dead already. "Wow, how does he look?" Brad exclaimed excitedly, as he quickened his step to the point Mandy was having trouble keeping up. They stopped at the elevator.

"It's a miracle, Brad. He looks good, like himself again."

"Praise God!" Brad exclaimed.

"He's been asking for you, so I came right down to get you," she explained cheerily.

At that moment the elevator door opened, Brad stepped forward, then backwards suddenly as he realized someone was exiting the elevator. The excitement in his heart faded as he stared into the smirking face of Blane Stevens. In a second, Brad's heart abandoned its state of jubilation and was suddenly filled with anger at the sight of this vile person. There was perhaps no other individual in the world who could evoke such a feeling in Brad.

"Hi, Bradford," Blane remarked in his usual snide way.

It was all Brad could do to keep his arm from punching Blane right in the face. Mandy sensing the tension, spoke in her compassionate manner. "Hi, Blane. What are you doing here?"

Blane stepped off the elevator, "Well, if it's any of your business, I'm here to pay my respects to Sammy. It looks like, thanks to your buddy Luke, he won't be around much longer. I can hardly wait to testify against him—me and about fifty other people who saw him do it."

"That is a lie, and you know it." Brad lunged at Blane and grabbed his shirt. Before he could stop himself, he had shoved Blane back into the elevator, slamming him against the back wall as the elevator doors closed behind him. They were all alone now and there was a moment of eerie silence as the clearly startled Blane came to his senses. Blane grabbed Brad's hands and shoved him back. Mandy, standing outside the elevator with her mouth open wide in disbelief, had quickly pressed the elevator button, and the door opened. Blane shoved Brad again and rebuked him loudly, "Don't you ever touch me again, or I'll have you arrested too, along with your murdering friend." Several people, including the G-men down the hall, looked up, hearing the skirmish.

"Bra-d!" Mandy exclaimed.

Brad quickly regained his composure, although he could feel the heat in his face from the encounter. *What am I doing?* He thought. *How could my joy be so quickly stolen and turned into nothing but pure hatred?* God's conviction swept over him.

Blane, who was now conscious of people staring, remarked, "Just like you Christians—Nothing but hypocrites." The words burned into Brad's conscience. Blane turned and walked down the hall.

"Blane," Brad called to him, "I'm sorry, I. . ."

Blane threw up his hand without turning, and retorted, "Yeah, right," and kept walking.

Brad watched him, helplessly, as he left the building. Then his eyes caught the stares, and he heard the whispers of the people in the lobby. He felt about two inches tall; wanting to run and hide. Mandy grabbed his hand and pulled him into the elevator. As the doors closed, Brad gazed down at the floor in a mental stupor. "I can't believe I just did that. Why am I so stupid?"

"Don't be so hard on yourself. You only did what I was thinking. That Blane Stevens just walks around trying to push people's buttons. I don't know why he takes such delight in getting people angry." She looked up with a sly smile as she touched his shoulder. "I guess it's just a gift he has."

Brad wanted to smile back at her attempt to break his sadness. "But I should know that by now and be ready for it. Why couldn't I have self-control like the Bible says? Why do I have so much hatred for him? The Bible says to love our enemies. I don't think it's possible to love him."

As the elevator doors opened to the third floor, Mandy simply said, "Pray for him."

Pray for him, Brad thought. *Huh. Why haven't I considered that? Perhaps I'm so angry at Blane that I don't want to pray for him. He deserves to roast in hell. He's the most contrary, boastful, hateful person I've ever met. But none of us deserves the grace of God. Blane was just a living exaggeration of all of us.* Brad was reminded of some of the times when he had acted just as self-centered as Blane. If Jesus Christ had not intervened in his life, he would be just like him. Even now at times, Brad knew he could be every bit as selfish and prideful. The incident that just occurred proved it. "I will begin to seriously pray for Blane," Brad announced to Mandy. "I just want to be able to control myself when I see him."

"Well, knowing God, I 'm sure that you will get another opportunity," she replied, with a cockeyed smile that broke through Brad's momentary depression.

He knew what that meant. He would face this challenge over and over again in the pursuit of getting it right.

They came to the door of Luke's room, where Marcia Finney and Brad's mom were apparently discussing some new problem. Brad's mom noticed them coming down the hall and waved. Brad could tell by her expression that something was wrong. Mrs. Finney turned, and they could see that her face was streaked with tears. They quickened their steps. Brad's heart sank. He feared that Luke's condition had changed for the worse, before he even got in to see him. As they approached, Brad heard his mom comforting Mrs. Finney, "God will take care of this too, Marcia," she submitted kindly. "He didn't bring Luke through so much to abandon him now. We have to keep our trust in Him." Marcia nodded in agreement.

"Mom?" Brad asked gently. "Is Luke alright?" Mrs. Finney turned and gave Brad a hug.

"Oh, Brad, I want to thank you for all you've done for Luke. I know that it was your prayers that have gotten him through this difficult time." Brad couldn't help feeling totally unworthy of such praise after what had just happened down in the lobby, but he thanked her. She turned and went back into Luke's room.

"What's going on, Mom? I thought Luke was doing better," Brad asked, trying to see into the room.

"Well, he was and still is, physically. But, he had a visitor a few minutes ago that seems to have upset him terribly. This teenage boy stopped in to see how he was doing. Since he was doing so well, we let him come in. Luke seemed to recognize him. We thought it might do Luke some good to visit with a friend, so we left them alone for a few minutes. But after the boy left, Luke started calling out for you. He was almost hysterical and had to be given a sedative. He's finally calmed down a bit but won't talk to anyone and is almost in a state of stupor."

"Blane." Brad asked, "Was the boy's name Blane?"

"Why, yes. I believe that is what Luke called him."

"Brad! I need to see Brad. Can you please get him?"

Hearing Luke call out his name, Brad hurried quickly into his room. "I'm here, Luke," Brad came close to Luke's bed and was amazed at the transformation from just an hour and a half before. God had truly worked a miracle. Except for an expression of turmoil on his face, Luke looked completely normal— eyes bright and clear. His color, although a little pale, was almost back to normal. The bloated look was gone, and his facial features were almost as sharp ever.

"Luke, it's a miracle! Look at you! You look amazing." Luke looked up at him and almost smiled. Then as if the burden of the whole world had fallen on him, declared, "Thank God you are here." Luke reached out and grabbed Brad's arm and held on to it. "Brad, the man in white, Jesus, He came to me. It was like I was trapped in my body. I was wrapped in chains, and no matter how hard I tried I couldn't break free. But He came to me and told me that He has a reason for me to live. That I should follow the narrow path, and I would be used for His purposes instead of the enemy's. It was amazing. He raised His hand toward me, and the chains fell off. Then, I awoke and could move."

"That's incredible! A bunch of the G-men are down in the lobby. We've been praying for you." Luke's eyes lowered, and Brad could see a look of fear on his face. Brad placed his hand on Luke's shoulder. "Look, I know that Blane was here. What did he tell you? Why are you so upset?"

Luke's eyes began to well up. "Brad, I've made such a mess of my life, I don't see how Jesus can ever use me. Blane said that I had been doing some drugs, and that I shot Sammy Dornberg in front of a whole bunch of people—That I'd better pray that Sammy didn't die so that I wouldn't be arrested for murder. Is that true?"

Brad shook his head, trying to control his anger at Blane. "No, that's not true. Don't you remember anything about what happened last night?"

Luke thought, "I remember being at your house and feeling that things were going to be better. Then, did we go to the old shed? The thumb drive—I remember shoving it into the compartment in my flashlight. Then, those guys grabbed me. Did you get it, the flashlight, I mean? Do you have it?" Luke looked intensely at Brad, "You do have it, right?"

"Well," Brad paused, wishing he could pull it out of his pocket. "I had it. But right now I don't."

"We need to get it and take it to Sgt. Shackleton. It has some very important evidence on it about Dragon and his whole operation. Can you go get it right now?"

Brad looked into Luke's hope-filled, brown eyes and then down at the floor feeling completely inept. "I don't know exactly where it is," he admitted.

"What happened to it?" Luke asked in dismay.

"Luke, I didn't know anything was hidden in it. I grabbed it and followed you through the woods. Those dudes brained me with something, so the world was sort of spinning. But I managed to follow them out to the road, only to see their tail lights disappearing in the darkness. Miraculously, Matt came along and we headed for the Dragon's Den. Anyway, I left it on a shelf in that back storage room, and it disappeared before I could get back to get it. I'm afraid one of Dragon's men might have it." He looked up at Luke whose mind was now racing.

"No, Dragon's men don't have it, because Blane asked me about it. He said that he knew about the thumb drive and that Dragon wanted it back. If I returned it, he told me, all of my problems would go away."

"I wonder how he knew about the flash drive?" Brad asked out loud.

"Well, Blane was a friend of Sammy's, at least until Sammy started having trouble with Dragon. Blane developed this almost god-worshiping devotion to Dragon. He'd found the thumb drive in Sammy's laptop and questioned him about it. Blane had walked in while Sammy was going through it. Sammy told him it was nothing, just some company reports. Obviously, he didn't realize how much of it Blane had seen. Blane likes to play the drums, so he and I had become friends. He told me about it, saying that Sammy was trying to set Dragon up. I think he wanted me to help him get rid of Sammy. Blane had definite designs on taking Sammy's place in the business."

"But how did you get the flash drive?" Brad pressed.

"Blane wound up stealing the thing, I think. I'm not sure. But, I had been in his office the day it went missing. Sammy thought that I had taken it. That's why he worked me over. I tried to tell him that I didn't have it. I had taken some money from him, but nothing else. It wasn't until days later that I found the thing. I was looking for change, in the cushions of the sofa at the house where all the guys stay. It must have fallen out of Blane's pocket that evening, when he was over drinking with the guys in the band. I was so angry with all of them, that I stuffed it in my little black bag and just took off. Then, I went home and hid it in my bass drum. Later, I was afraid that they would search my room and find it. I had found that old shed by your house and decided it was a good place to hide it. Brad, we really need to get it back. I'm more convinced than ever that Dragon is not only evil, but dangerous. I also believe he will hurt you if you get in his way."

A dull rapping sound on the door interrupted their conversation. The boys turned to see Bart and Matt standing in the doorway. "How are things going, dude?" Matt asked, as he held up his clenched fist and Luke raised his to meet it.

Luke smiled, still a little on edge from his encounter with Blane. "I'm doing much better. The doctor says that I might be able to get out of this place tomorrow."

"Wow, that's amazing," Matt responded. "Just a few hours ago, we were afraid that you weren't going to make it."

"Yeah," Luke said. "I know that it was you guys praying for me that made all the difference."

"By the way, this is a friend of ours I don't think you've met. His name is Bart Graham." Brad explained as Bart reached out his hand and shook Luke's.

"Good to meet you Bart. Thanks for praying for me."

"Glad to do it," Bart replied with a big smile.

"I hope that you will continue to pray. I need all the prayer I can get," Luke replied, overwhelmed with emotion, as his eyes became glassy, and a big teardrop trickled down his cheek.

"You can be sure of that, Luke," Matt agreed, placing a hand on Luke's shoulder. Matt wondered at Luke's overt display of emotion. He looked at Brad as concern furrowed his brow.

"Luke had a visitor this afternoon—none other than our old friend Blane, who proceeded to tell him how he, and fifty other people watched Luke shoot Sammy."

Matt shook his head. "That's not right, Luke. Brad and I were there. We saw you put the gun down on the stage floor. Don't you remember that?"

"I don't remember much of anything about that night." Suddenly, Luke's mind flashed back and he could see the first few rows of a crowd through bright lights that hurt his eyes. They were cheering and then totally silent. "Wait—I remember being on stage," Luke confided, closing his eyes, trying to remember. Standing on the stage, he could see his arms stretched out straight in front of him with a shiny silver object protruding from his tightly clasped hands. "I did have a gun!" Luke recounted, his voice trembling as he relived the moment in his mind. Straight in front of him stood a confused Sammy Dornberg. "And— it is pointing at . . ." He paused. "Sammy!" he acknowledged in distress.

Brad wanted to intervene and stop the obvious emotional pain of his friend. But he also felt the need to know what he went through, so he let him continue in his thoughts.

As he sat there shaking, Luke sank deeper into thought. Almost like a bad dream, Luke saw another figure who stalked slowly toward him, his back to the crowd. Luke cut his eyes toward him. Dressed all in black, only his face seemed to catch the light, giving the eerie impression of a head floating in mid air. Luke looked back at Sammy. He could see fear in Sammy's eyes. *He should fear,* Luke thought, *after what he did to me.* "He's always treated me like some scrawny little mutt that he could kick around whenever he didn't get what he wanted," Luke vented aloud. He could still feel the sharp pain in his mouth from the cuts made when the back of Sammy's hand made contact with his face, as well as the bruises on his arms. "He should die. He was nothing but a murdering thug anyway."

Brad gasped at Luke's statement, but tried to control his reaction.

Luke's vision continued: Dragon moved closer. Luke could see his lips moving, but could hear nothing. Things in Luke's mind were beginning to get foggy. He stared, mesmerized by Dragon's moving lips. "Shoot him." Luke repeated aloud, as he understood what Dragon was saying. "Shoot the alien, now." Luke remembered how his finger moved on the trigger, and he could feel the sharp resistance of the slender piece of metal. He looked back at Sammy, whose eyes suddenly flashed a brilliant green. "H-he is an alien!" Luke stuttered, reliving his hypnotic state.

Brad looked at Matt in astonishment as Luke continued his trance-like account.

"I must obey the words of the floating head—but it's not right." Luke's body was trembling. He looked up, eyes wide. "Suddenly, a voice called out from the darkness beyond. I didn't understand exactly what it said, except for one distinct word, "Jesus." He paused. "Jesus!" Luke cried out, his hands over his face. "I saw a flash and heard a booming loud noise and everything went black."

Tears were now streaming down his face as Luke turned to Brad, who was watching him relive this traumatic incident. "Did I really shoot Sammy? I did have a gun I my hand."

Brad's heart was moved by the turmoil of his friend. The thought of his taking another life was more than Luke could bear.

"Is Sammy going to make it? I don't know that I could be forgiven for killing another human being."

"Luke, you didn't shoot him. Matt and I were both there. We saw you put the gun down. Don't you remember putting the gun on the floor?"

Luke thought again. He closed his eyes. All he could see was that floating head and the mouth saying, "Shoot him, now!" Luke clasped his face with both hands and shook his head. Wearily, he said, "All I can see is Dragon's face saying, 'Shoot him.'"

Brad looked over at Matt, whose jaw was set tight in anger. Finally, Matt spoke. "I would never have believed this if I hadn't seen it, but I believe that you were under Dragon's spell of hypnosis. I believe that Dragon must have hypnotized you and planted the thought that Sammy was an alien and that you were to kill him."

"Yeah," Brad agreed. "He's just like the devil. He played off your feeling of hatred for Sammy and tried to get you to carry out his evil desires. You said yourself that he was trying to get rid of Sammy."

Luke's face turned from a look of sadness and remorse to deep thought. He had often seen Dragon put people "under," as he called it. Although Blane and some of the others took it seriously, Luke had never thought much about it. He had thought that they were on some sort of Harry Potter trip, with all that magical stuff. He consoled himself with the idea that it was all just a gimmick to attract kids to the Den. The truth was, however, it did make him nervous. He'd seen people do some strange things. Luke had tried to keep his distance from all that stuff, but now realized that he wasn't immune from its influence. He liked things that he could understand with his mind. Perhaps that's why he struggled with God and Jesus so much. There was so much about it that he didn't understand. Luke was now being forced to come to grips with a fact he'd never considered before. *Some forces of this world, which we can't see, have real control over a person's life, whether or not we understand them, or even believe in them. There is much more to this world than what we can see with our physical eyes.* Just as Brad had tried to tell him several times before, there is no neutral ground. If we are not being used by God in his kingdom for good, then we are sitting ducks for the enemy. Satan uses people whether they realize it or not. "I've been such a fool," Luke said angrily. "I've been a part of Dragon's movement, as he calls it, all for the sake of fun and fame, not wanting to see the truth. He just wants to control people's lives for his own selfish purposes. Brad, I now understand what you said about 'no neutral ground.' This hypnotism thing is just a means of getting people to do what he wants— tricking them into thinking it's what they want."

"That's exactly what the enemy of God does," Matt agreed. "He gets people to believe that what he wants is fun and exciting and that it's what they desire, even though it is totally destroying their life." Satan uses our weaknesses to ensnare us. We think everyone who tries to tell us otherwise is just against us and doesn't understand. We're just suckered into sin, and Satan doesn't care whether it destroys our life. All he wants to do is keep us hooked."

Shaking his head, Luke added. "I can't believe I've been so stupid. Why haven't I seen this before?"

"Luke, the Bible says that Satan has blinded the eyes of those in the world, and that we can only see when we turn to God and He opens our eyes. Remember yesterday evening before all this happened, you asked Jesus to come into your heart? Now, you are beginning to see things as they really are. There really are only two kingdoms: one of darkness and one of light. One focuses on freedom from sin and doing what is right, led by Jesus and His Father. The other kingdom focuses on keeping people bound in selfishness and evil desires, ruled by Satan and all of his demons. Matt and I prayed for you when you were up there on stage, and when you heard the name of Jesus it broke the power of his hypnotic spell. I could see it. A change came over you. That's when you put the gun down," Brad explained, hoping to encourage Luke to completely trust God.

"Then, I didn't shoot Sammy! But who did?" Luke wondered aloud.

"It had to have been Dragon," Matt deduced. "He was the only one near the gun. He made it look like he was trying to keep you from firing the gun. But, I believe that when he saw you weren't going to do it, and the lights went out, he took the opportunity."

"I know for sure Sammy thought Dragon wanted him out." Luke confirmed.

Chapter 29

Dragon Is Setting Us All Up

A sudden commotion in the hall turned the guys heads toward the door. Luke's mother was talking loudly, in somewhat of a frantic state. "That's impossible! Luke would never do a thing like that!"

Matt, Brad, and Bart all walked over, hearing Luke's mother in a heated exchange with Officer Henson. He and another officer were apparently checking on Luke's condition.

"I'm sorry, Mrs. Finney, but some very serious allegations have been made against your son, and we really need to question him. Numerous eyewitnesses say that Luke pointed a gun at a Sammy Dornberg, who is just down the hall struggling for life from a gunshot wound," Officer Henson stated in a matter-of-fact tone.

"That is simply not true," Brad interrupted. "I was there. I saw the whole thing. Luke didn't shoot Sammy." Brad could see Officer Henson's look of annoyance.

"You are the young man accused of trespassing and vandalism, are you not?" Brad glared at him but held his tongue. "You are also a friend of the young man in question, are you not?" Henson continued, "I guess you can see then how your testimony might appear to be somewhat biased."

"Well, we almost lost Luke a few hours ago. He's in no condition to talk to you right now," Mrs. Finney stated with frustration.

"Mom!" Luke called out. "It's OK. I'll talk to them. I'll be happy to tell them everything that I know about what happened."

Brad walked back over to Luke and whispered, "There's something funny about that Henson guy. Tell him you want Sgt. Shackleton to be here." Luke nodded. As the men approached, Luke mustered a smile and looked up at them.

"Boys, if you could step outside for a moment, we need to ask Luke a few questions." The friendly officer, whose name was Murphy, moved aside to let the boys file out into the hall, while Luke's mom followed the officers into the room. Brad stopped just outside the door and cupped his ear, straining to hear every word.

"Hello, son. My name is Officer Murphy, and this is Officer Henson. We are investigating the events which took place last night at the Dragon's Den. Are you familiar with that place?"

"Yes, sir. I know it. I play in a band there."

"Are you aware that there was a shooting there last night?"

"Yes, I've been told that Sammy was shot, and that people say that I did it. However, I don't remember much about last night, other than I was kidnapped and taken there by force."

"Kidnapped?" Officer Henson exclaimed.

"Yes, and if I could please speak to Sgt. Shackleton I would be happy to explain all that I can remember to him."

"He is not assigned to this case," Officer Henson snapped. Overcoming his apparent irritation, he added, "All we are here to do is take preliminary information. If you don't cooperate, then we can get a warrant and take you to the station."

Luke saw Officer Murphy roll his eyes. Seeing the officer's response to his overzealous partner, Luke decided to milk the situation. He was a little nervous at the tone of Officer Henson's voice. He closed his eyes and began to fidget. "I'm not feeling so well. It's so hot in here." Luke massaged his forehead with one hand and began to rub his eyebrows with his thumb and forefinger.

His mother, who was standing behind the officers, was visibly upset. "Gentlemen, could we continue this at some other time? I don't believe that my son is quite ready for this."

Officer Henson bristled, but realized that he was getting nowhere.

"Yes, ma'am," Officer Murphy replied politely, and tried to console Mrs. Finney. "Luke indicated that he would feel more comfortable talking to Sgt. Shackleton. Perhaps we can set up a time to come by on Monday to speak with him if Luke is feeling better."

She smiled and thanked him. "Yes, I think that would be much better."

Officer Henson, clearly not happy, turned to Brad as he was leaving. "Mr. Johnson, we need to talk with you about your involvement in vandalizing that building. You will need to be available Monday afternoon. Your father will receive a call as to the time." He tipped his hat and nodded as if to say: "there, take that you little troublemaker." Brad couldn't understand why Officer Henson seemed to have it in for him. Brad had never been in any trouble before. It was very strange.

The officers left, and Luke called Brad back over. "What was he talking about? He mentioned that you vandalized some building." Brad explained how he had gone back into the building and seen Dragon toss the lantern that set it ablaze again. Then, how he had carried Brittany to the back where Matt and Bart met him, and how they all had fled in Matt's car, only to be pursued by Dragon's men.

"Man, what a night!" Luke declared. "Now, Dragon's setting you up, too. He's setting us all up." A look of concern came into his eyes. "I knew you shouldn't have gotten involved in this," Luke lamented, his concern deepening into worry. "I had it coming to me, because I was stupid. But it's not right that they're out to get you, too. You weren't doing anything, but trying to help me."

Brad could see that guilt was trying to overtake Luke. "Hey, don't worry, man. God is in control. He will take care of it." Brad was preaching to himself as much as to Luke. The truth was, he was also battling fear over this. Dragon's lawyers could twist these events in a way that would be difficult to explain.

"Why did you go back into the Den anyway?" Luke asked, as he thought through all of the events.

"I went back in for the flashlight, remember?" Brad recounted with a sigh.

"The flashlight," Luke repeated. "That's right. You said you lost it in there. I sure wish we had that thing. That little thumb drive could change everything. All that evidence of many of Dragon's illegal activities would sure come in handy right now. It also shows his teachings on hypnotism along with video of some of his 'experiments in hypnosis', as he calls them. I know it's the reason he wanted Sammy dead. I sure wish we could find it." Luke paused, and then asked curiously, "Was the Den burned down completely?"

"No. Bart told me that the sprinkler system came on in the newer part, and that the fire was confined to the bar and dining area."

"What about the offices?"

"No. They were spared except for smoke damage. Why, what are you thinking?" Luke was about to respond when Bart and Matt reentered from the hallway.

"What's up with that Officer Henson guy?" Bart asked Matt. "He seems bent on getting both Brad and Luke thrown in jail."

Matt frowned. "I'd like to say that he's just doing his job. I don't like to speak ill of anyone on the force. I know personally that police officers are some of the most dedicated people on the planet, but I don't know about him. He seems to be out to make my dad look bad, because it was my car that sped away from the Dragon's Den last night."

"It looks to me that he is trying a little too hard to promote the gospel according to Dragon. Doesn't he know that Dragon is a drug-pushing thug?" Bart questioned angrily.

"Well," Matt replied calmly, "Dragon has never been convicted of any serious crimes. Someone else always seems to take the fall. It could be said that Officer Henson is just making sure that all the evidence is fully explored."

"Yeah, right," Brad huffed. "I guess we're the ones to take the fall this time." As soon as he said it, Brad wished he could suck those words right back into his mouth. He could see that Luke was blaming himself for all of their trials. Luke turned and faced the wall away from them. Matt, seeing Luke's countenance change, interjected, "Look, guys, all of this is in God's hands. He doesn't allow the wicked to go unpunished, nor the innocent to pay the price of the wicked. We need to trust Him and just tell the truth."

"Amen," Brad agreed. Luke was still facing the wall, fighting to keep control of his emotions. Finally he admitted, as he again rubbed his eyes," Guys, I'm not feeling too great right now. I think I'd like to rest a while." He closed his eyes and nodded slowly.

Brad studied him, concern filling his heart. "OK, man. But, I'll be back first thing in the morning to check on you." Luke nodded again slowly. All three boys moved quietly out of the room. Brad gave Mrs. Finney a hug as he left.

None of them said a word until they reached the elevator. "Brad, you know Luke better than all of us. What do you think just happened?" Matt asked, concerned.

"He's feeling so guilty about getting us all into trouble. We need to pray for him. I'd feel better if I could stay here and keep an eye on him, but I don't think my parents would go for that," Brad confided.

"Well, you had a rough twenty-four hours yourself. Besides, his parents will be here."

The elevator door opened with a "ding". Mandy and Brad's mom greeted the boys. "Brad, we are about ready to head home. Are you ready?"

"I guess so," Brad replied, hesitantly. They all agreed to continue to pray for Luke as they exited the elevator and made their way out of the hospital. Brad's heart was still heavy about leaving his friend on such a down note.

"Maybe, if you're up for it, Brad, I could pick you up early for church tomorrow. We could come by the hospital first and see how Luke is in the morning."

Matt is amazing, Brad thought. *He always seems to know how to lift my spirit.* Brad smiled at Matt. "Thanks, man. That would be great."

"I'm concerned about him, too. He's a babe in Christ, and I know that he's facing some heavy stuff. We need to stay close by."

Brad just nodded and agreed, "Amen, bro'. See you in the morning."

Bart, who was talking to some of the other guys, waved. Brad waved back as he turned and walked with his family to the car. He was beat. His body was beginning to ache, and his knee was throbbing again.

Brad's mother noticed him limping. "Young man, when we get home, I want you to go straight to bed," she stated, with all the passionate rights of a mother's protective nature.

"But Mom, I'm starving," Brad whined.

"Well, I guess I'll just have to bring some rations up to your cell."

Brad smiled. He didn't like being sick, but he had fond memories of how his Mother would dote over him when he wasn't feeling well. Even though he was almost sixteen, he turned into a big baby when he was sick and let her take care of him.

Brad followed orders when he arrived home. It was almost five o'clock in the afternoon. He hobbled up the stairs and into his room. Plopping down on his bed, he pulled off his shoes, and reclined. It felt so good to lie down. He stared up at the ceiling, and then around at the posters in his room. For some reason, his computer screen caught his attention. He still had the Draegon computer game disc in the player. It seemed to be making a soft pulsating noise. Brad sat up and rolled onto his stomach, with his head toward the foot of the bed. Reaching over to his desk, he hit the space bar. Instantly, the screen came to life. Thousands of tiny golden-green dancing specks of light swirled and glistened across the black background. Finally, two red dots appeared about two inches apart. The red dots grew in size to about the size of a dime. Then a vertical black slit formed in the middle of each, forming the reptilian eyes of the serpent head that was now appearing, as the florescent specs gathered into the shape of a writhing dragon. A deep gravelly growl emanated from the speakers as the creature seemed to dare Brad to play the game. Brad frowned, exhausted. "Oh, shut up," he grumbled under his breath, as he hit the button that turned off the machine. After his battle with the real Mr. Dragon he was in no mood to deal with one that lived in the imagination of cyber land.

Rolling onto his back, Brad heard heavy footsteps coming down the hall. He turned to see his dad standing in the doorway, a forced smile on his face. Brad could tell when his Dad had something to say that he really didn't want to say. Kind man that he was, he tried to put the best face on difficult situations. "I guess Officer Henson called," Brad lamented, followed by a heavy sigh.

"Actually, it was a Detective Pierce. He wants to meet with us on Monday at four-thirty. Are you available?"

Brad's stomach churned as a feeling of dread crept over him. He reached over and pulled a pillow over his head. "Tell him I'll check my schedule and get back with him," Brad's muffled voice said through the pillow.

"Son, you really don't have anything to worry about, if you just tell the truth. After all, you were just rescuing a pretty damsel in distress."

Brad slid the pillow off his head and looked over with a half smile. "But, you don't know that Officer Henson. He seems to think that we sneaked in there to burn the place down. It's no secret that I was helping to organize a prayer meeting to pray against the performance Dragon was planning at school. Blane and some of Dragon's groupies from school have made me out be a religious fanatic who's just trying to destroy everyone's fun. Why is it so easy, when you are trying to do what is right, for the enemy to make you into the bad guy?"

His dad thought for a moment as he leaned against the door frame. "I think you're making more out of it than you ought. Remember young David? He slew that giant, the same one the entire army of Israel had made out to be undefeatable, and he did it with just a small stone. The Bible says, 'If God be for us, who can be against us?' Don't forget that God is in this. I don't believe all of it has happened for nothing. God desires that the forces of evil be pulled down, and although he uses us in the process, it is ultimately His battle to win. Remember, He has a plan. Often we don't see it until after the fact. That's where faith comes in. We must trust Him in the midst of the battle and not give up."

Brad lay there and let the truth of his father's words sink into his spirit. His dad was right. He frowned as he realized that he was once again giving in to the fear and lies of the enemy. *Why is fear so powerful? It destroys our trust in the most powerful force in the universe, the God who created all things and holds all things together by the power of His might.* "I'm so stupid sometimes, Dad. Why do I so quickly give in to the lying schemes of the enemy?"

Brad's dad picked up the pillow that Brad had let fall onto the floor and smacked him across the chest with it. A startled Brad broke into a laugh. "So, there. Stop it." His dad smiled. "Brad, believe me, I have the same problem. We all let our fears get the best of us sometimes. That's why it's so important to stay close to Jesus. He is the Author and Finisher of our faith. Only the power of His Holy Spirit can keep us strong enough to overcome the forces of darkness. Remember, Jesus is fearless against them. They run in terror from Him."

Brad pictured that in his mind. He remembered how that huge, slimy, snarling, hell-fire spewing dragon had shrunk down to a scrawny, sniveling wimp when he saw Jesus standing with Brittany. Brad clasped his hands behind his head as he lay there. "That's awesome," he acknowledged with a smile.

"Make way. Ration patrol coming through." Brad could smell the savory aroma of his mom's beef stew before she had gotten completely into his room.

"Um-m-um," Dad remarked excitedly, expressing his appreciation of her mastery of the culinary arts.

Brad sat up, ready to dive in to the delectable morsels sizzling on the tray. "Thanks, Mom. You're a keeper."

"OK, mister." She turned to Dad, "Stop drooling over your son's food. Yours is awaiting you downstairs, if you'll kindly go down, and set the table."

Brad feasted and soon his mom came up for the tray. She noticed that Brad eyes were red and had dark circles under them. She bent down and kissed him on the forehead. "Dear, you look so tired. I know it's early but maybe you need to just go to sleep."

With a yawn, he replied, "I think you're right, Mom. I feel like I've been carrying around a sack of bricks all day." She kissed him on the cheek, and took the tray. Brad got up and got ready for bed, and then sat down on the bed. He noticed his Bible sitting on the nightstand. His eyelids were heavy. He looked at his alarm clock. *It's only 5:15. Man it seems later than that.* Looking back at the Bible, it was as if it were calling out to him. He reached over and pulled it close.

The word dragon seemed to be on his mind a lot lately, so he turned to the concordance in the back of his Bible. *D- Dragon, there it is.* He was curious about the word Dragon in the Bible. He thought that there was a mention of a dragon, in Revelation. He turned the pages in the book of Revelation to chapter twelve. He began to read about the great red dragon whose tail swept away a third of the stars. Brad studied the commentary on the side of the page, and learned that this dragon was Satan. The stars represented fallen angels or demons who had followed Satan in his rebellion. Verse seven spoke of a great war in heaven. The Devil and all of his angels were defeated and cast out of heaven, down to earth to deceive the whole world. Brad stopped and thought. *That's really just what Satan spends all of his time doing, deceiving the world. He's trying to get everyone to believe that God either doesn't exist or doesn't care about what we do.*

"Lord, how can we resist him? We're just humans, and he was an angel with supernatural power," Brad asked out loud. Then he looked down and read verse ten: "Then I heard a loud voice saying, Now salvation and the power and the kingdom of our God and the authority of His Christ have come, for the accuser of our brethren has been thrown down, he who accuses them both day and night." Brad paused again, *That's what he does alright. He's always accusing me of something. He's always accusing Christians of being the problem in the world.* He continued and read verse eleven once, then again and again. Finally, he read it out loud: "And they overcame him because of the blood of the Lamb and because of the word of their testimony, and they did not love their lives even when faced with death." Brad understood now what he must do. He had been washed in the blood of the Lamb, Jesus, and now he must testify to the truth no matter what it cost him. *People need to know, not only who Mr. Dragon is, but more importantly who Jesus is. Jesus is the only one who can defeat this enemy.* Brad knew he had to try to find that thumb drive and expose this evil force in their community, before it swept up so many unsuspecting young people in its hypnotic fervor.

"Jesus," Brad prayed, "help me find that little black thumb drive. It will help us defeat this evil Dragon." Although tired, he continued to pray for his friends.

Chapter 30

Can A Computer Have A Demon?

Suddenly, Brad's computer beeped. The room seemed to be fading into darkness except for his computer monitor. Brad's eyes focused on the glowing blue screen, as he sat wondering if it was possessed or something. Within a split second, it lit up, and once again the image of the Dragon appeared. As Brad stared, dumbfounded at the snarling beast, it seemed to take on a three dimensional effect. His room was completely, dark except for the neon image spewing forth from the flat screen. Larger and larger it grew, so that the image was no longer on the computer, but now filled the entire side of the room. The image on the screen had now morphed into a real silver, scaly, creature. It was so tall that it's long neck and head hovered along the ceiling. If it could have stood upright, it would have been at least fourteen feet tall. Its color changed from silver to bright green, then finally to a bloody red. Brad, petrified at the bizarre image, scrambled back against the headboard of his bed.

His Bible slipped from his fingers, cascaded onto the floor—the pages flying shut. Slime dripping from its mouth, the head swung around. Its red gleaming serpent eyes, focused on various objects in the room. Then, with a snake-like twitch of its head, the curving neck of the serpent flew straight at Brad, stopping right in front of Brad's wide-open eyes. Brad could feel his heart pounding in his chest. He wanted to cry out, but his voice was gone. It was as if he couldn't even breathe. He wanted to close his eyes, but no matter how hard he tried, he could not shut out the terrifying image right there in his face. Again, the hot putrid breath filled his mouth and lungs to the point he felt like throwing up. Brad's body was frozen in place—completely paralyzed. All he could do was gaze on the grotesque head with its steaming, flaring nostrils, over two rows of gleaming, bloody fangs. A slender, fleshy, forked tongue slipped out of its mouth. It fluttered momentarily, and then popped back inside, leaving a thin trail of clear, greenish saliva that dripped down, forming a web-like string. As Brad watched, completely grossed out, the head began to contort and change. The protruding snout began to shrink back into the head which slowly became more rounded. The eyes now appeared more human and the coarse scales that covered it became smooth, like skin. Before his eyes, in a matter of ten or fifteen seconds, the head of the dragon had transformed into the now all-too-familiar face of Mr. Dragon, complete with the graying goatee.

Brad didn't know what to think, but his fear was now turning to anger at the vision of this individual who was attempting to destroy so many lives. Brad's mind raced back to the text he had just read in Revelation. It said that the Dragon had seven heads. Is this what it meant? The dragon took on many different forms as it went about carrying out its cruel designs.

Brad marveled at the spectacle before him. Attached to this huge, winged, scaly body of a reptile, whose tail circled most of the room, was the face of a man who had become a very real enemy to Brad.

The unusually red face of Mr. Dragon began laughing at him and spoke, "So, boy, you think that you can destroy me. Who do you think you are? I will tell you who you are. You are nobody. You are nothing but a scared little boy; one of millions of nameless, meaningless lives who dwell on this miserable little planet. You have the audacity to think you can somehow stop me, but you can't. If you try, foolish boy, I promise it is you who will be destroyed. No human can stand against me. Do you hear me!"

Brad, still paralyzed, and speechless, began to think through what the face had just said. It was right. He was just a nobody. There was nothing Brad Johnson could do against such a powerful entity. All he could think was, *Jesus.* As soon as the thought entered his mind, the beast seemed to intensify its rhetoric. "No one can help you. Just like every other loser in this world, you are a failure, and you will die a failure, useless to anyone, a sniveling coward just like your friend, Luke. You think you can free him from my power, but it is too late. He's gone too far and cannot be brought back. If I go down I will take him with me, and there is nothing you can do." The face sneered, "Even now he is returning to me, and there is not a thing you can do about it."

Brad decided to set his mind on the only source of real strength he knew. He continued to think about Jesus and the verse in Revelation that said, "*the salvation and the power and the kingdom of our God have come.*" Before he knew it, his tongue had been loosed and Brad was speaking. "A-a-nd the authority of His Christ has come, for the accuser of the brethren has been thrown down."

The face of Mr. Dragon screamed a blood curdling cry. "Shut up, you fool. I am the ruler of this place. You will see what I can do." With that, the monster reared back one of his wiry, sickle-like claws, and with one mighty swipe, ripped through the flesh across Brad's chest. Hot searing pain shot through Brad's body. His mouth agape, he looked down at his ripped t-shirt. Blood poured out of four deep, open wounds from the middle of his rib cage and below. Brad's breath was short, as each breath brought great pain. The face of Mr. Dragon smirked triumphantly, as if he had just silenced an impudent little dog.

I'm going to die, Brad thought. A cold chill ripped through his body as this revelation ran through his mind. *Jesus,* was again all he could think. At that, his mind was again drawn to the scripture he had just read. "And they overcame him by the blood of the lamb, and because of the word of their testimony, and they did not love their lives even when faced with death."

"Jesus, h-h-help." Brad managed to mutter as he felt the last of his strength draining away. His head dropped down, and he stared at his blood-soaked midsection. Suddenly, things began to change. He felt a warmth in his abdomen, taking away the pain. Before his very eyes, the blood began to disappear, and the flesh began to mend. He looked up at the ridiculous-looking face of the man, who called himself Dragon, stuck so oddly onto this huge body. Brad could now feel strength coming back to him, a strength that he knew did not originate with him. In the power of the Spirit of Almighty God, Brad spoke, "You are a liar, and you have been a liar from the beginning." Dragon's face contorted in anger. Then, a look of absolute terror came over it, and the huge head recoiled as it recognized the words of Jesus.

Brad was suddenly aware of another presence in the room. Beside him on his bed, a shimmering light had appeared in the shape of a human form. Just as before, the once fearless beast now began to shrink, smaller and smaller until it was only about two feet tall. It writhed, squirmed and spewed out horrible words until finally the radiant Man said, "Be gone from this place and never return!" Instantly, it vanished into a reddish vapor which trailed out through the partially open widow.

Brad felt as if a heavy burden had been lifted from him. He turned to the man sitting beside him. Tears filled Brad's eyes as he looked into a shining face so warm and genuine that Brad felt he never wanted to look away. It was the perfect antithesis of Dragon's wretched grotesqueness. "Thank you," Brad said. Jesus just smiled at him. "Is it really too late for Luke?" Brad asked hesitantly.

"No. That is what the enemy wants Luke to think. I'd like for you to help him see the truth. He will need your help."

Abruptly, a jingling tone startled Brad. He jerked and felt a dull pain in his neck. He awoke and lifted his head to see his room empty. His light was still on and his Bible had fallen onto the bed next to him. He ought to have been used to this by now, but he couldn't help feeling a little let down that this was just another of his fantastic dreams. The phone had stopped ringing before Brad awakened enough to figure out what it was. *Boy, is my neck stiff.* He massaged it, realizing he had fallen asleep while sitting up, reading the Bible. *It really doesn't matter that it was only a dream,* he thought. He had learned that Jesus could speak some powerful things into his life through dreams. Out of the corner of his eye, Brad caught a glimpse of movement. His door had been cracked opened slightly, and then shut. "I'm awake. Is it for me?"

Mandy's head appeared in the partially open door. "I wasn't sure. Just five minutes ago I thought a freight train was idling in here. Yes, it's for you."

Who could be calling at this hour? Brad wondered as he looked over at the clock. He couldn't believe it. The clock read 8:38 pm. It felt to Brad more like one or two in the morning. Mandy handed him the receiver.

"Hello—Brad?"

"Yeah. Hey, Matt. How's it going?"

"I'm sorry if I woke you, but I was wondering if you have heard from Luke."

"Luke? No," Brad replied wondering.

"My dad just called from the office. Luke 's parents called and reported he had disappeared from the hospital."

"Disappeared!" Brad exclaimed. "Do you mean someone abducted him or something?"

Matt could hear the excitement building in Brad's voice. "Calm down, dude. They don't think that, because his clothes are missing. His mom said that she went into the hallway to talk to a friend, and when she came back, he was in the bathroom for a while. He came out of the rest room and got back into the bed. She thinks he must have put his clothes on under his hospital gown. She went down to get a snack at about seven o'clock, and when she returned he was gone. It took a few minutes before she realized he was missing, because he had shut the bathroom door and left the light on. She thought he was in there again."

Brad's mind was racing. "He hasn't been here, but we have to go look for him."

"Brad, don't be silly. It's almost nine o'clock and you are in no condition to be out hunting down a fugitive."

"A fugitive. I bet that's what that Officer Henson dude is calling him. He already thinks Luke's a killer."

"Don't worry, Brad. They have half of the police force looking for him," Matt tried to console him.

"Well, I hope it isn't Officer Henson who finds him. Matt, we've got to do something. I'm not going to just sit here. If you're not going to look for him, then I'm going to take out on my bike."

"Brad, you're crazy. With that bum knee of yours you won't get two blocks away before you'll be lying in a ditch somewhere, that leg blown up like a balloon. Besides, your mom will never let you out of the house."

Brad knew he was right. "Matt, I had another dream, and I told Jesus I would help Luke. He needs help. I believe the enemy is trying to take him out. I just can't sit here and do nothing."

There was a few seconds of silence on the other end of the phone. "I'll be there in fifteen minutes."

"Thanks, friend. I knew a G-Man wouldn't leave a man in trouble to fend for himself."

"OK, OK. I said I was coming."

Brad laughed. "Bye." He hung up the phone and threw on his clothes and started putting on his shoes. Matt was right about one thing. His Mom would never let him out of the house. He didn't feel right about sneaking out of the house, but what could he do?

Suddenly his door flew open and a voice asked, "Bradford Johnson, what do you think you are doing?"

Drat, already busted, Brad thought as his mind raced for a proper defense. *Wait a minute, that wasn't Mom's voice.* He turned to see his sister standing there, arms folded, tapping her foot in the exact manner of his Mom. For a moment he wondered if she wasn't the product of some sinister cloning experiment. "Mandy, you sure know how to take years off of a person's life."

"Br-ad, why are you putting on your shoes?" she contested, using most serious tone a girl of almost fifteen could exude.

"I think that you're taking this maternal instinct thing a bit too far right now. Let's just say I need some exercise. Call it therapy, OK?"

"At this hour?" she questioned. "I don't think Mom and Dad would approve."

Brad wondered why Mom hadn't come in herself. "Are they already asleep?"

"No, they went to the hospital. Mrs. Finney called. I guess you know Luke is missing. They went over to see his parents."

"Look Mandy. Matt is coming over, and we are going to look for Luke. Mom might not like it, but I'm sure Dad will understand.

"Brad, I know that this is upsetting, but. . ." she stopped in mid-sentence, seeing the determined look on his face. "Oh, just be careful."

Brad got up and walked through the doorway into the hall. He gave her a peck on the cheek as he passed. "I will. Thanks for understanding," he replied, turning on his brotherly charm.

She followed him down the stairs. "I understand, but I don't like it. Don't do anything foolish," she exclaimed, one hand on her hip.

Brad frowned and shook his head. "Oh, ye of little faith," he muttered as he watched out the window for Ruby. Headlights flashed in the street in front of the house and Brad could hear the unmistakable rumble of horsepower waiting to be exercised. "Don't worry. I'll be with Matt. He'll keep us out of trouble." He smiled as he slipped out the door.

"Yeah, just like last time," she called back.

He popped his head back in. "You'll let Mom and Dad know where I am, won't you."

She rolled her eyes. "Sure, leave me to do your dirty work." He closed the door and started quickly toward the headlights shining in his face, ignoring a dull ache in his knee. He opened the car door and sat down. "I really appreciate this," Brad acknowledged.

"You know I appreciate the challenge," Matt replied. "But, I did call Dad and let him know what we were doing. He told me to be careful and to call him if we discovered anything."

"Fair enough," Brad replied.

"I'm not sure where we should start looking, but we need to swing by the hospital and pick Bart up first," Matt explained as he slowed for a stop sign.

"Bart? Why's he still at the hospital?"

"Bart is a great guy, a real faithful brother. He called me right after I talked to you. Something wasn't right in his spirit. He felt that the Holy Spirit was prompting him to stay and pray for Luke there in the hospital lobby after everyone left. He wound up falling asleep on one of the sofas."

Brad laughed.

"But," Matt continued, "He woke up just in time to see the back of a kid who looked a lot like Luke going out the front entry of the hospital. He jumped up and stumbled over to the door and outside. It was dark, but he managed to follow the kid at a distance. The kid met another guy who was waiting by a car. As Bart got closer, he saw them both get into the car and drive off."

Brad sighed heavily, "So, he did go of his own free will. He just took off again."

"That's not all," Matt looked soberly at Brad. "The guy standing by the car was none other than our old pal, Blane."

"I knew it. That hateful dude is out to get Luke." Brad could feel the heat of anger rising inside him. *Think Brad*, he said to himself. *No, pray.* He began to pray. "Lord, we cry out for Luke once again. I know that you desire for us to help him, but I don't know how, right now. Direct our steps, Lord. Give us insight to where he could be." Brad's mind went back to his conversation with Luke earlier in the day, at the hospital. Luke had told him about Blane visiting him. Blane's words kept playing over and over in Brad's mind. "If you return that little device, all your troubles will be over." Brad remembered telling Luke that he had lost the flashlight, with the device hidden inside, at the Dragon's Den. He also remembered Luke asking him if the offices were damaged.

"That must be where he's going," Brad announced, thinking out loud.

"Where?" Matt asked, turning into the hospital parking lot. "There's our man." Bart came running over to the car as Brad opened the door, and Bart jumped into the back seat. Bart was breathing heavily from his jog over to them.

"Hey Bart," Brad greeted. "Thanks for keeping an eye on Luke."

"Well, I tried. I guess I now know why Jesus was disappointed at His disciples when they fell asleep in the garden. I almost missed everything."

Matt laughed, "Don't be too hard on yourself. I think the Holy Spirit woke you just in time."

Bart nodded. "Do you think that Blane is heading to that old house? You know, the one that the band stays in out in the country?"

"No, I don't think so," Brad replied. "I think they're heading for the burned out Dragon's Den."

"The Dragon's Den?" Matt repeated. "Why would they want to go there?"

"He's looking for something." Brad explained, as Matt pulled out of the parking lot heading in the direction of the dreaded hell-hole. "He's looking for a thumb drive. According to Sammy Dornberg, it has enough evidence on it to put Mr. Dragon away for a long time."

"Something that small could be anywhere."

Brad was going over, in his mind, the night he lost the flashlight. He knew that he last saw it in that back room. A large dark SUV passed and caught Brad's eye. Matt could see Brad's double take when the vehicle passed. "Relax, man, it was dark green not black. You sure are jumpy."

Brad smiled, "Yeah, and after the dream I had tonight, you'd think I would never be afraid of anything again."

"Did you say that Jesus was in this one, too?" Matt asked.

Bart's ear perked up. "You dreamed about Jesus? Cool, what happened?"

"Well, I think it was a dream. They seem so real." As they drove to the Den, Brad recounted the events of the dream, ending with the words of Jesus asking him to help Luke.

"That's awesome, man!" Bart could hardly contain his excitement, "I would love to have a dream like that. Well, I don't know about the dragon ripping my guts out, but the part where Jesus talks to you; that's incredible."

"Yeah," Brad responded. Then thought to himself, *it is incredible.* He really didn't understand why. He wasn't anything special, and he certainly was not perfect. But then he realized maybe that was why. Maybe, he just wasn't used to listening, and this thing with Luke and Dragon was so important to the whole community that Jesus had to really get his attention. Before, he had taken so many things for granted, thinking that someone else would do something. He had just been content to sit on the sidelines and be a spectator. The dreams had provoked him into action. Whatever the reason, Brad was grateful to be a part of God's plan to destroy this evil invasion of their land.

"Do you think Jesus will ever talk to me like that? Bart asked.

Brad caught a sly grin on Matt's face. "Yeah, sure he will, Bart. You're half way there. You've got the sleeping part down."

Bart laughed. He knew they would rag him for a while about falling asleep at the hospital.

"Bart, I think He already speaks to you, more than me. Or maybe, you listen more. You always seem to be at the right place at the right time. You are so used to hearing and responding to God that he doesn't have to appear to you in a dream," Brad encouraged.

"Really?" Bart beamed. "I never thought of it that way." He paused, musing on Brad's words. "But it still would be way cool to have a dream like that."

Suddenly, Brad realized that they were only about a half a mile from the Den. "Slow down, Matt. No, keep going. We'll drive by and see if any cars are there. We can park on that same path in the woods as we did before."

"Then what," Matt asked?

Brad gave him a dumbfounded look and said, "Duh. We sneak over and find out what they're up to."

Matt rolled his eyes. "Remember what happened last time? We were, like, accused of trespassing. Remember, there was Lumas with a gun, and the place caught on fire. Not to mention that we are accused of arson at this very moment."

"Technicalities," Brad replied, "merely a ploy by the enemy to side-track us. We've got to help Luke."

"There's no telling what kind of hypnotic spell he's under," Bart chimed in.

"So, you're ganging up on me now? OK, but I 'm going to call my Dad and tell him where we are."

"Great," Brad replied. "But, at least wait until we see if they are even there."

The Dragon's Den came into view.

Chapter 31

Deranged Boy Goes Berserk

The building was dark, but the lights illuminating the parking lot broke the blackness of the night. It seemed to Brad as if there was always a hazy mist creating an eerie ring around the street lights dotting the parking lot of the place. He wondered how that could be. It was sort of like the way there was always a storm that was only over the Munster's house. The parking lot on the left side of the building was empty. They passed in front of the building and the other side came into view. The building itself was in better shape than Brad thought it would be. The front entry was boarded up along with the windows. The only evidence of a fire was a dark, sooty coating around the tops of the windows near the front, along with a generous draping of yellow caution tape around the large columns near the entry. "There they are," Brad announced. "Bart, is that the car you saw Luke get into?"

Bart studied the small red hatch back.

"Yep, that's it." Seeing the cars in the lot, Matt began to increase his speed. Driving by the building to the wooded area, Matt found the old logging path and pulled onto it. He dug his cell phone from his pocket, and scrolled down to his father's number and quickly hit send. He could hear the ringing tone through the speaker. Finally, a voice responded. Matt started to speak but realized there was only a recording on the other end. The recording stated: "Sgt. Shackleton, head of special investigations is not available, please leave a brief message at the tone. BE-E-EP."

"Dad," Matt wasted no time with extraneous details. "We're out at the Dragon's Den. We believe we've found Luke. Please send units, thanks."

"What do we do now?" Bart asked.

"I think we wait for back up," Matt admonished.

"But, what if they are torturing Luke or something?"

"Didn't he go of his own free will?" Matt replied.

"Yes, but I think that he felt responsible for getting us in so much trouble and is trying to deal with it himself. Luke's probably not thinking very clearly at the moment. You know as well as I do that you can't trust Blane as far as you can throw him. We have to see what they're up to. You've called your Dad, and as soon as he gets the message, he'll be here," Brad reasoned.

"OK," Matt sighed. "But, let's stick together."

Brad pulled the door handle and muttered, "You can be sure of that." He had no intention of winding up alone with that crowd again.

They started down the dark path toward the road with Brad in the lead. Bart's foot caught a low branch, and he stumbled. "Too bad we don't have a flashlight," he whispered, as he picked himself up.

"Wait a minute," Matt stated, as he dashed back to the car and reached under the driver's seat. He came jogging back, a dim beam of light emanating from his right hand. "OK. Let's go," he asserted, as he moved past them to take the lead.

Making their way along the edge of the road, Brad couldn't seem to shake the feeling of de'ja- vu. It was only two nights ago that he had taken this same dubious path along this lonesome road in the middle of the night. Coming to the darkened edge of the lit parking lot, Matt turned off the light and shoved it into his pocket. The air was cooler and the night sky was illuminated by the moon. A myriad of twinkling stars peeked through patches of thin clouds, not heavy thunderheads as before. They continued around the edge of the parking lot, again to avoid the lights in the parking lot. Before they got too close to the building, Matt pulled out his cell phone to try his father's number. Again, it went directly to his voice mail. Frustrated, Matt set the phone on the vibrate mode to be safe from detection if it rang.

Continuing to the back of the building, and the same familiar door near the dumpsters, the trio stopped to listen. Everything was quiet, except for their own breathing and the occasional chirping of a cricket near the dumpsters. Brad pulled on the door. To his amazement, it opened. Matt started to protest, but it was too late. Brad was already inside. Once inside they all stopped again to listen. Absolute quiet dominated for about thirty seconds. It was almost totally black in the long storage room that led to the metal staircase. Brad was about to suggest that they keep their eyes peeled for the lost flashlight when they heard a sound coming from farther inside the building. Matt slowly moved forward in the darkness through the mess of overturned shelves. He got to the doorway at the top of the stairwell and listened. Brad and Bart followed.

"What is it?" Bart asked in a whisper.

"Voices," Matt replied. He pulled the flashlight out of his pocket and covered it with his shirt so that the light wouldn't be as bright. It produced a dim yellow glow, which helped the boys make their way down the steps. When they all got to the bottom of the steps, Matt dowsed the light. The large metal door, that led to the hallway, was only open about twelve inches. Matt knew, that in every old movie he'd ever seen, it was an undisputable fact that old metal doors inevitably squeaked when moved. So, as quietly as he could, he directed them to follow as he sucked in his gut and squeezed between the space in the doorway. Once he got through, it would be no problem for the two skinnier boys to make it. Bart made it with no problem. Brad followed suit. He was about halfway through when a loud, rather high pitched cry broke through the quiet. Brad was so startled by the creepy sound, that his body jerked. His recuperating knee caught the corner of the door, sending fresh, hot pain right up his leg all the way to his eyes, which began to water. Brad bit his tongue to keep from crying out, and froze. Luckily, the stiff heavy door didn't move, and the sound of the impact was no more than a muffled thud, hardly loud enough for Bart and Matt to hear. Bart turned and helped him through the doorway.

Matt continued to lead, feeling his way along the wall. A thick, smoky smell filled their lungs and began to sting the back of their throats. The guys turned the corner of the hallway. They could see a dim light shining through one of the swinging doors that led into the auditorium beside the stage. It was propped open by a little doorstop at the base. They stopped again to listen, as a muffled voice could again be heard from the auditorium. It wasn't quite loud enough to understand, but Brad recognized the slithery, soothing voice of Mr. Dragon. Brad quietly took another step toward the open door.

"No, no, no. Leave me alone," A pitiful, slurring voice again cried out. *Is that Luke?* Brad wondered. If it was, he sounded emotionally tormented. Brad got close enough to look through the corner of the small square window placed about three quarters of the way up the door. He could see Luke sitting in a chair with a lantern on the floor in front of him. Dragon was seated in a chair, which he had turned backward, his legs spread and arms propped on top of the back of the chair. Blane sat on the drum stool nearby. Lumas and the other goon stood on each side of Luke.

Dragon spoke loud enough so that Brad could understand his words. "Luke, my dear friend, you know that I only want to spare your friends any further trouble. If you will just co-operate, this will all be over very soon. If you don't, then my associate, Mr. Lumas, here, will have to get a little nasty; and that's really the last thing we want." Luke, whose head was facing down, looking at the floor, didn't say anything. Brad heard a deep sigh of frustration from Dragon. "Lumas, I don't believe Mr. Hunter here is paying attention to me." Immediately, Lumas stepped forward, pulling his shiny revolver from under his coat. He reached out and grabbed a fist full of Luke's hair pulling his head up so that Luke had to face Dragon. Luke yelped, but Brad could tell he stopped and sucked up the pain. His eyes were wide with fear, but then his countenance changed, like he remembered something. His eyes focused on Dragon and became cold and steely. Dragon stared back, affirming, "There, that's better." Then Dragon pulled out a small black pen-shaped item and pressed a button on it. A tiny but bright red light on the top began to flash, slowly, at regular intervals. On, off, on, off, on. . . Holding it right in front of Luke's face, Dragon instructed, "Now, Luke, I want you to focus on the light. Let everything go. Relax, and look into the light. It will guide you to the right thoughts."

Luke stared at the light. Lumas let go of his hair. Brad was amazed at how quickly Luke went under the spell of Dragon's hypnotic power. "Luke, you will not remember anyone being here tonight with you. You came here tonight with one purpose in mind. You were looking for something. You searched the office and found the hiding place of this piece." Dragon pulled a small silver handgun from his pocket, and held it up in front of Luke. "Sammy Dornburg," Dragon continued in a peaceful, comforting voice, "is the source of all your troubles. As long as he lives, you will never be free. He's out to kill your friend, Brad Johnson. He must be stopped. Only you can do it, Luke."

Brad turned to the other guys, who were now standing right behind him. Matt held a finger up to his lips. Dragon gave the gun to Luke. *OK,* Brad thought. *Luke is just faking it. He's going to take that gun and force his way out.* Then Brad saw that Lumas had his weapon carefully trained on the back of Luke's head. Luke took the gun, but kept his eyes fixed on Dragon. "Now put the gun in the pocket of your sweatshirt." Brad could tell that Luke's mind was responding in slow motion. After a couple of seconds, he slowly did what Dragon commanded. "You are now on a mission," Dragon continued. "You have one desire: to return to the hospital and kill Sammy Dornburg. You will not touch the gun until you see Sammy's face. Once you see Sammy's face, you will point the gun at his chest and fire. You did it, because Sammy tortured you and made your life a living hell." Dragon called Blane over. "Take him out and drop him off about a block from the hospital. Make sure no one sees you. Then go home and lay low for a few days."

Brad motioned for Matt and Bart to follow him back down the hall around the corner. "We need to head back out and watch for Luke to come to the hospital, "Brad whispered.

"Matt, we can take him to your dad and tell him what we've witnessed," Bart added.

"I wouldn't have believed it if I hadn't seen it with my own eyes," Matt replied. They quietly headed back to the stairs.

"Stop right where you are!" A familiar, snide sounding voice declared. The boys stopped dead in their tracks. Brad knew that voice. He had become very familiar with it within in the last forty-eight hours.

"Officer Henson?" Brad whispered. "Is that you? They've got Luke in there and they are planning. . ."

"Quiet!" Officer Henson commanded a little too loudly. "I'll do the talking. Move back toward the stage doors," The man ordered, as he pulled a flashlight from his pocket and shined the light into their faces. "So, the vandals return to finish the job."

The boys walked toward the stage doors. Lumas, alerted by the commotion, appeared in the doorway. Pointing his gun at them, he yelled, "Who's there?"

"Careful where you point that thing," Henson replied.

As the boys came closer, Lumas grabbed Matt. He yanked him through the doorway, and then shoved him backward onto the floor. Matt was incensed and jumped back to his feet, only to run right into the powerful fist of Lumas. He staggered, but held his ground. Lumas laughed. "I guess that will teach you to respect your elders, boy."

Dragon was enraged. "How did they get in here? You were supposed to be watching the place."

Henson who was not in uniform, stammered, "L-Look, this place has five entries. How can one man watch them all?"

"This changes everything. There's no telling what they heard. We'll have to lock them up until I can think of a suitable accident." Thinking quickly, Dragon appeared to have a brainstorm. He turned slowly, thinking. He stared at Luke, who was sitting silently in the chair, still under his hypnotic influence. "Is it possible," Dragon wondered mockingly out loud, "that a confused drugged out boy could turn on his supposed friends who were harassing him with their fanatical Christian views? Yes, I think it's plausible. I can see it in the papers now: Deranged Boy Goes Berserk." Dragon looked at Brad with a sly grin then walked over to Lumas and spoke in a low evil tone.

Brad noticed Luke's eyes cut toward him for a split second, and then back into nothingness. *Could it be?* Brad wondered.

"We'll let our little mind slave do our dirty work. Half the town already believes that he shot poor Sammy," Dragon droned on.

Matt, who was down on his knee, holding his bleeding mouth, looked at Brad and slightly nodded his head. Brad understood this meant he was about to do something. Abruptly, Matt leaped forward, and with all of the force he could expend, caught Lumas behind his legs at the knees. This sent the giant careening backward. With a loud "SMACK," the back of his head came into contact with the edge of the stage. Brad instantly lunged toward Henson and knocked the gun from his hands. Bart scrambled after it, only to receive the heel of Dragon's hard black boot in his back. Henson regained his balance and pushed Brad aside. Henson picked up his gun and pointed it at Matt's head. "I have had all the trouble I can take out of you," Henson said, glaring angrily down at Matt, who was lying on his back facing his assailant.

BANG! A shot rang out. Matt grabbed his head. Henson unexpectedly grabbed his own right shoulder, whirled around, staggered, and fell to his knees. The shot had not come from Henson's gun, but from out of the darkness in the back of the auditorium. Lumas was now on his feet, his weapon drawn, eyes squinted to see where the shot had come from. Pointing the gun toward the back of the auditorium, he fired. A second later another blast came from out of the darkness. Brad saw a section of Lumas' trousers rip open near his thigh and blood spew forth. Everyone on the stage was now on the floor scrambling to take cover from flying bullets, including Luke who seemed to have been freed from his trance-like state. Lumas grabbed his leg and held it, grimacing in pain. Suddenly, a powerful flashlight beam illuminated Lumas from the back of the auditorium. Brad saw something he never thought he would see from this giant of a man. A look of fear spread across his face as he realized that he was a sitting duck and that the next bullet could be right through his heart. Dragon crouched behind a speaker, trying to figure out who was firing at them.

A voice, strong and clear, boomed from the back of the room, "Throw your weapons into the front row of seats, and place your hands on top of your heads." Brad watched the Dragon, who was studying the situation—peering into the blackness. Brad could tell that Dragon was confused but not afraid, his mind working through some sort of scheme to rid himself of this irritating situation.

"This is the police. Please do as you are told, so that no one gets hurt."

Dragon turned, and made a subtle hand motion to Blane. Blane nodded.

What is he up to? Brad wondered.

Lumas and Henson threw their weapons into the auditorium. Brad could make out two figures coming into the golden ring of the lantern light. Brad now knew whose voice was speaking to them. Sgt. Shackleton's serious face emerged along with another officer. Sgt. Shackleton went straight to his son and knelt down. Matt was holding his bleeding head. "It's about time you got here," Matt chided with a smile.

"How you doing, son?" he asked in a gentle voice.

"Much better now that you're here. Where were you when I called?" Matt asked curiously.

"Around." His father winked at him and helped him to his feet.

"I want all of these boys arrested right now for trespassing," Dragon raged. "After all the damage they've already caused, we caught them in the act of trying to finish the job."

Brad marveled at Dragon's audacity. *He must just live in his own little world of reality,* Brad thought as he shook his head at Dragon's ridiculous accusations.

Sgt. Shackleton walked over to Dragon, looking him squarely in the eyes. "If that was true, you should have called the police when you caught them."

Luke, who was now on his feet, came over toward Sgt. Shackleton, smiling. Watching him, Brad thought, *Wow, what a transformation.* Luke seemed to be his old self again.

Sgt. Shackleton turned to Luke. "Luke, are you OK?"

"Yes sir, I'm fine. Did we get all the evidence we need?" Luke asked, his dark eyes shining.

"I believe so." Sgt. Shackleton reached into the hood on the back of Luke's navy blue sweatshirt and pulled out a tiny device with a cord attached. "Thank you for your willingness to help."

I knew it! Brad thought to himself. *Luke was just playing along the whole time. The whole thing was a set up to get Dragon to hang himself.*

Dragon, knowing it was hopeless to deny anything, said nothing. He stood there, thinking, one hand in his pocket. Brad noticed that Blane had disappeared. He looked around, but Blane was nowhere to be found. Quietly, he had disappeared into the darkness.

"I guess you will need this for evidence." Luke pulled the gun from his sweatshirt pocket and held it out to Sgt. Shackleton.

Suddenly, Dragon shoved Sgt. Shackleton with one hand and grabbed Luke's wrist, jerking Luke close to him. He seized the gun, putting it to Luke's head. "Give me that device," he growled, holding his hostage tight.

Sgt. Shackleton shook his head. "Dragon, you're only adding to your problems. Why don't you just give up?" Sgt. Shackleton tried to reason.

Dragon sneered, "Just throw that thing on the floor now, or I will put a bullet through his head. You know I have nothing to lose." The sergeant complied, tossing the little black rectangular device, onto the floor at the feet of the desperate man. Dragon picked up his foot, and with one crushing blow of his boot, reduced it to a mangle of wires, metal and bits of plastic. Dragon shuffled off the stage toward the double doors dragging Luke helplessly with him. He stopped suddenly and boldly taunted, "You fools. You will never stop the Dragon. This world is mine." While keeping the gun trained on Luke's head, he reached into his pocket. Then, with an evil laugh, he raised his hand and with a flourish, tossed a small, round ball toward the stage.

Brad gasped. The very second Dragon's wicked laugh permeated the auditorium; Brad could have sworn that his eyes flashed with a reddish light, just like the dragon on his computer game. Brad realized that he had not been battling the Draegonian Invasion all this time, but the invasion of the Dragon. *Could it be that Mr. Dragon was "THE" dragon?*

Chapter 32

Fear Not, For I Am With You

The little ball hit the stage floor and exploded into a greenish cloud of gas, sending everyone into a fit of coughing. Gasping for breath, Brad could hardly see and put his sleeve over his mouth. His watering eyes were focused on the door. Before he could think, he was running toward the double doors through which he had just seen Dragon disappear with his friend, Luke. Brad stumbled into the darkness of the hallway and felt his way along the wall. He stopped and could hear footsteps on the metal stairway.

"Move, you little fool, or I'll kill you right here." Brad ran toward the sound, but hit something in the middle of the floor and tripped. He felt a handle and the head of a mop. The footfalls were now off the stairs. Brad picked himself up. He quickly made his way to the door of the stairwell, and then up the stairs. He could now see Dragon in the doorway, and Luke being pulled out of the door. A bright light silhouetted them. *It's too weird,* Brad thought. *This is just like the very first dream— Luke disappearing through the doorway into a glaring light.* Fear tried to grab hold of him. But this time the words "Fear not, for I am with you," resounded in his spirit. Brad continued up the stairs and made his way through the storage room. He burst through the threshold behind Dragon into the brilliant bluish light. Brad realized the light in the background was coming from the headlights of Blane's sports car. Dragon was forcing Luke into the back seat.

Not knowing exactly what to do, Brad followed an impulse and yelled, "In the name of Jesus, I bind your power, Satan."

Dragon was so stunned that he turned around, trying to figure out where the words had come from. When he did, Luke seized the moment, and with a shove, bolted out of the car. Running blindly, he tripped and crashed to the ground about four feet to the side of where Brad was standing. Luke was now on his knees, about to get up, when Dragon stood and pointed his gun, taking aim at Luke's back. Without thinking, Brad lunged sideways, knocking Luke over on his side. Brad heard the blasts of a gun, three shots in rapid fire. Sharp searing pain burned into his chest. He tumbled over on top of Luke. In a blur, he could see the car screeching off, throwing gravel through the parking lot. Brad could hear Luke's voice calling his name. He tried to move, but the pain paralyzed him. *Is this the end,* Brad wondered. *Am I dying?* Brad thought about all the people he had been meaning to tell about Jesus. Why hadn't he? *There's so much more I would like to do. And, what about Luke? Oh Jesus, I thought You wanted me to help Luke,"* he wondered as consciousness drifted away.

All was quiet for a few moments as a brilliant light formed in front of him. Brad's fear turned into peace as he heard the words of a gentle voice say, "And they loved not their lives even unto death." Then, right before him, he could see the kind, radiant face of the Friend he had come to trust so in these trials of fear. Emmanuel said to him. "Fear not, for you have much to do. Your time has not yet come. You will show many the way." With that, Brad drifted off into peaceful sleep.

Brad woke to the beep of medical devices perched near his bed. He heard a man's voice speaking. "It is nothing short of a miracle. This young man has a lot to be thankful for. A half-inch difference and one bullet would have pierced his heart and the other his backbone."

"I have never seen so many young people praying for someone. The lobby has been full of people—many of them kids. Do you think he will make it, doctor?" a female voice queried.

"Well, when he was brought in, he was practically dead already. I didn't give him any hope. But, I've witnessed nothing short of a miracle. He's made it through the last forty-eight hours. With all of those prayers, he will make it."

A few minutes later Brad opened his eyes. The room appeared somewhat fuzzy, and the glare of a florescent light behind his bed hurt his eyes. *I'm alive,* Brad thought. He knew it because of the pain he felt in his body. He never thought that he would be glad to feel pain, but it meant he was alive. It wasn't too bad, but he felt as if he had a bowling ball sitting on his chest. The room was full of medical equipment and he knew from his visits with Luke, that he was in the ICU.

The nurse, who had her back to him, turned. Seeing that Brad's eyes were open, she said, "Well, good morning, Mr. Johnson. So nice of you to join us."

Brad's mom, resting in a recliner, heard the nurse and leapt to her feet. In an instant, her face was smiling down at him. Her eyes filled and big tear drops rolled down her face. He felt her warm hand take his, and he could hear her soft voice. "Thank you, Jesus. Praise be to Your Name." Brad hadn't said a word. His throat was sore and he had tubes running into his nose. "Brad, can you hear me?" his Mom asked.

He nodded his head and squeaked out a barely audible, "Yes."

Brad could hear men's voices in the background; his father talking to the doctor. A moment later the blue eyes of his father beamed down at him, as he joined his wife beside the bed. He, too, was wiping tears from his eyes. "God did it, Brad. He brought you through." Brad could feel warm tears flowing down the sides of his own face as gratitude filled his heart. Looking up at his precious parents, he knew that everything was going to be all right. He closed his eyes, drifting off, back to sleep.

He awoke six hours later to the jingle of a cell phone. Brad felt better and realized that the tubes in his nose were gone. He tried to turn a bit, to look over at his mother. A sharp pain shot across his chest reminding him to take it slowly. Brad could hear his mom's voice. "Yes, he's doing so much better. Thank you. Yes, I think that will be fine."

Brad wondered who she was talking to. He woke up with Luke on his mind. *Had he been shot too?* Brad's mind ran through what he could remember of the night's events. When Mrs. Johnson got off the phone, Brad called out to her, "M-mom." He said in a raspy voice. Although they had been removed, his throat stung with rawness from the tubes. As she came over to his side, he asked almost in a whisper, "I-is Luke OK?"

"Luke?" she responded. "I believe he's just fine." She was interrupted by a knock on the door. She turned to see who it was and then looked back at Brad with a smile. "Well, dear. I believe you can ask him yourself."

Brad looked toward the door and saw Luke entering the room. "I-is it OK to come in?" he asked timidly.

Brad smiled and nodded, and his mom replied, "Sure. Brad was just asking about you. I think he could use a little company right now." Mrs. Johnson said as, she gave Brad a cup of warm liquid which soothed his throat.

Luke came over to the side of the bed. Concerned, he asked, "How are you feeling?"

"Well, I have felt better. But I praise God for a little pain because it means I'm alive."

Luke smiled. "I sure like the way you look at things. I'm still struggling with all that has happened. Brad, I'm sorry that you had to go through all of this. I know it's all my fault."

"It's not your fault." Brad insisted. He paused and sipped from the styrofoam cup.

"Luke," Mrs. Johnson responded, "God allows things to happen for His purposes. He used this situation to teach us all something, and to bring about His will."

Brad agreed, "I believe He used it to stop the evil plans of Dragon and keep him from building a stronghold through a drug culture here in our town. God used us to stop it. If that meant a little pain in the process, it was worth it."

"Yes, but it should be me lying in that bed, not you. I owe you my life."

"No, Luke—we both owe our lives to Jesus. He put it on my heart to try to help you. The dreams I had about you, showed me what was going on in your life—And how to break out of my own fear and complacency. God is the one who gave me the strength to pursue this battle."

Luke looked down and then back up at Brad. "I thank you both then."

"How are you doing Luke? Are you still interested in following Jesus?"

Luke furrowed his brow and gave him a funny look. "Are you kidding? After all He's brought me through? There is no one else to follow. I've definitely seen that all other roads lead to nothing but despair and misery." He paused. "I'm afraid, however. There are some people who still think that I shot Sammy. I hate that. I believe that will dog me all of my life."

Brad's heart went out to him. "Don't worry. I believe God will turn that around in time. By the way, what happened to Dragon?" Brad inquired.

"That's the irritating thing. He disappeared. When the police finally caught up with Blane, Dragon wasn't in the car. He had obviously dropped him somewhere, and now they think he's up north. But, if you can believe it, his lawyer is still pursuing the case against us. He's still accusing me of shooting Sammy and you guys of arson and vandalism."

Brad shook his head. "I can't believe the nerve of that guy. Will he never give up? With all the evidence against him, I don't know why he's pursuing it."

"That's the problem, Brad. There isn't that much real evidence. The recorder was destroyed and Dragon has accused Sgt. Shackleton of trying to frame him. He is charging misconduct and entrapment. It's all a big mess. I sure wish we could have found that little flash drive."

Luke was interrupted by some commotion in the hallway, and then a knock on the door. Mrs. Johnson greeted them and asked, "Bradford, can you take a few more visitors?" Brad could see Matt leading the way with a broad smile. Matt's Dad, and Bart, followed through the doorway.

"How's it going?" Matt asked, as he reached over and gently touched Brad's arm, being careful of the IV tube. They all, in turn, greeted Brad and Luke.

"Brad, I'm so glad that you are doing better. When we found you and Luke two nights ago, I must confess, I had my doubts about you making it. God surely worked a miracle here," Sgt. Shackleton acknowledged.

"You're so right, sir. I know that He did. I just pray that somehow Dragon will be brought to justice. I can't believe that he's not in jail."

"Well, we'll get him. Eventually, things will be exposed, and the truth will be known. Unfortunately, the system can take a while to work, and evidence can be skewed and twisted by slick lawyers."

Brad noticed Matt was holding something. It was a silvery gray cylinder. "Matt, what's that in your hand?"

"This?" Matt held it up, "It's your flashlight."

"No. That's it! It's *my* flashlight!" Luke exclaimed.

"Your flashlight?" Matt asked, confused, looking at Brad. "But Brad, Bart mentioned that you were looking for a flashlight, so I thought this was yours."

"Yes –Yes!" Brad replied with as much excitement as he could in his condition. "I've been frantically looking for that thing. Didn't you know that? Where did you get it?"

"You left it on a shelf in that room at the Den. I thought we might need it, so I grabbed it and shoved it in my pocket. I totally forgot about it until later, when I got in my car. I stuck it under the seat. I'm sorry, but I didn't know that you were looking for it until Bart mentioned it last night." Brad shook his head in amazement, as it dawned on him that Matt had a flashlight the night he was shot. He had it the whole time, completely unaware of the secret it held. Brad realized that every time he was about to mention it, some sort of distraction had prevented him from actually telling Matt about it.

Luke excitedly took the light from Matt's hand and slid a little piece of metal sideways. The small compartment on its side opened. Luke shook it a bit; and a small, black plastic, rectangular device fell into his hand. He turned to Sgt. Shackleton, "Sir, this should give you all the evidence you need to convict Dragon and shut down his operation for good."

Sgt. Shackleton looked at the tiny object. "Such a small thing can do all that?" he marveled. "What all is on it?"

"I can answer that," a voice called from the doorway. It was Sammy Dornberg guiding his wheelchair into the room. "There are names and dates of drug deals and payments, as well as directives to take out certain people. There are also videos of Dragon putting people under—what they said and did. He used those videos to blackmail them into doing whatever he wanted. Dragon is a master of using fear to enslave people. I want to offer my complete cooperation."

Luke was stunned at Sammy's turn-around. Brad wondered too, remembering his arrogance and hatefulness in their past meetings. Then his mind traveled back to the night he was shot and the look of desperation in his eyes. Sammy moved over toward Brad, as the group parted to let him through. He looked directly at Brad. Brad could see the man's eyes turning glassy.

"Did you really mean what you said to me that night at the Den? Is it true that God will help me? I know that He must be real. I've seen His enemy and the power he has to blind people. All I ever thought about was myself and what I could get. Then, I see you guys who are seriously trying to help others, so much so that you would take a bullet for your friend."

"That's two bullets," Luke interjected.

Brad looked at Sammy, the joy of the Holy Spirit filling his heart. "Most definitely Sammy; God is the only one who can really help you." Brad responded. "Jesus cares about you, and wants you in His kingdom. Sammy, the question is: are you willing to turn away from the sinful life you've been living?" Brad asked.

Sammy thought for a minute, and replied. "You mean this life that has made me completely miserable, and almost gotten me killed several times. All the money and stuff I could want isn't worth the pain I have in my heart. Yeah, I want to change, but I'm not sure I can."

"Sammy," Sgt. Shackleton intervened, "I won't say that it's easy, but with Jesus truly living in your heart, it will happen."

Bart spoke up, "It happened to me, a year ago, Sammy. God totally changed my way of thinking. He helped me to understand the Bible, and it became real to me."

Matt put his hand on Sammy's shoulder. "Sammy, we're all here to help you and pray for you. Why don't we pray right now? Are you ready for that; to ask Jesus to come into your heart and clean you up?"

Brad was amazed. Sammy's eyes were glazing over with tears. He would never have imagined this crass, tough, brute of a guy could show such emotion. They all in turn, prayed for Sammy; that God would come into his heart and give him the power to change and follow the leading of God's Holy Spirit.

Finally, Brad said, "Sammy, now God wants to hear it from your own mouth. You need to repent and ask Him to come into your heart and live there. Tell Him that you are willing to follow Him."

Sammy nodded. He bowed and was silent for a few seconds. "Oh, God, I've made a real big mess of my life and have sinned against You and so many others. I'm so sorry. I need Your help to change. I want to change. I want to live for You. Please help me do this—I need Your help to do it."

As Brad listened to him cry out to God in his tough New Jersey accent, he began to praise God. His mercy and kindness had led this hardened, self-centered thug to repentance. Brad thought, *what a huge difference this would make in the world. Now, instead of a life of crime and leading people into the bondage of drugs and sin, Sammy would be used by God to set them free from the prison of sin.*

Suddenly, Brad's thoughts were transported back to that dark, ominous corridor of his dream, filled with people trapped in the mirrored cubes. As Brad approached one of them, it lit up and Brad could see Sammy inside, weeping and struggling to find a way out. He wondered why he wasn't free. One side was open, but it was as if he couldn't see it. As Brad watched, he once again felt the warmth of his shimmering Friend standing beside him. Jesus turned to Brad and smiled. "You see, you helped more than Luke in this quest."

Brad smiled back and nodded. "But, Lord, he's still trapped in the cage."

Jesus looked at Brad and smiled, "Not anymore." He raised His mighty arm and, with one blow, shattered Sammy's glass prison into a million tiny pieces.

Clapping and cheering erupted in the room, which brought Brad out of his vision and back into the hospital room. The prayers were finished, and now Sammy's walk with Jesus would begin. Brad understood more than ever what life was really all about. *God truly desires to bring about His purposes in everything that happens. Either we follow Him on the great adventure and grow closer to Him, or we don't. What a shame,* Brad thought to himself, seeing all the joyful faces in that small room. *What a shame it would have been to have let fear rule me and to have missed out on the great joy of looking into Jesus' grateful eyes.* Sure, there was some pain, and he had faced fear like he had never known before. *But look at what God has done through it.*

Brad listened as Sgt. Shackleton encouraged Sammy, "Sammy, you will need to be honest about everything and trust God to take care of you. You know that you'll have to pay the consequences of the crimes you've committed. But, if you cooperate fully and are helpful in getting the bigger fish, I'm sure that the judge will be lenient."

Sammy nodded. "Thank you Sergeant. I appreciate your help."

Brad called out to Sammy, "Sammy, keep in mind that the real Judge is now your Friend, and He has paid the price for all of your sins. Your job is to follow Him and let Him continue to set you free from everything that would hinder your walk with Him."

Sammy's face lit up. "One thing I know: he didn't spare my life so that I could do nothing. I've been to prison before. I know that God can use me there. Whatever happens to me, I won't forget that night at the Den, and realizing that someone actually cared about me. I've done a lot of thinking since then. You will stay in touch with me, won't you? I might be kind of hard to get to, you know."

Brad smiled. "Oh, I'll find a way. You can be sure of that."

"And you too squirt," Sammy said to Luke. Then, he got really serious. Luke looked at him and tried to smile. They had struggled together in many ways. "Luke, I know that it wasn't you who shot me, even though I deserved it. I hope you can forgive me for the way I've treated you."

Luke nodded. "Sammy, how could I not forgive you? Isn't that what Jesus is all about? Besides, you actually did me a favor by showing me how miserable life is without God." Luke reached out and shook Sammy's hand. "I'll pray for you, if you'll pray for me," Luke affirmed.

"You've got a deal. And I hope you know I don't really believe you're a squirt. You're one of the biggest guys I know."

Sgt. Shackleton and Sammy said goodbye and moved toward the door just as Brad's dad entered the crowded room along with Luke's parents. Brad was glad to hear that the Finneys were all planning to come to church this week. Brad's dad explained that they were also going to come over once a week for Bible study.

"That's not all," Mom added excitedly. "I did some research and found that Luke's dad, Dave here, is a direct descendant of the great preacher, Charles Finney. "

Luke looked up at Dave, his step-dad, who was standing near him—then over to Brad.

"That's quite a heritage, Mr. Finney," Brad remarked, trying to ease the way for the two of them.

"Yes, and I would love to learn more about it. Maybe Luke and I could learn together," Mr. Finney replied.

Luke looked up, a huge smile spreading across his face. His eyes sparkled with the life of God. "Dad, I would really like that."

As the group began to leave, Brad realized how tired he was. Brad's mom was the only one left. Brad, why don't you get some sleep, son? Your body needs to heal.

"Yes," Brad agreed. "Sleep. That's what I need." As he made himself comfortable and closed his eyes, he suddenly wondered, "Or do I?"

To learn more about following Jesus, visit me at www.fredjackson.org

CPSIA information can be obtained at www.ICGtesting.com
Printed in the USA
BVOW072302110213

312933BV00002B/5/P

9 781462 714438